Collected Stories

Collected Stories

BRUNO SCHULZ

Translated from the Polish by Madeline G. Levine

Foreword by Rivka Galchen

NORTHWESTERN UNIVERSITY PRESS

EVANSTON, ILLINOIS

Northwestern University Press

www.nupress.northwestern.edu

English translation copyright © 2018 by the Polish Book Institute.
Foreword copyright © 2018 by Rivka Galchen. Published 2018 by Northwestern
University Press. All rights reserved.

 This book has been funded by the Polish Book Institute © POLAND
Translation Program.

The source for this translation is the annotated Polish National Library edition of
Bruno Schulz, *Opowiadania. Wybór esejów i listów* [*Stories: Selection of Essays and Letters*],
edited by Jerzy Jarzębski and published in Poland in 1989 by Zakład Narodowy im.
Ossolińskich.

Printed in the United States of America

10 9 8 7 6 5 4 3 2 1

Library of Congress Cataloging-in-Publication Data

Names: Schulz, Bruno, 1892–1942, author. | Levine, Madeline G., translator.
Title: Collected stories / Bruno Schulz ; translated from the Polish by Madeline G.
    Levine ; foreword by Rivka Galchen.
Other titles: Short stories. English
Description: Evanston, Illinois : Northwestern University Press, 2018.
Identifiers: LCCN 2017039986| ISBN 9780810136601 (pbk. : alk. paper) |
    ISBN 9780810136618 (ebook)
Subjects: LCSH: Schulz, Bruno, 1892–1942—Translations into English.
Classification: LCC PG7158.S294 A2 2018 | DDC 891.8537—dc23 LC record
    available at https://lccn.loc.gov/2017039986

CONTENTS

Other Stories

FOREWORD

Rivka Galchen

Simply because it is an ending, death can take on the misleading appearance of an explanation, as if it is the unhappy resolution to a riddle. Consider the story of the death of Homer. The Oracle of Delphi had prophesied Homer would die on the island of Ios. When he reached the island, he asked some fishermen there what they had caught. One replied: "What we caught, we threw back; what we didn't, we kept." Homer resolved not to leave Ios until he solved the riddle. Never divining the answer, he died there. It's a bit of a drastic end, for one of the greatest of poets to be undone by a schoolboy's sort of riddle. Let us try, for at least a spell, not to think of the story of Bruno Schulz in this way.

What characterizes the world made by the words of Bruno Schulz? For one, the inanimate is regularly made to seem alive, even self-aware. Doors are "witnesses," lamps are "dejected and peevish," and the "mournful grayness of the city" besieges a family on all sides. We read of this grayness "blossoming in the windows as the dark rash of dawn, the parasitical fungus of twilight . . ." Strange and uncanny botanies appear in other guises as well: "The city is under the sign of the weed, of wild, passionate, fanatical vegetation," Schulz writes of Warsaw in "The Republic of Dreams." Even Schulz's more literal biological descriptions read as phantasmal. Here he is, describing ordinary growth: "From a pinch of chlorophyll it brings forth and expands in the fire of these days that lush, vacant tissue, the green pulp disseminated a hundred times onto millions of leafy surfaces, greenly pierced with light and veined, diaphanous with watery, vegetative, herbal blood, moss covered and hairy, with a pungent, weedy, rustic odor." Schulz is often compared to Kafka, but this seems more a matter of history than of imaginative affinity. Kafka's worlds, with their paradoxes and recursive anxieties, have the immaculate quality of mathematics and physics. Schulz's world by contrast has the inescapable and encroaching biology of a voyage through the tropics, even as his literal latitude runs through a cold eastern Europe.

The tendency of the inanimate world to feel and reproduce at times crosses over into its logical inverse, with people becoming things. At one point the father asks, "Am I to pass over in silence that my cousin, as a consequence of a lengthy incurable illness, changed progressively into a coil of rubber intestines, that on winter nights his poor wife carried him around day and night on pillows, humming endless lullabies to the unhappy creature? Can there be anything sadder than a man changed into an enema hose?" This is funny and tragic, and it's also the father's way of feeling. A sentient inanimate world requires refined, even impossible, sympathies. The father in the stories says at one point, "Who knows how many suffering, crippled, fragmentary forms of life there are, how artificially pieced together is the life of wardrobes and tables violently hammered together . . . silent martyrs to cruel human ingenuity . . . How much old, wise torment there is in stained rings of wood, in the veins and grains of our old respected wardrobes." If life is everywhere, the labor of feeling is boundless. How to contain it?

In one story, the son is sure that a stuffed condor in the living room is his father. (His mother tells him that he should know his father is just away, a traveling salesman.) It may not be true, but it seems like a viable emotional solution.

These transformations are essential to Schulz's dark humor, a humor whose timing relies on the irregular movements of Schulzian time. Time in these stories is said to leave a character and walk by itself across a room. Time also passes unevenly "making knots, as it were, in the passing of hours, swallowing up somewhere entire empty intervals of duration." We encounter "threadbare time," "regurgitated time" and "the rapid disintegration of time that is not supervised with constant vigilance." Even a new extra month turns up, "a thirteenth false month," and though we have the option of straightforwardly understanding this as the month of Adar II, a month added into the Jewish solar and lunar calendar every few years to keep the seasons in check, we can also, through the detailed metaphoric description of that "thirteenth false month," see it as a fantastical outgrowth.

In "The Sanatorium under the Hourglass," time even reverses (or at least the doctor says it does). The narrator has gone to the sanatorium to visit his father, though we are told that his father has already died. We learn from Dr. Gotard that although the father's death "casts a certain shadow on his existence here," the father is also still very much alive. He is even, we are told, capable of recovering. This is because at the sanatorium "we have turned back time" and are "late by an interval whose length is impossible to define."

I first came to the work of Schulz through an old copy of *The Street of Crocodiles* (the title under which *Cinnamon Shops* appeared in its first English translation). The image that stayed with me most from that first read comes at the end of the story "Uncle Karol." As Uncle Karol exits his room, we learn that "moving without haste in the opposite direction, into the depths of the mirror, was someone who always had his back turned, moving through an empty enfilade of rooms that did not exist." As the "real" Uncle Karol walks out of our gaze, his correlate in the mirror holds our attention indefinitely, even infinitely. But why, I later wondered, did I remember that moment most vividly? The "Uncle Karol" story is only a few pages, has little straightforward "event," and concerns a minor character. The dominant figures in *Cinnamon Shops* are the charismatically mad father, the dreamy boy watching, and the assured servant girl Adela. Yet in one of those coincidences that can feel (maybe misleadingly) meaning-besotted, I've twice found myself speaking with people about Schulz and heard them recall the same moment to me as their favorite. The door through which Uncle Karol exits is a common entrance into the universe of Schulz. It leads into the vivid rooms "that did not exist" and which, in Schulz, receive their due prominence.

The master of this world seems to be the father figure, whose wild imaginings appear sometimes as burdens, sometimes as genius. In an early story, the father spends large amounts of money importing exotic bird eggs. He gives these eggs to large chickens to incubate, eventually making a (filthy) aviary in an upper room of the home, behind a door which seems to the rest of the family to only sometimes be findable. The project collapses. The father also wants to make mannequins of people. He spends time in a world no one else can see except apparently his cat. And yet, in another story, the narrator says, "That avian project of my father's was the last explosion of color . . . Only today do I understand the lonely heroism with which he, all by himself, waged war on the boundless element of boredom stupefying our city."

In moments, the boy takes on the imaginative power of his father. In "Cinnamon Shops," the young boy is sent to fetch his father's forgotten wallet at home while his parents are at the theater. He doesn't make it home, naturally, but ends up searching for a correlate of home, searching for the shops he boyishly terms "cinnamon shops" because they are "paneled with dark, cinnamon-colored wainscoting." At the shops, he explains, "You could find Bengal lights there, magic boxes, stamps of long-vanished countries, Chinese decals, indigo, colophony from Malabar, the eggs of exotic insects, parrots, toucans, live salamanders and basilisks, mandrake root, windup toys from Nuremberg, homunculi in flowerpots, microscopes and telescopes, and, above all, rare and unusual books, old folios full of the strangest etchings and stunning stories." They are basically junk shops. But also they contain entire worlds—the vanished, the distant, the invisible to the human eye—in a small space, one available in the hometown which Schulz himself almost never left.

But the young boy, on this eve, visits the eponymic cinnamon shops only in his imagination. He finds neither the shops, nor his father's wallet, but instead, as if in a dream, arrives at the back entrance to his *Gymnasium* building. He doesn't recognize it at first, seen from the other side. This space, we learn, is where an evening drawing class was sometimes held. And here the story becomes a prophecy of sorts. Bruno Schulz himself, after the publication of this story, which did not make him wealthy or famous, became the unusual and unstrict arts and crafts professor at a Jewish school for boys.

I didn't mention the "answer" to the schoolboyish riddle at Homer's end. In some versions of the story it's actual schoolboys rather than fishermen who offer the riddle. The answer is lice. A pretty humble answer, and maybe not even a very tricky one. It's hard not to imagine that Homer—at least the mythic Homer—couldn't have solved it. Maybe that is part of what is useful about the story. It allows us to think it's not true. The story allows us to think that Homer didn't die in that way, or maybe even at all. And at the same time the story shifts the scale to the tiny comic creatures, who surely bear us no ill will, and for whom we as humans constitute a kind of planet.

The mix of obscured hopefulness and degradation in this anecdote remind me of Schulz. Schulz was born in 1892, in the town of Drohobych, which was then Austrian Galicia and today is in Ukraine. He was Jewish, the son of a cloth merchant. He wrote in Polish, and was also fluent in German. One of the stories told of Schulz is that when he was a young boy his mother saw him feeding the last grains of sugar to the houseflies, and when she asked him what he was doing, he said he was helping the flies make it through the winter.

People and creatures don't quite die in Schulz's work, even when they do. Schulz often asks us to see our real world, like that very real thirteenth month, as false. The Street of Crocodiles itself, which is presented to us as unequivocally real—"an industrial-mercantile district with a strikingly emphatic character of sober utilty"—becomes, by the end of the story, a place best described as " a paper imitation, a photo montage assembled from musty cutouts, from last year's newspapers."

The story of Schulz's death is infamous. He was shot dead in the street by an SS officer in an exchange. Supposedly one SS officer said, "I have killed your Jew," to which the other replied, "All right, now I will go and kill yours." There are other variants on this terrible story, and we can't really know if it's true or just a telling. But also there are other stories about Schulz. The Israeli writer David Grossman wrote in the *New Yorker* about meeting an elderly Jewish man in Israel who told him that Schulz had been his art teacher, from 1939 to 1941. The man told Grossman, "In Schulz's class, there were mainly kids who were disciplinary problems, and he knew he would be fresh meat for them and their ridicule, and I think he realized very fast that he could save himself only if he did something different . . ." Schulz told the kids stories, extemporaneous stories, and "we listened—even the wildest animals listened."

Schulz's narrator in "The Sanatorium under the Hourglass" not only finds his dead father at the sanatorium, but moves into the sanatorium himself. "Since the moment of my arrival," the narrator tells us, "during which certain appearances of hospitable thoughtfulness were spun out for the newcomer's sake, the administration of the sanatorium has not troubled itself in the least to give us even the illusion of some kind of care." In this way, the sanatorium perfectly mirrors our own everyday life, in which we are left to attend to ourselves. Yet it's also the place where the dead continue to live.

TRANSLATOR'S NOTE

In 1963, Celina Wieniewska, a Polish-born literary translator, introduced Bruno Schulz to readers of English. Schulz had been dead for more than twenty years and his brilliant literary creations had seemed doomed to remain a treasure available only to readers of Polish. That first book of Schulz's stories in English, faithfully titled *Cinnamon Shops and Other Stories*, has been known ever since as *The Street of Crocodiles*, the title under which it was brought out by its American publisher.[1] In 1977 Wieniewska published a second volume of previously untranslated stories under the title *Sanatorium under the Sign of the Hourglass*.[2]

I fell in love with Bruno Schulz's stories through the undeniable magic of Wieniewska's English version of *Sklepy cynamonowe*, which I read soon after its appearance in the United States. I was not alone. Wieniewska's translations have been enchanting readers ever since they appeared. They have also served as the basis for translations into many other languages by translators who did not work from the original Polish. Instytut Książki, the Polish Book Institute, under the leadership of its then director, Grzegorz Gauden, sought to remedy that situation by commissioning new translations directly from the Polish. All of the new translations were to be based on the 1989 scholarly edition, which contained a lengthy foreword, a selection of Schulz's essays and letters, and the annotated texts of his two published short-story collections—*Cinnamon Shops* and *The Sanatorium under the Hourglass*—as well as the four separately published stories collected here under the heading, "Other Stories." This edition was not, of course, available to Celina Wieniewska. The present translation was part of the Instytut Książki's ambitious project. I am deeply grateful for the Institute's support.

Why undertake a new English translation of Bruno Schulz's fiction? Because a translation is not a clone of the original, there can be no perfect rendering into another language. The richer the original, the more interpretations it can sustain. Translation is both a scholarly art and a form of performance.[3] Celina Wieniewska did not publish an explanation of her approach, but her translations reveal that she intended to convey the visual images and often bizarre events that distinguish Schulz's stories and to make his writing more accessible by taming his prose. It appears that she did not try to convey the linguistic tics and mannerisms of Schulz's style.

The present translation attempts to get closer to the texture of Schulz's prose by stretching English syntax to make it accommodate the sinuosity of Schulz's longer sentences rather than reining them in. It uses repetition as often as Schulz did—of individual words and of alliterative word combinations—and, as frequently as possible, it deploys the prefix "dis-" (the English equivalent of Polish *roz-*), which is one key to his view of the world, as has been so persuasively argued by Michał Paweł Markowski.[4]

I have benefited immensely from the advice of Professor Markowski, who generously read my draft translation against the original word by word and phrase by phrase. He caught and corrected errors, offered suggestions for more accurate wording, and through his queries challenged me to find equivalents for verbal tricks I thought defied analogous rendering in English. No translator could ask for a more engaged reading. I am profoundly grateful for the collegial spirit in which his assistance was offered. I am likewise grateful to the attentive anonymous reader who reviewed the translation for Northwestern University Press. The reviewer raised questions about points of style, cautioning me not to risk betraying Schulz by too rigid an interpretation of "faithfulness." She or he inspired me through the generous deployment of yellow highlighting—the software equivalent of a raised eyebrow—to make numerous revisions throughout the translation before I decided, reluctantly, that it was time to stop tinkering.

Finally, for his faith in the translation and for initiating the publication process in his former role as editor at this press, I offer my thanks to Mike Levine—no relation despite the shared surname, but always an engaging interlocutor and friend. Responsibility for any errors of interpretation is, of course, mine alone.

Notes

1. Bruno Schulz, *Cinnamon Shops and Other Stories*, trans. Celina Wieniewska (London: MacGibbon & Kee, 1963); Bruno Schulz, *The Street of Crocodiles*, trans. Celina Wieniewska (New York: Walker & Co., 1963).

2. Bruno Schulz, *Sanatorium under the Sign of the Hourglass*, trans. Celina Wieniewska, with an introduction by John Updike (London: Picador, 1978).

3. This idea that translation of a literary work is akin to performance of a musical score is elaborated in Robert Wechsler, *Performing without a Stage: The Art of Literary Translation* (North Haven, Conn.: Catbird Press, 1998).

4. Michał Paweł Markowski, *Powszechna rozwiązłość: Schulz, egzystencja, literatura* (Kraków: Wyd. Uniwersytetu Jagiellońskiego, 2012).

Cinnamon Shops

August

I

In July, my father left to take the waters, abandoning my mother, my older brother, and me as prey to the dazzling summer days that were white with heat. Dazed by the light, we browsed the great book of vacation, whose every page was on fire from the radiance and which contained in its depths the languorous sweet flesh of golden pears.

Adela would come back on those luminous mornings like Pomona from the fire of the blazing day, pouring from her basket the colorful beauty of the sun—the glistening sweet cherries, full of water beneath their transparent skin; the mysterious dark sour cherries, whose aroma far exceeded their flavor; apricots whose golden flesh held the core of long afternoons; and next to this pure poetry of fruit she would unload racks of flesh with their keyboards of veal ribs, swollen with energy and nourishment; seaweeds of vegetables that resembled slaughtered cephalopods and jellyfish—the raw material of dinner with a taste as yet unformed and bland, the vegetative, telluric ingredients of dinner with a smell both wild and redolent of the field.

Every day, the great summer passed in its entirety through the dark apartment on the second floor of the apartment house on the market square: the silence of shimmering rings of air, squares of radiance dreaming their passionate dreams on the floor, the melody of a barrel organ drawn from the day's deepest golden vein, two or three measures of a refrain played over and over again on a piano somewhere, fainting away in the sunshine on the white sidewalks, lost in the fiery depths of the day. The housework done, Adela would draw the linen drapes, releasing shade into the room. Then the colors dropped an octave lower, the room filled with shade as if submerged in the light of ocean depths and was reflected even more dimly in the green mirrors, and all the sweltering heat of the day was breathing on the drapes, which were billowing gently with noon-hour dreams.

On Saturday afternoons Mother and I would go for a walk. From the semidarkness of the vestibule one stepped immediately into the sunny bath of the day. The people walking past, wading in gold, had their eyes half closed

3

from the heat, as if glued together with honey, and their retracted upper lips exposed their gums and teeth. And everyone wading in this golden day had that grimace of scorching heat as if the sun had placed upon its followers one and the same mask—the golden mask of the sunshine brotherhood; and all who walked along the streets today, who met one another and passed by, old men and youths, children and women, exchanged greetings in passing with that mask painted in thick golden paint on their face, grinned that Bacchic grimace at one another—the barbaric mask of a pagan cult.

The market square was empty and yellow from the heat, swept clean of dust by hot winds, like a biblical desert. Thorny acacias that had grown out of the golden square's emptiness were seething above it with their bright foliage, bouquets of nobly articulated green filigrees, like the trees in old Gobelins tapestries. The trees appeared to be commanding a gale, theatrically agitating their crowns to demonstrate in their pathetic contortions the elegance of their leafy fans with their silvery underbellies like the furs of noble foxes. The old houses, polished by the winds of many days, took on the reflected colors of the great atmosphere, the echoes and memories of hues diffused in the depths of the colorful weather. It seemed that entire generations of summer days (like patient stucco workers chipping off the mildew of plaster from old facades) were hammering away at the deceitful glaze, extracting from one day to the next the ever more clearly authentic countenance of the houses, the physiognomy of the fate and life that formed them from inside. Now the windows, blinded by the radiance of the empty square, were sleeping; the balconies confessed their emptiness to the sky; the open vestibules smelled of coolness and wine.

A throng of urchins who had survived the fiery broom of sweltering heat in a corner of the market square besieged a section of a wall, throwing buttons and coins at it to test it, as if it were possible to read from the horoscope of those metal disks the true secret of a wall etched with the hieroglyphs of scratches and cracks. In any event, the market square was empty. One expected the Good Samaritan's donkey, led by the bridle, to arrive under the shade of the swaying acacias at the vaulted entranceway with its wine merchant's barrels and two servants to cautiously lower the sick man from the burning saddle in order to carry him carefully up the cool stairs to the floor above, fragrant with the Sabbath.

So, Mother and I strolled down the two sunny sides of the market square, leading our broken shadows across all the houses as if across piano keys. The pavement squares passed slowly under our soft, flat steps—some of them pale pink, like human skin, others golden and dark blue, all of them flat, warm, and velvety in the sunshine like the faces of sundials trampled by feet until they are unrecognizable, unto blissful nothingness.

Until finally, at the corner of Stryjska Street, we entered the shade of the apothecary shop. A large show globe with raspberry juice in the broad apothecary window symbolized the coolness of the balms with which all suffering could be soothed there. A couple of houses more and the street could no longer maintain its urban decorum, like a fellow who, returning to his native village, sheds his city elegance along the way, slowly changing into a ragged peasant the closer he gets to his village.

The bungalows on the city's outskirts were subsiding along with their windows, sunken in the luxuriant, jumbled blooming of their small gardens. Forgotten by the great day, all the herbs, flowers, and weeds multiplied luxuriantly and silently, gladdened by this pause that they could sleep through outside the margin of time, on the borders of the endless day. An immense sunflower, held up on a powerful stem and sick with elephantiasis, awaited in yellow mourning dress the final, sad days of its life, sagging beneath the excess growth of its monstrous corpulence. But the naive suburban bluebells and the modest little muslin flowers stood there helpless in their starched pink and white little shirts, with no understanding of the sunflower's great tragedy.

II

The tangled thicket of grasses, weeds, wild plants, and milk thistles is blazing in the fire of the afternoon. The garden's afternoon nap buzzes with a swarm of flies. The golden stubble cries out in the sunshine like a red locust; crickets scream in the torrential rain of fire; seed pods explode softly, like grasshoppers.

And over near the fence a sheepskin coat of grasses rises like a protuberant hillock-hump, as if the garden has turned onto its other side in its sleep and its thick peasant shoulders are breathing the silence of the earth. On these shoulders of the garden the slovenly female fecundity of August expanded into dense hollows of enormous burdocks, proliferated in lobes of shaggy sheets of leaves, in luxuriant tongues of fleshy vegetation. There, those bulging burdock bodies goggled like lolling gorgons, half consumed by their own frenzied skirts. There, the garden was selling at no cost the cheapest groats of wild lilac, a coarse porridge of plantain, stinking like soap, wild firewater of mint, and all the worst August trash. But on the other side of the fence, behind this lair of summer in which the imbecility of demented weeds had spread, there was a garbage dump wildly overgrown with milk thistle. No one knew that it was precisely there, during that summer, that August was celebrating its great pagan orgy. On this garbage dump, propped against the fence and overgrown with wild lilac, stood the bed of Tłuja the idiot girl. That's what we all called her. On a pile of garbage and scraps, old pots, shoes, rubble and trash, stood a green-painted bed, supported, in place of a missing leg, by two old bricks.

The air above the rubble, gone wild from the heat, slashed by the lightning flashes of glistening horseflies, enraged by the sun, crackled as if from invisible rattles, exciting one into a frenzy.

Tłuja sits there, squatting amid her yellow bedding and rags. Her large head bristles with a mop of black hair. Her face is contractile, like the bellows of an accordion. Every moment or so a grimace of weeping folds the accordion into a thousand transverse pleats, then amazement opens it up again, smooths out the pleats, reveals the slits of her tiny eyes and the moist gums with yellow teeth beneath a snoutlike, fleshy lip. Hours filled with heat and boredom pass during which Tłuja babbles under her breath, dozes, grumbles quietly, and grunts. A thick swarm of flies settles on the immobile girl. But suddenly this whole pile of dirty tattered clothes, of rags and scraps, begins to move, as if animated by the rustling of rats breeding inside it. Startled, the flies wake up and rise in a great, roaring swarm full of furious buzzing, flashes, and flickering. And while the tattered clothes slip onto the ground and scatter across the garbage dump like frightened rats, the heart of the dump digs its way out from them, the core slowly unwraps itself and emerges from its shell: a half-naked, dark imbecile slowly rises and stands there, looking like a little pagan idol on short, childlike legs, while from her neck, which is swollen with an influx of fury, from her flushed face growing dark with rage, on which the arabesques of swollen veins resembling primitive paintings are efflorescing, a bestial shriek escapes, a throaty shriek, produced from all the bronchi and pipes of this half-bestial, half-godlike breast. The milk thistles, burned by the sun, are screaming, the burdocks puffing up and flaunting their shameless flesh, the weeds drooling glistening poison, and the imbecile girl in a wild convulsion, hoarse from her shrieking, with frenzied passion thrusts her fleshy groin against an elderberry trunk that, bewitched by this whole beggars' chorus to perverted pagan fecundity, creaks softly beneath the urgency of dissolute lust.

Tłuja's mother hires herself out to housewives to scrub their floors. She's a small woman, yellow as saffron, and she also seasons with saffron the floors, fir tables, benches, and fold-down beds that she cleans in the homes of poor people. Once, Adela took me to that old Maryśka's house. It was early in the morning; we entered a small room whitewashed with a bluish tint, with a tamped-down clay layer on the floor on which the early sunlight lay, brilliant yellow in the morning quiet that was measured out by the frightful clanging of the peasant clock on the wall. Stupid Maryśka was lying on straw in a chest, as pale as a communion wafer and as silent as a glove from which a hand has been withdrawn. And as if taking advantage of her sleep, the silence chattered away, yellow, glaring, evil silence, it soliloquized, quarreled, loudly and vulgarly carrying on its nonsensical, maniacal monologue. Maryśka's time, the time imprisoned in her soul, emerged from her terrifyingly real and walked by itself across the room, raucous, roaring, infernal, rising in the glaring silence of the morning from the noisy mill clock like bad flour, powdery flour, the stupid flour of madmen.

III

In one of these cottages, surrounded by brown palings and drowning in the lush greenery of the garden, lived Aunt Agata. Going in to see her, we passed in the garden colored glass balls perched on top of slender poles, pink, green and violet balls, in which entire luminous, glowing worlds were spellbound, like those ideal, happy pictures enclosed in the matchless perfection of soap bubbles.

In the dim vestibule with its old oleographs eaten away by mold and blind from old age, we would discover a familiar smell. In that reliable old odor the life of these people was contained in a marvelous simple synthesis, a distillation of race, the blood type and secret of their fate, enclosed imperceptibly in the quotidian transience of their own distinct time. The old, wise doors, whose dark sighing admitted these people and let them out, silent witnesses to the comings and goings of the mother, daughters, and sons, opened noiselessly like a wardrobe's doorframe, and we entered into their life. They sat as if in the shade of their own fate and did not defend themselves; in their initial awkward gestures they revealed to us their secret. Were we not related to them by blood and fate?

The room was dark and velvety from the navy-blue upholstery with its gold pattern, but here, too, the echo of the flaming day trembled in the brass on the picture frames, the door handles, and gold moldings, although filtered through the dense greenery of the garden. Aunt Agata stood up from beside the wall, huge and luxuriant, her flesh round and white and spotted with the red rust of freckles. We sat down near them as if on the shore of their fate, a little embarrassed by the defenselessness with which they revealed themselves to us without reservation, and we drank water with rose syrup, a most peculiar drink, in which I discovered what seemed to be the deepest essence of that sweltering Saturday.

My aunt complained. That was the basic tone of her conversations, the voice of that white and fecund flesh, already expanding lushly as if beyond the boundaries of her person, only loosely controlled in concentration, in the constraints of individual form, and already multiplied even in this concentration, ready to distend, to disintegrate, to discharge into a family. It was an almost self-generating fecundity, femaleness deprived of brakes and pathologically rampant.

It seemed that the very scent of masculinity, the smell of tobacco smoke, a bachelor's joke, could stimulate this inflamed femaleness to a depraved parthenogenesis. And truly all her complaints against her husband, against the servants, her worries about the children were only the capriciousness and sulking of unsated fecundity, a continuation of the surly, irate, and tearful coquetry that she visited, in vain, upon her husband. Uncle Marek, small, hunched over, with a face drained of sex, sat in his gray bankruptcy, resigned to his fate, in the shade of the boundless contempt in which he seemed to rest. The garden's distant glow, spread wide-open in the window, smoldered in his gray eyes. Occasionally, he would attempt to register a reservation with a weak motion, to put up resistance, but the wave of self-sufficient femaleness thrust that meaningless gesture aside, moved triumphantly past it, flooded with its broad stream the feeble convulsions of masculinity.

There was something tragic in this untidy and unconstrained fecundity; it was the abjection of a creature struggling on the border of nothingness and death, it was a kind of heroism of femaleness triumphing with its fecundity even over a deformity of nature, over the insufficiency of the male. But the progeny demonstrated the rightness of that maternal panic, that frenzy for giving birth, that exhausted itself in unsuccessful creatures, in an ephemeral generation of phantoms without blood or faces.

Łucja came in, of average height, with a full-blown head too mature for her childlike, plump body with its white, delicate flesh. She gave me her doll-like hand that seemed to be only now putting out buds, and immediately her whole face blossomed, like a peony overflowing with rosy repletion. Unhappy because of her blushes that spoke shamelessly of the secrets of menstruation, she half closed her eyes and flushed even more under the touch of the most neutral questions, since every one of them contained a secret allusion to her oversensitive maidenhood.

Emil, the oldest of the cousins, with a light-blond mustache and a face from which life seemed to have wiped away every expression, paced back and forth in the room, his hands in the pockets of his pleated trousers.

His elegant, expensive attire bore the stamp of the exotic countries from which he had returned. His faded, opaque face appeared to forget about itself from one day to the next, to become an empty white wall with a pale net of veins in which, like the lines on a faded map, the dying memories of this stormy, wasted life were entangled. He was a master of card tricks, smoked long, elegant pipes, and gave off the strange smells of foreign countries. His gaze wandering over distant memories, he told the strangest anecdotes, which, at a certain point, would suddenly break off, disconnect, and disperse into nothingness. I gazed at him wistfully, yearning for him to pay attention to me and to rescue me from the torment of boredom. In fact, it did seem that he winked at me as he went into another room. I followed him. He sat sunk low on a small couch, his knees crossed almost at the level of his head, which was as bald as a billiard ball. It seemed as if it were his clothing alone lying there pleated, crumpled, tossed over the seat. His face was like the breath of a face—a streak that some unknown passerby had left in the air. In his pale hands, with their light-blue glaze, he was holding a wallet in which there was something he was looking at. The bulging white of a pale eye emerged with difficulty from the mist of his face, enticing me with impish winking. I felt an irresistible attraction to him. He took me between his knees, and shuffling photographs before my eyes with skillful hands, he showed me images of naked women and boys in strange positions. I stood there, leaning against him, and looked with distant, unseeing eyes at those delicate human bodies, while the aura of vague agitation with which the air had suddenly grown thick reached me and ran down me as a shudder of anxiety, a wave of sudden understanding. But at the same time that faint mist of a smile that had sketched itself beneath his soft, beautiful mustache, the germ of desire that was as taut on his temples as a pulsing vein, the tension holding his features in concentration for a moment collapsed back into nothingness and his face departed into absence, forgot about itself, dissipated.

A Visitation

I

At that time our city was already falling ever deeper into a chronic twilight grayness and becoming overgrown at the edges with a patchy rash of shadow, puffy mold, and iron-hued moss.

Scarcely had the day been disentangled from the dark brown smoke and morning fogs than it immediately started listing toward a low amber afternoon, becoming for a moment transparent and golden, like brown ale, only to descend beneath the repeatedly segmented, fantastic vaults of brightly colored, expansive nights.

We lived on the market square, in one of those dark houses with empty, blind facades that make it so difficult to distinguish one from another.

This can cause endless mistakes. Having entered the wrong vestibule and the wrong stairwell, one usually wound up in a veritable labyrinth of unfamiliar apartments and passageways, unexpected exits into unfamiliar courtyards, and one forgot the original goal of the expedition, until, many days later, while returning on some gray dawn from the uncharted territories of strange, matted adventures, one remembered amid pangs of conscience one's family home.

Our apartment, full of large wardrobes, deep couches, pale mirrors, and tawdry artificial palm trees, was falling ever deeper into a state of neglect owing to the indolence of Mother, who sat in the shop all day, and to the negligence of slender-limbed Adela, who, unsupervised by anyone, spent her days in front of mirrors at her lengthy toilette, leaving traces of herself everywhere in the form of brushed-out hair, combs, discarded slippers and stays.

Our apartment had no fixed number of rooms since no one ever remembered how many of them were rented out to unknown tenants. Occasionally, one of these forgotten rooms would be opened by accident and discovered to be empty; the tenant had long since moved out and unexpected discoveries were made in drawers that had not been touched for months. The salesclerks lived in the downstairs rooms, and occasionally we were awakened at night by their groans, voiced under the influence of nightmares. In the winter, it was still pitch-black night outside when Father descended to those cold, dark rooms, his candle startling flocks of shadows that flew sideways along the floor and walls; he was on his way to awaken the loudly snoring men from their rock-hard sleep.

By the light of the candle he placed there, they wriggled out lazily from under their dirty bedding; seated on their beds, they stuck out their bare, ugly feet and, holding a sock in their hand, surrendered for just one more moment to the sensual pleasure of yawning—of yawning drawn out to the point of voluptuousness, to a painful spasm of the palate as happens during powerful bouts of vomiting.

In the corners sat huge cockroaches, motionless, turned gigantic by their own shadows affixed to them by the burning candle, shadows that did not detach themselves even when one of those flat, headless torsos suddenly set off running with uncanny, spidery moves.

At that time, my father's health began to fail. Already in the first weeks of that early winter there were periods when he spent entire days in bed surrounded by bottles, pills, and the account books that were brought to him from the office. A bitter odor of illness settled on the bottom of the room, whose wallpaper teemed with a very dark tangle of arabesques.

In the evenings, when Mother returned from the store, he would be excited and inclined to squabble; he accused her of inaccuracies in maintaining the accounts, grew red in the face, and worked himself up to the point of insanity. I remember that once, having awakened late at night, I saw him, barefoot and in his nightshirt, running back and forth on the leather couch, documenting his irritation in this way before my bewildered mother.

Other days, he would be calm and collected and thoroughly engrossed in his books, lost in the labyrinths of convoluted computations.

I can see him in the light of a smoking lamp, squatting among the pillows, against the great carved headboard of the bed, with the enormous shadow of his head on the wall, nodding in silent meditation.

From time to time, his head would emerge from the accounts as if to catch its breath; he would open his mouth, smack his dry and bitter tongue with disgust, and look around in bewilderment, as if searching for something.

It often happened then that he would run silently from the bed to a corner of the room, to the wall on which his trusted instrument hung. This was a sort of water hourglass or a large glass flask, calibrated in ounces and filled with a dark fluid. My father connected himself to this instrument by means of a long rubber hose that was like a twisted, sickly umbilical cord, and connected thus with the pitiful apparatus, he froze in concentration and his eyes grew darker until an expression of suffering or of some kind of illicit pleasure appeared on his pale face.

Then again came days of quiet, focused work, interspersed with lonely monologues. When he sat like that in the light of the table lamp amid the pillows of his great bed while the room grew enormous above him in the shadow of the lampshade that connected him with the great element of the city night beyond the window, he sensed without looking that the pulsing thicket of the wallpaper, full of whispers, hisses, and lisps, was contracting the expanse around him. He heard without looking a conspiracy full of blinks signaling mutual understanding, flirtatious winks blossoming among the flowers of his ears' attentive shells and dark smiling lips.

Then he appeared to delve even deeper into his work, he counted and added up, afraid of betraying the anger that was gathering in him and struggling against the temptation to blindly hurl himself backward with a sudden shout, grabbing fistfuls of those curly arabesques, those bunches of eyes and ears that the night had produced in swarms and that grew and multiplied, hallucinating flowers and ever newer sprouts and shoots from the darkness's maternal umbilicus. He would finally calm down when, with the ebbing of night, the wallpaper withered, curled up, dropped its leaves and flowers, and grew autumnally sparse, letting in the distant dawn.

Then, amid the twittering of the wallpaper birds, in the golden winter dawn, for an hour or two he would fall into a deep, black sleep.

For days and weeks, when he appeared to be immersed in complex running accounts, his thoughts had been secretly straying into the labyrinths of his own intestines. He would hold his breath and listen closely. And when his gaze, grown pallid and vague, returned from those depths, he calmed it with a smile. He did not yet believe, he dismissed as absurd, those claims, those propositions that weighed on him.

During the day they were like reasoned arguments and persuasions, lengthy, monotone deliberations, conducted in a muted voice and full of humorous interludes, of playful bantering. But at night the voices resounded more passionately. The demand returned all the more clearly and portentously, and we heard him conversing with God, as if pleading and recoiling from something that insistently demanded and enjoined.

Until there came a night when the voice resounded, menacing and undeniable, commanding him to bear witness with lips and entrails. We heard the spirit enter him, and he rose from his bed, long and growing with prophetic anger, choking on vociferous words that he expelled like a light machine gun. We heard the pounding of a struggle and my father's groan, the groan of a titan whose hip is broken but who rages on.

I had never seen the Old Testament prophets, but at the sight of this man, brought down by divine wrath, straddling an enormous porcelain chamber pot with his legs spread wide apart, screened by the whirlwind of his arms, by a cloud of despairing contortions above which his voice, alien and hard, rose even higher, I understood the divine wrath of holy men.

It was a menacing dialogue, like the speech of thunderbolts. The flailing of his arms shredded the sky into pieces, and the face of Jehovah appeared in the cracks, swollen with wrath and spitting out curses. Without looking, I saw him, the menacing Demiurge, as he, reclining on the darkness as on Mount Sinai, his powerful hands supported by the curtain rail, pressed his enormous face to the upper panes of the window against which his monstrously fleshy nose was flattened.

I heard his voice in the intervals between my father's prophetic tirade; I heard the powerful snarls from those swollen lips rattling the panes and mixing with the eruptions of my father's entreaties, lamentations, and threats.

At times the voices grew quiet and fumed softly, like the chattering of wind in a chimney at night, then they exploded anew in a great tumultuous uproar, a storm of intermingled sobs and curses. Suddenly, the window opened with a dark yawn, and a sheet of darkness wafted across the room.

In the brightness of a lightning flash I caught sight of my father in a billowing nightshirt as he, with a terrifying curse, poured out the contents of his chamber pot through the window into a night that roared like a seashell.

II

My father was slowly disappearing, withering before our eyes.

Crouched against his great pillows, with clumps of his gray hair bristling wildly, he engaged in conversation with himself in a low voice, utterly engrossed in some convoluted internal affairs. It might seem that his personality had disintegrated into many quarreling and divergent selves, for he argued with himself out loud, negotiated vehemently and passionately, persuaded and pleaded, but then again he would seem to be presiding over a meeting of many customers whom he was striving to reconcile by expending all his ardor and eloquence. But every time, these noisy gatherings, full of hot tempers, splintered apart in the end amid curses, imprecations, and abuse.

Then came a period of subsidence of some kind, of inner consolation, a blessed cheerfulness of the soul.

Once again the great folios were spread about on the bed, on the table, on the floor, and in the light shed by the lamp a kind of Benedictine calm of work settled over the bed's white sheet, over the bowed gray head of my father.

But when Mother returned from the shop late at night, Father would grow animated, call her over, and proudly show her the splendid, colorful decals that he had pasted assiduously all over the pages of the main ledger.

We all noticed then that Father had started shrinking from one day to the next, like a nut shriveling inside its shell.

No loss of his powers accompanied this decline. On the contrary, the state of his health, humor, and mobility appeared to improve.

He often laughed now, out loud and chirpily; he simply roared with laughter, but he also would knock on his bed and reply to himself, "Come in" in various tones for hours on end. From time to time he crawled out of bed, climbed onto the wardrobe, and, crouching under the ceiling, attempted to make order among the old, rust-filled, dusty junk.

At times, he would place two chairs across from each other, and, supporting himself with his hands on their armrests, he would swing his legs back and forth, searching with a radiant gaze for expressions of amazement and encouragement on our faces. It seemed that he had made his peace with God. At times, the face of the bearded Demiurge would show itself in the bedroom window at night, bathed in the dark purple of Bengal lights, and for a moment it would look good-naturedly at the soundly sleeping man whose melodious snoring appeared to be wandering far afield through the unknown territories of his dreamworlds.

During the long, semidark afternoons of that late winter, from time to time my father would disappear for hours at a time into corners densely packed with old junk, doggedly searching for something.

And sometimes at dinnertime, as we were all sitting down to the table, it turned out that Father was missing. Then for a long while Mother would have to keep calling "Jakub!" and banging a spoon on the table until he crawled out from some wardrobe, covered in rags of cobwebs and dust, his vacant gaze fixed on some complicated matters that preoccupied him, visible to him alone.

At times he would clamber up onto the curtain rail and assume an immobile pose, mirroring the great stuffed vulture that hung on the wall on the other side of the window. In that motionless, crouching pose, with clouded gaze and slyly smiling expression, he would sit for hours until suddenly he would flap his arms like wings upon someone's entrance and crow like a rooster.

We stopped paying attention to these eccentricities in which he was becoming more enmeshed from one day to the next. As if totally divested of bodily needs, taking no food for weeks on end, with every passing day he plunged deeper and deeper into complicated and bizarre affairs that we found incomprehensible. Unreachable by our persuasive arguments and pleas, he replied with fragments of his internal monologue, whose course could not be disturbed by anything external to it. Perpetually overwrought, pathologically animated, with a flush on his dry cheeks, he did not notice us but looked right past us.

We grew accustomed to his harmless presence, to his quiet babbling, to the childlike self-absorbed twittering whose trills somehow proceeded along the margins of our time. By then he was already disappearing, at times for many days, vanishing somewhere in the distant recesses of the apartment, and it was impossible to find him.

Gradually, these disappearances ceased to make an impression on us; we grew accustomed to them, and when he would appear again after many days, thinner and a couple of inches shorter, this did not hold our attention for long. We simply stopped taking him into account, so distant had he become from everything human and real. Knot by knot, he loosened his ties with us; point by point, he lost the bonds connecting him with the human community. What remained of him was a small amount of corporeal casing and that handful of senseless eccentricities—they could disappear one day, as unnoticed as the gray pile of trash collecting in a corner that Adela carried out every day to the garbage bin.

Birds

The yellow winter days arrived, filled with boredom. A threadbare table-cloth, too short and pocked with holes, covered the rust-colored earth. On many roofs it wasn't big enough and there were black or rust-colored thatched roofs and arks concealing in themselves the sooty expanse of attics—black, charred cathedrals, bristling with the ribs of rafters, purlins and tie beams, the dark lungs of winter gales. Every dawn revealed new chimneys and smoke vents that had sprung up during the night, inflated by a nighttime gale, the black pipes of the devil's organs. The chimney sweeps could not repel the crows that, in the shape of live black leaves, would cover the branches of the trees near the church in the evening, take flight again, flapping, in order finally to settle, each one clinging to its own place on its own branch, and then at dawn they would fly away in great flocks—storm clouds of soot, flakes of lampblack, undulating and fantastic, staining with their flickering croaking the dull-yellow streaks of dawn. The days hardened from cold and boredom like last year's loaves of bread. They were cut open with dull knives, without appetite, with a lazy somnolence.

Father no longer left the house. He lit the stoves, studied the never fully investigated essence of fire, detected the salty, metallic aftertaste and the smoky odor of the winter flames, the cool caress of the salamanders licking the sparkling soot in the chimney's throat. During those days he lovingly undertook all the repairs in the upper regions of the room. He could be seen at any time of day as, squatting on the top rung of a ladder, he tinkered with something near the ceiling, near the cornices of the high windows, the balls and chains of the chandeliers. As was the custom of painters, he used the ladder like enormous stilts and felt comfortable in that bird's-eye perspective close to a painted heaven, to the arabesques and birds of the ceiling. He was departing farther and farther from the affairs of practical life. When Mother, concerned and worried by his condition, tried to draw him into a conversation about business, about the bills coming due on the nearest *ultimo*, he listened to her distractedly, full of anxiety, with twitches showing on his distracted face. And it would happen that he interrupted her suddenly with a commanding movement of his hand in order to run to a corner of the room, press his ear to a crack in the floor, and, with the index fingers of both hands raised to express the high importance of his scrutiny, would listen attentively. We did not yet at that time understand the sad background of these extravagances, the lamentable complex that was developing deep inside him.

Mother had not the slightest influence on him, whereas he bestowed great respect and attention on Adela. The cleaning of his room was a great and important ceremony for him that he never neglected to witness, following all Adela's manipulations with a mixture of terror and delight. He ascribed deeper, symbolic meaning to all her activities. When the girl, with youthful and bold movements, pushed a brush on a long pole over the floor, that was almost beyond his strength. Tears would flow from his eyes, his face would be overwhelmed with quiet laughter, and a delightful orgasmic spasm would shake his body. His sensitivity to tickles grew to madness. It sufficed for Adela to point her finger at him with a gesture indicating tickling and immediately he would flee through all the rooms, slamming the doors behind him, finally to collapse belly down on a bed in the last room and writhe in convulsions of laughter under the influence of the internal image that he could not resist. Thanks to this, Adela had almost unlimited power over Father.

It was then that for the first time we observed in Father a passionate interest in animals. Initially, it was simultaneously a hunter's and an artist's passion, perhaps also the deeper zoological sympathy of a creature for its kin, also for different forms of life, experimentation in untested registers of being. Only in its later phase did this matter assume the incredible, tangled, deeply sinful and unnatural turn that it would be best not to expose to the light of day.

It began with incubating birds' eggs.

With great expenditure of labor and money, Father imported from Hamburg, from Holland, from African zoological stations fertilized birds' eggs that he gave to enormous Belgian chickens to incubate. This was an exceedingly absorbing procedure for me, too—this hatching of the chicks, true freaks in shape and coloring. It was impossible to perceive in those monsters with enormous, fantastic beaks that ripped themselves wide-open immediately after birth, hissing greedily in the abysses of their throats, in those lizards with the frail, naked bodies of hunchbacks, the future peacocks, pheasants, capercaillies, and condors. Placed in baskets, in cotton, this dragonlike brood lifted their blind, walleyed heads on their thin necks, squawking soundlessly from mute throats. My father, wearing a green apron, walked back and forth along the shelves like a gardener patrolling his hotbeds of cacti and lured out of nothingness those blind bladders pulsing with life, those awkward bellies taking in the external world only in the form of food, those outgrowths of life groping their way blindly toward the light. A couple of weeks later, when these blind buds of life burst open to the light, the rooms were filled with the colorful murmuring, the flickering chirping of its new inhabitants. They perched everywhere, on the curtains' cornices, the wardrobe moldings, they nested in the thicket of tin branches and arabesques of the many-branched chandeliers.

While Father studied his great ornithological compendia and leafed through their colorful plates, the feathered phantasms seemed to fly out from them and fill the room with colorful fluttering, with petals of crimson, scraps of sapphire, verdigris, and silver. During feeding, they created on the floor a colorful, undulating flower bed, a living carpet that disintegrated upon someone's careless entrance, dispersed into mobile flowers, flapping in the air, only to settle themselves in the end around the upper regions of the room. One condor in particular, an enormous bird with a naked neck, a face wrinkled and rank with growths, remains in my memory. He was a thin ascetic, a Buddhist lama, full of unshakable dignity in his entire demeanor, who conducted himself with the iron decorum of his great race. When he sat facing Father, motionless in his monumental stance of the ancient Egyptian gods, his eye veiled with a whitish film that he drew over the pupil from the side in order to lock himself completely in the contemplation of his own dignified solitude, he seemed with his stony profile to be my father's older brother. The same bodily fabric, the tendons and wrinkled, tough skin, the same gaunt, bony face, the same corneous, deep eye sockets. Even Father's hands, strong and knotted, his long, slender hands with their curved fingernails, had their analogue in the condor's talons. Seeing him asleep like this, I could not resist the impression that there was a mummy in front of me—the desiccated and therefore shrunken mummy of my father. I believe that this amazing similarity did not escape Mother's notice either, although we never touched on that subject. It was characteristic that the condor shared the chamber pot with my father.

Not content with hatching ever new specimens, my father arranged bird weddings in the attic, sent out matchmakers, tethered alluring, yearning fiancées in the attic's gaps and cavities, and in fact succeeded in turning the roof of our house, an enormous gabled and shingled roof, into a veritable avian inn, a Noah's ark, to which all sorts of winged creatures flocked from far-off places. Even long after the liquidation of the avian household, that tradition of our house lived on in the world of birds, and in the season of springtime migrations there often descended on our roof entire swarms of cranes, pelicans, peacocks, and birds of every kind.

This project, however, suddenly—after its brief magnificence—took a sad turn. For soon it became necessary to effect Father's final transfer into the two garret rooms that served as junk rooms. A mingled clangor of birds' voices reached us from there as soon as dawn broke. The wooden boxes of the attic rooms, assisted by the resonance of the roof's expanse, rang with noise, with fluttering, crowing, tooting, and gurgling. That is how we lost sight of Father for several weeks. Only rarely did he descend into the apartment, and then we were able to notice that apparently he had grown smaller, lost weight, and shriveled. Sometimes, out of forgetfulness, he would leap up from his chair at the table and, flapping his arms like wings, emit a protracted crowing, while his eyes became clouded with a misty film. Then, abashed, he would laugh along with us and attempt to turn the incident into a joke.

Once, during a time of general housecleaning, Adela appeared unexpectedly in Father's avian kingdom. Stopping in the doorway, she wrung her hands at the stench that rose in the air, as well as at the piles of excrement covering the floor, tables, and furniture. Immediately resolute, she opened a window, through which, with the help of her broom, she set the entire bird mass whirling. A hellish dust cloud of feathers, wings, and shrieking arose, in which Adela, like a mad maenad, shielded by the whirling of her thyrsus, danced her dance of destruction. Along with the flock of birds, my father, in a state of terror, flapping his arms, attempted to rise into the air. Slowly, the winged cloud thinned out until finally Adela alone remained on the battlefield, exhausted and out of breath, and my father, with a troubled, embarrassed face, was ready to agree to any terms of capitulation.

A moment later, my father descended the steps from his dominion—a broken man, a banished king who had lost his throne and his kingdom.

Mannequins

That avian project of my father's was the last explosion of color, the last splendid countermarch of a fantasy that that incorrigible improviser, that swordsman of imagination, produced on the earthworks and trenches of barren, empty winter. Only today do I understand the lonely heroism with which he, all by himself, waged war on the boundless element of boredom stupefying our city. Deprived of all support, without recognition on our part, that most peculiar man defended the lost cause of poetry. He was a wonderful mill into whose hoppers the bran of empty hours poured that it might bloom within its cogwheels with all the colors and fragrances of the spices of the East. But, accustomed to the splendid juggling of that metaphysical prestidigitator, we were inclined simply to accept the value of his sovereign magic, which saved us from the lethargy of empty days and nights. Adela was not met with a single rebuke for her thoughtless, stupid vandalism. On the contrary, we felt a kind of low gratification, a shameful satisfaction from the suppression of these expansive exuberances, which we tasted greedily until we were satiated, only afterward to perfidiously shirk any responsibility for them. And perhaps there was in this betrayal a secret bow in the direction of victorious Adela, to whom we vaguely ascribed a kind of mission and commissioning from powers of a higher order. Betrayed by everyone, Father retreated without a struggle from the locations of his recent glory. Without crossing swords, he conveyed into the hands of the enemy the domain of his former magnificence. A voluntary outcast, he withdrew to the empty room at the end of the hall and entrenched himself there with his solitude.

We forgot about him.

The mournful grayness of the city besieged us on all sides, blossoming in the windows as the dark rash of dawn, the parasitical fungus of twilight, and proliferating into the fluffy fur coat of winter nights. The wallpaper in the rooms, which had been blissfully relaxed during those days and open to the colorful flights of that winged swarm, closed in upon itself again, thickened, became entangled in the monotony of bitter monologues.

The lamps grew black and withered like old teasels and milk thistles. Now they hung dejected and peevish, tinkling softly like little glass crystals when someone groped his way through the gray twilight of the room. In vain did Adela insert colorful candles into all the arms of these lamps, an unsuccessful surrogate, a pale remembrance of the splendid illuminations with which their hanging gardens had recently blossomed. Alas! Where was that twittering budding, that hasty and fantastic fruiting in the bouquets of these lamps from which, as from bursting magical tortes, winged phantasms flew out, disrupting the air into decks of magic cards, distributing them as colorful applause, pouring down in thick scales of azure, of peacock and parrot-green, in metallic sparkles, drawing lines and arabesques in the air, glimmering traces of soaring and circling, displaying colorful fans of flutters, holding still for a long time after their passage through the rich and sparkling atmosphere? Even now, the echoes and the possibilities of colorful flashes were hiding in the depths of the colorless aura, but no one bored a hole with a flute or sampled with a drill the murky rings of air.

Those weeks were under the sign of a peculiar somnolence.

The beds, left unmade throughout the day, heaped with bedclothes crumpled and rolled about in because of disturbing dreams, stood like deep boats ready to sail off into the damp, tortuous labyrinths of some black, starless Venice. At the break of dawn Adela would bring us coffee. We dressed lazily in cold rooms by the light of a candle reflected multiple times in the black panes of the windows. Those early mornings were filled with disorganized bustling, desultory searching in various drawers and wardrobes. The slap-slap of Adela's slippers could be heard throughout the apartment. The salesclerks lit their lanterns, received the great keys to the shop from Mother's hand, and went out into the dense, swirling darkness. Mother could not cope with getting dressed. The candles burned down in the candelabra. Adela would disappear somewhere in the distant rooms or in the attic, where she was hanging up the linens to dry. It was impossible to call her. A still young, dull, dirty fire in the stove licked the cold, glittering accretions of soot in the chimney's throat. A candle went out, the room sank in darkness. With our heads on the tablecloth, amid the remains of breakfast, we dozed off, half dressed. Lying with our faces on the furry belly of the darkness, we sailed away on its undulating breath into starless nothingness. Adela's noisy housecleaning woke us up. Mother could not handle getting dressed. Before she had finished brushing her hair, the salesclerks were returning for dinner. The darkness in the marketplace acquired the color of yellowish smoke. In a moment, colors of the most beautiful afternoon might disentangle themselves from those smoky honeys, those murky ambers. But the happy moment passed, the amalgam of dawn faded, the swollen ferment of the day, nearly attainable by now, subsided into helpless grayness. We took our seats at the table, the salesclerks rubbed their hands, red from the cold, and suddenly the prose of their conversations instantly introduced the day in its fullness, a gray and empty Tuesday, a day without traditions and without a face. But when a platter of fish in glassy aspic appeared on the table, two large fish lying side by side and head to tail like a figure from the zodiac, we recognized in them the day's coat of arms, the calendrical emblem of a nameless Tuesday, and we hastily divided it among ourselves, filled with relief that in it the day had recaptured its proper physiognomy.

The salesclerks ate solemnly, with the gravity due a calendric celebration. The smell of pepper wafted through the room. And when they had wiped the last bit of aspic from their plates with a roll, contemplating in their thoughts the heraldry of the coming days of the week, and only the heads with their boiled eyes remained on the platter, we all felt that the day had been conquered by our collective strengths and that the rest was beside the point.

In fact, Adela did not stand on ceremony with the rest of the day, which was consigned to her mercies. Amid the clatter of pots and splashes of cold water she energetically liquidated the couple of hours until dusk while Mother slept through them on the ottoman. Meanwhile, in the dining room the stage set for the evening was already being prepared. Polda and Paulina, the young seamstresses, were setting themselves up with the props of their trade. Carried in their arms, a silent, immobile woman, a lady made of wisps and canvas, with a black wooden knob instead of a head, entered the room. But once mounted in the corner between the door and the stove, the quiet lady became mistress of the situation. From her corner, standing motionless, she supervised the girls' work in silence. With criticism and disfavor, she received their efforts and courtship as they knelt before her measuring fragments of a dress marked with white basting stitches. They catered attentively and patiently to the silent idol whom nothing could satisfy. That Moloch was implacable, as only female Molochs can be, and constantly sent them back to their work, while they, spindle shaped and slender, like the wooden spools from which the threads were unwound, and just as restless, manipulated the pile of silk and cloth with deft movements, cut into its colorful mass with clanking shears, made their machine whir, pressing its pedal with a cheap little patent leather foot, while around them rose a pile of scraps, varicolored strips and rags like spat-out shells and husks around two fastidious, wasteful parrots. The crooked jaws of the shears opened with a creaking sound like the beaks of these colorful birds.

The girls trampled carelessly on the colorful trimmings, wading in them obliviously as if in the trash heap for a possible carnival, the junk room of some great masquerade that never came to pass. They brushed the scraps of cloth off themselves with a nervous laugh, tickled the mirrors with their eyes. Their souls, the rapid sorcery of their hands, were not in the boring dresses that remained on the table but in the hundreds of sheared-off pieces, the hasty, frivolous clippings with which they could shower the entire city like a colorful, fantastic snowstorm. Suddenly they felt hot and opened a window so that in the impatience of their seclusion, in their hunger for strangers' faces, they might at least see the nameless face of night pressed against the window. They fanned their burning cheeks before the winter night, which was swelling the curtains; they bared their burning décolletés, filled with hatred for each other and rivalry, ready to enter into battle for whatever Pierrot a dark breeze of night might blow into the window. Ah! how little did they demand from reality. They had everything in themselves; they had an excess of everything in themselves. Ah! a Pierrot stuffed with sawdust would have sufficed for them, the word or two for which they had long been waiting, that they might fall into their long-prepared role, which had long since been pressing onto their lips, full of sweet and terrible bitterness, racing wildly, like the pages of a romance devoured at night along with the tears shed onto their blushing cheeks.

During one of his evening wanderings through the apartment undertaken in Adela's absence, my father happened upon that quiet evening performance. He stood for a moment in the dark doorway of the adjacent room with a lamp in his hand, enchanted by that scene full of fever and blushes, that idyll made of face powder, colorful tissue paper, and atropine, for which the winter night served as a background full of meaning, breathing amid the billowing window curtains. Putting on his glasses, he took a couple of steps closer and walked around the girls, illuminating them with the lamp he held in his hand. A draft from the open door lifted the curtains at the window, the young women allowed themselves to be examined, twisting at the hips, glistening with the enamel of their eyes, the lacquer of their creaking slippers, the buckles of the garters under their skirts that the wind was billowing out; the scraps of cloth took off across the floor like rats, escaping toward the half-open door of the dark room, while my father gazed attentively at the snorting young ladies and whispered under his breath, "*Genus avium* . . . if I'm not mistaken, *scansores* or *psitacci* . . . worthy of attention in the highest degree."

That accidental meeting was the start of an entire series of performances during which my father quickly managed to enchant both young ladies with the charm of his peculiar personality. Repaying him for his conversation, which was full of gallantry and wit, and which filled the emptiness of the evenings for them, the girls allowed the fervent researcher to study the structure of their slim, tawdry bodies. This took place in the course of conversation, with dignity and refinement, such that it removed any suggestive appearance from the most risky points of these investigations. Slipping a stocking off Paulina's knee and studying with infatuated eyes the compact and noble structure of the joint, my father said, "How full of charm and how fortunate is the form of being that you ladies have chosen. How beautiful and simple is the thesis that you were granted to reveal with your life. But with what mastery, with what finesse you discharge that task. If, casting aside respect for the Creator, I should wish to entertain myself with a critique of creation, I would cry out, 'Less content, more form!' Ah, how that diminution of content would relieve the world. More modesty in intentions, more restraint in pretensions, gentlemen demiurges, and the world would be more perfect!" my father cried, precisely at the instant when his hand stripped the tether of her stocking from Paulina's white calf. At that moment, Adela appeared in the open dining room door, bearing a tray with afternoon tea. It was the first meeting of these two enemy powers since the time of the great crackdown. All of us who were present at this meeting experienced a moment of great anxiety. It was inexpressibly painful for us to be witnesses to a new humiliation of this already so sorely tested man. Very embarrassed, my father got up off his knees, his face coloring with wave after wave of a progressively darker flood of shame. But Adela unexpectedly found herself equal to the situation. She walked over to Father with a smile on her face and tweaked his nose. At this signal Polda and Paulina clapped their hands joyfully, stamped their little feet, and, hanging on Father's arms on either side, danced around the table with him. In this way, thanks to the girls' good hearts, the germ of bitter conflict dissipated in general gaiety.

That was the beginning of the greatly interesting and peculiar lectures that my father, inspired by the charm of this small and innocent audience, delivered during the succeeding weeks of that early winter.

It is worth noting how, in contact with that unusual man, all things somehow retreated to the root of their being, reconstructed their appearance down to the metaphysical core, returned to some extent to the primal idea, in order to betray it at that point and incline toward those dubious, risky, and ambiguous regions that we shall here refer to, in short, as the regions of the great heresy. Our heresiarch walked among things like a mesmerist, infecting them and seducing them with his dangerous charm. Am I to name Paulina, too, as his victim? She became his student during those days, a disciple of his theories, the model for his experiments.

Here I shall attempt to lay out with appropriate caution, avoiding any outrage, the exceedingly heretical doctrine that possessed my father for many long months at that time and controlled all his actions.

A Treatise on Mannequins; or, The Second Book of Genesis

"The Demiurge," said my father, "had no monopoly on creation; creation is a privilege of all spirits. Matter has been granted infinite fecundity, an inexhaustible vital force, and at the same time, a seductive power of temptation that entices us to create forms. In the depths of matter indistinct smiles take shape, tensions are reinforced, experimental shapes solidify. All matter flows from the infinite possibilities passing through it in faint shivers. Awaiting the life-giving breath of the spirit, it overflows endlessly within itself, tempts with a thousand sweet curves and the softness it hallucinates in its blind imaginings.

"Lacking in initiative, lasciviously submissive, malleable like a woman, compliant in response to every impulse, it becomes a space outside the law, open to every sort of charlatanry and dilettantism, the domain of every abuse and dubious demiurgic manipulation. Matter is the most passive, defenseless being in the cosmos. Anyone can knead it, shape it; it obeys everyone. Every organization of matter is impermanent and unfixed, easily reversed and dissolved. There is no evil in the reduction of life to new and different forms. Murder is not a sin. Often, it is a necessary act of violence against unyielding, ossified forms of being that are no longer satisfying. In the interest of an intriguing, important experiment it may even constitute a service. Herein is the starting point for a new apologia for sadism."

There was no end to my father's glorification of the bizarre element that is matter.

"There is no dead matter," he instructed us; "lifelessness is only an external appearance behind which unknown forms of life are hiding. The scale of these forms is infinite, their shades and nuances inexhaustible. The Demiurge possessed vital and interesting creative recipes. Thanks to them he created a multitude of species that renew themselves by their own power. Whether these recipes will ever be reconstructed is unknown. But this is not necessary, for even if those classical methods of creation should turn out to be forever inaccessible, there remain certain illegal methods, an infinity of heretical, extreme methods."

Moving on from these general principles of cosmogony, the closer my father came to the area of his narrower interests the lower his voice dropped, sinking to a penetrating whisper; his lecture grew increasingly difficult and convoluted, and the conclusions he was aiming for were lost in increasingly dubious and perilous regions. His gesticulating acquired an esoteric solemnity. He closed one eye, placed two fingers against his forehead, and the cunning in his gaze became simply uncanny. He bored into his interlocutors with that cunning, he violated their shyest, most intimate reserve with the cynicism of that gaze, and he reached the retreating girls in the farthest corner, pinned them to the wall, and tickled them, scratching with his ironic finger until a flash of comprehension was tickled out of them, along with laughter, the laughter of acknowledgment and acceptance to which it was necessary, at last, to capitulate.

The girls sat motionless, the lamp smoked, the cloth had long since slipped out from under the machine's needle, and the machine, empty, was still clattering away, quilting the black, starless cloth unwinding from the warp of the winter night outside the window.

"Too long have we lived under the terror of the Demiurge's unsurpassable perfection," said my father. "Too long has the perfection of his creation paralyzed our own creativity. We do not wish to compete with him. We have no ambition to equal him. We wish to be creators in our own, lower sphere, we desire creative work for ourselves, we desire creative delight, we desire, in a word, demiurgy."

I do not know in whose name my father proclaimed these postulates, what community, what corporation, sect, or order bestowed pathos upon his words by its solidarity. As for us, we were far removed from any demiurgic temptations.

But my father, in the meantime, had developed a program for this second demiurgy, an image of the second generation of creatures that was to stand in open opposition to the present era.

"We do not care about creations with long-lasting breath, about creatures for the long run. Our beings will not be the heroes of multivolume romances. Their roles will be short, concise, their characters without plans for the future. Often, for a single gesture, for a single word, we shall undertake the labor of bringing them to life for just that one moment. We confess this openly: we will not insist on the permanence or solidity of our workmanship; our creations will be provisional, as it were, constructed for a single use. If they are to be people, we will give them, for example, only one side of a face, one arm, one leg—namely, the one that will be necessary for their role. It would be pedantic to worry about the other leg, which does not come into play. In the back, they can simply be stitched up with canvas or whitewashed. We shall encapsulate our aspiration in this proud motto: For every gesture a differ-ent actor. To serve each word, each deed, we shall bring to life an individual human being. Such is our fancy; it will be a world based on our taste. The Demiurge was fond of refined, splendid, complex materials; we give pride of place to tawdry. Quite simply, the cheapness, the shoddiness, the tawdri-ness of material thrills and excites us. Do you understand," asked my father, "the profound meaning of this weakness, this passion for gaudy tissue paper, for papier-mâché, for lacquer paint, for scraggly hair, and sawdust? This is," he said with a pained smile, "our love for matter as such, for its puffiness and porosity, for its unique, mystical consistency. The Demiurge, that great master and artist, makes it invisible, commands it to disappear beneath the game of life. We, on the contrary, love its discord, its resistance, its scruffy shapelessness. We like to see beneath its every gesture and every movement the leaden exertion, the torpor, the sweet bearishness."

The girls sat motionless with glassy eyes. Their faces were elongated and stupefied from attentive listening; their cheeks appeared to be powdered with blushes. It was difficult to say at this moment if they belonged to the first or the second generation of creation.

"In a word," my father concluded, "we want to create man for the second time, in the image and likeness of a mannequin."

Here, for the sake of reportorial fidelity, we must describe a certain minor, insignificant incident that occurred at this point in the lecture and to which we attach no weight. This incident, entirely inexplicable and nonsensical in the said course of events, can perhaps be explained as a certain type of ves-tigial automatism, without antecedents and without continuation, a type of maliciousness of an object transferred into the psychological realm. We advise the reader to ignore it just as casually as we have done.

This is how it unfolded: At the moment when my father was pronouncing the word *mannequin*, Adela glanced at her wristwatch, after which she and Polda exchanged a glance communicating their agreement. Now she slid for-ward a few inches with her chair, lifted the hem of her dress, slowly extended her foot in its tight-fitting black silk, and flexed it like a serpent's head.

She sat like that throughout the entire time of this scene, absolutely rigid, her great fluttering eyes made deeper with the azure of atropine, and with Polda and Paulina at either side. All three, their eyes wide-open, looked at Father. My father cleared his throat, fell silent, bent down, and suddenly turned very red. In an instant the deep lines of his face, until then so lively and vibrant, froze into subdued features.

He, that inspired heresiarch only just released from a gale of exultation, suddenly folded in upon himself, collapsed, and curled up. Or perhaps he had been exchanged for someone else. That other man sat rigid, very red, with downcast eyes. Miss Polda approached and bent over him. Patting him lightly on his back, she said in a tone of gentle encouragement, "Jakub will be reasonable, Jakub will listen, Jakub will not be stubborn. Come now . . . Jakub, Jakub . . ."

Adela's outstretched slipper trembled slightly and glistened like a serpent's tongue. My father rose slowly, his eyes downcast, took one step forward like an automaton, and sank onto his knees. The lamp hissed in the silence, meaningful glances ran back and forth in the thicket of the wallpaper, the whispers of poisonous tongues, zigzags of thoughts, flew about . . .

A Treatise on Mannequins, Continued

The next evening, with renewed eloquence, Father took up his dark and intricate theme. The deep lines of his wrinkles expanded and contracted with exquisite cunning. A projectile of irony was concealed in each spiral. But at times inspiration expanded the circles of his wrinkles, and they rose like an immense, whirling menace, escaping in silent volutes into the depths of the winter night.

"The figures in waxworks, dear ladies," he began, "are pathetic church-fair parodies of mannequins, but be wary of treating them lightly even in this form. Matter knows no jokes. It is always full of tragic dignity. Who dares to think that it is possible to play with matter, to shape it for the sake of a joke, that the joke will not grow into it, will not instantly eat into it like fate, like predestination? Can you sense the pain, the dumb captive suffering, the suffering embedded in matter of this grotesque hag that does not know why it exists, why it must endure in this form, this parody, imposed on it by an act of violence? Do you understand the power of expression, of form, of appearance, the tyrannical willfulness with which it throws itself upon a defenseless log and masters it like its own tyrannical, controlling soul? You impose upon some head made of tufts of hair and canvas an expression of anger and you leave it once and for all with that anger, that convulsion, that tension, locked up with a blind fury for which there is no outlet. The crowd laughs at this parody. Weep, my ladies, over your own fate, seeing the misery of imprisoned matter, tormented matter, matter that does not know who it is and why it exists, nor where that gesture that has been imposed on it once and for all is leading it.

"The crowd laughs. Do you understand the terrible sadism, the intoxicating demiurgic cruelty of this laughter? All the same, we should weep, my ladies, over our own fate at the sight of this misery of matter, violated matter, upon which a terrible injustice has been committed. From this, ladies, there follows the terrible sadness of all those clownish golems, all those hags tragically brooding over their comical grimaces.

"Here is the anarchist Lucchesini, the murderer of Empress Elisabeth; here is Draga, the demonic, unfortunate queen of Serbia; here is a brilliant young man, the hope and pride of his people, destroyed by an unfortunate addiction to onanism. Oh, the irony of those names, of those appearances!

"Is there really something of Queen Draga in this hag, her double, even the most distant shadow of her essence? The similarity, the appearance, the name calms us and prevents us from asking who this unhappy creature thinks it is. And yet it must be someone, my ladies, someone anonymous, someone menacing, someone unhappy, someone who has never in its dumb life heard of Queen Draga . . .

"Have you heard at night the terrible howling of those waxwork dummies locked inside fairground stalls, the pitiful chorus of those bodies made of wood and porcelain, hammering with their fists against the walls of their prisons?"

On my father's face, distorted by the horror of the things he was summoning out of darkness, a vortex of wrinkles had formed, a deepening funnel on the bottom of which blazed the terrible eye of a prophet. His beard bristled strangely; the wisps and tufts of hair shooting out from his warts, his moles, his nostrils rose straight up from their roots. He stood there rigid, with burning eyes, trembling from inner agitation, like an automaton that has gotten stuck and is at a standstill.

Adela got up from her chair and asked us to turn a blind eye to what, in a moment, was going to happen. Then she walked over to Father and, hands on hips, adopting a pose of emphatic determination, insisted most explicitly . . .

The girls sat stiffly, with downcast eyes, in a peculiar state of numbness . . .

A Treatise on Mannequins, Conclusion

On one of the following evenings my father continued his lecture with these words: "It was not about these embodied misunderstandings, nor about these sad parodies, my dear ladies, these fruits of a coarse and vulgar intemperance, that I wanted to speak when delivering my speech about mannequins. I had something else in mind."

Here my father began constructing before our eyes an image of his dreamed-of *generatio aequivoca*, a generation of beings only half organic, a kind of pseudoflora and pseudofauna, the result of the fantastic fermentation of matter.

They were creatures similar in appearance to living beings, to vertebrates, crustaceans, arthropods, but this appearance was deceptive. They were, in fact, amorphous beings without an internal structure, the fruits of the imitative tendency of matter that, endowed with memory, repeats out of habit forms that are already established. The scale of morphology to which matter is subservient is in general limited, and a certain inventory of forms continually replicates itself on the various levels of existence.

It was possible to obtain these beings—mobile, sensitive to stimuli, and yet far from true life—by suspending certain complex colloids in solutions of kitchen salt. These colloids took shape over several days, organized themselves into particular densities of substance that resemble the lower forms of fauna.

In beings that have arisen in this manner it was possible to confirm a process of respiration, the transformation of matter, but chemical analysis did not demonstrate in them even a trace of albuminous tissue or any carbon compounds at all.

Nevertheless, these primitive forms were as nothing in comparison with the wealth of shapes and the magnificence of pseudofauna and flora that sometimes appear in certain narrowly delimited environments. These environments are old apartments, saturated with the emanations of many lifetimes and events—worn-out atmospheres, rich in the specific ingredients of human daydreams, and rubble, abounding in the humus of reminiscence, nostalgia, sterile boredom. On such soil the pseudovegetation sprouted rapidly and superficially, parasitized abundantly and ephemerally, pushed out short-lived generations that burst into bloom abruptly and magnificently only to suddenly fade away and vanish.

The wallpaper in such apartments must be very worn-out and bored by incessant wandering among all the rhythmic cadenzas; no wonder that they lose their way in distant, risky delusions. The core of furnishings, their substance, must already be loose, degenerate, and susceptible to extreme temptations; then, on that sick, exhausted, wild soil there will blossom, like a beautiful rash, a fantastic coating, a colorful, lushly flourishing mold.

"You know, ladies," said my father, "in old apartments there are rooms that people have forgotten about. Not visited for months at a time, they shrivel in their abandonment between the old walls, and it happens that they withdraw into themselves, become encased in bricks, and, lost to our memory once and for all, slowly lose their own existence, too. The doors leading into them from some backstairs landing may be overlooked for so long by the residents that they take root, grow into the wall that obliterates any trace of them in a fantastic drawing of cracks and scratches.

"Once," said my father, "early one morning toward the end of winter, after many months of absence, I entered such a half-forgotten tract and was astounded by the look of those rooms.

"From every crack in the floor, from every molding and frame, thin sprouts shot out and filled the gray air with a glimmering filigree of lacy foliage, with a conservatory's openwork thicket, full of whispers, shimmers, swinging, a kind of spurious and blissful spring. Around the bed, beneath a many-armed lamp, along the wardrobes, clusters of delicate trees were swaying, spraying upward into luminous crowns, into fountains of lacy foliage, striking with their atomized chlorophyll right up against the painted sky of the ceiling. In an accelerated process of blooming, enormous white and pink flowers were sprouting in that foliage, blossoming before one's eyes, shooting out lushly from the center as pink pulp, then overflowing their edges, dropping their petals, and disintegrating in rapid conclusion to the flowering cycle.

"I was happy," my father said, "at this unexpected blossoming that filled the air with a twinkling rustle, a gentle sound pouring down like colored confetti through the branches' slender twigs.

"I saw how from the trembling of the air, from the fermentation of the excessively rich atmosphere, this accelerated blossoming separated out and materialized, this overflowing and disintegration of fantastic oleanders that filled the room like a rare, indolent snowstorm of great pink sprays of flowers.

"Before night fell," my father concluded, "there was no longer any trace of that splendid flowering. That entire illusory fata morgana was only a mystification, a case of the wonderful make-believe of matter that passes itself off as life."

My father was strangely animated that day; his glances, his sly, ironic glances burst with verve and humor. Then, suddenly growing serious, he again considered the infinite range of forms and shades that polymorphic matter assumes. He was fascinated by boundary forms, uncertain and problematic, like the ectoplasm of somnambulists, pseudomatter, the cataleptic emanation of the brain that in certain instances grew out of the mouth of a sleeping person into an entire table and filled an entire room, like a lushly expanding tissue, an astral dough on the border between body and soul.

"Who knows," he said, "how many suffering, crippled, fragmentary forms of life there are, how artificially pieced together is the life of wardrobes and tables violently hammered together with nails, the life of crucified wood, of the silent martyrs to cruel human ingenuity. The terrible transplantation of alien races of wood that hate one another, their being shackled together into a single unhappy individual.

"How much old, wise torment there is in stained rings of wood, in the veins and grains of our old respected wardrobes. Who will recognize in them the old features, smiles, glances, planed and polished beyond recognition?"

My father's face as he was saying this dissolved into a pensive line drawing of wrinkles; it began to resemble the knots and rings of an old board from which all recollections have been planed away. For a moment we thought that Father would fall into the torpid condition that sometimes came upon him, but suddenly he came to, regained his senses, and continued.

"The ancient mystical tribes embalmed their dead. Bodies and faces were immured and set into the walls of their houses; in the drawing room was the father, who was stuffed; the tanned mother, deceased, was the rug beneath the table. I knew a certain captain who had in his cabin a Melusina lamp, a chandelier made from his murdered lover by Malayan embalmers. She had enormous antlers on her head.

"In the quiet of the cabin that head, stretched between its branches of antlers up near the ceiling, would slowly open its eyelashes; on its parted lips a film of saliva glistened and popped from a quiet whisper. Cephalopods, tortoises, and enormous crabs, suspended on the ceiling's rafters like candelabras and chandeliers, were moving their legs constantly in that endless silence, walking and walking in place."

My father's face suddenly acquired an expression of concern and sorrow while his thoughts, on the paths of who knows what associations, moved on to new examples:

"Am I to pass over in silence," he said in a lowered voice, "that my cousin, as a consequence of a lengthy incurable illness, changed progressively into a coil of rubber intestines, that on winter nights his poor wife carried him around day and night on pillows, humming endless lullabies to the unhappy creature? Can there be anything sadder than a man changed into an enema hose? What disillusionment for his parents, what disorientation of their feelings, what dashing of all hopes connected with the promising young man! And yet my poor cousin's faithful love accompanied him in this transformation, too."

"Oh! I can't take this any longer, I can't listen to this!" moaned Polda, slumping in her chair. "Silence him, Adela."

The girls stood up, Adela walked over to Father, and with one extended finger made a motion suggesting tickling. Father, disconcerted, fell silent, and, filled with terror, started retreating before Adela's waggling finger. She kept following him, threatening him venomously with her finger, forcing him step-by-step from the room. Paulina yawned and stretched. She and Polda, arm in arm, looked into each other's eyes and smiled.

Nimrod

Throughout August of that year I played with a splendid little puppy that had turned up one day on our kitchen floor, feeble and whimpering, still smelling of milk and infancy, with an unformed, roundish, trembling little face, its molelike paws sprawled along its sides, and with the most delicate, downy fur.

At first sight, that little speck of life captured all the rapture, all the enthusiasm of my boy's soul.

From what heaven did this favorite of the gods, dearer to the heart than the most beautiful of toys, drop down so unexpectedly? And just to imagine that old, utterly uninteresting washerwomen at times can hit upon such splendid ideas and bring from the outskirts of town such a puppy—at an utterly early, transcendentally early, morning hour—to our kitchen!

Ah! one was still, alas, not there, not yet delivered from the warm bosom of sleep, but already that happiness had come into being, already it was waiting for us, lying awkwardly on the cool kitchen floor, unappreciated by Adela and the members of the household. Why wasn't I awakened earlier? A saucer of milk on the floor bore witness to Adela's maternal impulses and also bore witness, alas, to the moments in a past that was lost to me forever, to the delights of foster motherhood in which I had played no part.

But an entire future still lay before me. What an infinity of experiences, experiments, discoveries was opening now! The secret of life, its most essential mystery, reduced to this most simple, most convenient and entertaining form, was exposed here to insatiable curiosity. It was inexpressibly interesting to have for one's own such a tiny bit of life, such a particle of the eternal mystery in such an amusing, new form, awakening endless curiosity and secret respect by dint of its otherness, its unexpected transposition of that very thread of life that is in us, too, into a form that is different from ours, an animal form.

Animals! the target of insatiable curiosity, exemplifications of the enigma of life, as if created to demonstrate man to man, dividing his richness and complexity into a thousand kaleidoscopic possibilities, each one pursued to a paradoxical extreme, to an exuberance replete with character. Unburdened by that fusion of exotic interests that muddy relations between people, my heart opened wide, full of sympathy for the alien emanations of eternal life, full of that loving collaborative curiosity that is the masked hunger for self-knowledge.

The puppy was velvety, warm, and pulsing with its small, rapid heart. His ears were two soft petals, his eyes light blue and bleary, he had a pink little mouth that you could put your finger into without any danger at all, delicate, innocent little paws with a touching pink little nipple-shaped bump on the back of each front leg just above the paw. He crawled into the bowl of milk with those paws, ravenous and impatient, slurping the drink with his little pink tongue, and then, sated, mournfully lifting his muzzle with a drop of milk on the chin, awkwardly backed away from his bath of milk.

His walk was an ungainly rolling, sideways and at a slant, in an undecided direction along a somewhat tipsy, wavering line. The dominant feature of his mood was a certain indefinite, fundamental sorrow, his orphanhood and helplessness—an inability to fill the emptiness of life with anything between the sensations of his meals. This manifested itself in the aimlessness and inconsistency of his movements, irrational attacks of nostalgia accompanied by pitiful whimpering, and an inability to find a place for himself. Even in the depths of sleep, in which he had to calm his need for support and snuggling by employing himself for that purpose, curled up into a trembling ball, a feeling of isolation and homelessness kept him company. Oh, life—young and fragile life, expelled from the trusted darkness, from the snug warmth of the maternal womb into a great, alien, luminous world, how it shrinks and retreats, how it recoils before the need to accept the project proffered to it— full of aversion and despondency!

But slowly little Nimrod (he had received that proud, martial name) begins to relish life. The exclusive dominance of the image of the maternal origin of all being yields to the charm of multiplicity.

The world begins to lay its traps for him: the unknown and enchanting taste of various foods, the rectangle of morning sunlight on the floor where it is so good to lie down, the movements of his own limbs, his own paws, tail, impishly summoning him to play with himself, the caresses of a human hand under which a certain friskiness is slowly maturing, gaiety opening out his body and giving rise to the need for all kinds of new, intense, risky movements—all this bribes, persuades, and incites him into acceptance, into making peace with the experiment of life.

And one more thing. Nimrod begins to understand that what approaches him here, despite the appearance of novelty, is fundamentally something that already has happened—has happened many times, an infinite number of times. His body recognizes situations, impressions, and objects. Fundamentally, none of this is overly surprising. In the face of each new situation he dives into his memory, into the deep memory of his body, and he searches blindly, feverishly—and it sometimes happens that he discovers in himself the appropriate reaction, already prepared: the wisdom of generations compounded in his plasma, in his nerves. He finds actions, decisions, which he himself had not known were already mature in him, already waiting to leap out.

The scenery of his young life, the kitchen with its fragrant buckets, with dishcloths and their complicated, intriguing aroma, with the slapping of Adela's slippers, with her noisy bustling about, no longer terrifies him. He has grown accustomed to considering it his domain, he feels at home in it and has begun to develop in relation to it a hazy feeling of belonging, of a fatherland.

Except that unexpectedly there descends on him a cataclysm in the form of floor scrubbing, the laws of nature overthrown, splashes of warm lye washing under all the furniture, and the menacing scraping of Adela's scrub brushes.

But the danger passes, the brush, calmed down and motionless, lies quietly in a corner, the drying floor smells sweetly of wet wood. Nimrod, restored to his normal rights and freedom in his own territory, feels a lively desire to grab the old blanket on the floor with his teeth and jerk it to right and left with all his might. This pacification of elements fills him with inexpressible joy.

Suddenly he stands as if rooted to the spot: in front of him, some three puppy steps away, a freak is moving about, a monster sliding along rapidly on little sticks that are its many jumbled legs. Shaken to his core, Nimrod follows with his gaze the oblique path of the glossy insect, tensely following the flat, headless, blind thorax carried along by the unbelievable mobility of its spidery legs.

Something rises inside him, something ripens, swells, something he himself does not yet understand, a kind of anger or terror, but rather pleasant and linked to a shudder of power, self-awareness, aggression.

And suddenly he collapses onto his front paws and projects a voice as yet unknown to him, alien, totally unlike his ordinary whimpering.

He projects it once, and once again, and yet again, in a thin high-pitched voice that keeps going off course.

But in vain does he apostrophize the insect in this new language born of sudden inspiration. In the categories of the cockroach mind there is no room for this tirade, and the insect continues on its oblique circuit toward the corner of the room, amid movements consecrated by an eternal cockroach ritual.

Feelings of hatred, however, do not yet hold permanence and power in the puppy's soul. His newly awakened joy in life transforms every feeling into gaiety. Nimrod keeps on barking, but the meaning of this barking has changed imperceptibly, has become a parody of itself—yearning, fundamentally, to express the inexpressible adequacy of this splendid project of life, full of piquancy, of unexpected little shivers, and of punch lines.

Pan

In a corner between the rear walls of the sheds and outbuildings was the dead end of the courtyard, the most distant, final branch locked in between a stall, an outhouse, and the rear wall of the chicken coop—a soundless bay from which there was no exit.

It was the most distant promontory, the Gibraltar of that courtyard, banging its head despairingly against the blind fence made of horizontal boards, the imprisoning, final wall of this world.

From under its moss-covered planks a trickle of black, smelly water oozed out, a vein of the putrid, oily marsh that was never dry—the only road that led across the boundary of the fence and into the world. But the despair of the stinking dead end had been hitting its head against this barrier for so long that it finally loosened one of the strong, horizontal boards. We boys finished the rest, we forced and pushed out the heavy, moss-covered board from its support. Thus, we created a gap and opened a window onto the sunshine. Standing with one foot on the board, which was thrown across the puddle like a bridge, a prisoner of the courtyard could squeeze through the crack, which would release him into a new, airy, expansive world. There was a big garden there, old, gone wild. Tall pear trees and spreading apple trees grew in huge, scattered clusters, sprinkled with a silvery rustling, a seething net of whitish sparkles. Lush, jumbled, unmown grasses covered this wavy terrain like a fluffy sheepskin cloak. There were the ordinary blades of meadow grasses with feathery tassels of grain; there were the delicate filigrees of wild parsley and carrots; the wrinkled, coarse little leaves of ground ivy and of blind nettles, which smelled like mint; fibrous, glistening ribwort plantain, spotted with rust, shooting out tufts of thick red buckwheat. All of this, matted and fluffy, was saturated with gentle air, lined with azure wind, and infused with sky. When you lay down in the grass, you were covered with a complete azure geography of clouds and floating continents, you breathed in the entire vast map of the heavens. From their relationship with the air, the leaves and shoots were covered with delicate hairs, a soft coating of fluff, a coarse bristle of hooks, as if intended for grasping and detaining the flow of oxygen. This delicate, whitish coating connected the leaves with the atmosphere, gave them the silvery gray gloss of waves of air, of shadowy pensiveness between two flashes of sunlight. And one of these plants, yellow and full of a milky liquid in its pale stalks, puffed up by the air, was already pushing out from its empty shoots just air itself, just fluff in the shape of feathery sow thistle spheres dispersed by a breeze and filtering soundlessly into the azure silence.

The garden was extensive, branching into several offshoots, and it had various zones and climates. On one side, it was open, full of the milk of the heavens and the air, and there it spread out for the sky the softest, most delicate, most downy greenery. But the deeper it descended into the depths of that long spur and plunged into the shade between the rear wall of the abandoned soda water factory and the long, collapsing wall of the stables, it grew visibly gloomier, turned surly and careless, let itself go wild and unkempt, grew fierce with nettles, bristled with thistles, turned mangy with all sorts of weeds, until at the very end between the walls, in a broad, rectangular bay, it lost all measure and fell into a rage. There, it was no longer an orchard but a paroxysm of madness, an explosion of fury, a cynical shamelessness and debauchery. There, completely out of control, the barren burdock cabbage heads proliferated, opening the floodgates to their passion—enormous witches, disrobing in broad daylight, shedding their ample skirts, flinging them off one after another, until their puffed-up, rustling, tattered rags buried under themselves with their frantic layers the rambunctious bastard tribe. But the ravenous skirts swelled and jostled one another, piled up one atop another, spread out and covered each other, growing together into a swollen mass made of sheets of leaves as high as the low eaves of the barn.

It was there that I glimpsed him for the only time in my life at a noon hour frantic from the heat. It was that moment when time, crazed and wild, breaks free from the daily grind of events, and like a fugitive tramp, races, shouting, across the fields. Then summer, deprived of all control, grows through the entire expanse without restraint or accounting, grows with wild abandon on every side, twofold, threefold, or into some other unnatural time, into an unknown dimension, into madness.

At that hour I would be overcome with a frenzy to catch butterflies, a passion for pursuing those flickering flecks, those erratic petals trembling in a clumsy zigzag in the blazing air. And it so happened that one of these bright flecks broke into two and then three pieces while in flight—and that shuddering, blindingly white triangle led me, like a will-o'-the-wisp, through the frenzy of thistles blazing in the sun.

I restrained myself only at the border of the burdocks, not daring to wade into that blind hollow.

Then, suddenly, I saw him.

Immersed up to his armpits in the burdocks, he was squatting in front of me.

I saw his thick shoulders in a filthy shirt and a scruffy scrap of frock coat. Ready to leap out of his hiding place, he was sitting like that—shoulders hunched over as if under a great weight. His body was panting from tension and sweat poured from his copper face, which glistened in the sunlight. Motionless, he appeared to be working hard, to be wrestling with some enormous burden, but without moving.

I stood there, nailed to the spot by his gaze that held me as if with pincers.

It was the face of a vagabond or a drunkard. A wisp of dirty tufts stuck up over his high, bulging brow like a stone nodule washed by a river. But that brow was deeply furrowed. It was unclear if pain, or the searing heat of the sun, or a superhuman tension had worked itself into that face and strained the features to the point of bursting. The black eyes drilled into me with the intensity of the highest despair or pain. Those eyes were looking at me and yet not looking, seeing me and not seeing me at all. They were bulging spheres, strained by the highest ecstasy of pain or a wild rapture of inspiration.

And suddenly, from those features, stretched to bursting, a kind of dreadful grimace erupted, shattered by suffering, and that grimace grew, took into itself the madness and the inspiration, swelled with it, kept on distorting itself more and more, until it broke into a roaring, rattling cough of laughter.

Shaken to the core, I saw him whooping with the laughter that emerged from his powerful chest as he slowly got up from his squatting position and fled, hunched over like a gorilla, with his hands in the drooping rags of his trousers, clomping in great leaps across the flapping sheets of the burdocks— Pan without his pipes, retreating in a panic to his native forest.

Uncle Karol

On Saturday afternoons my uncle Karol, a grass widower, would set out on foot to a summer resort located an hour from the city, to see his wife and children, who were vacationing there.

Since his wife's departure, the apartment had not been cleaned, the bed had never been made. Uncle Karol came back to the apartment late at night, worn-out and battered by the nocturnal carousing that those hot and empty days dragged him through. The crumpled, cool, wildly scattered bedding was a kind of blessed harbor for him at that time, an island of safety that he had chanced upon with his last remaining strength, like a castaway swept for nights and days across a storm-swept sea.

Groping his way in the darkness, he collapsed somewhere among the whitish mountains, ranges, and drifts of cool down, and slept flat on his back in an unknown direction, head hanging down, his temple driven into the fluffy pulp of the bedding as if he wanted in his sleep to drill through, to wander straight across, the mighty massifs of the bedding that mounted up at night. He struggled with the bedding in his sleep like a swimmer in water, crushed it and pounded it with his body as if he had collapsed into an enormous kneading trough of dough, and woke up in the gray dawn, panting, drenched in sweat, cast out onto the bank of that pile of bedding that he had been unable to subdue in the strenuous nighttime wrestling match. Thus, half expelled from the watery deep of sleep, he would hang semiconscious on the edge of night, seizing air with his chest, while the bedding rose around him, swelled and fermented—and grew to cover him again in a pile of heavy, whitish dough.

He slept like that until late in the morning while the pillows arranged themselves into a great, white, flat plain through which his now calm sleep wandered. Along those white high roads he slowly returned to himself, to the day, to consciousness—and finally he opened his eyes like a sleeping passenger when the train comes to a stop at the station.

A lingering semidarkness reigned in the room along with the sediment of many days of loneliness and silence. Only the window seethed with the morning's swarm of flies and the curtains shone brightly. With a yawn, Uncle Karol expelled the remains of yesterday from his body, from the depths of his bodily cavities. This yawning took hold of him convulsively as if it wanted to turn him inside out. Thus he expelled from himself the sand, the burdens—the undigested residues of the day before.

Having relieved himself in this fashion, and feeling much freer, he jotted down his expenses in a notebook, calculated, summed up, and daydreamed. Then he lay motionless for a long while, with glassy eyes that were the color of water, protuberant and moist. In the watery semidarkness of the room, brightened by the reflection of the hot day behind the curtains, his eyes, like tiny mirrors, reflected every glittering object: the white spots of sunlight in the cracks of the window, the gold rectangle of the curtains, and they duplicated, like a drop of water, the entire room with the silence of carpets and empty chairs.

In the meantime, the day beyond the curtains resounded more and more feverishly with the buzzing of the sun-maddened flies. The window could not contain that white fire and the curtains fainted from its bright surges.

Then he extricated himself from the bedding and sat on the bed for some time, unconsciously groaning. His thirty-something body was beginning to incline toward corpulence. In this organism, swelling with fat, worn-out from sexual excesses but still flooded with abundant juices, it seemed that in this silence, slowly maturing, was his future fate.

While he was sitting there in a vacant, vegetative stupor, completely transformed into circulation, respiration, and the deep pulsing of his juices, there arose from the depths of his body, sweaty and covered with hair in numerous places, an unknown, unformulated future, like a monstrous growth, sprouting fantastically into an unknown dimension. He was not horrified by it, because he already sensed his identity with this unknown and enormous thing that was supposed to arrive, and he grew together with it, without objection, in surprising agreement, frozen with calm dread, recognizing his future self in these colossal eruptions, in these fantastic piles that were ripening before his inner gaze. One of his eyes then turned slightly toward the outside, as if departing for another dimension.

Then, from these mindless stupors, from these blinking distances, he came back to himself and to the moment; he saw his feet on the sofa, fleshy and dainty as a woman's, and slowly removed the gold cuff links from his dress shirt. Then he went into the kitchen and located in a shadowy corner the bucket of water, the disk of a quiet, sensitive mirror waiting for him there—the sole living, cognizant being in this empty apartment. He poured water into a basin and tested on his skin its bland, stale, sweetish wetness.

He performed his toilette carefully and at length, without haste, inserting pauses between individual manipulations.

The empty, abandoned apartment did not recognize him; the furniture and walls followed him with silent criticism.

Entering into their silence, he felt like an intruder in this underwater, inundated kingdom in which a different, distinct time was floating.

Opening his own dresser drawers, he felt like a thief and despite himself walked around on tiptoe, afraid of waking the noisy, excessive echo irritably waiting for the slightest excuse to explode.

When finally, walking softly from one wardrobe to another, he located, piece by piece, everything he needed and finished getting dressed amid the furniture that tolerated him in silence and with an absent air, when finally he was ready, then, standing with hat in hand, ready to walk out, he was embarrassed that at the last moment, too, he could not find a word to dissolve that hostile silence, and, resigned, he walked toward the door slowly, with bowed head—while in the meantime, moving without haste in the opposite direction, into the depths of the mirror, was someone who always had his back turned, moving through an empty enfilade of rooms that did not exist.

Cinnamon Shops

During the period of the shortest, sleepy days of winter that are demarcated from morning and evening on both sides by furry edges of twilight, when the city branches out ever more deeply into the labyrinths of the winter nights and is summoned back by a brief dawn to reflection, to a return home, my father was already lost, sold, sworn to that other sphere.

His face and head were overgrown at that time, luxuriantly and wildly, with gray hair that protruded irregularly in wisps, bristles, long tufts shooting out from his warts, his eyebrows, his nostrils—which lent his physiognomy the appearance of an old bristly fox.

His senses of smell and hearing had sharpened exceedingly and one could tell by the play of his silent, intense face that through the intercession of those senses he remained in constant contact with the invisible world of dark nooks and crannies, mouse holes, moldy empty spaces under the floor, and chimney flues.

All the rustling sounds, the nighttime crashes, the secret, creaking life of the floor had an infallible, sensitive observer in him, a spy and a coconspirator. It absorbed him to such a degree that he immersed himself completely in this sphere to which we had no access, and that he made no effort to explain to us.

Sometimes he had to flick his fingers at it and laugh softly to himself when the invisible sphere's antics became too absurd; he would exchange an understanding glance then with our cat, which, just as initiated into the secrets of that world, would lift its cynical, cold, striped face and out of boredom and indifference narrow even more the slanted slits of its eyes.

It might happen that at dinnertime, in the middle of eating, he would suddenly lay down his knife and fork and, with his napkin tied under his chin, get up with a feline movement, steal on the pads of his toes to the door of the adjacent empty room, and with the greatest caution peer through the keyhole. Then he would return to the table as if embarrassed, with a puzzled smile, grumbling and muttering indistinctly in response to the internal monologue in which he was engrossed.

To create a bit of a distraction for him and tear him away from his unhealthy investigations, Mother would drag him out for evening strolls that he went on silently, without resistance, but also without conviction, distracted and absent in spirit. Once, we even went to the theater.

We found ourselves once again in that great, poorly illuminated, filthy hall, full of the sleepy buzz of people's voices and chaotic disorder. But once we had waded through the crush of people, an enormous, pale-blue curtain emerged before us like the sky of another firmament. Great painted pink masks with puffed-out cheeks were wallowing in the immense canvas expanse. The artificial sky was expanding and floating lengthwise and sideways, swelling with the enormous breath of pathos and grand gestures, with the atmosphere of that artificial world, full of radiance, that was being constructed there on the thundering scaffolding of the stage. The shudder flowing across the great countenance of that sky, the immense canvas's breath from which the masks were growing and coming back to life, betrayed the illusory nature of that firmament, caused that trembling of reality that, in metaphysical moments, we perceive as a glimmer of mystery.

The masks fluttered their red eyelids, their colorful lips whispered something voicelessly, and I knew that the moment would come when the tension of the mystery would reach its zenith, and then the swollen sky of the curtain would truly crack, rise up, and reveal unprecedented, dazzling things.

But it was not my fate to live to see that moment because just at that time Father began manifesting certain symptoms of anxiety; he clutched at his pockets and finally declared that he had forgotten his wallet with money and important documents.

After a brief consultation with Mother, during which Adela's honesty was subjected to a hurried wholesale evaluation, it was suggested to me that I should set out for home in search of the wallet. According to Mother, there was still a great deal of time before the start of the show, and, given my agility, I could make it back in time.

I walked out into the winter night, colorful with the sky's illuminations. It was one of those clear nights in which the starry firmament is so widespread and wide-ranging that it seems to have disintegrated, disconnected and distributed itself into a labyrinth of individual skies sufficient for the dispersal of an entire month of winter nights and for overlaying all their nocturnal occurrences, adventures, scandals, and carnivals with its silver, painted lampshades.

It is unforgivable thoughtlessness to send a young boy on an important and urgent mission on such a night, for in its half-light the streets multiply, get mixed up, and change places with one another. Duplicate streets, doppelgänger streets, lying and deceptive streets, so to speak, reveal themselves in the depths of the city. The imagination, enchanted and led astray, creates illusory maps of the city, supposedly long familiar and well known, in which these streets have their place and name, but the night in its inexhaustible fecundity has nothing better to do than supply constantly new and imaginary configurations. These temptations of the winter nights usually begin innocently from a desire for a shortcut, an unusual life but a quicker pathway. Tempting schemes arise for cutting short one's complicated route with some untried cross street. But this time it began differently.

Having gone a few steps I noticed that I did not have my coat. I wanted to turn back, but after a moment that seemed an unnecessary waste of time since the night was not at all cold; on the contrary, it was veined with stripes of strange warmth, with the breaths of a kind of false spring. The snow had shrunk into fluffy white clouds, into an innocent, sweet fleece that smelled of violets. The sky, in which the moon was doubling and tripling, demonstrating in this multiplication all its phases and positions, had melted away into just such clouds.

That day, the sky laid bare its internal structure on many anatomical slides, as it were, which revealed spirals and rings of light, cross sections of the aquamarine blocks of night, the plasma of the sky, the tissue of nocturnal reveries.

On such a night it is impossible to walk along Podwale Street or any other of the dark streets that are the reverse side, the lining, so to speak, of the market square's four sides, and not recall that at this late hour it sometimes happens that several of those peculiar and so enticing shops about which one forgets on ordinary days are still open. I call them cinnamon shops because they are paneled with dark, cinnamon-colored wainscoting.

These truly noble businesses, open late at night, were always a subject of my fervid daydreams.

Their dimly lit, dark, and formal interiors were redolent of the deep odor of dyes, sealing wax, incense, the aroma of distant lands and rare materials. You could find Bengal lights there, magic boxes, stamps of long-vanished countries, Chinese decals, indigo, colophony from Malabar, the eggs of exotic insects, parrots, toucans, live salamanders and basilisks, mandrake root, windup toys from Nuremberg, homunculi in flowerpots, microscopes and telescopes, and above all, rare and unusual books, old folios full of the strangest etchings and stunning stories.

I remember those old merchants, full of dignity, who served customers with downcast eyes, in discreet silence, full of wisdom and sympathy for their most secret desires. But above all there was one bookstore there in which I once examined rare and forbidden editions, the publications of secret clubs that lifted the curtain concealing oppressive, intoxicating mysteries.

It was such a rarity to have an opportunity to visit these shops, and furthermore with a small but sufficient sum of money in my pocket. It was impossible to let this occasion pass despite the seriousness of the mission entrusted to our zealousness.

According to my calculations it was necessary to venture into a side street and pass two or three intersections in order to reach the street of the nighttime shops. That took me away from my goal, but it was possible to make up for the delay by returning via the saltworks.

Given wings by my yearning to visit the cinnamon shops, I turned into a street that I knew and flew more than walked, taking care not to lose my way. I had already passed the third or fourth intersection, but the street I wished for was still not there. In addition, even the configuration of the streets did not correspond to my anticipated image. No sign of the shops. I was walking along a street whose buildings had no entrances anywhere, just tightly closed windows, blinded by the moon's reflection. The right street from which these buildings are accessible must be on the other side of these buildings, I thought. Uneasy, I picked up my pace, relinquishing in my soul any thought of visiting the shops. Just let me get out of here quickly and into the city's familiar quarters. I was approaching the street's outlet, filled with anxiety about where it would take me. I emerged onto a broad, sparsely built-up highway, very long and straight. Immediately, I was enveloped in a breath of air from a broad expanse. Picturesque villas, the ornate houses of the rich, stood either beside the street or deep within gardens. In the spaces between them parks and the walls of orchards could be seen. From a distance the image called to mind Lesznianska Street in its lower, rarely visited regions. The moonlight, diffused in thousands of fluffy cloud fragments, in silvery flakes of sky, was pale and as bright as daytime; the parks and gardens alone appeared black in this silvery landscape.

Having stared attentively at one of the houses, I arrived at the conclusion that what was in front of me was the back, the never-before-seen aspect of the *Gymnasium* building. In fact, I was approaching the gate, which, to my astonishment, was open, the hallway illuminated. I entered and found myself on the red carpet of a corridor. I hoped that I would manage to steal through the building unobserved and exit by the front gate, happily shortening my route home.

I remembered that one of the elective classes that was conducted in the late evening and for which we gathered in winter, burning with a noble enthusiasm for drawing lessons that our excellent teacher inspired in us, must be meeting in Professor Arendt's classroom at this late hour.

The small group of diligent pupils was practically lost in the great dark room on whose walls the shadows of our heads, cast by two small candles burning in the necks of bottles, would loom large and then break up.

To tell the truth, we did little drawing during those hours, and the professor did not make excessively strict demands. Some of us brought pillows from home and lay down on the benches for a light nap. Only the most diligent would draw beside a candle, in the golden circle of its radiance.

We usually waited a long time for the professor's arrival, growing bored with our sleepy conversations. At last, the door to his room would open and he would enter—short, with a beautiful beard, full of esoteric smiles, discreet silences, and the aroma of mystery. He would quickly and firmly close the office door behind him, through which at the moment of its opening a throng of plaster shadows crowded behind his head, classical fragments, mournful Niobes, Danaës, and Tantaluses, an entire sad and sterile Olympus that had been withering away for years in that museum of plaster casts. The twilight in this room was opaque in the daytime, too, overflowing drowsily from plaster daydreams, empty glances, fading ovals, and reveries that disappeared into nothingness. We often liked to eavesdrop outside the door—listening in on the silence filled with the sighs and whispers of this storage room that was moldering away in spiderwebs, this twilight of the gods disintegrating in boredom and monotony.

The professor paraded majestically, full of solemnity, alongside the empty benches among which, scattered about in small groups, we would be drawing something in the gray reflection of the winter night. It was snug and sleep inducing. Here and there my classmates lay down to sleep. The candles slowly burned down in their bottles. The professor rooted around in a deep display case filled with old volumes, old-fashioned illustrations, engravings, and prints. He showed us among the esoteric romances old lithographs of evening landscapes, nocturnal thickets, avenues in winter parks that appeared black on the white moonlit roads.

Time passed imperceptibly amid our sleepy conversations and ran unevenly, making knots, as it were, in the passing of hours, swallowing up somewhere entire empty intervals of duration. Imperceptibly, without transition, we would discover the crowd of us already on the return path, white with snow and flanked by a black, dry thicket of brushwood. Long after midnight, we would walk along this shaggy edge of darkness, brushing against the ursine fur coat of the brushwood that crackled beneath our feet on a bright moonless night, a milky false day. The diffused whiteness of that light, drizzly from the snow, from the pale air, from the milky skies, was like the gray paper of an engraving on which the lines and hatchings of dense undergrowth intertwined with deep blackness. Now the night would repeat long after midnight that series of nocturnes, Professor Arendt's nighttime engravings, continuing his fantasias.

In the black thicket of the park, in the shaggy pelt of undergrowth, in the mass of brittle brushwood, there were in some places niches, nests of the deepest, downy blackness, full of tangles, secret gestures, formless sign-language conversations. It was snug and warm in these nests. We would sit there on the summery light snow in our shaggy overcoats, gorging ourselves on the nuts with which the hazel thicket was full in that springlike winter. Martens, weasels, and mongooses wove their way silently through the brushwood, furry, snuffling little beasts with stinking pelts, stretched out on low paws. We suspected that among them were specimens from the classroom that, although eviscerated and balding, were feeling in their empty innards on this white night the voice of ancient instinct, the call of the rut, and were returning to their lairs for a short, illusory life.

But slowly the phosphorescence of the spring snow would grow opaque and die out and the thick, black, predawn darkness arrive. Some of us fell asleep in the warm snow; others fumbled about in the thicket of the entrances to their homes, groped their way into the dark interiors, into their parents' and brothers' sleep, into the continuation of deep snoring that they had been catching up with on their tardy paths.

For me, these nocturnal séances were full of mysterious charm; even now I could not let pass the opportunity to glance for a minute into the art room, resolving that I would not allow myself to stop there longer than a brief while. But entering by the back cedar stairs, full of a sonorous resonance, I realized that I was in a strange, never-seen side of the building.

Not even the lightest murmur interrupted the solemn silence. The corridors were more spacious in this wing, covered with a plush carpet and full of elegance. Small, dimly burning lamps shone where they turned a corner. Having passed one such bend, I found myself in an even larger corridor, elegant with palatial splendor. One of its walls opened out into broad, glass galleries onto the interior of an apartment. Straight ahead there began a long enfilade of rooms leading deep into the interior and furnished with dazzling magnificence. My gaze ran along a line of silk tapestries, gilded mirrors, expensive furniture, and crystal chandeliers into the fluffy pulp of these luxurious interiors, full of colorful whirling and glimmering arabesques, entwined garlands and budding flowers. The profound silence of these empty drawing rooms was filled only with the secret glances that the mirrors reflected back to one another and the panic of the arabesques, running as friezes high up along the walls and disappearing in the stuccowork of the white ceilings.

I stood facing this splendor with wonder and respect. I surmised that my nocturnal escapade had unexpectedly led me into the headmaster's wing in front of his private apartment. I stood glued to the spot with curiosity, my heart racing, ready to flee at the slightest murmur. How could I, if apprehended, justify my nocturnal spying, my impudent inquisitiveness? The director's daughter might be sitting in one of those deep plush armchairs, quiet and unobserved, and she might suddenly lift her eyes from her book to look at me—black, sibylline, calm eyes, whose gaze none of us could endure. But I would have accused myself of cowardice were I to retreat in the middle of my route without having accomplished the plan I had adopted. In any case, a deep silence reigned throughout these interiors, so filled with splendor and illuminated by the dim light of this indefinite time. Through the corridor's arcade I saw at the other end of the great drawing room large glass doors leading onto a terrace. It was so quiet all around that I gathered courage. To descend the couple of steps leading to the level of the hall, to race in a few leaps across the great, expensive carpet and find myself on the terrace from which I could easily reach a street I knew well did not seem to be linked to excessive risk.

That is what I did. After descending to the parquet floor of the salon under great palm trees that shot up from vases all the way to the arabesques of the ceiling, I observed that I was already actually on neutral ground since the drawing room did not have a front wall at all. It was a kind of grand loggia connected by a few stairs to a city square. It was a branch, as it were, of that square and some of its furniture was already on the sidewalk. I ran down the several stone steps and found myself once again on the street.

The constellations were already standing upright on their heads, all the stars had turned over onto their other side, but the moon, buried in the feather beds of clouds that it illuminated with its invisible presence, appeared to have before it an as yet unfinished journey, and, immersed in its convoluted celestial proceedings, it was not thinking about the dawn.

Several droshkies shone black on the street, ramshackle and dilapidated like crippled, sleeping crabs or cockroaches. A coachman leaned down from his high coach box. He had a small, red, kindly face.

"Shall we drive, young master?" he asked.

The carriage shuddered in all the joints and hinges of its multilimbed body and began to move on its light tires.

But who on such a night will entrust himself to the whims of an unpredictable droshky driver? Amid the clatter of the springs, the rumbling of the box and boot, I could not communicate with him about the goal of this journey. He nodded heedlessly and indulgently at everything while humming to himself and driving on a roundabout route through the city.

In front of some tavern or other there was a group of droshky drivers, waving at him in a friendly way. He said something joyfully to them and then, without stopping the coach, he threw the reins onto my knees, dropped down from the coach box, and joined the group of his colleagues. The horse, an old, wise, droshky horse, looked back briefly and set off at an even droshky trot. Actually, this horse aroused confidence; it seemed wiser than the driver. But I did not know how to drive; I had to rely on his wishes. We drove into a suburban street bordered on either side by gardens. These gardens gave way slowly, in keeping with our progress, to parks with many trees, and they, in turn, to woods.

I shall never forget that luminous drive on that brightest winter night. The colorful map of the skies grew into an immense, boundless cupola on which fantastic continents, oceans, and seas were piled up, lined with contours of astral vortexes and currents, the luminous contours of celestial geography. The air became easy to breathe and bright, like silver gauze. It smelled of violets. From under the snow, woolly like white karakul, trembling anemones peeked out, with a spark of moonlight in their delicate calyxes. The entire forest appeared to be illuminated with thousands of lights and stars, plentifully dropped by the December firmament. The air smelled of some kind of secret springtime, the ineffable purity of snow and violets. We were driving into hilly terrain. Lines of hills that looked shaggy with their naked twigs rose up like blissful sighs toward the sky. I noticed on these joyful slopes entire groups of wanderers gathering from among the moss and bushes fallen snow-wet stars. The road became steep, the horse kept slipping and had a hard time pulling the coach, which was making music with all its joints. I was happy. My chest inhaled the blessed spring of the air, the freshness of stars and snow. A rampart of white snowy foam built up higher and higher in front of the horse's chest. The horse struggled to dig his way through the pure, fresh mass. Finally, he stopped. I got down from the droshky. He was breathing heavily, his head drooping. I hugged his head to my chest; tears glistened in his great black eyes. Then I noticed a round black wound on his belly. "Why didn't you tell me?" I whispered through tears. "My dear one, it's for you," he said and became very small, like a wooden toy horse. I left him. I felt amazingly light and happy. I considered whether to wait for the little local train that came by here or to return to the city on foot. I started walking down the steep serpentine road through the woods, walking at first with a light, elastic stride, and then, gathering speed, I transitioned into a sliding happy run that suddenly changed into a ride as if on skis. I was able to regulate my speed at will, steering my ride by means of slight shifts of my body.

Nearing the city I slowed my triumphal run, changing it to a decorous strolling pace. The moon was still high. There was no end to the transformations of the sky, the metamorphoses of its multiple vaults into ever more artistic configurations. Like a silver astrolabe the sky opened its inner mechanism on this magical night and revealed in endless evolutions the golden mathematics of its wheels and cogs.

In the market square, I met people enjoying strolls. Everyone, enchanted by the spectacle of that night, had his face uplifted and silver from the magic of the sky. Concern about the wallet completely deserted me. Father, immersed in his eccentricities, had certainly forgotten about its loss, and I was not concerned about my mother.

On such a night, the only one in the year, happy thoughts come, stirrings, prophetic touches of the finger of God. Filled with ideas and inspirations, I wanted to go directly home, when my schoolmates, with books under their arms, crossed my path. They had set out for school too early, awakened by the brightness of this night that did not want to end.

We set out in a group for a stroll along the steeply descending street from which a light whiff of violets wafted, uncertain if that was still the magic of the night shimmering silvery on the snow or if dawn was already breaking . . .

The Street of Crocodiles

My father kept hidden in the bottom drawer of his deep desk an old and beautiful map of our city.

It was a complete *in folio* volume of sheets of parchment that, originally pieced together with scraps of canvas, created an enormous wall map in the shape of a bird's-eye-view panorama.

Hung on the wall, it occupied almost all the space in the room and opened up a distant view of the entire valley of the Tyśmienica River, which meanders sinuously like a pale-yellow ribbon, and of the entire lake region of widely overflowing marshes and ponds, onto the undulating foothills extending to the south, occasionally straight ahead, and then in ever more numerous ranges, like a chessboard of roundish hills, growing smaller and smaller, fainter and fainter, as they moved off toward the golden, smoky haze of the horizon. From this withered distance of its peripheries the city emerged and grew toward the front, even more toward the front in undifferentiated complexes, in compact blocks and masses of buildings, intersected by the deep ravines of streets, in order, even closer, to separate into individual apartment houses etched with the sharp clarity of views examined through a telescope. On these nearer planes the engraver had brought out all the tangled, manifold hubbub of the streets and alleys, the sharp clarity of cornices, architraves, archivolts, and pilasters, shining in the late, dark gold of an overcast afternoon that plunges every curve and window frame into the deep sepia of shadow. The blocks and prisms of this shadow, like slabs of dark honey, cut into the gorges of the streets, flooding in its warm, juicy substance here an entire half of a street, there the empty gap between buildings, dramatizing and orchestrating with the gloomy romanticism of shadow that manifold architectonic polyphony.

On this map, produced in the style of Baroque panoramas, the Street of Crocodiles district appeared as empty whiteness, the way polar regions and unexplored lands, the existence of which was doubtful, used to be depicted on geographic charts. Only the lines of several streets were drawn in with black marks and provided with names in a simple, unadorned script, to distinguish them from the noble Roman type of other labels. Evidently, the cartographer resisted recognizing this quarter as belonging to the city itself and expressed his reluctance in this distinct, dismissive rendition.

In order to understand this reservation we must now turn our attention to the ambiguous and dubious character of that quarter that was so different from the fundamental tone of the city as a whole.

It was an industrial-mercantile district with a strikingly emphatic character of sober utility. The spirit of the time, the mechanism of economics, had not spared our city, either, and it had put down greedy roots on the patch that was its periphery, where it developed into a parasitic quarter.

While in the old city there still reigned a nocturnal, illicit trade, full of a solemn ceremoniousness, in this new quarter there had immediately developed modern, sober forms of commercialism. Pseudo-Americanism, grafted onto the old, moldy ground of the city, here exploded as the luxuriant, but empty and colorless, vegetation of a tawdry, shoddy pretentiousness. Cheap, poorly constructed apartment houses with grotesque facades, covered with monstrous stuccowork made of cracked gypsum, could be seen there. Crooked old suburban cottages received hastily patched-together portals that only upon closer inspection were unmasked as miserable imitations of metropolitan installations. Defective, blurry, and dirty windows, distorting in wavering refractions a dark reflection of the street, the unfinished wood of the doors, the gray atmosphere of those barren interiors, depositing spiderwebs and clumps of dust on high shelves and shabby, crumbling walls, imprinted on the shops here the stamp of a wild Klondike. Tailors' shops, ready-to-wear clothing stores, china shops, drugstores, barber shops were lined up one after the other. Their big gray display windows bore oblique or semicircular inscriptions made of gilded artistic letters: CONFISERIE, MANICURE, KING OF ENGLAND.

The native inhabitants of the city kept their distance from this quarter, inhabited as it was by scum, by rabble, by creatures without character, without solidity, by veritable moral garbage, the tawdry variant of man that emerges in such ephemeral environs. But on the days of their fall, in hours of low temptation, it would happen that one or another of the city's inhabitants would stray half accidentally into that dubious quarter. The best people were not free at times from the temptation of voluntary degradation, of leveling borders and hierarchies, of wallowing in this shallow swamp of community, easy intimacy, filthy commingling. The quarter was an El Dorado for such moral deserters, such fugitives from the banner of personal dignity. Everything there seemed suspect and ambiguous, everything invited one to unclean hopes with a secret batting of the eye, a cynically performed gesture, a bold wink, everything delivered a low nature from its shackles.

It was the rare person who beheld, unbiased, the singular oddity of the quarter: the lack of colors, as if in that tawdry, hurriedly arisen city it was impossible to allow oneself the luxury of color. Everything there was gray, as in monochrome photographs, as in illustrated brochures. The similarity went beyond ordinary metaphor since, at times, wandering through this part of the city, one in fact had the impression that one was leafing through some kind of brochure, or in the boring columns of commercial advertisements among which suspect announcements, touchy notations, dubious illustrations had parasitically made themselves at home; and these wanderings were as sterile and without result as excitations of fantasy driven by the pages and columns of pornographic publications.

One enters a tailor's shop to order a suit—a suit of cheap elegance, so characteristic of that quarter. The premises are large and empty, very high and colorless. Enormous multistoried shelves rise one above the other to the indeterminate height of the room. The tiers of empty shelves conduct one's gaze upward as far as the ceiling, which may be the sky—the quarter's miserable, colorless, shabby sky. However, the storerooms farther along, which can be seen through the open doors, are filled all the way to the ceiling with boxes and cartons, towering like an enormous card index that disintegrates at its top beneath the tangled sky of the attic into the cubage of a void, the sterile building material of nothingness. Through the big gray windows, divided into multiple squares like sheets of graph paper, no light enters, since the shop's space is already filled, as if with water, with an indifferent gray afterglow that casts no shadow and accentuates nothing. Suddenly some slender youth turns up, surprisingly obliging, flexible, and amenable, to satisfy our wishes and flood us with the cheap, easy eloquence of a salesclerk. But when, chattering away, he unwinds enormous bales of cloth, pleats and drapes the endless stream of material flowing through his hands, forming out of its folds illusory frock coats and trousers, all this manipulation appears to be something insubstantial, a sham, a comedy, a veil thrown ironically over the true meaning of the matter.

The shopgirls, slender and dark, each with some defect in her beauty (characteristic for that quarter of defective goods), go in and out, stand in the stockroom doorway, probing with their eyes whether the particular matter (entrusted to the salesclerk's experienced hands) will mature to the appropriate point. The salesclerk cajoles and minces, at times producing the impression of a transvestite. One would like to grab him under his weakly defined chin or pinch his powdered, pale cheek when, with a knowing sideways glance, he discreetly directs one's attention to the brand name on the goods, a mark of transparent symbolism.

Slowly, the business of choosing a suit moves to the next level. That spoiled youth, soft to the point of effeminacy, full of understanding of the customer's most intimate stirrings, now slides before his eyes noteworthy trademarks, an entire library of brand names, the discriminating collector's cabinet. It becomes apparent then that the ready-to-wear clothing shop was only a facade behind which was concealed a secondhand bookstore, a collection of highly ambiguous publications and private editions. The attentive sales-clerk opens up additional stockrooms that are filled to the ceiling with books, prints, photographs. These vignettes, these prints, exceed our most daring dreams a hundred times over. We have never sensed such culminations of depravity, such sophistication of debauchery.

The shopgirls move more and more frequently between the rows of books; they are gray and papery like the prints, but full of pigment in their depraved faces—the dark pigment of brunettes with their shiny, greasy blackness, which, hidden in their eyes, would suddenly race out on a shiny cockroach's zigzag course. But in their burning blushes, as well as the piquant stigmata of their beauty spots, the embarrassing signs of dark down, their race of thick black blood was betrayed. That color with its overly intense power, that thick, aromatic mocha seemed to stain the books that they took into their olive-green hands, their touch seemed to dye them and to leave in the air a dark rain of freckles, a smudge of snuff, like a puffball with its arousing animal odor. Meanwhile, the general dissoluteness increasingly relaxed all restraints on appearances. The salesclerk, having exhausted his insistent activity, slowly transitioned to feminine passivity. Now he was lying on one of the many sofas arranged here and there among the regions of books, wearing silk pajamas displaying a feminine décolleté. The shopgirls demonstrated to one another the figures and positions from the book-jacket illustrations; others were already nodding off on makeshift beds. The pressure on the customer was loosening. He was released from the circle of importunate interest and left to his own devices. The salesgirls, busy chatting, no longer paid any atten-tion to him. With their backs or sides turned toward him, they remained in arrogant contrapposto, shifting from one foot to the other, toying with their coquettish shoes, allowing the serpentine play of their limbs to pass from top to bottom along their slender bodies, attacking with it the aroused spectator, whom they ignored behind their heedless irresponsibility. Thus they retreated, deliberately slipped into the background, opening a free space for the guest's activity. Let us profit from this moment of inattention to escape the unfore-seen consequences of this innocent visit and make our way out into the street.

No one detains us. Through the corridors of books, between long racks of journals and periodicals, we make our way out of the shop, and here we are at the place on the Street of Crocodiles where, from its highest point, one can see almost the entire length of this broad tract, all the way to the distant, unfinished buildings of the railway station. It is a gray day, as always in this district, and the entire scene seems at moments like a photograph from an illustrated newspaper, so gray, so flat are the houses, people, and vehicles. This reality is as thin as paper and betrays its imitative quality with its many gaps. At times one has the impression that only on this little scrap before us does everything compose itself in exemplary fashion into this most effective image of a metropolitan boulevard, while at the same time the improvised masquerade is already dissolving and disconnecting on either side and, incapable of remaining in its role, is disintegrating behind us into plaster of Paris and oakum, into the junk room of an enormous, empty theater. The tension of the pose, the artificial solemnity of the mask, the ironic pathos trembles on this outer skin. But we are far from desiring to unmask the spectacle. Although we know better, we feel ourselves drawn to the tawdry charm of the quarter. After all, in the image of the city there is also no lack of certain self-parodic features. Rows of small one-story suburban cottages alternate with multistoried apartment houses that, as if constructed from cartons, are a conglomeration of shop signs, blind office windows, glassy-gray displays, advertisements, and numbers. Alongside the buildings flows the river of the crowd. The street is as broad as a metropolitan boulevard, but the roadway, like village squares, is made of compacted clay, full of potholes, puddles, and grass. The street traffic in the quarter is a source of comparisons in the city; the inhabitants speak of it with pride and with a knowing sparkle in their eyes. This gray, impersonal crowd is highly excited by its role and full of fervor in demonstrating its metropolitan appearance. Nevertheless, despite its preoccupation and self-interest, one has the impression of a vague, monotonous, aimless wandering, a kind of sleepy procession of marionettes. An atmosphere of surprising insignificance penetrates the entire scene. The crowd flows monotonously, and, strange to say, one sees it indistinctly, the figures flowing past in an intermeshed, gentle turmoil without achieving complete clarity. Sometimes all we can pick out from amid the many heads in this hubbub is a dark, lively gaze, a black bowler hat pulled way down on the head, a half face broken by a smile, with a mouth that has just said something, a leg extended in a step and already forever frozen.

A peculiarity of the quarter is the driverless droshkies that run independently along the streets. It is not that there are no droshky drivers here, but mingling in the crowd and busy with a thousand matters, they pay no attention to their droshkies. In this quarter of appearances and empty gestures, no undue weight is attached to the precise goal of a trip, and the passengers entrust themselves to these errant conveyances with the recklessness that characterizes everything here. Often, it is possible to see them on dangerous curves leaning far forward on a broken coach box as, with the reins in their hands, they tensely carry out a difficult passing maneuver.

We have trams in this quarter, too. Here, the ambition of the local councillors celebrates its highest triumph. But the sight of these carriages made of papier-mâché, with their bent walls crumpled from many years of use, is pitiful. Often they have no front wall at all, so that one can see the passengers as they ride past, sitting stiffly and behaving with great dignity. These trams are pushed by local porters. But the most amazing thing is the train system on the Street of Crocodiles.

Occasionally, at irregular times of the day toward the end of the week, one can observe a crowd of people waiting for a train at a bend in the street. It is never certain if it will come and where it will stop, and it often happens that people are standing at two different places, unable to agree on where the stop is. They wait for a long time and stand in a black, silent crowd along the barely marked traces of the track, their faces in profile, like a row of pale paper masks cut into a fantastic line of abstraction. Then at last it pulls in unexpectedly; it has already entered from a side street where no one was waiting for it, low like a snake, a miniature, with a small, wheezing, squat locomotive. It rides between the two black rows, and the street becomes dark from the line of carriages sowing coal dust. The dark wheezing of the steam engine and the puff of strange power that is full of sorrow, muffled haste, and nervousness transform the street for a moment into a railroad depot in the rapidly descending winter dusk.

Agiotage in train tickets and bribery are a plague in our city.

At the last minute, when the train is already at the station, negotiations with the bribed railroad clerks are proceeding in nervous haste. Before these negotiations are concluded, the train starts moving, accompanied by a slowly drifting, disenchanted crowd, which accompanies it for a long way only to scatter in the end.

The street, compressed for a moment into this improvised train station, full of twilight and the breath of distant roads, grows bright again, widens, and again permits the carefree, monotonous crowd of strollers to pass through its channel and wander amid the din of conversation past the shop windows—those dirty, gray rectangles full of tawdry goods, large wax mannequins, and hairdressers' dolls.

Provocatively dressed in long lace dresses, the prostitutes walk past. They could be, of course, the wives of hairdressers or coffeehouse bandmasters. They walk with a predatory, slinky gait and have a slight flaw in their unpleasant, depraved faces that defines them: they squint with a crooked black squint, or their lips are torn, or they're missing the tip of a nose.

The inhabitants of the city are proud of this odor of corruption that emanates from the Street of Crocodiles. "We do not need to deny ourselves anything," they think with pride, "we can afford even true metropolitan debauchery." They declare that every woman in this quarter is a coquette. In truth, one need only turn one's attention to one of them, and immediately one is met with that persistent, titillating gaze that chills us with delightful certainty. Even the schoolgirls here wear their hair ribbons in a certain characteristic way, arrange their slender legs in a specific manner, and in their gaze they have the impure flaw in which their future depravity exists preformed.

And yet . . . , and yet, are we to betray the final secret of this quarter, the carefully concealed secret of the Street of Crocodiles?

Several times in the course of our report we have placed certain warning signs, we have expressed our reservations in a delicate fashion. The observant reader will not be unprepared for this final turn of the matter. We have spoken of the imitative and illusory character of this quarter, but these words have too final and categorical a meaning to define the partial, unresolved character of its reality.

Our language does not possess definitions that can, as it were, apportion a degree of reality, define its density. Let us put it bluntly: the fatal flaw of this quarter is that nothing in it is ever realized, nothing reaches its *definitivum*, all movements that are initiated hang in the air, all gestures are exhausted prematurely and cannot proceed beyond a certain dead end. Already, we could observe the great exuberance and profligacy—in intentions, in projects, and in anticipations—that characterize this quarter. It is in its entirety nothing other than the prematurely exuberant fermentation of desires, and therefore it is powerless and void. In its atmosphere of excessive ease, the slightest whim and every passing tension swells and develops into an empty, bulging growth, shoots out gray, lightweight vegetation of fluffy weeds, colorless hairy poppies, made of the weightless tissue of delirium and hashish. Over the entire quarter rises a lazy and dissolute fluid of sin, and the buildings, shops, people often appear to be shivers on its feverish body, goose bumps on its febrile dreams. Nowhere do we feel as threatened by possibilities as here, as shocked by the closeness of fulfillment, as pale and powerless before the exquisite terror of consummation. But that is also where it ends.

Having passed a certain point of suspense, the surge stops and retreats, the atmosphere fades and withers, possibilities droop and disintegrate into nothingness, the mad, gray poppies of exaltation are dispersed into ash.

We will regret for all eternity that we walked out for a moment from the storehouse of ready-to-wear clothing of suspect behavior. We will never happen upon it again. We will wander from sign to sign and be mistaken hundreds of times. We will visit scores of shops, happen upon entirely similar ones, wander through aisles of books, leaf through magazines and prints, confer at length and circuitously with young ladies with excessive paint and flawed beauty who will not succeed in understanding our wishes.

We will become entangled in misunderstandings until all our fever and arousal evaporate in unnecessary effort, in a doomed, vain pursuit.

Our hopes were a misunderstanding, the ambiguous appearance of the premises and staff a pretense, the ready-to-wear clothing was real ready-to-wear clothing, and the salesclerk had no concealed intentions. The female world of the Street of Crocodiles is distinguished by an utterly mediocre depravity, stifled by thick layers of moral prejudices and banal vulgarity. In this city of cheap human material there is also a lack of exuberance of instinct, a lack of unusual, dark passions.

The Street of Crocodiles was our city's concession to modernity and metropolitan depravity. Evidently, we could not afford anything other than a paper imitation, a photo montage assembled from musty cutouts, from last year's newspapers.

Cockroaches

It was in the period of gray days that arrived after the splendid colorfulness of my father's age of genius. They were long weeks of depression, hard weeks without Sundays and holidays, under a closed sky and in an impoverished landscape. Father was already gone by then. The upstairs rooms had been thoroughly cleaned and rented out to a woman telephone operator. Of the entire avian household a single specimen, a stuffed condor standing on a shelf in the sitting room, remained. In the chilly semidarkness of drawn curtains, he stood there as he had in life, on one foot, in the pose of a Buddhist sage, and his bitter, dried-up ascetic's face was petrified into an expression of ultimate indifference and abnegation. The eyes had fallen out, and sawdust was sifting through his wept-out, teary orbits. Only the horny Egyptian protuberances on the bare, powerful beak and bald neck, the protuberances and lumps of a faded blue color lent the elderly head something dignifiedly hieratic.

His feathery garment was already eaten in many places by moths and had lost the soft, gray feathers that Adela swept up once a week along with the room's nameless dust. In the bald spots one could see the coarse, burlap cloth from which shreds of hemp had slipped out. I bore a hidden grudge against Mother for the ease with which she moved on past the loss of Father to daily routine. She never loved him, I thought, and because Father was not rooted in the heart of any woman, he also could not grow into any reality and floated eternally on the periphery of life, in half-real regions, on the edges of actuality. He had not even merited an honest civil death, I thought; everything in him had to be eccentric and dubious. I decided to surprise Mother at an appropriate moment with an open conversation. On that day (it was a heavy winter day and already since morning the light puff of twilight was filtering down), Mother had a migraine and was lying on the sofa alone in the sitting room.

In this rarely visited grand room exemplary order had reigned, tended by Adela with wax and brushes ever since Father's disappearance. The furniture was covered with dustcovers; all the furnishings submitted to the iron discipline imposed by Adela in this room. Only the bunch of peacock feathers in a vase on the chest of drawers would not submit to being reined in. It was a playful element, carefree, with an elusive revolutionary nature, like an unruly class of *Gymnasium* girls, full of piety when someone was watching and of riotous playfulness when out of sight. Those eyes looked piercingly all day long and drilled holes in the walls, winked, crowded together fluttering their eyelashes, with a finger near their mouth, one beside the other, full of giggling and pranks. They filled the room with twittering and whispering, they scattered like butterflies around the multiarmed lamp, in a colorful crowd they collided with the matte, senile mirrors that had grown unused to movement and gaiety, peeped in through the keyholes. Even in the presence of Mother, who was lying on a sofa with what looked like a bandage on her head, they could not control themselves; they winked, signed to one another, spoke in a mute, colorful alphabet full of secret meanings. That mocking understanding, that twinkling conspiring behind my back irritated me. With my knees pressed against Mother's sofa, investigating with two fingers, pensively, as it were, the delicate material of her dressing gown, I said as if in passing, "I have wanted to ask you for a long time now, 'Is it true that that's him?'" And although I did not indicate the condor even by a glance, Mother guessed immediately, grew very embarrassed, and lowered her eyes. I deliberately allowed a moment to pass in order to savor her embarrassment, after which, with complete calm, mastering my growing anger, I asked, "In that case, what sense is there in all these rumors and lies that you are spreading about Father?"

But her features, which were about to fall apart in panic during the first moment, began to organize themselves again.

"What lies?" she asked, blinking her eyes, which were vacant and flooded with a dark azure obscuring the whites. "I'm aware of them from Adela," I said, "but I know that they come from you. I want to know the truth."

Her lips trembled slightly; her pupils, avoiding my gaze, wandered to the corner of her eyes. "I haven't lied," she said, but her lips swelled and at the same time became small. I felt that she was flirting with me, like a woman with a man. "With those cockroaches, it's true; you remember that yourself . . ."

I was confused. Indeed, I remembered that invasion of cockroaches, that flood of a black swarm that filled the nighttime darkness with spiderlike running around. Every chink was full of quivering antennae, every crack could suddenly shoot out a cockroach, from every swelling in the floor that black lightning, flying in a crazed zigzag across the floor, might be hatched. Oh, that wild madness of panic, written in a glittering, black line on the tablet of the floor. Oh, those cries of Father's terror as he leaped from chair to chair with a dart in his hand. Taking neither food nor drink, with a feverish flush on his face, with a convulsion of disgust etched around his mouth, my father had gone completely wild. It was clear that no organism could long endure that tension of hatred. The terrible revulsion had changed his face into a frozen tragic mask in which only the pupils, concealed behind the lower lid, lay in wait, tensed like bowstrings, in eternal distrust. With a wild growl he would suddenly leap up from his seat, fly blindly into a corner of the room, and already he'd be holding up the spear on which an enormous cockroach was skewered, desperately twitching the jumble of its legs. At that moment Adela would come to help him as he stood pale from terror and take away the lance along with its entangled trophy in order to drown it in a pail. Already then, however, I would not have been able to say whether it was Adela's stories that had instilled these images in me or if I had witnessed them myself. My father no longer possessed the resistant strength that defends healthy people from the fascination of revulsion. Instead of fencing himself off from the terrifying attractive power of that fascination, my father, a prey to madness, became more and more entangled in it. We didn't have to wait long for the sad results. Soon, the first suspicious signs appeared, filling us with dread and sorrow. Father's behavior changed. His frenzy, the euphoria of his excitement, abated. In his movements and mimicry signs of a guilty conscience began betraying themselves. He started avoiding us. He hid in corners all day long, in wardrobes, under the quilt. I often saw him observing his own hands as if in contemplation, studying the consistency of the skin, the nails, on which black spots were beginning to appear, glittering black spots, like the scales of a cockroach.

During the day he still resisted with the remnants of his strength, he struggled, but at night the fascination struck him with powerful attacks. I would see him late at night in the light of a candle placed on the floor. My father would be lying on the ground naked, spattered with the black spots of a totem, marked with lines of ribs, with a fantastic drawing of an anatomy transparent to the outside; he was lying on all fours, possessed by the fascination of the aversion that dragged him into the depths of its tortuous paths. My father was moving with the many-limbed, complicated movement of a strange ritual in which I recognized, horrified, an imitation of a cockroach ceremony.

From then on, we gave up on Father. The similarity to a cockroach became clearer with every day—my father was turning into a cockroach.

We began to grow accustomed to this. We saw him less and less frequently; he would disappear somewhere for entire weeks on his cockroach paths, and we were no longer able to distinguish him, for he had merged completely with that uncanny black tribe. Who could say if he was still living somewhere in some chink in the floor, or running around the rooms at night, entangled in cockroach affairs, or if perhaps he was among those dead insects that Adela found every morning lying belly up, bristly with legs, that she collected with loathing on her dustpan and discarded.

"And yet," I said, disconcerted, "I am certain that that condor and he are one and the same."

Mother glanced at me from under her eyelashes. "Don't torment me, my dear, I already told you that Father is traveling about the country as a traveling salesman. After all, you know that sometimes he arrives home at night only to drive on before dawn."

The Windstorm

During that long, empty winter the darkness produced an immense, hundredfold harvest in our city. For too long, it seemed, no one had cleaned the attics and junk rooms, pots were piled upon pots and bottles jammed next to bottles, empty batteries of bottles were allowed to accumulate endlessly.

There in the scorched, multiraftered forests of attics and roofs, the darkness began to degenerate and wildly ferment. There, those black parliaments of pots began, those garrulous and empty rallies, those mumbling bouts between flasks, those burblings of bottles and jugs. Until one night, the phalanxes of flasks and pots rose up beneath the expanse of shingles and floated out into the city in a great, compact mass.

The attics, attacking each other, proliferated one out of another and shot out in black rows, and through their spacious echoes ran cavalcades of girders and beams, cavortings of trusses kneeling on fir knees so as to fill the expanses of the night with the galloping of rafters and the tumult of purlins and tie beams now that they had fallen out into freedom.

It was then that those black rivers, the meanderings of barrels and jugs, poured out and floated through the nights. Black, glossy, clamorous throngs of them besieged the city. For nights on end the dark turmoil of pots and pans swarmed and pressed on, like armies of voluble fish, an unrestrained invasion of brashly talking pails and delirious buckets.

Banging their bottoms, the buckets, barrels, and bottles bunched up, potters' clay pots dangerously dangled, old caps and dandies' hats clambered on top of one another, climbing to the sky in columns continuously disintegrating.

And all of them rattled awkwardly with their knobs of wooden tongues, ground ineptly in their wooden mouths a gibberish of curses and invectives, blaspheming with mud on the entire expanse of the night. Until finally they blasphemed and cursed their way to getting what they wanted.

Summoned by the cackling of utensils, their gossiping spread from border to border, at last the caravans approached, the powerful trains of the gale drew near and came to a standstill above the night. An immense encampment, a black, movable amphitheater, began to descend in mighty circles toward the city. And the darkness exploded in an enormous, agitated windstorm and raged for three days and three nights . . .

"You're not going to school today," Mother said in the morning; "there's a terrible windstorm outside."

A delicate veil of smoke, smelling of resin, rose in the room. The stove howled and whistled as though an entire pack of dogs or demons were tied up inside it. The large, crudely executed picture painted on its bulging belly contorted its face with a colorful grimace and made a fantastic image with its puffed-out cheeks.

I ran over to the window on my bare feet. The sky was windswept across its length and breadth by the winds. Silvery white and spacious, it was streaked with lines of intensity strained to bursting, into severe grooves, like frozen veins of tin and lead. Divided into energy fields and shuddering from the voltages, it was full of latent dynamism. Outlined on it were diagrams of the windstorm that, itself invisible and elusive, charged the landscape with power.

One could not see it. It was recognized by the houses, the roofs into which its fury was driving. One after another the attics seemed to grow and explode with madness when its force entered into them.

It stripped the squares bare, it left behind a white emptiness on the streets, swept clean entire tracts of the market square. Here and there, a lone person was bent low beneath it, flapping as he clung to a corner of a building. The entire market square appeared to be ballooning and glistening like a bare bald head beneath its powerful gusts.

In the sky, the wind exhaled cold, dead colors, verdigris, yellow, and lilac streaks, the distant vaults and arcades of its labyrinth. Beneath those skies the roofs stood black and crooked, full of impatience and expectation. The ones that the gale entered into rose up in inspiration, grew higher than the neighboring houses, and prophesied beneath the disheveled sky. Then they collapsed and died away, unable to restrain any longer the powerful breath that flew on and filled the entire expanse with tumult and horror. Then again other houses rose up with a shriek, in a paroxysm of clairvoyance, and prophesied.

The enormous beech trees near the church stood with upraised arms, like witnesses to terrifying revelations, and screamed and screamed.

Farther on, beyond the roofs of the market square, I saw distant walls of fire, the bare gables of the outskirts. They were climbing on top of one another and rising, rigid with terror, stupefied. The distant, cold red reflection tinted them with belated colors.

We did not eat dinner that day, because the fire in the stove kept returning to the room as clouds of smoke. It was cold in the rooms and it smelled of wind. Around two in the afternoon a fire exploded in the outskirts of the town and spread rapidly. Mother and Adela started packing the bedclothes, fur coats, and jewelry.

Night came. The gale had grown in force and violence, expanded beyond measure, and encompassed the entire expanse. It was no longer visiting houses and roofs but was erecting above the city a multistoried, multifold expanse, a black labyrinth rising in endless stories. From this labyrinth it shot out in entire galleries of rooms, brought out in a flash wings and roadways, rolled out with a boom long enfilades, then allowed itself to sink into these imagined stories, vaults, and dungeons and soared even higher, shaping the formless vastness with its own inspiration.

The room trembled slightly, the pictures on the walls jangled. The windowpanes shone with the lamp's greasy reflection. The curtains hung swollen on the window, filled with the breath of that stormy night. It occurred to us that Father had not been seen since morning. Early that morning, we conjectured, he must have made his way to the shop, where the windstorm overtook him, cutting off his return.

"He's eaten nothing all day," Mother moaned. Teodor, the senior salesclerk, took it upon himself to head out into the night and windstorm in order to bring him some food. My brother joined the expedition.

Wrapped in great bearskin furs, they loaded down their pockets with irons and mortars, ballast intended to prevent their being carried away by the windstorm.

The door leading out into the night was cautiously opened. Scarcely had the salesclerk and my brother in their bulging overcoats taken a single step into the darkness than the night swallowed them right on the doorstep of our house. The gale instantly erased any trace of their having gone out. Not even the lantern they had with them could be seen through the window.

After swallowing them, the gale subsided for a moment. Adela and Mother again attempted to get a fire going in the stove. Their matches went out and ash and soot puffed out through the stove's little door. We stood next to the front door and listened intently. In the lamentations of the gale all kinds of voices, arguments, exhortations, and gossiping could be heard. It seemed to us that we were hearing Father, lost in the windstorm, calling for help, then again, my brother and Teodor chatting unconcernedly outside the door. That impression was so deceptive that Adela opened the door and, as a matter of fact, caught sight of Teodor and my brother struggling to emerge from the windstorm in which they were trapped up to their armpits.

Winded, they entered the vestibule, pushing the door closed behind them with great effort. For a moment they had to prop themselves up against the doorjamb, so powerfully did the gale storm the gate. Finally, they slid the bolt home and the wind pressed onward.

They told us incoherently about the night, the windstorm. Their fur coats, soaked with wind, now smelled of air. They fluttered their eyelids in the light; their eyes, still full of night, bled darkness with every beat of their eyelids. They had not been able to reach the shop; they had lost their way and barely managed to return home. They did not recognize the city; it was as if all the streets had been rearranged.

Mother suspected that they were lying. In truth, the entire scene gave the impression that they had stood there in the darkness under the window for that quarter of an hour, not going one bit farther. But perhaps the city and the market square really were no longer there, and the gale and the night had surrounded our house with only dark coulisses filled with howling, whistles, and groans. Perhaps those immense, miserable expanses that the gale had suggested to us did not exist at all; perhaps the lamentable labyrinths, those many-windowed stories and corridors on which the gale had played as if on long black flutes did not exist at all. More and more the conviction strengthened in us that this entire storm was only a nocturnal quixotism imitating in the narrow space of the coulisses the tragic boundlessness, the cosmic homelessness and orphanhood of the windstorm.

More and more frequently the hall door opened now to admit a guest wrapped in cloaks and shawls. A panting neighbor or acquaintance slowly unwound himself from scarves and overcoat and blurted out tales in a breathless voice, disjointed disconnected words that increased fantastically, falsely exaggerating the immensity of the night. We were all sitting in the brightly illuminated kitchen. Behind the kitchen hearth and the wide black hood of the chimney a couple of stairs led to the attic door.

On these stairs Teodor, the senior salesclerk, sat and listened intently to how the attic was being played by the gale. He heard the bellows of the attic ribs collapsing into their pleats during the pauses in the windstorm and the roof growing slack and hanging down like enormous lungs from which the breath had fled, then again gathering breath, adjusting itself with palisades of rafters, rising like Gothic vaulting, spreading out as a forest of beams, full of a hundredfold echo, and roaring like a box of enormous basses. But then we forgot about the windstorm; Adela was pounding cinnamon in the resonant mortar. Aunt Perazja came to pay us a visit. Tiny, energetic, and full of thriftiness, with the lace of a black shawl on her head, she started bustling about in the kitchen, helping Adela. Adela was plucking a rooster.

Aunt Perazja set fire to a handful of paper under the chimney hood and wide flakes of flame flew up into the black maw. Adela, holding the rooster by its neck, lifted it over the flames in order to singe its remaining feathers. The rooster suddenly flapped its wings in the fire, crowed, and burst into flames. Then Aunt Perazja began quarreling, swearing, and cursing. Shaking with rage, she threatened Adela and Mother with her fists. I did not understand what she was upset about, but she grew more and more heated in her anger and became a single bundle of gesticulations and curses. It seemed that in her paroxysm of rage she would discombobulate herself into pieces, that she would disintegrate, divide, disperse into a hundred spiders, distribute herself over the floor in a black, twinkling cluster of crazed cockroach races. Instead, she abruptly started to shrink, to contract, while continuing to be jittery and spilling over with curses. Suddenly, hunched and tiny, she toddled over to the corner of the kitchen where there was kindling and, cursing and cough-ing, began feverishly sorting through the resonant pieces of wood until she found two thin, yellow splinters. She grasped them with agitatedly flying hands, measured them against her feet, after which she climbed up on them as if on stilts and started walking on those yellow crutches, clattering on the boards, then running back and forth along a diagonal line on the floor, faster and faster, then she clambered onto a fir bench, hobbling on the thudding boards, and from there onto a shelf with plates, a resonant, wooden shelf that circled the kitchen walls, and she ran along it, bent at the knees on the crutches, until finally, somewhere in a corner, growing smaller and smaller, turning black, curled up like a limp piece of smoldering paper, she burned up completely into a flake of ash and crumbled into dust and nothingness.

We all stood there, helpless in the face of this raving fury of rage that consumed and devoured itself. We watched with sympathy the sad course of this paroxysm and returned with a certain feeling of relief to our own affairs when the lamentable process reached its natural end.

Adela again made the mortar ring by grinding cinnamon, Mother contin-ued her interrupted conversation, and Teodor the salesclerk, listening to the attic prophesies, made funny grimaces, lifted his eyebrows high, and laughed to himself.

The Night of the Great Season

Everyone knows that in the course of ordinary, normal years every once in a while eccentric time brings forth from its womb different years, peculiar years, degenerate years onto which, like a sixth little finger on a hand, grows a thirteenth false month.

We say "false" because rarely does it reach maturity. Like children who are conceived late in life, it remains retarded in growth, a little hunchback month, a half-withered shoot more implied than real.

The guilt for this resides in the senile incontinence of the year, its dissolute, belated vitality. It happens at times that August passes, but from habit the stout, old trunk of the year continues to bring forth, pushing out from its rotten wood these wilding days, weed days, sterile and idiotic; for good measure and free of charge it throws in stalk days, empty and inedible—days that are blank, astonished, and unnecessary.

They grow out irregular and uneven, undeveloped and fused, like the fingers of some monstrous hand, budding and curling into a fig.

Some people compare these days to apocrypha inserted secretly between chapters of the great book of the year, to palimpsests covertly incorporated among its pages, or to those blank, unprinted sheets onto which one's eyes, sated with reading and replete with content, can bleed images and shed colors onto their empty pages, making them paler and paler until at last they repose upon their nothingness before being drawn into the labyrinths of new adventures and chapters.

Ah, that old, yellowed romance of the year, that great, disintegrating book of the calendar! It languishes forgotten somewhere in the archives of time, and its content keeps on growing between the covers, swelling unceasingly from the month's garrulousness, from the rapid self-generation of claptrap, from the babbling and ravings multiplying within it. Ah, writing down these narratives of ours, arranging these stories about my father on the worn margin of its text, am I not surrendering to a secret hope that someday, unnoticed, they will take root among the yellowed pages of this most magnificent, disintegrating book, that they will enter into the great rustling of its pages that will swallow them?

What we are about to speak of here took place in the thirteenth, super-numerary, and somehow false month of that year on the dozen or so blank pages of the great chronicle of the calendar.

Mornings at that time were strangely biting and refreshing. One could tell from the subdued and cooler tempo of time, from the entirely new smell of the air, the changed consistency of the light, that we had entered into a different series of days, into a new region of God's Year.

One's voice trembled sonorously and freshly beneath these new skies as in a still new and empty apartment full of the smell of varnish and dyes, of things begun and not yet assayed. With a strange emotion one assessed the new echo, bit into it with curiosity, as one tastes a slice of coffee cake on a chilly, sober morning on the eve of a journey.

My father was seated once again in the shop's back office, in a small room with a vaulted ceiling, a room divided, like a hive, into squares, into the many-celled boxes of file cabinets, perpetually shedding layers of paper, letters, and invoices. From the rustling of sheets of paper, the endless leafing through of pages, arose the gridlike empty existence of this room; with the ceaseless reordering of files, the countless letterheads of firms, the apotheosis of a manufacturing city was renewed in the air as seen from a bird's-eye view, bristling with smoking chimneys, surrounded by rows of medals, and captured in the flourishes and swirls of pompous "& Co.'s."

There sat Father as in an aviary, on a high stool, and the dovecotes of the registries rustled with piles of paper, and all the nests and hollows were filled with the twittering of figures.

The interior of the great shop grew darker and richer from day to day with stocks of cloth, cheviot-wool serge, velvet, and twill. On the dark shelves, in those granaries and stockrooms of cool felt color, the dark, sedimented hues increased a hundredfold in value, and autumn's mighty capital multiplied and was sated. There the capital grew and loomed ever darker and settled down among the shelves as if in the galleries of a great theater, continuing to replenish itself and multiply every morning with new loads of goods in boxes and crates that were carried in along with the morning chill on the bearlike shoulders of groaning, bearded porters amid vapors of autumnal freshness and vodka. The salesclerks unloaded the new stocks of color-saturated silks and painstakingly filled all the cracks and gaps in the tall cabinets with them, as if they were putty. It was a gigantic register of every type of autumn color, arranged in layers, sorted by hues, moving up and down as if on resonant steps, on the scales of every octave of color. It began at the bottom, timidly and mournfully attempting alto slides and semitones, then passed on to the faded ashes of distance, to the greens and azures of Gobelins tapestries, rising upward in wider and wider chords until it reached the dark navies, the indigo of distant forests, and the plush of soughing parks, from there to traverse all the ochers, oxbloods, reds, and sepias, to enter the rustling shade of wilted gardens, and arrive at the dark smell of mushrooms, the breath of rotted wood in the depths of an autumn night, and the muffled accompaniment of the darkest basses.

My father walked alongside these arsenals of a fabric autumn, calming and quieting those masses, their surging might, the peaceful power of the Season. He wished to preserve for as long as possible these reserves of stored-up color. He was afraid of breaking his resolve, of cashing in the iron capital of autumn. But he knew, he sensed, that the time would come when an autumn gale, a devastating, warm gale, would blow across these cabinets and then they would give way, and nothing would be capable of stemming the flood, the streams of color in which they would explode across the entire city.

The time of the Great Season was approaching. The streets grew livelier. At six o'clock in the evening the city blossomed with fever, the buildings became flushed, and people wandered about, animated by a sort of inner fire, vividly made-up and berouged, their eyes shining with a festive, beautiful, mischievous fever.

On the side streets, in the quiet back lanes that flowed into the night district, the city was empty. Only children were playing beneath the balconies in the small squares; they played breathlessly, boisterously, and absurdly. They affixed little bladders to their mouths in order suddenly to inflate them and to puff up dramatically and turkeylike into great, gobbling, splattered wattles, or they cocked their heads into stupid rooster masks, red and crowing, into colorful autumn monsters, fantastic and absurd. It seemed as if thus inflated and crowing, they would rise into the air in long colorful chains and, like autumn wedges of birds, would fly over the city—fantastic flotillas made of tissue paper and autumn weather. Or they rode around shouting in noisy little wagons that made music with a colorful rattling of wheels, spokes, and shafts. The wagons rode downhill laden with their shouting and tumbled down the street all the way to the shallow, overflowing yellow evening stream, where they disintegrated into the rubble of small disks, wheels, and sticks.

And while the children's games became more and more raucous and confused, the city's flushes darkened and blossomed into purple, and suddenly the whole world began to wilt and turn black, and a hallucinatory dusk that infected everything rapidly exuded itself from it. This pestilence of dusk spread everywhere treacherously and poisonously, moved from one thing to another, and whatever it touched decayed instantly, turned black, disintegrated into rotten wood. People fled from the dusk in quiet panic and suddenly the leprosy was catching up with them, spilling onto their foreheads as a dark rash; they lost their faces, which fell off in great, shapeless patches, and they kept on walking without features now, without eyes, losing mask after mask along the way so that the dusk swarmed with these discarded terrifying masks showering down in the wake of their flight. Then everything began to be overgrown with black rotting bark that peeled off in great pieces, in sick scabs of darkness. And when everything had gone to pieces in this quiet turmoil, in the panic of rapid disintegration, up above, the silent alarm of the evening glow held steady and rose higher and higher, trembling with the twittering of a million quiet bells, gathering in its upward flight a million invisible larks merging in their flight into a single great, silver infinity. Then, suddenly, it was already night—a great night, still growing, expanding on gusts of wind. In its manifold labyrinth bright nests were carved out— the shops, great, colored lanterns full of stacked-up goods and the clamor of customers. Through the bright panes of these lanterns one could follow the clamorous rite, full of the bizarre ceremony of autumn shopping.

That great, flowing autumn night, growing larger with shadows, expanded by wind, concealed within its dark folds shiny pockets, little sacks containing colorful gewgaws, gaudily wrapped chocolates, fruitcakes, a motley colonial mix. These booths and stalls, cobbled together from empty sugar boxes, gaudily papered with advertisements for chocolates, full of soaps, cheery tawdry things, gilded trifles, tinfoil, bugles, wafers, and colorful mints, were stations of frivolity, noisemakers of lightheartedness, scattered among the thickets of the enormous, labyrinthine, wind-flapped night.

Large, dark throngs drifted in the darkness in raucous confusion, in the shuffling of a thousand feet, the clamor of a thousand mouths—a swarming, tangled migration streaming through the arteries of the autumn city. Thus the river flowed on, full of clamor, of dark glances, sly winks, dismembered by conversation, chopped up by chatter, a great mash of gossip, laughter, and din.

It seemed as though desiccated, autumn poppy heads, scattering their poppy seeds—noisemaker heads, rattle people—were moving along in crowds.

My father, nervous and flushed with color, with glittering eyes, was pacing back and forth in the brightly lit shop and listening attentively.

Through the panes of the display window and door the noise of the city reached here from afar, the muffled clamor of the flowing throng. Above the quiet of the shop a kerosene lamp, suspended from the great ceiling, burned brightly, displacing the slightest trace of shadow from every nook and cranny. The empty, great floor creaked in the silence and by this light it counted—up, down, and across—its gleaming squares, a chessboard of great tiles conversing in the silence by means of creaks, answering one another now here, now there, with a resounding crack. The bales of cloth, however, lay there in their felt fluffiness, silent, mute, sending glances along the walls behind Father's back, exchanging quiet knowing signals from shelf to shelf.

Father was straining to hear. In this nocturnal silence his ear seemed to lengthen and branch out beyond the window—a fantastic coral, a red polyp undulating in the underworld of the night.

He listened intently and he heard. He heard with growing anxiety the distant incoming tide of the approaching crowds. Horrified, he looked around the empty shop. He was searching for the salesclerks. But those dark, redheaded angels had flown off somewhere. He alone remained, in terror of the crowds that any minute now would inundate the quiet of the shop in a plundering, rowdy throng and dismantle among themselves and auction off the entire rich autumn, collected for many years in the great secluded granary.

Where were the salesclerks? Where were those handsome cherubs who were supposed to defend the dark cloth ramparts? Father suspected, with a painful thought, that they were sinning with the daughters of men somewhere in the depths of the house. Standing motionless and filled with worry, his eyes gleaming in the bright silence of the shop, he heard with his inner ear what was going on in the depths of the house, in the back chambers of that great colorful lantern. The house opened before him, room by room, chamber by chamber, like a house of cards, and he saw the salesclerks' pursuit of Adela through all the empty, brightly illuminated rooms, down the stairs and up the stairs, until she eluded them and fled into the bright kitchen, where she barricaded herself behind the kitchen cupboard.

There she stood, out of breath, glowing, and in high spirits, smilingly fluttering her long lashes. The salesclerks were giggling, crouched outside the door. The kitchen window was opened onto the great, black night, full of reveries and confusion. The half-opened black panes glowed with the reflection of distant illumination. The gleaming pots and flagons stood motionless around her, their greasy glaze shining in the silence. Adela cautiously leaned her head out the window, her rouged face with its fluttering eyes brightly colored. She was searching for the salesclerks in the dark courtyard, certain they were waiting in ambush. And then she caught sight of them as they crept toward her window, proceeding cautiously in single file along the narrow ledge that ran beneath the windows of the upper story wall, which was red with the reflection of the distant illumination. Father cried out in anger and despair, but at that moment the clamor of voices drew near and suddenly the bright windows of the shops were peopled with approaching faces distorted by laughter, chattering faces with noses flattened against the shining panes. Father turned purple from agitation and leaped onto the counter. And when the crowd stormed that fortress and invaded the shop in a raucous throng, my father clambered onto the shelves of cloth in a single leap and, suspended high above the crowd, blew with all his might on a great trombone made of horn and trumpeted the alarm. But the ceiling did not fill with the sound of angels rushing to his aid, and instead each groan of the trumpet was answered by the great laughing choir of the crowd.

"Jakub, trade! Jakub, sell!" they all were crying, and this cry, continuously repeated in that chorus, became a rhythmic chant and slowly turned into the melody of a refrain sung by every throat. At that point my father gave up, jumped down from the high ledge, let out a yell, and headed for the barricades of cloth. Gigantic with anger, his head swollen into a crimson fist, he ran to the cloth ramparts like a battling prophet and began to rage against them. He pushed against the huge bales of wool with his whole body, dislodging them from their foundation, slipped under those enormous bales of cloth, and hoisted them onto his bowed shoulders so that he could hurl them from the height of the gallery to land on the counter with a dull thud. The bales flew, unfurling in the air into enormous flapping banners, the shelving exploded on every side with explosions of draperies, waterfalls of cloth, as if struck by a blow from Moses's rod.

Thus did the stock on the shelves pour out, vomiting violently, flowing in wide rivers. The colorful contents of the shelves flowed out, grew, multiplied, and inundated all the counters and tables.

The walls of the shop disappeared beneath the mighty formations of this cloth cosmogony, beneath these mountain ranges towering in their mighty massifs. Broad valleys opened up between the mountain slopes, and the contours of continents thundered amid the broad pathos of the uplands. The shop's space expanded into a panorama of an autumn landscape, full of lakes and vales, and against the backdrop of this scenery Father strolled among the folds and valleys of a fantastic Canaan, taking large steps as he strolled, his arms outstretched prophetically in the clouds, and gave form to the land with strokes of inspiration.

And down below, at the feet of this Sinai that had risen up from Father's anger, the people were gesticulating, cursing, and worshiping Baal, and trading. They scooped up full armloads of soft folds, draped themselves in colorful cloth, wrapped themselves in improvised dominoes and robes, and babbled incoherently and endlessly.

My father, stretched taller by anger, was suddenly rising above these groups of hagglers and thundering from on high at the idolaters with his mighty word. Then, overcome with despair, he was climbing up to the high galleries of the shelving, running crazily along the shelves' trussed beams and the reverberating planks of the bare scaffolding, pursued by images of the shameless debauchery that he sensed behind his back in the interior of the house. The salesclerks had just reached the iron balcony at the level of the window and, clinging to the balustrade, had grabbed Adela by the waist and pulled her through the window, her eyes fluttering and her slender legs in their silk stockings trailing behind her.

While my father, appalled by the hideousness of sin, was merging into the terror of the landscape through the rage of his gestures, down below Baal's carefree rabble was indulging in unbridled merriment. Some parodic passion, some plague of laughter ruled over the mob. How could one demand gravity from them, from this mob of noisemakers and nutcrackers! How could one demand from these mills that were continuously grinding out a colorful mash of words any understanding of Father's great concerns! Deaf to the thundering of prophetic anger, these merchants in their silk bekishes squatted in small groups around the folded mountains of material, volubly, amid laughter, deliberating over the quality of the goods. That black stock exchange dismantled on their quick tongues the noble substance of the landscape, they shredded it with the mincing action of their chatter, and practically gulped it down.

Elsewhere, groups of Jews in colorful gabardines and fur kolpiks stood in front of high waterfalls of bright materials. They were the men of the Great Assembly, distinguished gentlemen full of solemnity, stroking their long, well-cared-for beards and conducting restrained, diplomatic conversations. But even in this ceremonial conversation, in the glances they exchanged, there was a twinkle of smiling irony. Common people, an amorphous crowd, a rabble without faces or individuality, threaded their way among these groups. To a certain extent they filled in gaps in the landscape, bestrewed the background with bells and rattles of mindless chattering. This was a buffoonish element, a dance-crazed crowd of Punchinellos and Harlequins, which, with no serious trading intentions of their own, with their buffoonish pranks carried to the absurd the transactions that, here and there, were being entered into.

Gradually, however, bored by their clowning, the merry little crowd dispersed in the distant districts of the landscape and slowly lost touch with one another among the rocky bends and valleys. In all likelihood, one after another these jokesters collapsed somewhere in the crevices and folds of the terrain, like children worn-out by playing in the corners and recesses of an apartment on the night of a ball.

In the meantime, the city fathers, the men of the Great Sanhedrin, promenaded in grave and dignified groups, engaging in quiet, profound debates. Dispersed across this entire great, mountainous country, they wandered in twos and threes along distant, winding roads. Their silhouettes, small and dark, peopled the entire barren uplands above which hung a heavy, dark sky, pleated and gloomy, and plowed in long parallel furrows, in silver and white overthrust faults that revealed in their depths ever more distant layers of stratification.

The lamplight created an artificial day in that land—a strange day, a day without dawn or evening.

My father slowly calmed down. His anger settled and hardened in the layers and strata of the landscape. Now he sat in the gallery of the high shelves, looking at the vast land shading into autumn. He saw that fishing was in progress on distant lakes. In each tiny husk of a boat, a pair of fishermen sat, lowering their nets into the water. On the banks, boys carried on their heads baskets full of the thrashing silver catch.

It was at that time that he noticed groups of wanderers in the distance lifting their heads toward the sky, pointing to something with upraised hands.

And presently the sky began to teem with a kind of colorful rash, scattering rippling patches that grew, matured, and presently filled the vast expanse with a strange mob of birds circling and wheeling in great intersecting spirals. The entire sky filled with their lofty flight, the flapping of wings, the majestic lines of silent soaring. Some of them, like enormous storks, floated motionless on calmly outstretched wings; others, resembling colorful plumes, barbaric trophies, were flapping heavily and clumsily in order to maintain themselves on currents of warm air; finally, other, unsuccessful conglomerations of wings, powerful legs, and plucked necks reminded one of badly stuffed vultures and condors from which the sawdust was sifting out.

Among them were two-headed birds, many-winged birds, crippled ones, too, limping in the air with a one-winged, awkward flight. The sky began to resemble an ancient fresco, filled with monsters and fantastic animals that circled, passed one another, and returned once again in colorful ellipses.

My father rose up on the support beams, bathed in a sudden glow, and stretched out his arms, summoning the birds with an ancient incantation. Filled with emotion, he recognized them. They were the distant, forgotten progeny of that avian generation that Adela had once driven out into all corners of the sky. They were returning now, degenerate and exuberant, this artificial progeny, this deteriorated avian tribe, internally stunted.

Foolishly exploded in size, grown absurdly enormous, they were empty inside and lifeless. The entire life force of these birds had passed into plumage, grown luxuriant to the point of fantasticality. It was like a museum of with-drawn species, a junk room in avian Paradise.

Several of them were flying on their backs; they had heavy, clumsy beaks that resembled padlocks and latches, they were burdened with colorful growths, and they were blind.

How moved Father was by this unexpected return, how amazed he was by the avian instinct, by this attachment to the Master that that exiled tribe had nursed, like a legend, in their soul, so that, at long last, after many genera-tions, on the final day before the tribe's extinction, it would be lured back to its primeval fatherland.

But those blind paper birds could no longer recognize Father. In vain did he call to them with his former incantation in the forgotten avian language; they neither heard him nor saw him.

Suddenly stones began whistling in the air. It was the jokesters, the stupid, witless tribe, aiming missiles at the fantastic avian sky.

In vain did Father warn them, in vain threaten them with supplicating gestures; they did not hear him, they did not notice him. And the birds were falling. Struck by a missile, they drooped heavily and were already wilted in the air. Before they flew down to earth they were already a shapeless pile of feathers.

In the blink of an eye, the uplands were covered with this strange, fantastic carrion. Before Father could run over to the place of slaughter, the whole glorious avian tribe was already lying dead, scattered about on the rocks.

Only now, close up, could Father observe the entire trashiness of that impoverished generation, the total absurdity of that tawdry anatomy.

They were immense bunches of feathers stuffed any which way like an old carcass. It was impossible to discern the head on many of them since this cudgel-shaped part of the body bore no signs of a soul. Some of them were covered with shaggy, matted fur, like bison, and they gave off a disgusting stench. Others reminded one of humped, bald, dead camels. Others, finally, were most evidently made of a certain type of paper, empty in the middle, but marvelously colorful on the outside. Some of them turned out to be, close up, nothing more than great peacock tails, colorful fans, into which some semblance of life had been breathed by some inconceivable means.

I saw my father's sad return. The artificial day was already slowly taking on the colors of an ordinary morning. In the devastated shop the highest shelves were suffused with the colors of the morning sky. Among the fragments of the fading landscape, among the demolished coulisses of the nighttime stage set, Father saw the salesclerks getting up from sleep. They were standing up among the bales of cloth and yawning at the sun. In the kitchen, on the second floor, Adela, warm from sleep, her hair tousled, was grinding coffee in a mill, pressing it to her white breast from which the beans took on a radiance and heat. The cat was licking itself clean in the sunlight.

The Sanatorium under the Hourglass

for Józefina Szelińska

The Book

I

I am calling it simply the Book, without any attributes or epithets, and in this abstinence and limitation there is a helpless sigh, a silent capitulation before the immensity of the transcendent, since no word, no allusion can manage to shine, smell, flow with that shudder of terror, that premonition of the thing without a name, the first taste of which on the tip of the tongue exceeds the capacity of our rapture. Of what help could the pathos of adjectives and the fluffiness of epithets be in relation to that thing without measure, that magnificence without a reckoning? After all, in any event the reader, the true reader on whom this narrative is counting, will understand when I look him deep in the eye and to my very depths begin to shine with that radiance. In that brief and mighty glance, in the transitory squeezing of his hand, he will grasp, accept, recall—and he will half close his eyes from rapture at that profound reception. For do we not all hold one another's hands in secret under the table that divides us?

The Book . . . Somewhere in the dawn of childhood, at the first daybreak of life, the horizon grew bright from its gentle light. The Book lay full of glory on Father's desk, and my father, quietly engrossed in it, with a saliva-moistened finger patiently rubbed the back of those decals until the blind paper started to blur, to grow opaque, to rave with a blessed premonition and suddenly peel off in tufts of tissue paper to reveal a border with peacock eyes surrounded by lashes, and one's gaze descended, fainting, into the virginal dawn of divine colors, the wondrous dampness of the purest azures.

Oh, that abrading of the film, oh, that invasion of radiance, O blessed spring, O Father . . .

Sometimes Father would get up from the Book and walk away. At those times I remained alone with it and the wind passed across its pages and the images rose up.

And when the wind quietly paged through those sheets, blowing away colors and shapes, a shudder ran through the columns of its text, releasing from among the letters the formations of swallows and skylarks. Thus did page after page fly away, scattering and sinking gently into the landscape, which

83

it saturated with color. Sometimes the Book slept and the wind blew it apart silently like a *centifolia* rose and opened its little leaves, petal by petal, eyelid by eyelid, all of them blind, velvety, dormant, concealing in their core, on the very bottom, an azure pupil, a peacock heart, a screeching nest of hummingbirds.

That was a very long time ago. Mother was not there yet. I spent my days alone with Father in our room, which was then as great as the world.

The prismatic crystals dangling from the lamp filled the room with diffuse colors, with a rainbow sprinkled over every corner, and when the lamp rotated on its chains, the whole room wandered like fragments of the rainbow, as if the spheres of the seven planets were moving ahead, spinning past one another. I liked to stand between Father's legs, embracing them on both sides like columns. Sometimes he would be writing letters. I would sit on the desk and with rapture follow the flourishes of his signature, intricate and swirling like a coloratura's trills. On the wallpaper, smiles were budding, eyes hatching out, pranks turning somersaults. To amuse me, Father would blow soap bubbles into the rainbow space with a long straw. They would strike the walls and burst, leaving their colors in the air.

Then Mother arrived and that early, bright idyll ended. Seduced by Mother's caresses, I forgot about Father, my life ran on a new, different track, without holidays and without miracles, and I might even have forgotten about the Book forever were it not for that night and that dream.

II

I woke up once on a dark winter dawn—deep down below, under piles of darkness, a gloomy sunrise was burning—and since I still had under my eyelids a swarm of misty figures and signs, I started raving incoherently and elaborately amid anguish and belated regret for the old, lost Book.

No one understood me, and, irritated by this obtuseness, I began more insistently to nag and importune my parents in my impatience and fever.

Barefoot, dressed only in my nightshirt and trembling with excitement, I rummaged through Father's library and, disappointed and angry, was helplessly describing to my stupefied audience this indescribable thing that no word, no image drawn with my trembling, elongated finger could equal. I exhausted myself endlessly in recitals full of confusion and inconsistencies, and I wept from impotent despair.

They stood over me helpless and perplexed, ashamed of their impotence. In the depths of their soul they were not without guilt. My vehemence, my impatient demanding tone, full of anger, lent me the appearance of legitimacy, the advantage of well-founded complaint. They ran to me with various books and thrust them into my hands. I rejected them indignantly.

One of them, a thick, heavy folio, my father kept offering me over and over again with timid encouragement. I opened it. It was the Bible. I beheld on its pages a great migration of animals floating down the high roads, branching out in processions across a distant land; I beheld a sky covered with flocks and fluttering, an enormous, upside-down pyramid whose distant summit was touching the Ark.

I lifted my eyes, full of reproach, to look at Father.

"You know, Father," I cried, "you very well know it; don't hide, don't try to wriggle out of it! This book has betrayed you. Why are you giving me this tainted apocrypha, this thousandth copy, this incompetent forgery? What have you done with the Book?"

Father looked away.

III

Weeks passed and my agitation subsided and abated, but the image of the Book still burned in my soul with a bright flame, a great, rustling Codex, an agitated Bible through whose pages the wind moved, ransacking it like an immense, crumbling rose.

Father, seeing that I was calmer, cautiously approached me once and said in the tone of a gentle proposition, "Fundamentally, there exist only books. The Book is a myth that we believe in our youth, but with the passing of years one stops treating it seriously."

By then, I already possessed a different conviction; I knew that the Book is a postulate, that it is a task. I felt on my shoulders the weight of a great mission. Filled with contempt and a furious, gloomy pride, I said not a word in response.

At that time I was already in possession of that scrap of a book, those pitiful remnants that a strange stroke of fate had smuggled into my hands. I carefully concealed my treasure from all eyes, grieving over the profound deterioration of this book about whose crippled remnants I would be incapable of winning anyone's understanding. This is how it happened.

One day that winter, I had caught Adela in the process of cleaning, with a broom in her hand, leaning against a lectern on which a tattered scrap of paper was lying. I bent over her arm, not so much out of curiosity as once again to intoxicate myself with the fragrance of her body, whose young charm had revealed itself to my recently awakened senses.

"Look," she said, putting up with my hugging without protest. "Is it possible that someone's hair could grow down to the ground? I would like to have hair like that."

I looked at the print. On a large *in folio* sheet was the image of a woman with a rather strong, thickset shape and a face full of energy and experience. From this lady's head flowed an immense pelt of hair, tumbling down heavily from her shoulders, the ends of its thick coils sweeping the ground. It was an improbable freak of nature, a voluminous, capacious cloak spun from the roots of her hair, and it was difficult to imagine that this weight did not cause her intense pain and disable the head that was burdened with it. But the owner of this splendor appeared to bear it with pride, and the text printed alongside it in bold type proclaimed the story of this miracle, beginning with these words: "I, Anna Csillag, born in Karlovice in Moravia, had a scant growth of hair . . ."

It was a long story, similar in construction to the story of Job. By an act of God, Anna Csillag was afflicted with a scant growth of hair. The entire little town grieved over this impairment, which they forgave her in view of her irreproachable life, although it could not have been entirely undeserved. And as a result of fervent prayers, it happened that the curse was removed from her head. Anna Csillag achieved the grace of enlightenment, received signs and instructions, and concocted a patent medicine, a miraculous medicine that returned fecundity to her head. She began to be covered with hair, and, as if that were not enough, her husband, brothers, and male cousins became felted from one day to the next with a sturdy black fur coat of facial hair. On the second page, Anna Csillag was shown six weeks after the revelation of her recipe, surrounded by her brothers, brothers-in-law, and nephews, men bearded down to the waist and mustachioed, and one looked with astonishment at this veritable explosion of genuine, ursine masculinity. Anna Csillag made the entire little town happy. A veritable blessing in the form of wavy mops of hair and immense manes flowed down on the town whose inhabitants swept the earth with their beards as if with wide brooms. Anna Csillag became an apostle of hirsuteness. Having made her native town happy, she yearned to make the entire world happy, and she asked, cajoled, pleaded that they accept for their salvation this gift from God, this miraculous medicine, whose secret she alone knew.

I read this story over Adela's shoulder and suddenly a thought struck me and I was completely aflame from its touch. So this was the Book, its final pages, its unofficial supplement, a rear annex full of waste and rubbish! Fragments of a rainbow were turning around in the swirling wallpaper; I yanked the scrap of paper from Adela's hands, and in a voice that refused to obey me I breathed out, "Where did you get this book?"

"Fool," she said, shrugging her shoulders, "it's always here, and we tear out pages from it every day for meat from the butcher stalls and for your father's breakfast . . ."

IV

I ran to my room. Utterly distressed, my face burning, I started leafing through the tattered pages with fluttering hands. Alas, there were scarcely a dozen of them. Not a single page of proper text, only advertisements and announcements. Right after the long-haired Sybil's prophecies came a page devoted to a miraculous medicine for all illnesses and handicaps. Elsa-Fluid with a Swan the balm was called, and it worked miracles. The page was filled with certified, moving reports by individuals for whom the miracle had worked.

From Transylvania, from Slavonia, from Bukovina, came convalescents full of fervor to testify, to relate their stories in burning, emotional words. They came bandaged and bent over, shaking their no longer needed crutches; they threw away the patches from their eyes and the bandages from their scrofula.

Behind these migrations could be seen distant, sad little towns with a paper-white sky, hardened by prose and everyday life. They were towns that had been forgotten in the depths of time where people were tied to their little fates from which they did not break away for even a minute. A shoemaker was thoroughly a shoemaker; he smelled of leather, had a small, lean face, myopic pale eyes above a colorless mustache that sniffed the air, and he felt himself a shoemaker through and through. And if their ulcers did not hurt, their bones did not break, dropsy did not lay them flat on their pallets, they were happy with a colorless, gray happiness, they smoked cheap tobacco, yellow Imperial-Royal tobacco, or daydreamed dully in front of the lottery office.

Cats ran across their path, first from the left, then from the right; a black dog appeared in their dreams, and their hands itched. Sometimes they copied letters from a letter-writing manual, carefully pasted on stamps, and entrusted them hesitantly, filled with distrust, to the letter box, which they struck with a fist as if to wake it up. And then white pigeons flew through their dreams with letters in their bills and disappeared in the clouds.

The next pages rose above the sphere of everyday affairs into regions of pure poetry.

There were accordions, zithers, and harps, the instruments of angel choirs in days of yore—today, thanks to advances in industry, available to the common man at popular prices, to a god-fearing people for strengthening hearts and decent entertainment.

Barrel organs were there, true marvels of technology, full of flutes concealed inside them, tiny throats and pipes, harmonicas warbling sweetly like nests of sobbing nightingales, a priceless treasure for the disabled, a source of lucrative earnings for cripples, and in general a necessity in every musical home. And one could see these barrel organs beautifully painted, wandering on the backs of modest gray old men whose faces, corroded by life, were as if wrapped in spiderwebs and completely blurred, faces with tearing, fixed eyes that were slowly leaking, faces drained of life, as discolored and innocent as tree bark cracked by all sorts of weather and, like it, smelling now only of rain and the sky.

They had long since forgotten their names and who they were, and thus lost within themselves they shuffled along with bowed knees, taking tiny, even steps in their enormous, heavy boots along an entirely straight, monotonous line amid the winding, tortuous roads of pedestrians.

On white, sunless mornings, mornings turned stale from the cold and immersed in the ordinary affairs of the day, they would extricate themselves stealthily from the crowd, set their barrel organs on sticks at an intersection beneath a yellow streak of sky crossed by a telegraph wire, and, among people hurrying dully with their collars up, begin their melody, not from the beginning but at the place where yesterday they had broken off, and play, "Daisy, Daisy, give me your answer true . . ." while white plumes of steam were puffing from the chimneys. And a strange thing: that . . . melody, scarcely begun, leaped immediately into an empty gap, into its own place at this hour and in this landscape, as if it had always belonged to this pensive, self-absorbed day, and the thoughts and gray cares of the hurrying people kept time with it.

And when after a certain time it ended with a long, drawn-out wheeze plucked from the entrails of a barrel organ, which was starting up from an entirely new barrel, the thoughts and cares paused for a moment, as if to change feet in a dance, and then without thinking began turning in the opposite direction in time to the new melody running out from the barrel organ's pipes—"Margarita, treasure of my soul . . ."

And in the dull indifference of that morning no one even noticed that the meaning of the world had changed fundamentally, that it was now running not to the beat of "Daisy, Daisy" but to exactly the opposite, "Mar-ga-rita . . ."

We turn the page again . . . What is this? A spring rain coming down? No, it is the twittering of birds sprinkling like gray buckshot onto umbrellas, for here genuine Harz Mountain canaries are on offer, cages full of goldfinches and starlings, baskets full of winged singers and chatterboxes.

Spindly and lightweight as if stuffed with cotton, leaping about in fits and starts, reversible, as if on smooth, warbling pivots, chirping like the cuckoos in a clock—they were a solace for loneliness, they were substitutes for bachelors lacking the warmth of a domestic hearth, they enticed from the hardest hearts the bliss of maternal feeling, so much did they have within them what is chicklike and touching, and besides, when a page was turned above them, they sent their mingled, alluring twittering after the departing person.

But farther along, this wretched document tumbled into ever steeper decline. Now it entered upon a roadless tract of some sort of dubious, fraudulent divination. Wearing a long overcoat, with a smile half swallowed up by his black beard, who was it presenting himself in service to the public? Signor Bosco from Milan, a self-proclaimed master of black magic, spoke at length and unclearly, demonstrating something on his fingertips that did not make the matter any more intelligible. And although in his own opinion he was reaching amazing conclusions, which he appeared to be weighing for a moment between his sensitive fingers before their elusive meaning escaped from his fingers into the air, and although he subtly marked the turning points of dialectics with a cautionary lifting of his eyebrows, preparing us for uncommon things, he was not understood, and, what is worse, no one yearned to understand anything and he was left with his gesticulations, with his subdued tone, and an entire range of dark smiles in order to rapidly leaf through the final pages, which were disintegrating into scraps.

On those final pages that were noticeably falling in an obvious manner into delirious gibberish, into evident nonsense, a certain gentleman was offering his infallible method for becoming energetic and resolute in one's decisions, and he said a great deal about principles and character. But all one had to do was turn the page to be totally disoriented in matters of resoluteness and principles.

There, with a tiny step, a Miss Magda Wang emerged, hobbled by the train of her dress, and informed us from the heights of her tight décolleté that she laughs at masculine resoluteness and principles, and that her specialty is breaking the strongest character. (Here, with a movement of her little foot, she arranged her train on the ground.) There are methods to this goal, she continued through clenched teeth, infallible methods that she does not wish to belabor, referring us to her memoirs, titled *From Purple Days* (Institute of Anthroposophy Publishing House in Budapest), in which she laid out the results of her colonial experiences in the field of breaking in people (that last expression with emphasis and an ironic gleam in the eye). And the strange thing is, that lady who spoke so sluggishly and unceremoniously appeared to be confident of the approbation of those about whom she was speaking with such cynicism, and amid her singular dizziness and glittering, it felt as if the directions of moral designations had strangely slipped away, and that we were here in a different climate in which the compass of emotions worked the other way around.

That was the final word of the Book, which left a taste of strange stupefaction, a mixture of hunger and arousal in the soul.

V

Bent over the Book, my face aflame like a rainbow, I burned in silence from ecstasy to ecstasy. Engrossed in reading, I forgot about dinner. My premonition had not deceived me. It was the Authentic, a holy original, even though in such a profound state of humiliation and degradation. And when, in late twilight, blissfully smiling, I put away the yellowed catalog in the deepest drawer, covering it with other books in order to conceal it, it seemed to me that I was putting the dawn to sleep in the bureau, a dawn that continually caught fire from within itself, moved through every flame and crimson, and returned once again and did not wish to stop.

How indifferent I became to all other books!

For ordinary books are like meteors. Each of them has a single moment, one moment when with a cry it soars like a phoenix, blazing with all its pages. For the sake of that single instant, that one moment, we love it afterward even though by then it is only ashes. And with bitter resignation we wander now and again, late at night, through those now-cold pages, shifting with wooden clacking their dead formulas, like rosary beads.

Exegetes of the Book assert that all books aim for the Authentic. They live only a borrowed life that, in the moment of soaring, returns to its ancient source. This means that books wane, but the Authentic grows. Nevertheless, we do not wish to bore the reader with a lecture about Doctrine. We would like only to turn his attention to one thing: the Authentic lives and grows. What follows from this? Well, when we open our yellowed pages next time, who knows where Anna Csillag and her loyal followers will be by then. Perhaps we will catch sight of her, a long-haired pilgrim, sweeping the highways of Moravia with her cloak, wandering through a distant land, through white towns engrossed in the everyday and prose, distributing samples of the balm of Elsa-Fluid among God's simpletons who are afflicted with oozing and itching. Oh, what will the worthy bearded ones of the town do then, immobilized by their enormous beards, what will that faithful community do, condemned to the tending and administration of their excessive harvests? Who can say that all of them will not buy real barrel organs from the Schwarzwald for themselves and follow their apostle into the world, seeking her throughout the land, playing "Daisy, Daisy" in every place?

O, Odyssey of the bearded ones wandering with their barrel organs from city to city in search of their spiritual mother! When will a rhapsodist worthy of this epopee be found? For who was that being to whom they left the city entrusted to their care, to whom did they bequeath the government of souls in the city of Anna Csillag? Can they not foresee that deprived of its spiritual elite, of its splendid patriarchs, the city will fall into doubt and apostasy and open its gates—to whom?—alas, to the cynical, perverse Magda Wang (Institute of Anthroposophy Publishing House in Budapest), who will establish in it a school for the training and breaking in of characters?

But let us return to our pilgrims.

Who does not know that old guard, those wandering Cimbrians, dark brunets with seemingly powerful bodies composed of tissue without brawn or sap? All their strength, all their might, went into their hair. Anthropologists have been racking their brains for ages over this peculiar race, dressed always in black clothing, with thick silver chains on their bellies and huge brass signet rings on their fingers.

I like them, these Caspars and Balthazars by turns, their profound dignity, their funereal decorativeness, these splendid masculine specimens with their beautiful eyes with the oily sheen of roasted coffee; I love their noble lack of vitality in bodies luxuriant and spongy, the morbidezza of vanishing tribes, their wheezy breathing from their powerful chests, and even the smell of valerian wafting from their beards.

Like Angels of the Countenance they sometimes stand unexpectedly inside the doors of our kitchens, enormous and wheezing, and easily exhausted—they wipe the sweat from their dewy brows, rolling the bluish whites of their eyes—and at that moment they forget their mission, and, astonished, searching for an exit, a pretext for having come there, they hold out their hands for alms.

We return to the Authentic. But we never abandoned it. And here we point out the strange characteristic of the yellowed Catalog, which is already clear to the reader: it unfurls during reading, it has borders on all sides that are open to all fluctuations and flows.

Now, for example, no one offers Harz Mountain goldfinches any longer, because those feathery wisps flutter out at irregular intervals from the barrel organs of the brunets, from the breaking and bending of the melodies, and the market square is showered with them as if with colorful type. Ah, what a proliferation, scintillating and full of chirping . . . Around every peak, pole, and weathercock, real colorful traffic jams are being created, flutterings and battles for space. And it is sufficient to place the curve of a walking stick through a window for it to be coated with a fluttering, heaving cluster when it is drawn back into the room.

Now in our narrative we are approaching with rapid steps that splendid, catastrophic epoch that in our biography bears the name of the age of genius.

In vain would we deny that now we are already feeling that contraction of the heart, that blessed anxiety, that holy nervous trembling that precedes ultimate things. Soon we will lack the colors in crucibles and radiance in the soul needed to place the highest accents, to delineate the most luminous and already transcendental contours in this picture.

What is the age of genius and when was it?

Here we are forced to become for a moment thoroughly esoteric, like Signor Bosco of Milan, and to lower our voice to a penetrating whisper. We must underline our conclusions with ambiguous smiles and rub on our fingertips, like a pinch of salt, the delicate matter of imponderabilia. It is not our fault if at times we will have the appearance of those purveyors of invisible fabrics who with elegant gestures demonstrate their fraudulent goods.

So, did the age of genius happen, or not? It is hard to give an answer. Yes and no. For there are things that totally, through and through, cannot happen. They are too great to fit into an event, and too splendid. They only try to happen, they try the ground of reality to see if it will bear them. And soon they retreat, fearful of losing their integrity in the imperfection of realization. And if they have put a crack in their capital, lost this and that in those attempts at incarnation, then envious, they soon withdraw their property, take it back, reintegrate themselves, and then those blank spots, fragrant stigmata, remain in our biography, those lost silver traces of the bare feet of angels, scattered in giant steps across our days and nights while the fullness of glory increases and completes itself unceasingly and culminates above us, surpassing rapture after rapture in triumph.

And yet in a certain sense it fits, complete and integral, within each of its imperfect, fragmentary incarnations. Here there occurs the phenomenon of representation and vicarious life. Some event, perhaps minor and modest with regard to its provenance and its own means, may, when brought close to the eye, reveal in its interior an infinite, radiant perspective thanks to the higher being attempting to express itself and fiercely blazing within it.

And so we will gather those allusions, those earthly approximations, those stations and stages on the roads of our life, like the shards of a shattered mirror. We will gather piece by piece that which is whole and indivisible, our great age, the age of genius of our life.

Perhaps, with diminishing fervor, terrorized by the uncontainable nature of the transcendent, we limited it excessively, questioned and disturbed it. For despite all reservations—it did exist.

It existed and nothing can take away from us that certainty, that luminous taste that is still on our tongue, that cold fire on our palate, that sigh, broad as heaven and fresh as a draft of pure ultramarine.

Have we prepared the reader to a certain extent for the things that will follow? Can we risk a journey into the age of genius?

Our stage fright has been transmitted to the reader. We sense his nervousness. Despite appearances of animation, we, too, have a heavy heart and are full of anxiety.

In the name of God then—all aboard!

The Age of Genius

I

Ordinary facts are lined up in time, strung onto its course as if on a thread. They have their antecedents there and their consequences, which crowd together closely, constantly stepping on one another's heels without leaving a gap. This also has meaning for narrative, whose soul is continuity and succession.

But what can be done with events that do not have their own place in time, with events that arrived too late, when all of time was already distributed, divided, disassembled, and now they've just been left there, unclassified, suspended in the air, homeless and errant?

Could it be that time is too narrow for all events? Can it be that all the seats in time are already sold? Worried, we run along the length of the entire train of events, preparing to ride.

For God's sake, can it be that here there is no type of agiotage of tickets for time? . . . Conductor, sir!

Just calm down! Without undue panic we will deal with this quietly in our own realm of action.

Has the reader heard something about parallel strands of time in two-track time? Yes, such spur lines of time do exist; true, they are a bit illegal and problematic, but when they carry contraband such as we do, such a supernumerary event that cannot be classified, one cannot be too fastidious. Let us attempt, then, to branch off just such a spur line, a blind track, at some point in the story in order to shunt onto it this illegal history. But do not fear. It will happen imperceptibly, the reader will not suffer any shock. Who knows, perhaps while we are speaking about it the dishonest manipulation is already behind us and we are already riding down a blind track.

II

My mother came running, terrified, and embraced my scream with her arms, wanting to cover it like a fire and stifle it in the folds of her love. She shut my mouth with her mouth and screamed together with me.

But I shoved her away, and pointing at the pillar of fire, the golden beam that hung slantwise in the air like a splinter and could not be pushed aside—full of radiance and the specks of dust swirling within it—I screamed, "Rip it out, tear it out!"

The stove swelled up with a large, colorful picture painted on its forehead; it was completely bloodshot and it seemed that from the convulsion of those veins, sinews and its entire anatomy distended to the point of bursting, it had freed itself with a garish, roosterlike crowing.

I stood there, arms outstretched in inspiration, with extended, elongated fingers I was pointing, pointing in anger, in fierce exaltation, as tense as a signpost and trembling in ecstasy.

My hand led me, alien and pale, dragged me along behind it, a stiff, wax hand, like great votive hands, like the hand of an angel raised in an oath.

Winter was coming to an end. The days stood in puddles and embers and had their palate full of fire and pepper. Glittering knives cut the honey pulp of the day into silver slices, into prisms, their cross sections full of colors and spicy piquancy. But the clockface of noon accumulated all the radiance of those days in a meager space and showed all the burning, fire-filled hours.

At that hour, unable to accommodate the heat, the day was shedding sheets of silver metal, crackling tinfoil, and exposing layer by layer its core of solid radiance. And as if that were not enough, the chimneys were emitting smoke, forming wreaths of glistening steam, and every moment exploding in a great soaring of angels, a storm of wings that the not yet satiated sky swallowed up, being constantly open to new explosions. Its bright battlements were exploding with white plumes, distant strongholds unfolded into silent fans of stacked-up explosions—all beneath a glistening cannonade of invisible artillery.

The room's window, entirely filled with sky, swelled with these endless soarings and overflowed with the curtains that, engulfed in flames, smoking in the fire, poured down gold shadows and the trembling of layers of air. The slanting, burning rectangle lay on the carpet, undulating with radiance, and could not tear itself from the floor. That pillar of fire disturbed me to the core. I stood there bewitched, my legs astride, and barked alien, hard curses at it in a changed voice.

On the threshold, in the hall, stood bewildered, terrified, hand-wringing people: my relatives, neighbors, aunts dressed to the nines. They approached on tiptoe and walked away, peered in through the door, full of curiosity. And I kept on screaming.

"You see," I screamed at Mother, at my brother, "I have always told you that everything is obstructed, walled in with boredom, not liberated. And now look, what an outpouring, what a flowering of everything, what bliss . . ."

And I wept from happiness and weakness.

"Wake up!" I cried, "hurry up and help me! Can I cope with this flood by myself, can I encompass this deluge? How can I, all by myself, answer the million dazzling questions with which God is inundating me?"

And when they remained silent, I cried in anger, "Hurry, collect bucketsful of this abundance, store up supplies!"

But no one could help me out; they stood there perplexed, looking around, and retreated behind their neighbors' backs.

Then I understood what I had to do, and full of enthusiasm I started pulling out from the cabinets old folios, Father's disintegrating business ledgers that were covered with his writing, and I threw them onto the floor under that pillar of fire that was lying upon the air and burning. It was impossible to supply me with enough paper. My brother and Mother came running with more and more new armfuls of old newspapers and diaries and threw them onto the floor in piles. And I sat among those papers, blinded by the radiance, my eyes full of explosions, rockets, and colors, and I drew. I drew hastily, in a panic, crosswise, at a slant, across printed and handwritten pages. Inspired, my colored pencils flew across columns of illegible texts, raced in brilliant scrawls, in neck-breaking zigzags, suddenly knotting into anagrams of visions, into rebuses of luminous revelations, and once again unwinding into empty, blind lightning flashes, seeking the trail of inspiration.

Oh, those luminous drawings, springing up as if under a stranger's hand; oh, those transparent colors and shadows! How often do I still find them today in dreams after so many years on the bottom of old drawers, gleaming and fresh as an early morning—still damp with the first dew of the day— figures, landscapes, faces!

Oh, those azures chilling the breath with a gasp of fear; oh, those greens that are greener than amazement; oh, those preludes and songs of colors only just anticipated, only just attempting to name themselves!

Why did I squander them then in the carelessness of excess with incomprehensible thoughtlessness? I allowed the neighbors to rummage through and ransack those piles of drawings. They gathered up entire bundles of them. To what homes did they wander off, on what trash piles were they lying about then! Adela wallpapered the kitchen with them to make it bright and colorful as if during the night snow had fallen outside the window.

That was drawing full of cruelty, ambushes, and attacks. When I sat taut as a bow, immobile and lying in wait, and in the sunshine around me papers were burning brightly, it sufficed that a drawing, pinned down by my pencil, should make the slightest movement toward escape. Then my hand, completely convulsed with new reflexes and impulses, would fling itself onto it with fury like a cat and already alien, savage, predatory, in lightning-fast bites would gnaw at the monster that wanted to escape from under the pencil. And it loosened its grip on the paper only when the already dead and motionless corpse displayed in the notebook, as if in a herbal, its colorful, fantastic anatomy.

It was murderous hunting, a battle to the death and life. Who, after all, could distinguish in it the attacker from the attacked, in this ball that was snarling with fury, in this tangle full of squealing and terror! It sometimes happened that my hand would begin to jump two or three times only to catch up with its victim on the fourth or fifth sheet of paper. Sometimes it cried from pain and terror in the claws and pincers of these monstrosities, writhing under my scalpel.

From hour to hour the visions swam up ever more densely, they crowded in, created roadblocks, until one day all the roads and paths were swarming and streaming with parades and the entire country branched out in migrations, dispersed in stretched-out processions—endless migrations of beasts and animals.

As in the days of Noah these colorful parades flowed past, these rivers of fur and manes, these undulating spines and tails, these heads, nodding ceaselessly in time to their tread.

My room was a border and a tollgate. Here they came to a stop, crowded together, bleating imploringly. They fidgeted, stamped in place anxiously and wildly—humpbacked and horned beings, sewn into all the costumes and armor of zoology, terrified of themselves, flustered by their own masquerade, they looked with anxious and astonished eyes through the openings of their hairy skins and mooed pitifully, as if gagged under their own masks.

Were they waiting for me to name them, to resolve their enigma that they did not understand? Were they asking me about their name, in order to enter into it and fill it with their essence? Strange monsters arrived—creature questions, creature propositions—and I had to shout and drive them away with my hands.

They retreated, lowering their heads and looking from under their brows, and lost themselves in themselves, returned, dissolving into nameless chaos, into a junk room of forms. How many flat and humped spines passed under my hand then, how many heads slipped by beneath it with a velvety caress!

I understood then why animals have horns. It was that—that incomprehensible thing that could not fit in their life, a wild and persistent caprice, an irrational and blind obstinacy. Some kind of idée fixe, grown beyond the borders of their being, higher than their head, and suddenly surfacing into the light, had solidified into a palpable, hard matter. There it acquired a wild shape, unpredictable and implausible, twisted into a fantastic arabesque invisible to their eyes but terrifying, into an unknown cipher, under whose threat they lived. I understood why these animals were inclined to incomprehensible, wild panic, to frightened frenzy: drawn into their own madness, they were unable to extricate themselves from the tangle of those horns among which, bowing their heads, they looked out sadly and wildly, as if seeking a passageway between their branches. These horned animals were far from being liberated and on their heads they bore with sorrow and resignation the stigma of their error.

But even farther from the light were the cats. Their perfection was frightening. Locked into the precision and exactness of their bodies, they knew neither error nor deviation. For a moment they would descend into the depths, to the bottom of their essence, and then, immobile in their soft fur coats, they settled down menacingly and ceremoniously, and their eyes grew round as moons, absorbing their gaze into their fiery craters. But after a moment, thrown out onto the brink, onto the surface, they yawned with their nothingness, disenchanted and without illusions.

In their lives, full of self-contained grace, there was no room for any alternative. And feeling bored in that prison of perfection without exit, overcome by spleen, they snarled with their wrinkled lips, full of aimless cruelty in their short faces made wider by stripes. Down below, martens, polecats, and foxes ran past stealthily, thieves among the animals, creatures with a bad conscience. In violation of the plan of creation, they seized their place in being by guile, intrigue, trickery; pursued by hatred, endangered, always on guard, always terrified about their place, they greedily loved their stolen life of hiding in burrows, prepared to let themselves be mauled in its defense.

Finally, they all had passed, and silence took up residence in my room. I began to draw again, engrossed in my scraps of paper, which breathed radiance. The window was open, and ring-necked doves and turtledoves quivered on the window ledge in the springtime air. Tilting their heads, they revealed a round glass eye in profile, as if they were terrified and full of flight. The days became soft toward the end, opalescent and luminous, then again pearly and full of hazy sweetness.

The Easter holidays arrived and my parents went away for a week to visit my married sister. I was left alone in the apartment, a prey to my inspirations. Adela brought me dinner and breakfast every day. I did not notice her presence when she stopped for a moment on the threshold in her holiday best, smelling of spring in her tulles and foulards.

Through the open window gentle breezes floated in, filling the room with a reflection of distant landscapes. For a moment, those windblown colors of bright distances paused in the air and suddenly dissolved, dispersed into azure shade, into tenderness and emotion. The flood of images calmed down somewhat, the outpouring of visions subsided and grew silent.

I was sitting on the ground. Around me on the floor lay crayons and tiny tins of paints, God's colors, blues breathing freshness, greens that had strayed to the extremes of amazement. And when I picked up a red crayon—into the bright world came fanfares of happy red, and all the balconies floated past in waves of red banners, and the houses lined up along the street in a triumphant double row. Processions of city firemen in raspberry uniforms paraded on the bright happy roads, and gentlemen doffed their cherry-red bowler hats in greeting. Cherry sweetness, the cherry song of the goldfinches, filled the air, which was full of lavender and of a gentle radiance.

And when I reached for the azure paint, the reflected light of a cobalt spring was walking down the streets through all the windows, and the panes opened, clattering, one after the other, full of azure and blue fire, the curtains rose as if at an alarm, and a joyous, light draft moved along this row amid fluttering muslins and oleanders on empty balconies, as if on the other end of this long, bright avenue someone had appeared in the distance and was approaching—radiant, preceded by news, by a presentiment, portended by the flight of swallows, by fiery runners scattered from mile to mile.

III

For the Easter holidays, at the end of March or the beginning of April, Shloma, Tobias's son, would get out of the prison where he had been confined for the winter after his summer and autumn scandals and rampages. One afternoon that spring I saw him through the window as he was leaving the shop of our barber, who alone served as our town's haircutter, dentist, and surgeon; with refinement acquired under prison discipline, Shloma was opening the gleaming glass door of the barbershop and descending the three wooden steps, refreshed and made younger looking with a precisely shorn head and wearing a frock coat that was a bit too short and checked trousers pulled up high—slender and youthful despite his forty years.

Holy Trinity Square was empty and clean at that time. After the spring thaws and the mud rinsed away later by torrential rains, the pavement was washed clean, dried out during many days of quiet, discreet weather, those days that were already great and too capacious, perhaps, for that early season, a trifle too lengthy, especially in the evenings when twilight, still empty in its depths, was endlessly prolonged, futile and sterile in its immense anticipation.

When Shloma closed the barbershop's glass door behind him, the sky entered through it immediately, as it did through all the small windows of that two-story house that was open to the pure depths of the shadowy horizon.

Having descended the steps, he found himself completely alone on the border of the great empty shell of the square, across which flowed the azure of a sky without a sun.

That great, clean square lay like a glass ball that afternoon, like a new, not yet begun year. Shloma stood on its bank, all gray and extinguished, overwhelmed by the azures, and did not dare to make a decision that might break that perfect globe of unspent day.

Only once a year, on the day he left prison, did Shloma feel so pure, unburdened, and new. The day would receive him into itself at that time washed clean of his sins, renewed, united with the world; with a sigh, it opened before him the pure circles of its horizons, crowned with quiet beauty.

He did not hurry. He stood on the edge of the day and did not dare to cross it, to scratch the gently vaulted conch shell of the afternoon with his tiny, young, slightly limping gait.

A transparent shade lay over the city. The silence of that third hour of the afternoon extracted from the buildings the pure white of chalk and laid it out noiselessly like a deck of cards around the square. Having dealt it out in one round, it began a new one, drawing reserves of white from the great baroque facade of Holy Trinity, which, like an enormous shirt of God sailing down from heaven and folded into pilasters, avant-corps, and embrasures, exploded by the pathos of volutes and archivolts, had hastily arranged on itself that great, turbulent garment.

Shloma raised his face, sniffing the air. A gentle breeze carried the fragrance of oleanders, the fragrance of holiday apartments and cinnamon. Then he sneezed mightily with his famous, mighty sneeze, which caused the pigeons on the police box to rise up terrified and fly away. Shloma smiled to himself: God was giving a sign through the convulsion of his nostrils that spring had arrived. It was a sign more certain than the arrival of the storks, after which the days would be punctuated with these detonations that, lost in the city's noise, now nearer, now farther away, annotated its events with witty commentary.

"Shloma!" I called out, standing in the window of our low second floor.

Shloma caught sight of me, smiled his kindly smile, and saluted.

"We're alone now in the entire market square, you and I," I said softly, because the swollen ball of the sky resonated like a barrel.

"You and I," he repeated with a sad smile. "How empty the world is today."

"We could divide it and give it a new name; it's lying there so open, defenseless, and ownerless."

On such a day the Messiah approaches the very edge of the horizon and from there looks down at the earth. And when he sees it so white and silent, with its azures and pensiveness, it can happen that in his eyes it loses its boundary, the bluish bands of clouds lie down to form a passageway, and, not knowing himself what he is doing, he descends to earth. And in its reverie the earth will not even notice the one who has descended onto its paths, and people will awaken from their afternoon naps and remember nothing. The entire story will be as if it had been blotted out and it will be as it was in primeval times, before history began.

"Is Adela home?" he asked with a smile.

"No one is here. Come in for a minute and I'll show you my drawings."

"If no one is there, I won't deny myself the pleasure. Open the door for me."

And, with the movements of a thief, looking to left and right in the entranceway, he came inside.

IV

"These are splendid drawings," he said, holding them away from himself with the gesture of a connoisseur. His face brightened with the reflections of colors and lights. Occasionally, he made a circle around his eye with his hand and looked through this improvised telescope, pulling his features into a grimace of gravity and connoisseurship.

"One could say," he said, "that the world had passed through your hands in order to renew itself, to molt in them and shed its skin like a marvelous lizard. Oh, do you think I would have stolen and committed a thousand follies if the world had not been so worn-out and degraded, if the things in it had not lost their gilding, the distant reflection of the hands of God? What can one do in such a world? How can one not doubt, not grow depressed, when everything is thoroughly locked up, walled in beyond its own meaning, and everywhere you are only knocking against a brick, as against a prison wall? Ah, Józef, you should have been born earlier."

We were standing in the semidark, deep room that grew longer in perspective toward the open window that faced the market square. Waves of fresh air reached us from there in gentle pulses, silently spreading out. Each incoming wave carried in a new load seasoned with colors of the distance, as if the previous one was already worn and exhausted. The dark room lived only through the reflections of distant houses outside the window; it reflected their colors in its depths like a camera obscura. Through the window, as if through the barrel of a telescope, the pigeons on the police sentry box could be seen, puffed up, strolling along the parapet of the attic. From time to time they all flew up together and executed semicircles above the market square. Then the room brightened for a moment from their open feathers, widened with the reflection of their distant fluttering, then faded as, descending, they closed their wings.

"To you, Shloma," I said, "I can reveal the secret of these drawings. From the start I was assailed by doubt as to whether I am in fact their author. At times they seem to me to be involuntary plagiarism, something that was hinted to me, handed to me . . . As if something alien served as my inspiration for goals that I do not know. Because I must confess to you," I added quietly, looking into his eyes, "I have discovered the Authentic . . ."

"The Authentic?" he asked, his face alight with a sudden glow.

"Yes, indeed, see for yourself," I said, kneeling beside the chest of drawers. I pulled out a silk dress of Adela's, a box of ribbons, her new high-heeled shoes. The smell of powder or perfume dispersed into the air. I lifted up a few books, too; indeed, at the bottom lay the dear yellowed catalog, long unseen, and it shone.

"Shloma," I said, moved, "look, it's lying here . . ."

But he was standing there sunk in thought, with Adela's shoe in his hand, observing it with profound seriousness.

"God did not say that," he said, "and yet, how profoundly this convinces me, pins me to the wall, takes away my final argument. These lines are irrefutable, apposite, final, and they strike, like lightning, to the very heart of the matter. With what do you defend yourself, what do you set against them, when you yourself are already bribed, outvoted, and betrayed by the most faithful allies? The six days of creation were divine and bright. But on the seventh day He sensed an alien thread under his hands and, terrified, removed his hands from the world although his creative fervor was calculated to last many more days and nights. Oh, Józef, beware the seventh day . . ."

And lifting Adela's slender slipper with horror, he spoke as if spellbound by the glossy, ironic eloquence of that empty lacquer shell:

"Do you understand the monstrous cynicism of this symbol on a woman's foot, the provocation of her dissolute tread on these ingenious heels? How could I leave you under the power of this symbol? God forbid that I would do this . . ."

Saying this, he slipped Adela's slippers, dress, and necklace under his jacket.

"What are you doing, Shloma?" I said, stupefied.

But he was hurriedly moving toward the door, limping slightly in his too-short, checked trousers. In the doorway he turned his still-gray, completely expressionless face toward me once more and raised his hand to his lips with a calming gesture. He was already outside the door.

Spring

I

This is the story of a particular spring, a spring that was more true, more dazzling, and brighter than other springs, a spring that simply took seriously its literal text, that inspired manifesto, written in the brightest holiday-red, the red of postal wax and the calendar, the red of a colored pencil and the red of enthusiasm, the amaranth of happy telegrams from over there . . .

Every spring begins this way, from those enormous and stunning horoscopes, more expansive than a single season of the year, in each of them—let me state this just once—there is everything: unending parades and demonstrations, revolutions and barricades, across each of which at a certain moment the hot gale of passion passes, that boundlessness of sorrow and intoxication seeking in vain its adequate counterpart in reality.

But then these exaggerations and culminations, these accumulations and ecstasies join the blooming, they enter entirely into the swinging of cool foliage, into spring gardens excited by the night, and the sound engulfs them. Thus do springs betray one another—one after the other, engrossed in the breathless rustling of blossoming parks, in their surges and inflows—they forget about their oaths, they drop leaf after leaf from their testament.

That single spring had the courage to endure, to remain faithful, to retain everything. After so many unsuccessful attempts, ascents, incantations, it wanted finally to truly constitute itself, to explode into the world as a universal and now final spring.

That gale of events, that hurricane of incidents: what a happy coup d'état were those bombastic, lofty, and triumphant days! I would like the pace of this story to capture their rousing, inspired rhythm, to take on the heroic tone of that epopee, to equal in its march the rhythm of that springtime "Marseillaise"!

How uncontained is the horoscope of spring! Who can be offended at spring for learning to read that horoscope in hundreds of ways, combining them blindly, sounding them out in all directions, feeling happy when successful at deciphering something amid the misleading guesswork of the birds? Spring reads the text backward and forward, losing its meaning and picking it up anew, in all versions, in thousands of alternatives, trills, and twitters. For the text of spring is marked entirely in hints, in understatements, in ellipses, dotted without letters in the empty azure, and the birds capriciously insert their conjectures and their divinations into the empty spaces between syllables. That is why this story, modeled on that text, has stretched out on many branching tracks and will be thoroughly interspersed with springtime dashes, sighs, and ellipses.

II

On those early spring nights, wild and expansive, covered with immense skies that were still raw and lacking in fragrance, skies that led through impassable aerial roads and tracts into an astral wilderness, Father would take me along to eat supper in a small garden restaurant, tucked in between the rear walls of the last houses on the market square.

We walked in the wet light of street lanterns creaking in gusts of wind, cut across the great vaulted square of the market, alone, crushed by the enormity of the aerial labyrinths, lost and disoriented in the empty spaces of the atmosphere. Father, his face bathed in a faint glow, would look up at the sky and gaze with bitter concern at the starry gravel scattered over the shoals of the broadly branching, overflowing whirlpools. Their irregular, uncountable density was not yet organized into any constellations, no figures were in control of those vast, stagnant pools. The sadness of the starry wilderness weighed upon the city, the streetlamps studded the night below with rays of light, indifferently tying them together from knot to knot. Under these streetlamps passersby stopped in twos and threes in the circle of light that created around them the transient illusion of a room in the light of a table lamp—in the indifferent, uninviting night that was disintegrating up above into irregular expanses, into wild aerial landscapes, frayed by blasts of wind, pitiful and homeless. Their conversations were halting, they smiled with their eyes in the deep shadow of their hats, listening pensively to the distant murmur of the stars toward which the expanses of that night were rising rapidly.

In the restaurant garden the paths were paved with gravel. Two lanterns on posts hissed pensively. Gentlemen in black frock coats were sitting in groups of two or three, hunched over little tables covered with white cloths, staring mindlessly at the gleaming plates. Seated like that, they were inwardly calculating the sequences and moves on the great black chessboard of the sky; they saw the knights galloping among the stars and the doomed pieces and the constellations immediately taking their place.

On the stage, magicians dipped their mustaches in mugs of bitter beer; they kept dully silent, deep in self-contemplation. Their instruments, violins and cellos with noble contours, lay off to the side, abandoned under the silently murmuring deluge of stars. Sometimes they picked them up and tried them on, tuning them plaintively to the pitch of their chests and testing the tone by clearing their throats. Then they laid them down again, as if they were still immature and not up to the measure of that night that flowed on, indifferent. Then, in the silence and ebb of thoughts, while forks and knives clinked softly over the white-clothed tables, a violin suddenly stood up on its own, prematurely grown-up and adult; only recently plaintive and uncertain, it now stood there eloquent, slender, with a narrow waist, and making its authority clear, took up the momentarily postponed human affair and pressed forward the lost cause before the indifferent tribunal of the stars among which the F holes and profiles of the instruments were drawn in watery print, fragmentary keys, unfinished lyres and swans—an imitative, thoughtless, astral commentary on the margins of music.

The photographer, who for some time now had been casting knowing glances in our direction from the neighboring table, finally sat down with us, transferring his mug of beer from his table to ours. He smiled ambiguously, struggled with his own thoughts, snapping his fingers, continually losing once again the elusive point of the situation. From the outset we sensed its paradoxical nature. This improvised restaurant encampment under the auspices of the distant stars was going bankrupt without help, was breaking apart pitifully, unable to cope with the limitlessly increasing grievances of the night. What could we oppose to these bottomless wastelands? The night was erasing the human performance that the violin was attempting in vain to defend; it was occupying the gap, dragging its constellations onto the regained positions.

We saw the disbanding encampment of tables, the battlefield of discarded napkins and tablecloths that the night, luminous and immeasurable, had crossed over in triumph. We stood up, too, while our thoughts, getting ahead of our bodies, had long since been running after the noisy starry rumbling of its dippers, the distant, widely scattered starry rumbling of those great, bright tracks.

So we walked under the rockets of its stars, with tightly shut eyes anticipating in our souls its ever higher and higher illuminations. Ah, that cynicism of triumphant night! Having taken possession of the whole sky, it was now playing dominoes on its expanse, carelessly and without keeping score, gathering up indifferently its millions of winnings. Then, bored, it drew transparent scribbles on the battlefield of overturned tablets, smiling faces, always one and the same smile in thousands of repetitions, a smile that a moment later was crossing over—already eternal—to the stars and crumbling into starry indifference.

Along the way we stopped at a café for some pastries. We had barely stepped through the rattling glass doors into its white, glacé interior, full of glistening sugars, when the night stood still and instantly was all stars, alert and watchful suddenly, curious as to whether we would lock it out. It waited patiently for us the entire time, standing guard at the doors, shining from on high through the panes with stationary stars while we, with profound deliberation, selected our pastries. Then, for the first time, I caught sight of Bianka. She was standing near the counter with her governess, in profile, wearing a white dress, slender and calligraphic, as if she had emerged from the zodiac. She did not turn around but stood in the exemplary contrapposto of young girls, eating a cream puff. I did not see her clearly as I was still thoroughly crisscrossed by the zigzags of starry lines. That is how our horoscopes, still very muddled, intersected for the first time. They met and then distanced themselves indifferently. We did not yet understand our fate in that early starry aspect and we walked out indifferently, rattling the glass doors.

Afterward, we returned home by a circuitous route through a distant suburb. The houses became lower and less frequent, finally they parted before us for the last time and we stepped into another climate. Suddenly we had entered into mild springtime, into a warm night that was turning silver along the mud with the young, newly risen, violet moon. That late winter night advanced in hasty tempo, anticipating feverishly its late phases. The air, still just recently laced with the usual tartness of that season, suddenly became sweet and cloying, full of the smell of rainwater, of wet loam, and the first snowdrops blossoming somnambulistically in the white magical light. It is a wonder that under this bountiful moon the night was not teeming with frog spawn on the silvery marshes, that it had not hatched out eggs, had not been chattering away with its thousand gossiping little mouths on those riparian gravel bars that leaked a glistening net of fresh water in every season. And it was necessary to infer and add in the croaking on that noisy, spring-fed night full of subcutaneous shudders so that, suspended for a moment, it might move on, and the moon might reach its fullest, ever whiter and whiter, as if it were pouring its whiteness from one goblet to another, ever higher and ever more radiant, ever more magical and transcendent.

Thus we walked on under the gathering gravitational pull of the moon. Father and the photographer supported me between them for I was dead on my feet from extreme sleepiness. Our footsteps crunched on the wet sand. I had been asleep while walking for a long time already and had under my eyelids the entire phosphorescence of the sky full of luminous signs, signals, and astral phenomena when we finally came to a stop in an open field. Father laid me down on a coat spread out on the ground. Through closed eyes I saw how the sun, the moon, and eleven stars formed a parade in the sky, marching past before me. "Bravo, Józef," Father cried out his approval, clapping his hands. It was an obvious plagiarism committed against that other Joseph and applying to entirely different circumstances. No one rebuked me for this. My father, Jakub, nodded his head and clucked his tongue, and the photographer set up his tripod on the sand, expanded the apparatus's bellows like an accordion, and plunged his entire body into the folds of black cloth: he was photographing that singular phenomenon, that shining horoscope in the sky, while I, with my head floating in the radiance, lay dazzled on the coat and feebly held up this dream for display.

III

The days became long, bright, and vast, almost too vast for their still meager, nondescript content. They were days to be grown into, days full of waiting, pallid from boredom and impatience. A bright breath, a shining wind, passed through the emptiness of those days; not yet disturbed by the exhalations of naked, sun-filled gardens, it blew the streets clean and they became long and bright, swept clean as if for a holiday, as if they were waiting for someone's still distant and unknown arrival. The sun was slowly heading toward the points of the equinox, it was slowing its course, approaching the model position in which it had to stand motionless in ideal equilibrium, emitting streams of fire, portion after portion, onto the empty, thirsty earth.

A bright, endless draft blew across the entire breadth of the horizon, arranging the rows of trees and the avenues under the pure lines of perspective; it grew smooth with great, empty blowing and finally came to a halt, breathless, immense and gleaming, as if it wished to capture in its all-encompassing mirror an ideal image of the city, a fata morgana extending into the depths of its luminous concavity. Then the world grew motionless for a moment, out of breath, dazzled, desiring to enter whole into that deceptive image, that provisional eternity that had been revealed to it. But the happy offer passed by, the wind was breaking up its mirror, and time once again took possession of us.

The Easter holidays arrived, long and impenetrable. Free from school, we wandered the city aimlessly and needlessly; we did not know how to make use of freedom. It was a freedom that was utterly empty, without definition, and useless. Still undefined ourselves, we expected a definition from time, which did not know how to find one, and time itself kept getting lost amid a thousand subterfuges.

In front of the café, small tables were already arranged on the pavement. Women sat at the tables in their bright, colorful dresses, swallowing the wind, like ice cream, in dainty bites. Their skirts made whirring sounds, the wind was nipping at them from below like a furious little dog, the ladies were beginning to blush, their faces were burned from the dry wind and their lips chapped. The entr'acte and the great boredom of the entr'acte were still in progress; the world, beset by stage fright, was slowly drawing near to a border of sorts, it was reaching the finishing line prematurely and was waiting.

We were all ravenous as wolves in those days. Dried out by the wind, we ran to our homes to consume enormous slices of bread and butter in dull pensiveness; in the street we bought large pretzels, crackling with freshness, and all of us sat in a row in the spacious entrance hall—empty and vaulted—of the apartment house on the market square without a thought in our heads. The white, clean market square was visible through the low arcades. Empty wine barrels stood in a row against the wall giving off their smell. We sat on the long counter on which, on market days, colorful peasant kerchiefs were sold, and we drummed our feet against the boards out of helplessness and boredom.

Suddenly Rudolf, his mouth stuffed with pretzel, took a stamp album from under his jacket and unfolded it before me.

IV

Now I understood why until then that spring had been so empty, hollow, and out of breath. Unaware of this, spring had calmed down internally, fallen silent, and withdrawn into its core; it had made room, opened itself up entirely into pure space, into empty azure, without belief or definition—a puzzled naked form for receiving unknown content. Hence that azure neutrality as if awakened from sleep, that great and seemingly indifferent readiness for everything. That spring kept itself entirely at the ready; unpopulated and vast, breathless, head over heels, it placed itself utterly at our disposition—it was waiting, in a word, for a revelation. Who, after all, could have foreseen that it would emerge completely prepared—fully equipped and dazzling—from Rudolf's stamp album?

They were the strangest abbreviations and formulas, recipes for civilization, handy amulets in which it was possible to grasp between two fingers the essence of climates and provinces. They were remittances for empires and republics, archipelagoes and continents. What more could tsars and usurpers, conquerors and dictators possess? Suddenly, I recognized the sweetness of power over lands, the prick of that hunger that can be sated only by dominion. Along with Alexander of Macedonia I desired the entire world. And not one handspan less of earth than the world itself.

V

Dark, ardent, full of festering love, I took in a parade of creation, marching lands, shining processions that I saw in intervals through purple eclipses, deafened by the blows of the blood beating in my heart in time to this universal march of all nations. Rudolf, preoccupied and filled with zeal, passed those battalions and regiments before my eyes, conducted the parade. He, the owner of this album, blinded and disoriented in his unclear, thoroughly ambiguous role, demoted himself voluntarily to the role of adjutant and ceremoniously made his report, which was full of emotion like an oath of fealty. Finally, in exaltation, in a flood of some kind of fanatical magnanimity, he pinned on my chest as if affixing a medal a pink Tasmania, fiery as May, and a Hyderabad swarming with the Gypsy gibberish of mingled alphabets.

VI

Then the revelation took place, the suddenly manifested vision of the flaming beauty of the world; then the good news arrived, the secret message, the special mission about the infinite possibilities of being. Vivid horizons opened wide, severe and breathtaking, the world trembled and flickered in its joints, tilted dangerously, threatening to break free from all measures and laws.

What is a postage stamp to you, dear reader? What is the profile of Franz Joseph I, his bald head crowned with a laurel wreath? Is it not a symbol of the quotidian, the determination of all possibilities, the guarantee of the impassable borders within which the world is once and forever confined?

The world at that time was enclosed on all sides by Franz Joseph I, and there was no getting away from him. That omnipresent, inescapable profile loomed up on every horizon, emerged from behind every corner, locked the world, like a prison, with a key. And then, when we had already lost hope, when full of bitter resignation we had made peace inwardly with the unambiguous nature of the world, with the strict immutability of which Franz Joseph I was the powerful guarantor—then, all of a sudden, You opened that stamp album before me, O God, as if it were some unimportant object; You allowed me to cast a passing glance at this Book that was shedding radiance, this stamp album peeling off its vestments, page after page, becoming ever more brilliant and ever more terrifying . . . Who can hold it against me that I was dazzled then, weak from emotion, and that tears poured from my eyes, which were filled to the brim with radiance? What dazzling relativism, what a Copernican feat, what fluidity of all categories and ideas! You gave so many means of existence, O God; so innumerous is Your world! It is more than I imagined in my most daring dreams. That early anticipation of the soul, which insisted despite all obviousness that the world is innumerous, is the truth!

VII

The world was bounded at that time by Franz Joseph I. On every postage stamp, on every coin and every postmark, his image affirmed the permanence of the world, the imperturbable dogma of its unambiguous nature. "Such is the world and you shall have no other worlds but this," proclaimed the seal with the Imperial-Royal old man. "Everything else is fantasy, wild pretension, and usurpation." Franz Joseph I lay down on everything and stopped the world in its growth.

We are inclined toward orthodoxy from the depths of our being, dear reader. The loyalty of our courteous nature is not insensitive to the charm of authority. Franz Joseph I was the highest authority. If that authoritative old man threw his whole weight onto the scale of that truth, there was no helping it; it was necessary to surrender the soul's fantasies, its ardent anticipation, to arrange oneself as best one could in this one possible world, without delusions and without romanticism—and forget.

But when the prison was closing irrevocably, when the last opening was bricked over, when everything conspired to silence You, O God, when Franz Joseph I barricaded and sealed the last gap so that You would not be noticed, then You rose up in the sounding cloak of the seas and continents and showed him to be a liar. You, O God, took upon Yourself the odium of heresy and exploded into the world with that immense, colorful, magnificent blasphemy. O, magnificent heresiarch! You struck me then with that burning Book; You exploded from Rudolf's pocket in the form of a stamp album. I did not yet know the album's triangular shape. In my blindness I mistook it for the paper pistol from which we used to shoot under the school bench in order to aggravate our teachers. Oh, how You shot from it, O God! It was

Your ardent tirade, Your fiery, holy philippic against Franz Joseph I and his state of prose; it was the genuine Book of Radiance!

I opened it and it shone there before me with the colors of worlds, the wind of boundless expanses, a panorama of whirling horizons. You walked through it, page after page, pulling behind You a train woven from every region and climate. Canada, Honduras, Nicaragua, Abracadabra, Hyporabundia . . . I understood You, God. It was all the contrivances of Your wealth, the first best words that came to You. You reached Your hand into Your pocket and showed me, like a handful of buttons, the possibilities swarming within You. You were not concerned with precision, You said whatever Your saliva deposited on Your tongue. You might just as well have said "Panfibras and Haleliva," and the wind would have started flapping among the palms with parrots drawn to power, and the sky, like an immense, hundredfold, sapphire rose, blown open down to its base, would have revealed its dazzling core, Your peacock eye, surrounded by eyelashes and terrifying, and it would have started sparkling with the glaring root of Your wisdom, gleaming with hypercolor, giving off a hyperaroma. You wanted to dazzle me, O God, to boast, to flirt with me, because You, too, have moments of vanity when You are enraptured with Yourself. Oh, how I love these moments!

How submerged you became, Franz Joseph I, you and your gospel of prose! In vain did my eyes seek you! In the end, I found you. You were in this crowd, too, but how small, dethroned, and gray. You were marching with the others in the dust of the highway right behind South America and in front of Australia and were singing along with the others: Hosanna!

VIII

I became a follower of the new gospel. I made friends with Rudolf. I marveled at him, vaguely sensing that he was only an instrument, that the Book was ordained for someone else. He seemed, in fact, to be more like its guardian. He catalogued, glued, unglued, locked it away in a cabinet. Indeed, he was sad, like one who knew that he would be diminished while I would rise. He was like the one who came to make straight the way of the Lord.

IX

I had many reasons to assume that the Book was predestined for me. Many signs pointed to the fact that it was addressed to me as an especial mission, a dispatch, a personal commission. I knew this by the fact that no one considered himself its owner. Not even Rudolf, who acted more as its servant. In fact, it was alien to him. He was like a reluctant, lazy servant duty bound to drudgery. At times, envy flooded his heart with bitterness. He rebelled inwardly against his role as steward of a treasure that did not belong to him. He looked with envy at the reflection of distant worlds that meandered in a quiet color scale across my face. A distant glow from those pages in which his soul had no share reached him only when reflected from my countenance.

X

Once, I saw a prestidigitator. He was standing on a stage, slender, visible from all angles, demonstrating his top hat, showing everyone its empty, white bottom. Having thus, beyond any doubt, guaranteed his art against suspicions of fraudulent manipulation, with his wand he drew in the air his tangled magic sign and immediately, with exaggerated precision and clarity, began extracting from the top hat with his wand paper ribbons, colorful ribbons, by cubits, by fathoms, and finally by kilometers. The room filled with the colorful, rustling mass; it grew bright from that hundredfold multiplication, from the frothy, lightweight tissue paper, the luminous accumulation, but he did not stop extracting that endless thread despite the horrified voices, full of enchanted protest, the cries of ecstasy, spasmodic weeping, until in the end it became as clear as could be that it was costing him nothing, that he was drawing this abundance not from his own resources, that celestial sources not in accordance with human measures and accounts had simply opened up for him.

Someone predestined to receive the deepest meaning of that demonstration walked home pensive and inwardly illuminated, penetrated to the core by the truth that had entered into him: God is innumerous . . .

XI

This is the place to develop a short parallel between Alexander the Great and myself. Alexander the Great was sensitive to the fragrances of countries. His nostrils sensed unheard-of possibilities. He was one of those over whose face God passed His hand in their sleep, so that they know what they do not know, they become filled with conjectures and suspicions, and the reflections of distant worlds pass through their closed eyes. However, he took divine allusions too literally. As a man of action, that is, of shallow spirit, he interpreted his purpose in life as a mission to be a world conqueror. His breast was filled with the same insatiability that filled my breast, the same sighs expanded it, entering his soul, horizon after horizon, landscape after landscape. He had no one to correct his mistake. Even Aristotle did not understand him. So he died disillusioned despite having conquered the entire world, doubting the existence of God, who was always eluding him, and His miracles. His portrait adorned the coins and stamps of every country. As punishment he became the Franz Joseph of his time.

XII

I would like to give the reader at least an approximate idea of what the Book was at that time, the Book in whose pages the decisive issues of that spring were preparing themselves and provisionally taking shape. An ineffable, distressing wind moved down the glistening rows of those stamps, down the decorated street of coats of arms and banners, zealously unfurling the crests and emblems waving in the breathless silence, in the shadow of clouds looming menacingly above the horizon. Then suddenly the first heralds appeared in the empty street in dress uniforms with red bands on their arms, glistening with sweat, confused, overwrought, and full of a sense of mission. They signaled silently, affected to their innermost core and filled with ceremonial gravity, and the street was already growing dark from the approaching demonstration, from all the cross streets the columns were growing darker with the crunching of thousands of approaching feet. It was an enormous display of countries, a universal May Day, a monster parade of worlds. As if it were taking an oath, the world was demonstrating with a thousand raised arms, flags, and banners, demonstrating with a thousand voices that it is not in favor of Franz Joseph I but of someone much, much greater. Above everything waved a bright red color, almost pink, the ineffable, liberating color of enthusiasm. From Santo Domingo, from San Salvador, from Florida, breathless, passionate delegations were approaching, all in raspberry-colored suits, and doffing their cherry-red bowler hats from under which clamorous goldfinches flew out in twos and threes. The glistening wind sharpened the radiance of the trumpets in happy flights, lightly and gently brushed the angles of the instruments, dropping onto all their edges silent wisps of electricity. Despite the crush, despite the march past of thousands, everything took place as it should have, the immense review unfurled as planned and in silence. There are moments when flags waving feverishly and violently from balconies, twisting in thin air in amaranthine bouts of nausea, in violent, quiet flapping, in vain flights of enthusiasm, stand up motionless, as if at roll call, and an entire street becomes red, garish, and full of mute alarm, while in the darkened distance the muffled salutes of a cannonade are counted down carefully—forty-nine detonations in the darkening air.

Then the horizon suddenly clouds over as before a spring storm, only the band instruments gleam brightly, and in the silence one can hear the murmur of the darkening sky, the sound of distant expanses, while from nearby gardens the fragrance of bird cherry wafts in concentrated bursts and discharges defenselessly in ineffable diffusion.

XIII

Then one day near the end of April the morning was gray and warm, people were walking, looking straight ahead at the ground, always at the square meter of damp earth in front of them, and not sensing that on both sides they were passing the park trees, which were branched out blackly, splitting in various places into sweet, festering wounds.

Enmeshed in the black branchy net of trees the gray, sultry sky—untidily stacked up, shapelessly heavy, and immense as a feather bed—lay on the backs of people's necks. People scrambled out from under it on their hands and knees, like cockchafers in that warm dampness sniffing the sweet clay with their sensitive antennae. The world lay mute, unfolding and rising somewhere above, somewhere behind and deep inside—blissfully powerless—and floated on. At times it slowed and vaguely resembled something, it branched out in trees, grafted onto the gray day a thick, glistening net of bird twittering that had been thrown over it, and moved deep into the subterranean snakelike tangle of roots, into the blind pulsing of worms and caterpillars, the muffled darkness of chernozem and clay.

Beneath this shapeless immensity crouched people deafened and without a thought in their head, crouching there with heads in hands, drooping, backs hunched, on park benches, with a sheet of newspaper on their knees from which the text had spilled into the great, gray vacuity of the day, hanging clumsily in a pose left over from yesterday, and unknowingly drooling.

Perhaps it was the compact rattles of twittering, the indefatigable poppy heads pouring out gray buckshot with which the air was growing dark that deafened them. They walked about drowsily beneath this lead hail and conversed by signs under this torrential downpour or, resigned to it, kept silent.

But when, at about eleven in the morning, somewhere at some point in space the sun pecked its way out as a pale sprout through the great bulging body of clouds—then all the buds suddenly shone densely in the branching baskets of the trees and the gray veil of twittering slowly detached itself from the face of the day as a pale gold net, and the day opened its eyes. And that was spring.

Then suddenly, in one instant, the avenue of the park that a moment before had been empty is sown now with people hurrying in various directions as though it were the hub of all the streets of the city, and it bursts into bloom with women's attire. Some of these quick, graceful girls are hurrying to work, to the shops and offices, others to a tryst, but for the couple of minutes during which they pass through the avenue's azure bower, which is breathing heavily with flower-shop moisture and is dappled with the trills of birds, they belong to that avenue and to that hour, they are without knowing it extras in this scene in the theater of spring, as if they had been born on the promenade at the same time as those delicate shadows of twigs and leaves budding before their eyes against the dark gold background of the damp gravel, and they will run for a couple of golden, burning, and costly pulses, then suddenly turn pale and drop into shadow, seep into the sand like transparent filigrees when the sun enters the pensiveness of the clouds.

But for one moment they swarm the avenue with their fresh haste, and the nameless odor of the avenue seems to flow from the rustling of their undergarments. Ah, those sheer blouses, fresh with starch, taken for a stroll beneath the azure shade of the springtime corridor, blouses with wet stains in the armpit, drying in the violet breezes of the distance. Ah, those young, rhythmical legs, hot from movement, in new stockings, the silk squeaking, beneath which lurk red spots and pimples—the healthy, springtime rashes of hot blood. Ah, this entire park is brazenly pimply and all the trees are pouring out buds of pimples that are bursting with twittering.

Then the avenue empties once more and along the vaulted promenade a baby carriage on slender springs softly jingles its wire spokes. In the lacquered little ship, sunk in a bed of tall, starched, feathery scarves, as if in a bouquet of flowers sleeps something even more delicate than they. The girl who is slowly pushing the baby carriage bends over it from time to time, tilts the floating basket, blossoming with white freshness, onto its rear wheels, its axles whimpering, and tenderly blows open the bouquet of tulle down to its sweet, slumbering heart through which sleep wanders like a fairy tale, while the carriage passes by streaks of shade—the flow of clouds and light.

Then at noon the budding flower garden is still weaving light and shade, and through the delicate eyelets of that net the chirping of tiny birds pours endlessly from branch to branch, pours like pearls through the wire mesh

cage of the day, but the women walking past along the edge of the promenade are already tired, their hair has come loose with migraine, and their
faces are worn-out with spring, and then the avenue is completely empty, and
slowly, across the afternoon silence, comes an aroma from the park pavilion
restaurant.

XIV

Every day at the exact same time Bianka walks along the park's avenue with
her governess. What shall I say about Bianka, how shall I describe her? I
only know that she is marvelously consistent with herself, that she fulfills her
program perfectly. My heart contracts with profound joy every time I see, as
if for the first time, how she enters step-by-step into her essence, light as a
ballerina, how she unconsciously hits the mark with every movement.

She walks in an entirely ordinary way, not with excessive grace, but with a
simplicity that grips the heart, and my heart contracts from happiness that
she can simply be Bianka, without artifice or effort.

Once, she slowly raised her eyes and looked at me, and the wisdom of that
glance penetrated me through and through, pierced me like a flying arrow.
Since then I have known that nothing is secret from her, that she has known
all my thoughts from the beginning. Since that moment I have put myself
at her disposal, entirely and unconditionally. She accepted with a barely perceptible lowering of her eyelids. This took place wordlessly, in passing, in a
single glance.

When I wish to picture her to myself, I can summon only one insignificant
detail: the chapped skin on her knees like a boy's, which is deeply moving
and leads my thoughts into torturous isthmuses of contradiction between
delightful antinomies. Everything else, higher and lower, is transcendent and
unimaginable.

XV

Today I immersed myself once again in Rudolf's stamp album. What a magnificent study! The text is full of cross-references, allusions, suggestions, full
of ambiguous flickering. But all the lines converge in Bianka. What delightful suppositions! My suspicion, ignited with luminous hope, runs from knot
to knot as if along a fuse—growing more and more dazzled. Ah, how painful
it is for me, how my heart contracts from the mysteries that I sense.

XVI

Every evening now in the city park a band is playing and a springtime promenade proceeds down the avenues. The people circle and turn back, pass
by and meet again in symmetrical, continuously repeating arabesques. The
young men wear new spring hats and hold their gloves nonchalantly in their
hands. Through the trunks of trees and the hedgerows the girls' dresses shine
in adjacent avenues. The girls walk in pairs, swaying their hips, puffed up with
the foam of feathers and flounces; like swans they carry along those pink and
white bustles—bells full of blooming muslin—and sometimes they alight on
a bench with them as if exhausted by the empty parade; they alight with all
that great rose of gauze and batiste that bursts, overflowing with petals. And
then their legs are revealed, placed one atop the other and crossed—braided
into a white shape full of irresistible eloquence, and the promenading young
men, passing them, fall silent and turn pale, stricken by the accuracy of the
argument, thoroughly convinced and conquered.

There comes the moment before twilight and the colors of the world grow
beautiful. All the hues turn theatrical, become festive, ardent, and sorrowful.
The park rapidly fills with a rosy varnish, a gleaming lacquer from which
things instantly turn very colorful and illuminated. But already in these colors
there is a blue that is too deep, a beauty that is too vivid and already suspect.
A moment later and the park's thicket, sparsely sprinkled with young greenery that is still bare and showing its branches, is suffused with twilight's rosy
hour, which has been subdued by the balm of coolness and saturated with the
ineffable sorrow of things that are forever mortally beautiful.

Then suddenly the entire park becomes an enormous, silent orchestra, solemn
and focused, waiting beneath the raised baton of the conductor for the music to
ripen in it and swell, and suddenly over this enormous, potential, ardent sym-
phony a rapid, colorful theatrical twilight descends as if under the influence of
tones swelling violently inside all the instruments—somewhere high above, the
voice of a golden oriole concealed in the thicket pierces the young greenery—and
suddenly on all sides it is solemn, solitary, and late, as in the woods at evening.

A barely perceptible breeze floats through the treetops from which a dry
dusting of bird cherry, ineffable and bitter, descends with a shudder. The bitter fragrance, into which the first stars are dropping their tears like the tiny
flowers of a lilac bush snipped from this pale, lilac night, pours out high
beneath the darkening sky and drifts down in a boundless sigh of death.
(Ah, I know: her father is a ship's doctor, her mother was a quadroon. Night
after night, a small dark steamer with wheels on its sides waits for her in the
harbor and does not light its lamps.)

Then, some kind of wondrous strength and inspiration enters into these circling couples, these young men and girls continually meeting in their regular rounds. Each of these men becomes a handsome, irresistible Don Juan, emerges from himself proud and victorious, and achieves in his glance that lethal power that terrifies girls' hearts. But the girls' eyes grow deeper, the dark, murmuring labyrinths of the parks, the deep gardens with avenues branching out, open wide in them. Their pupils enlarge with a festive radiance, they open without resistance and admit those conquerors into the alleys of their dark gardens branching off in paths repeatedly and symmetrically like the stanzas of a canzone in order to meet and find themselves, as in a sad rhyme, on pink squares, around circular flower beds, or near fountains burning with the late-twilight fire, and then once again to part and disperse among the black masses of the park, the evening thickets, ever thicker and noisier, in which they vanish and get lost in the intricate coulisses, the velvet portieres, and secluded alcoves. And no one knows when, through the chill of these gloomy gardens, they will enter into entirely forgotten, strange recesses, into a different, darker rustling of trees flowing like a funereal pall in which darkness ferments and degenerates and stillness putrefies over the course of years of silence, and decomposes fantastically, as in old forgotten wine barrels.

Groping their way in the black plush of these parks, they meet at last in a lonely glade beneath the final crimson of twilight, beside a pond that from time immemorial has been overgrown with black slime, and on a crumbling balustrade somewhere on the borderline of time, at the back gate of the world, they find themselves once again in some long-past life, in a distant preexistence, and, incorporated into an alien time, in the costumes of bygone eras, they sob endlessly over the muslin of a train and, climbing toward unattainable vows and entering upon the steps of passion, they advance toward peaks and boundaries beyond which is only death and the numbness of unnamed delight.

XVII

What is springtime dusk?

Have we reached the heart of the matter, does the road now lead no farther? We are at the end of our words, which are already becoming hallucinatory, delirious, and insane. And yet, only beyond their border does what is boundless and ineffable in this spring begin. The mystery of dusk! Only beyond our words, where the power of our magic cannot reach, does that dark, boundless element resound. Here, the word disintegrates into elements and dissolves, returns to its etymology, enters again into its depths, into its dark root. What do you mean, into its depths? We understand this literally. It is growing dark, our words are lost among obscure associations: Acheron, Orcus, Hades . . . Can you feel how it is growing dark from these words, how it is crumbling like a molehill, how a wind arose from the depths, the cellar, the grave? What is springtime dusk? Once more we pose this question, this ardent refrain of our inquiries to which there is no answer.

When the roots of trees wish to speak, when a great deal of the past, many tales and ancient stories, pile up under the sod, when too much breathless whispering, inarticulate pulp, and the dark thing that is short of breath and precedes every word accumulate under the roots—then the bark of the trees blackens and jaggedly disintegrates into thick scales and deep ridges, and the pith opens up with dark pores, like a bear's pelt. Bury one's face in that fluffy fur coat of dusk and in a moment it will be totally dark, soundless and without breath as if under a sealed lid. Then one must press one's eyes like leeches to the blackest darkness, apply light force, squeeze them through what is impenetrable, shove them straight through the dense soil—and suddenly, there we are, at the finish line, on the other side of things, we are in the innermost place, in the Underworld. And we see . . .

It is not, as one might assume, totally dark here. On the contrary—the whole interior is pulsing with light. It is, obviously, the interior light of the roots, a pale phosphorescence, the faint veins of an afterglow with which the darkness is marbled, the wandering, luminous ravings of matter. In just the same way, after all, when we sleep, cut off from the world, lost in deep introversion, in a reverse pilgrimage back to oneself—we also see, we see distinctly under our closed eyelids, because it is then that thoughts are ignited in us from an inner piece of kindling and they smolder hallucinatorily along lengthy fuses, flaring up from knot to knot. Thus does regression play out in us along the entire line, a retreat into the depths, a reverse journey to the root. Thus do we branch out into the depths through anamnesis, shuddering from the subterranean shivers that run across us, and dreaming subcutaneously beneath the entire phantasmal surface. Because only above, in the light— this must be stated once—we are a trembling, articulate cluster of melodies, a luminous skylark summit; in the depths we disintegrate once again into black muttering, into babble, into a host of interminable stories.

Only now do we see what this spring is growing on, why it is so inexpressibly sad and heavy with knowledge. Ah, we would not have believed it if we had not seen it with our own eyes. Here are the labyrinths of the interior, the storehouses and granaries of things; here are the still-warm graves, the dry rot and muck. Ancient stories. Seven levels, as in ancient Troy, corridors, chambers, treasuries. So many gold masks, mask upon mask, flattened smiles, eroded faces, mummies, empty chrysalids . . . Here are the columbaria, the drawers for the dead, in which they lie desiccated, black as roots, and await their time. Here are the great apothecaries where they stand on sale in lachrymal urns, crucibles, jars. They have been standing for years in their display cabinets, in long, ceremonial rows, although no one purchases them. Maybe they have already come back to life in the compartments of their nests, already completely recovered, pure and fragrant as incense—chirping specifics, awakened impatient medicines, balms and morning unguents weighing their early taste on the tip of their tongue. These walled-in dovecotes are full of beaks pecking out and the first, exploratory, luminous twittering. How early in the morning and before all time it suddenly becomes in these empty, long alleys where the dead awaken in a row, profoundly refreshed—to an entirely new dawn! . . .

But this is not the end; we are descending deeper. Don't be afraid. Give me your hand, please; one more step and we are at the roots, and right away it seems as if there are branches everywhere and gloom and roots as in a deep woods. It smells of sod and dry rot, roots wander in the darkness, become entangled, and juices, inspired, rise up in them as if in drinking-water pumps. We are on the other side, we are in the lining of things, in darkness basted with intricate phosphorescence. What circulation, movement, and crowding! What a swarm and pulp, tribes and generations, bibles and iliads multiplied a thousand times! What wandering about and tumult, what muddle and clamor of stories. This road goes no farther. We are at the very bottom, at the dark foundations, we are at the Mothers. Here are the endless infernos, the hopeless Ossianic expanses, the pitiful Nibelungen. Here are the great breeding grounds of stories, the fabulous factories, the fogbound forges of fictions and fables. Now, finally, that great, sad mechanism of spring is understood. Ah, it grows on stories. How many events, how many histories, how many fates! Everything that we ever read, all the stories we ever heard and all those—never heard—that have haunted us since childhood, here and nowhere else is their home and their fatherland. Where else would writers have taken their concepts, where else would they have gathered the courage to invent had they not sensed behind them these reserves, this capital, these hundredfold accounts with which the Underworld vibrates? What a tangle of whispers, what a murmuring din of earth! Inexhaustible persuasion pulsates against your ear. You walk with eyes half shut in this warmth of whispers, smiles, and proposals, endlessly besieged, pricked a thousand times over by questions as if by millions of sweet mosquito proboscides. They wish you would take something from them, anything, even just a pinch of those incorporeal, whispering histories, and accept it into your young life, into your blood, and preserve and continue to live with it. For what is spring if not the resurrection of stories? It alone is alive among these incorporeal things; it is actual, cool, and knows nothing. Oh, how these specters, all these phantoms, masks, and Farfarellos are drawn to spring's young, green blood, to her vegetal ignorance. And defenseless and innocent she takes them into her dream, and sleeps with them, and awakens unconscious at dawn and remembers nothing. That is why spring is so heavy with the entire sum of what has been forgotten, and so sad, because she alone must live for so many lives, be beautiful for so many rejected and forsaken . . . And to do this she has only the bottomless fragrance of bird cherry, flowing in one eternal, endless stream in which there is everything . . . For what does it mean to forget? During the night new greenery grew on the old stories, a soft, green coating, a bright, thick budding sifted out of all the pores in even bristles like the hair on the heads of boys after it has been closely cropped. How spring turns green with forgetfulness, how those old trees recover their sweet, naive ignorance, how they awake with branches unencumbered with memory, their roots immersed in old histories! That green will read them once again as if they are new and sound them out from the beginning, and from that green the stories will rejuvenate and begin once again as if they had never taken place.

There are so many unborn histories. Oh, those pitiful choirs among the roots, those tales conversing with each other, those inexhaustible monologues among suddenly exploding improvisations! Is there sufficient patience to hear them out? Before the oldest story that was heard there were others that you did not hear, there were nameless predecessors, novels without a name, enormous epopees, pale and monotonous, shapeless tales of old, irregular trunks, giants without faces filling the horizon, dark texts beneath the evening dramas of the clouds, and farther still—legend books, neverwritten books, eternal-book aspirants, lost and doomed books *in partibus infidelium* . . .

Among all these stories that crowd together, not disentangled, at the roots of spring, there is one that long ago had already become the property of night, had settled forever on the bottom of the firmaments, an eternal accompaniment and the backdrop of starry skies. Throughout every spring night, whatever might happen during it, that story passes by with great steps above the immense croaking of frogs and the endless running of mills. A man walks beneath the starry grist sifting down from the hand mills of night, he walks with great strides across the sky, cradling a baby in the folds of his cloak, always on the road, in a ceaseless wandering through the infinite expanses of night. Oh, the enormous pity of loneliness; oh, immeasurable orphanhood in the expanses of night; oh, the radiance of distant stars! In this story time can no longer change anything. At every moment this story is just now crossing the starry horizons, passing us with great strides, and thus it will be forever, constantly anew, for once having been derailed from the tracks of time it has become ungrounded, bottomless, never exhausted by repetition. The man walks on and cradles the child in his arms—we deliberately repeat this refrain, this pitiful motto of night, in order to express the intermittent continuity of crossing over, at times veiled by a tangle of stars, at times completely invisible for long, mute intervals through which eternity blows. Distant worlds approach very close—terrifyingly vivid, they send across eternity violent signals in mute, inexpressible relations—and he walks on endlessly soothing the little girl, in a monotone and without hope, powerless in the face of that distant whisper, those terrifyingly sweet persuasions of the night, that single word into which the lips of silence form when no one is listening to the night . . .

This is a story about an abducted changeling princess.

XVIII

And when late at night they return quietly to the vast villa among the gardens, to the white low room in which a long, black, glossy piano stands and is silent with all its strings, and through the great glass wall, as if through the panes of a conservatory the entire spring night bends down, pale and drizzling stars, from every flask and vessel there is the bitter smell of bird cherry above the cool linens on the white bed—then, anxieties and attentive listening run through the great, sleepless night and the heart chatters in its sleep and flies and stumbles and sobs through the vast, dewy night that is swarming with moths, bitter with bird cherry, and luminous . . . Ah, it is the bitter bird cherry that expands the bottomless night, and the heart, distressed by flights, worn-out from lucky chases, would like to fall asleep for a moment on some aerial border, on some thinnest edge, but from this pale night without end a new night, forever renewed, detaches itself, increasingly pale and more incorporeal, scratched into luminous lines and zigzags, into spirals of stars and pale flights, pierced a thousand times over by the proboscides of invisible mosquitoes, which make no sound and are sweet with maidens' blood, and the tireless heart once again babbles in its sleep, insane, enmeshed in astral, complex affairs, in breathless hurrying, in moonlight panics, rapturous and hundredfold, braided into pale fascinations, into torpid, somnambulistic dreams and lethargic shudders.

Ah, all the abductions and chases of that night, the betrayals and whispers, Negroes and helmsmen, balcony grilles and nighttime window blinds, muslin dresses and veils billowing behind a breathless escape! . . . Until at last, during a sudden onset of darkness, a hollow black pause, the moment arrives—all the puppets lie in their boxes, all the curtains are drawn, and all the breaths, long since determined, go peacefully back and forth across the whole width of the stage, while on the expansive, hushed sky dawn is silently building its distant pink and white cities, its bright, bulging pagodas and minarets.

XIX

Only now for the attentive reader of the Book does the nature of this spring become clear and legible. All these morning preparations of the day, its entire early toilette, all the hesitations, doubts, and scruples regarding choice reveal their core to him who has been initiated into stamps. Stamps lead into the intricate game of morning diplomacy, into those protracted negotiations, atmospheric maneuverings that precede the final version of the day. From the russet mists of the ninth hour—it is clearly visible—a gaudy, flaming Mexico with a serpent writhing in a condor's beak, hot and splotched with a vivid rash, would like to spill out, but in an azure interval a parrot in the high green of trees stubbornly keeps repeating "Guatemala" at regular intervals with identical intonation, and from that green word it slowly becomes cherry colored, fresh, and leafy. And thus, slowly, amid difficulties and conflicts, voting takes place, the course of the ceremony is set, the parade list, the diplomatic protocol of the day.

In May, there were days that were pink like Egypt. In the market square radiance poured out, rippling, from every border. In the sky, the pile of summer clouds knelt, all fleecy, beneath fissures of radiance, volcanic, vividly outlined, and—Barbados, Labrador, Trinidad—everything passed into red as if seen through ruby-colored spectacles, and through those two, three pulses, through growing darkness, through the red eclipse of blood pounding against the head, the great corvette of Guyana sailed across the entire sky, exploding with all its sails. Bulging, it glided along, its canvas snorting, towed cumbersomely amid its extended lines and the clamor of the towboats, through commotions of seagulls and the red radiance of the sea. Then the immense, jumbled rigging of ropes, ladders, and poles rose up to the entire sky and expanded immensely in breadth and, booming on high with its unfurled canvas the manifold, many-storied aerial spectacle of sails, yards and clew lines opened out, while in the hatches small, agile Negro boys appeared for a moment and then scattered in that canvas labyrinth, disappearing among the signs and figures of the fantastic sky of the tropics.

Then the scene changes, and in the sky, in the massifs of clouds, as many as three pink eclipses were coming to a climax at the same time, glowing lava was smoking, outlining with a luminous line the threatening contours of the clouds, and—Cuba, Haiti, Jamaica—the core of the world was moving into the depths, growing more and more vividly, making its way to the heart, and suddenly the pure essence of these days poured out: the murmuring oceanicity of the tropics, of archipelagic azures, of happy brooks and whirlpools, and equatorial salty monsoons.

With the stamp album in my hand I read the spring. Was it not a great commentary of the times, a grammar book of its days and nights? That spring declined through all the Colombias, Costa Ricas, and Venezuelas, for what, in essence, are Mexico and Ecuador and Sierra Leone if not some kind of ingenious nostrum, some intensification of the taste of the world, some extreme, refined finality, a blind alley of aroma into which the world rushes in its quests, testing and practicing on every keyboard?

The main thing, let us not forget—like Alexander the Great—is that no Mexico is the ultimate one, that it is a transitional point that the world passes by, that beyond every Mexico a new Mexico opens up, even more vivid, hypercolorful, and hyperaromatic . . .

XX

Bianka is completely gray. Her dusky complexion seems to include as one of its ingredients dissolved dead ashes. I think that the touch of her hand must surpass everything imaginable.

Entire generations of training reside in her disciplined blood. Her resigned submission to the requirements of tact is touching, testifying as it does to defeated defiance, broken rebellions, quiet sobs at night, and the violence done to her pride. With every movement, full of goodwill and sorrowful grace, she robes herself in prescribed forms. She does nothing that is not required, every gesture of hers is stingily measured out, barely fulfilling its form, entering into it without enthusiasm as if only out of a passive sense of duty. From the depths of these experiences of mastery Bianka draws her precocious experience, her knowledge of all things. Bianka knows everything. And she does not smile at the knowledge, her knowledge is serious and full of sorrow, her lips are tightly closed over it in a line of absolute beauty, her eyebrows are drawn with stern accuracy. No, she does not draw from her knowledge any incentive for relaxation of discipline, for softness and dissoluteness. On the contrary. As if it were possible to cope with the truth on which her sad eyes are focused only by intense alertness, only by the strictest adherence to form. And there is in this unwavering tact, in this loyalty to form an entire ocean of sorrow and of arduously mastered suffering.

And yet, although broken by form, she has emerged from under it victoriously. But with what sacrifice did she pay for that triumph!

When she walks, slender and erect, no one knows whose pride she is carrying with simplicity in the modest rhythm of her stride, whether her own defeated pride or the triumph of the principles to which she has submitted.

But, when she gazes with a simple, sorrowful lifting of her eyes—suddenly she knows everything. Youth has not protected her from guessing the most secret things. Her quiet serenity is a consolation after long days of weeping and sobbing. That is why she has dark rings around her eyes and there is a moist, burning glow in them, along with that unfailing purposefulness of glances that are indisposed to recklessness.

XXI

Bianka, marvelous Bianka, is a mystery to me. I study her stubbornly, passionately—and despairingly—on the basis of the stamp album. How can that be? Does the stamp album also treat of psychology? A naive question! A stamp album is a universal book, it is a compendium of all knowledge about that which is human. Naturally, in allusions, hints, insinuations. A certain perspicacity is required, a certain courage of the heart, a certain imaginativeness, to discover the thread, the fiery trace, the lightning flash running through the pages of the book.

There is one thing that must be guarded against in these matters: a narrow pettiness, pedantry, a dull literalism. All things are interconnected, all threads lead back to a single ball. Have you noticed that among the verses of certain books swallows fly in great numbers, entire lines of trembling, pointed swallows? One must read the flight of those birds . . .

But I return to Bianka. How touchingly beautiful are her movements. Each one of them is performed with deliberation, decided centuries ago, taken resignedly, as if she knew beforehand the entire course, the inevitable trajectory of her fate. It happens that I want to ask her about something with a glance, to inquire about something in my thoughts—sitting across from her in one of the park avenues—and I attempt to formulate my claim. And before I succeed, she has already answered. Answered with sorrow with one deep, brief glance.

Why does she hold her head down? What are her eyes gazing at attentively, pensively? Are the depths of her fate so abysmally sad? And yet, despite everything, does she not bear that resignation with dignity, with pride, as if that is exactly how it was supposed to be, as if the knowledge depriving her of joy bestowed upon her in exchange a certain inviolability, a certain higher freedom found at the bottom of voluntary obedience? This gives her submission the charm of triumph and thereby overcomes it.

She sits opposite me on the bench beside her governess, both of them reading. Her white dress—I have never seen her in a different color—lies like an open flower on the bench. Her slender, dusky legs are crossed with ineffable charm. To touch her body must be painful from the intense holiness of contact.

Then they both stand up, having laid down their books. In one brief glance Bianka receives and returns my ardent greeting and, as if untroubled, goes away with the meandering interweaving dance step of her feet falling melodically into the rhythm of her governess's great elastic strides.

XXII

I investigated the entire estate from every angle. Several times, I circled the extensive terrain that was protected by a tall fence. The white walls of the villa with its terraces and extensive verandas kept appearing to me in ever new aspects. Beyond the villa stretches a park, and beyond it a treeless plain. Strange structures stand there, half factories, half farm buildings. I pressed my eyes to a gap in the fence, and what I saw had to have stemmed from an illusion. In the springtime atmosphere, thinned by sweltering heat, sometimes distant things appear, reflected across entire miles of shimmering air. And yet my head is bursting from the most contradictory thoughts. I must consult the stamp album.

XXIII

Is it possible? Is Bianka's villa an extraterritorial territory? Her home under the protection of international treaties? To what astonishing discoveries does the study of the stamp album lead me! Am I the only one in possession of this amazing truth? And yet it is impossible to ignore all the circumstantial evidence and arguments that the stamp album is amassing around this point.

Today I studied the entire villa from up close. For weeks I have been circling around the great artistically wrought gate with its coat of arms. I took advantage of a moment when two great empty equipages drove out from the garden of the villa. The wings of the gate stood wide-open. No one closed them. I entered with a casual step, pulled a sketchbook out of my pocket, and, leaning against one of the gate's pillars, I pretended to be drawing a certain architectonic detail. I was standing on the gravel path down which Bianka's light little foot had so often walked. My heart fell silent from happy terror at the thought that her slender shape in a light white dress might emerge through one of the balcony doors. But green drapes had been drawn across all the windows and doors. Not the slightest rustle betrayed the life hidden in that house. The sky was clouding over on the horizon; in the distance there were flashes of lightning. There was not the slightest breeze in the warm, thin air. In the silence of the gray day only the chalk-white walls of the villa spoke with the voiceless but stirring expressiveness of richly cohering architecture. Its easy eloquence radiated in pleonasms, in thousands of variants of the same motif. Along a bright white frieze flatly sculpted garlands ran to left and right in rhythmical cadences and, indecisive, came to a stop at the corners. From the height of the central terrace a marble staircase descended—pathetic and ceremonial, amid rapidly parting balustrades and architectonic vases—and, having flowed down expansively to the ground, appeared to gather and draw back its swelling robe in a deep reverence.

I have an oddly sensitive sense of style. That style irritated and disturbed me as something incomprehensible. Behind its fervent classicism, mastered with great difficulty, behind that apparently cool elegance, imperceptible little thrills were concealed. That style was too fervid, too sharply pointed, full of unexpected beauty marks. A drop of some unknown poison injected into the veins of this style was turning its blood dark, explosive, and dangerous.

Internally disoriented, trembling from contradictory impulses, I walked around the villa's front on tiptoe, startling the lizards asleep on the stairs.

The earth around the dried-up, round pool was cracked by the sun and still bare. Only here and there did a bit of ardent, fanatical greenery shoot up from a crack in the soil. I ripped out a clump of those weeds and placed it in my sketchbook. I was trembling all over from inner agitation. Above the pool the air was gray, exceedingly transparent and lustrous, undulating from the heat. The barometer on a nearby post was indicating a catastrophic drop. Silence shrouded everything in the vicinity. Not a single twig was stirred by a breeze. The villa slept with lowered blinds, shining with its chalky whiteness in the boundless torpor of the gray atmosphere. Suddenly, as if the stagnation had reached a critical point, the air precipitated a colorful ferment, disintegrated into colorful petals, into glittering flutterings.

They were enormous, languid butterflies, in pairs, busy with their amorous frolicking. The awkward, trembling flapping persisted for a moment in the dead atmosphere. They took turns pulling ahead by several inches and then again uniting in flight, shuffling an entire deck of colorful flashes in the darkening air. Was it only a rapid disintegration of the exuberant atmosphere, a fata morgana of air full of hashish and whims? I slapped at it with my cap, and a heavy, plush butterfly dropped onto the ground, fluttering its wings. I picked it up and pocketed it. One more proof.

XXIV

I figured out the secret of that style. The lines of that architecture kept on repeating with persistent fluency the same incomprehensible phrase until after a long time I grasped the perfidious code, the wink, the tickling mystification. It was in truth an exceedingly transparent masquerade. In those sophisticated, energetic lines of excessive elegance there was a certain overly sharp paprika, a certain excess of hot piquancy, there was something spritely, ardent, too vividly gesticulating—in a word, something colorful, colonial, with leering eyes . . . That's it, the style had at its bottom something incredibly repulsive—it was dissolute, fanciful, tropical, and incredibly cynical.

XXV

I need not explain how this discovery shocked me. Distant lines draw close and unite, connections and parallels unexpectedly converge. Filled with excitement, I shared my discovery with Rudolf. He turned out to be only slightly moved. He even snorted reluctantly, accusing me of exaggeration and fabrication. More and more frequently he accuses me of bluffing, of deliberate mystification. If I still had for him, as the owner of the album, a certain sentiment, his envious eruptions, full of unrestrained bitterness, are alienating me from him more and more. However, I don't express my resentment to him; alas, I am dependent on him. What, after all, would I do without the stamp album? He knows this and takes advantage of his dominance.

XXVI

Too much is happening this spring. Too many aspirations, boundless grievances, overflowing and unfulfilled ambitions distend these dark depths. Spring's expansion knows no limits. The administration of this immense, branching, lush affair is beyond my powers. Wishing to dump a part of the burden onto Rudolf, I named him coregent. Anonymously, of course. Together with his stamp album, the three of us are an unofficial triumvirate on whom rests the burden of responsibility for this entire unfathomable and ungraspable affair.

XXVII

I lacked the courage to walk around the villa and reach the other side. I would undoubtedly have been noticed. Why, despite this, do I have a feeling that I had been there once upon a time—very long ago? Could it be that in fact we already know beforehand all the landscapes that we will encounter in life? Is it possible that something can still happen that is entirely new, that we have not in our deepest reserves long had a presentiment of? I know that someday, at some late hour, I will stand on the threshold of the garden there hand in hand with Bianka. We will enter those forgotten recesses where, enclosed within old walls are the poisoned parks, the artificial paradises of Poe, full of cowbane, poppy, and narcotic bindweed blazing beneath the dark gray sky of ancient frescoes. We will awaken the white marble of a statue with vacant eyes in the marginal world beyond the border of the faded afternoon. We will startle its only lover, the red vampire bat asleep on its bosom with wings folded. It will fly away soundlessly, soft, supple, fluttering, a weak, incorporeal, bright-red scrap without skeleton or substance; it will whirl, flap wildly, break apart without a trace in the motionless air. Through a small wicket we shall step into a completely empty meadow. The vegetation there will be burned like tobacco, like prairies in late Indian summer. Perhaps it will be in the state of New Orleans or Louisiana—countries are only pretexts, after all. We will sit down on the stone wall of a square pond. Bianka will wet her white fingers in the warm water full of golden leaves and will not raise her eyes. On the other side, a slender black figure will be seated, completely veiled. I will ask about it in a whisper, and Bianka will shake her head and say softly, "Don't be afraid, she's not listening, she's my dead mother, who lives here." Then she will tell me the sweetest, quietest, saddest things. There will be no further consolation. Dusk will be falling . . .

XXVIII

Events are chasing one another at an insane tempo. Bianka's father arrived. Today I was standing at the intersection of Fountain and Scarab Streets when a gleaming, open landau, its body broad and shallow like a conch, drove up. I caught a glimpse of Bianka in that white silk shell half reclining in a tulle dress. Her gentle profile was shaded by a ruffle on her hat, which was pulled down and held in place with a white ribbon under her chin. She was practically drowning in the feathers of a white foulard and was seated beside a gentleman in a black frock coat and white piqué vest on which shone a heavy golden chain with numerous pendants. Under a black bowler hat, worn way back on the head, was a gray, closed, gloomy face with sideburns. I began to tremble to the very core at this sight. There could be no doubt. It was de V——. . .

As the elegant conveyance passed by me, its flexible body thudding discreetly, Bianka said something to her father, who turned around and directed at me a glance through his large, black eyeglasses. He had the face of a gray lion without a mane.

Ecstatically, almost unconscious from the most contradictory feelings, I cried out, "Count on me! . . ." and, "To the last drop of my blood . . . ," and I fired into the air with a pistol I retrieved from under my jacket.

XXIX

Many things testify to the fact that Franz Joseph I was essentially a powerful, sad demiurge. His narrow eyes, dull as little buttons, seated in triangular deltas of wrinkles, were not the eyes of a man. His hairy face, with its milk-white sideburns combed toward the back as on Japanese demons, was the face of an old, dejected fox. From a distance, from the height of a Schönbrunn Palace terrace, that face, thanks to the arrangement of its wrinkles, seemed to be smiling. From up close, the smile was unmasked as a grimace of bitterness and mundane reality not brightened by the glimmer of a single idea. At the moment when he appeared on the world's stage in the green plume of a general, in a turquoise cloak down to the ground, somewhat stooped and saluting, the world had reached a certain happy boundary in its development. All forms, having depleted their contents in endless metamorphoses, already hung loosely on things, half flaked off, ready to be sloughed off entirely. The world was metamorphosing violently, hatching in young, chirpy, unbelievable colors, happily dissolving in all sorts of knots and joints. It would have taken very little for the map of the world, that sheet full of patches and colors, to have flown away in the air, fluttering and full of inspiration. Franz Joseph I sensed this as his personal danger. His element was a world that was constrained by the rules of prose, the pragmatics of boredom. The spirit of chancelleries and district offices was his spirit. And an amazing thing. This desiccated, dull old man, who had nothing appealing in his being, managed to attract a great part of creation to his side. All loyal and far-seeing fathers of families felt threatened along with him and breathed a sigh of relief when that powerful demon lay down with his burden on top of things and halted the world's ascent. Franz Joseph I divided the world into columns, regulated its course with the help of decrees, constrained it within procedural lines, and made it safe from derailment into the unforeseen, the adventurous, and the utterly unpredictable.

Franz Joseph I was not an enemy of decent, God-fearing joy. It was he who dreamed up in a kind of visionary affability the Imperial-Royal lottery for the people, Egyptian dream books, illustrated calendars, and Imperial-Royal tobacco stores. He standardized the celestial civil service, dressed them in symbolic sky-blue uniforms, and sent out into the world, divided into dicasteries and ranks, the personnel of angelic hosts in the form of letter carriers, conductors, and finance clerks. The most wretched of these sky-blue couriers still retained on his face the reflection of primeval wisdom borrowed from the Creator and a jovial smile of grace enclosed in a frame of sideburns, even when his feet, because of considerable earthly wanderings, stank of sweat.

But has anyone heard about the thwarted conspiracy at the very foot of the throne, about the great palace revolution nipped in the bud at the very start of the Omnipotent One's glorious government? Thrones wither if they are not fortified with blood; their vitality increases with the mass of injury, of negated life, of the eternally other that they have marginalized and denied. Here we are revealing things secret and forbidden, we are touching upon state secrets locked up a thousand times over and sealed with a thousand seals of silence. The Demiurge had a younger brother whose spirit and ideas were entirely different from his. Who does not have such a one in some form or another who accompanies one like a shadow, like an antithesis, like a partner in an eternal dialogue? According to one version, he was only a cousin; according to another, he had not even been born. He was deduced only from the Demiurge's trepidations, from his ravings overheard while he was asleep. Perhaps he had made him up haphazardly, substituted just anyone for him in order to play out this drama only symbolically, to repeat ceremoniously and ritually once more or for who knows how many times this prestatutory, fatal act that a thousand repetitions could not exhaust. This provisionally born, to a certain degree professionally wronged, antagonist, unhappy as a consequence of his role, was named Archduke Maximilian. The very name, uttered in a whisper, renews the blood in our veins, makes it brighter and redder, pulsing rapidly with that vivid color of enthusiasm, of postage seal and red pencil, with which happy telegrams from over there are stamped. He had rosy cheeks and radiant azure eyes; all hearts ran toward him, swallows, chirping with joy, cut across his path, placed him over and over again between shuddering quotation marks—a fortunate quote, penned in festive cursive, and twittered in all directions. The Demiurge himself secretly loved him, although he was contemplating his destruction. First he named him commander of the Levantine squadron in the hope that while pursuing adventures in the southern seas he would drown miserably. Soon thereafter, however, he made a secret pact with Napoléon III, who surreptitiously drew him into the Mexican adventure. Everything had been planned. The young man, full of fantasy and enthusiasm, ill served by his hope of establishing a happy new world in the Pacific, gave up all his agnate's rights of succession to the throne and the Habsburg inheritance. Aboard the French liner *Le Cid* he sailed straight into the ambush that had been prepared for him. The records of that secret conspiracy have never seen the light of day.

Thus was dissipated the last hope of the malcontents. After his tragic death, Franz Joseph I, under the pretext of court mourning, proscribed the color red. Black and yellow became the official colors for mourning. Since then, the color of amaranth, the billowing flag of enthusiasm, waves only secretly in the hearts of its adherents. The Demiurge did not manage, after all, to uproot it entirely from nature. It is, after all, potentially a component of sunlight. It is enough to shut one's eyes in spring sunshine to absorb it, burning hot, under one's eyelids, wave after wave. Photographic paper burns with precisely that red in the springtime radiance overflowing beyond every boundary. Bulls led down a sunny city street with a cloth over their horns see it in bright patches and lower their heads, poised to attack the imaginary toreadors escaping in panic in fiery arenas.

Sometimes an entire day goes by vivid in explosions of sunshine, in stacks of clouds luminously and chromatically encircled at their borders, all their edges full of a red that is breaking through. Dazed by the light, people walk with their eyes shut, exploding inside themselves from rockets, Roman candles, and kegs of gunpowder. Then, toward evening, the drumfire of light diminishes, the horizon becomes round and beautiful, fills up with azure like a garden crystal ball containing a miniature, luminous panorama of the world, with successfully arranged plans over which, like a final consummation, the clouds form into ranks above the horizon, stretched out in a long row like rolls of gold medals or the pealing of bells complementing one another in rosy litanies.

People congregate in the market square, silent beneath that immense, luminous cupola; they form groups despite themselves and merge into a great, stationary finale, a rapt scene of anticipation; the clouds pile up ever more rosily, at the back of every eye there is a deep peace and a reflection of the luminous distance, and suddenly, while they are waiting, the world reaches its zenith, matures to the highest perfection in two or three final beats. By now the gardens are arranging themselves definitively on the crystal bowl of the horizon, the May greenery is foaming and boiling like glittering wine ready at any minute to overflow its rim, the hills model themselves on clouds: having passed the highest peak, the beauty of the world separates and ascends—with enormous fragrance it enters into eternity.

And while the people are still standing motionless, their heads lowered, still full of bright and enormous visions, spellbound by the great, luminous ascent of the world, suddenly he whom they had been awaiting unknowingly runs out from the crowd, a breathless courier, all rosy in beautiful raspberry tights, with little bells, medals, and orders dangling all over him, runs across the clean market square that is encircled by the quiet crowd, still full of flight and annunciation—a supplementary surplus, pure profit discarded by the day, which happily sets it apart from all that radiance. Six and seven times he runs around the market square in beautiful mythological circles, in circles beautifully curved and delineated. He runs slowly in full view, his eyes lowered as if in embarrassment, his hands on his hips. His slightly heavy belly sags, shaken by his rhythmic running. His face, crimson from exertion, shines with sweat beneath his black Bosnian mustache, and on his brown exposed chest his medals, orders, and little bells bounce rhythmically like a wedding harness. He can be seen from a distance as, turning a corner in a tense, parabolic line, he draws near with the janissary band of his little bells, beautiful as God, unbelievably rosy, with his rigid torso, repelling with a sideways glitter in his eye and with blows of his riding crop the pack of hounds that are baying at him.

Then Franz Joseph I, disarmed by the universal harmony, proclaims a silent amnesty, grants permission for red, permits it for this one May evening in a diluted, sweet, caramel form, and, reconciled with the world and with his antithesis, stands in the open window of Schönbrunn beneath which on clean market squares ringed by silent crowds rosy sprinters are running; he can be seen at this moment throughout the world, on all horizons, he can be seen as an enormous imperial-royal apotheosis against a background of clouds, leaning with his gloved hands on the window balustrade in his turquoise-blue frock coat with the ribbon of a commander of the Maltese order, his eyes narrowed inside deltas of wrinkles as if from smiling—sky-blue buttons without kindness and without mercy. He stands like that with his snowy sideburns smoothed back to create the effect of kindness—an embittered fox—and from afar he imitates a smile with his face that lacks humor and genius.

XXX

After lengthy hesitation I told Rudolf about the events of the past days. I could no longer keep to myself the secret that was threatening to burst out of me. His face grew dark, he shouted, accused me of lying, and finally exploded openly with envy. "It's all a lie, a blatant lie," he cried, running around with his hands in the air. Extraterritoriality! Maximilian! Mexico! Ha-ha! Cotton plantations! Enough of that, it's over, he won't think of using his stamp album for such wickedness anymore. The partnership's done with. Termination of the contract. He clutched his hair in agitation. He was completely out of control, ready for anything.

I began explaining to him, calming him down; I was very frightened. I admitted that at first glance the matter is truly unbelievable. I myself, I confessed, cannot get over my astonishment. It's not surprising that it is difficult for him, who was unprepared for this, to accept it immediately. I appealed to his heart and his honor. Can he square it with his conscience that precisely now, when the matter is nearing the decisive stage, he will deny me his help and ruin things by retracting his participation? Finally, I attempted to prove to him on the basis of the stamp album that everything is, word for word, the truth.

Somewhat mollified, he opened the album. Never had I spoken with such eloquence and fire; I outdid myself. Arguing on the basis of the stamps, not only did I refute all his accusations, dispel all his doubts, but going beyond that I reached such simply revelatory conclusions that I myself was dazzled by the perspectives that opened up. Rudolf, defeated, kept silent; there was no longer any talk of dissolving our partnership.

XXXI

Can it possibly be an accident that precisely during those days a great theater of illusions arrived, a magnificent wax museum, and set up camp on Holy Trinity Square? I had long foreseen this and triumphantly informed Rudolf about it.

It was a windy, startled evening. It was threatening rain. On the yellow, fading horizons the day was already preparing to depart; it was hastily pulling gray waterproof covers over its string of wagons that stretched out in a line toward the late, chilly world beyond. Under the already half-lowered, darkening curtain the distant, last traces of sunset appeared for a moment, sinking like a great, flat, endless plain full of far-flung lake districts and reflective surfaces. Yellow and terrified, the already doomed reflection was moving diagonally across the sky away from these bright trails, the curtain was falling rapidly, roofs sparkled pale in their wet reflection, it grew dark, and a moment later the rain gutters began singing monotonously.

The waxworks was already brightly illuminated. In that nervous, hasty dusk people like dark silhouettes, covered with umbrellas, were thronging in the pale yellow light of the setting day to the illuminated vestibule of the tent where, respectfully, they paid the entrance fee in front of a colorful lady in a low-cut dress, who sparkled with jewels and the gold filling in her teeth—a living plaster bust laced up and painted, but fading below by some incomprehensible means in the shadow of velvet drapes.

We entered through a half-open curtain into a brilliantly illuminated space. It was already full of people. Groups wearing rain-soaked overcoats, their collars up, moved about in silence from place to place, forming tight semicircles. Among them I easily recognized those who only ostensibly belonged to the same world, while in reality they lived separate, representative, mummified lives on a pedestal, lives exposed to view and ceremonially empty. They stood in terrifying silence, dressed in formal frock coats, in Prince Albert frock coats, and in tailcoats of fine cloth, made to measure; they were very pale, with rashes from the final illnesses from which they had died, and their eyes glittered. There had not been a single thought in their heads for a long time, only the habit of showing themselves from every angle, the bad habit of representing their empty existence that sustained them with a final effort. They ought to have been in bed a long time ago after taking a teaspoonful of medicine, wrapped up in cool sheets, their eyes closed. It was abusive to keep them up so late into the night on their narrow plinths and armchairs on which they sat stiffly in tight patent leather shoes, miles away from their former existences, with glittering eyes and utterly devoid of memories.

From each of their mouths hung, like the tongue of someone who has been strangled, the last dead cry with which they had left the lunatic asylums where, assumed to be maniacs, they had spent time as if in purgatory before crossing these final thresholds. Yes, they were not in fact completely authentic Dreyfuses, Edisons, and Lucchenis; to a certain extent, they were impostors. Perhaps they were truly insane, caught in flagrante at the moment when a dazzling idée fixe had entered into them, the moment when their insanity was momentarily the truth and—skillfully distilled—it became the core of their new existence, pure as an element, staked in its entirety on that single card and already immutable. Since that time each had had that one thought in his head, like an exclamation mark, and stood upon it, on one foot, as if in flight, arrested in half motion.

I searched for him with my eyes in that crowd, full of anxiety, walking from group to group. At last I found him, not at all in the splendid uniform of an admiral of the Levantine squadron in which he had set sail from Toulon on the flagship *Le Cid* in that year when he was supposed to ascend the Mexican throne, nor in the green dress coat of a cavalry general that he wore so eagerly in his final days. He was dressed in an ordinary frock coat with a long, pleated skirt and light-colored trousers; a high collar with a stiff shirt-front supported his chin. Respectfully and with emotion both Rudolf and I stopped among the group of people who were surrounding him in a semicircle. Suddenly, I froze to my core. Three steps away from us, in the first row of spectators, stood Bianka in a white dress with her governess. She stood and looked. Her little face had grown pale and thin in the last few days, and her eyes, rimmed with dark rings and filled with shadow, were watching, deathly sad.

She stood motionless with her little hands clasped and hidden in the folds of her dress, glancing occasionally from under her grave eyebrows with eyes full of profound mourning. My heart contracted painfully at the sight. Involuntarily, I let my gaze follow her deathly sad glance, and this is what I saw: his face began to move as if awakened, the corners of the mouth lifted in a smile, the eyes flashed and started rolling in their sockets, the chest, sparkling with medals, rose with a sigh. It was not a miracle; it was an ordinary mechanical trick. Properly wound up, the archduke, in response to the mechanism's laws, performed a *cercle* artistically and ceremoniously as he had been accustomed to do in life. He glanced in turn at each of the people present, holding his gaze gravely for a moment on each one.

Thus, their eyes made contact for an instant. He trembled, hesitated, swallowed saliva, as if wishing to say something, but after a moment, already obedient to the mechanism, he looked away, gazing at the remaining faces with the same encouraging, radiant smile. Was he aware of Bianka's presence, did she enter his heart? Who could possibly know? After all, he was not even himself in the full sense of the word; he was a barely distant clone of himself, very reduced and in a state of deep prostration. But based on the facts, it was necessary to accept that he was somehow his closest agnate; he was, perhaps, even himself, insofar as, in general, it was still possible to be so in that state of things, so many years after his death. It was undoubtedly difficult in that wax resurrection to enter exactly into himself. Against his will something new and threatening must have availed itself of the opportunity to steal into him, something foreign must have mixed in from that brilliant maniac who had contrived him in his megalomania, and this must have filled Bianka with dread and terror. After all, a person who is very ill slips away and grows distant from his former self, to say nothing of those who have been improperly resurrected. How was he behaving now toward his nearest blood relative? Full of artificial gaiety and bravura, he played his buffoonish-imperial comedy, smiling and grand. Did he have to wear such a mask, was he so afraid of the attendants, who spied on him from all sides while he was on display in this hospital of wax figures where all of them lived under threat—of hospital discipline? Could it be that laboriously distilled from someone's madness, pure, cured, and at last a survivor, he did not have to tremble from fear that they might cast him back into disorder and chaos?

When my gaze again sought Bianka, I noticed that she had hidden her face in her handkerchief. The governess had her arm around her, her enamel eyes glittering emptily. I could look at Bianka's pain no longer; I felt a spasm of weeping about to overcome me, and I tugged at Rudolf's sleeves. We headed toward the exit.

Behind our backs the berouged ancestor, that grandfather in his prime, continued to distribute his radiant monarchical greetings all around; he even raised his hand in an excess of fervor, almost threw kisses at us in that motionless silence amid the hissing of acetylene lamps and the soft pattering of rain on the canvas of the tent, rising on tiptoe with his remaining strength, sick as can be, and, like every one of them, yearning for his mortal remains.

In the vestibule the cashier's berouged bust started speaking to us, sparkling with diamonds and a gold filling, against the black background of magical draperies. We exited into the night, dewy and warm from the rain. Roofs glistened, dripping water, and rain gutters wept monotonously. We ran through the splashing downpour that was illuminated by the blazing streetlamps clinking in the rain.

XXXII

O, abyss of human perversity, O, truly hellish intrigue! In whose mind could this poisonous, satanic thought have taken root, outstripping in its boldness the most refined inventions of fantasy? The deeper I penetrate into its abysmal baseness, the greater does amazement seize me at the unbounded perfidy, the flash of brilliant evil in the heart of this criminal idea.

So, my foreboding did not mislead me. Here, right beside us, amid apparent lawfulness, amid universal peace and the full power of treaties, a crime was being committed that makes one's hair stand on end. The grim drama was playing out here in perfect silence, so masked and conspiratorial that no one could imagine it and track it down among the innocent guises of this spring. Who could suspect that between that gagged, mute mannequin rolling its eyes and the delicate, so carefully educated and so well-mannered Bianka a family tragedy was playing out? Who was Bianka, after all? Must we finally expose an edge of the mystery? What does it matter that she was not descended either from the legitimate queen of Mexico or even from the illegitimate wife, the morganatic Izabella d'Orgaz, who conquered the archduke with her beauty from the stage of a traveling opera?

What does it matter that her mother was the little Creole woman to whom he gave the pet name Conchita and who entered history under that name—as if by way of the kitchen stairs? The information about her that I managed to gather on the basis of the stamp album can be summarized in a couple of words.

After the emperor's fall Conchita, with her little daughter, left for Paris, where she lived on her widow's pension, remaining indomitably faithful to her royal beloved. Here, history loses any further trace of this touching figure, ceding words to conjectures and intuitions. We know nothing about the marriage of the young daughter and her later fate. However, in the year 1900 a certain Mme de V., a person of unusual and exotic beauty, travels on a false passport with her little daughter and husband from France to Austria. In Salzburg, on the Bavarian border, just as they are changing trains for Vienna, the entire family is detained by the Austrian gendarmerie and placed under arrest. What is baffling is that after inspection of his false documents, M. de V. is released, yet he makes no effort to secure the release of his wife and little daughter. He returns to France that same day and all trace of him vanishes. Here, all threads are lost in total darkness. Through a kind of revelation I discovered their return track, shooting along a fiery line in the stamp album. My contribution, my discovery will always be the identification of the aforementioned M. de V. as a certain highly suspicious personage appearing under an entirely different name and in a different country. But shh! . . . Not a word about this yet. It is enough that Bianka's lineage has been confirmed beyond a doubt.

XXXIII

So much for canonical history. But the official story is incomplete. There are deliberate lacunae in it, long pauses and silences in which spring quickly inserts itself. It overgrows these lacunae rapidly with its marginalia, overpays with uncountable drooping foliage, expands into races, misleads with the absurdities of birds, with these winged creatures' contentions that are full of contradictions and lies, naive questions without answers, and stubborn, pretentious repetitions. A great deal of patience is needed to discover the true text behind that muddle. What will lead to it is a serious analysis of the spring, the grammatical parsing of its sentences and passages. Who, what? Of whom and of what? One must eliminate the misleading chattering of the birds, their pointed adverbs and prepositions, their skittish reflexive pronouns in order to slowly separate out the healthy grain of meaning. The stamp album serves me as an excellent guidepost. Foolish, unsophisticated spring! It overgrows everything indiscriminately, confuses sense and nonsense, eternally playing the fool—a sly jester, utterly thoughtless. Could it be that spring, too, was in league with Franz Joseph I, that it is tied to him with the knots of their mutual conspiracy? One must remember that every ounce of meaning hatching out in this spring is immediately obscured with hundreds of lies, with babbling of all sorts of nonsense. The birds erase the traces here, they mix up the word order with incorrect punctuation. In this way, truth is expelled on every side by this luxuriant spring that instantly overgrows every free inch of space, every chink, with its leafy flowering. Where else would the cast-out one take shelter, where find asylum, if not where no one is looking for her—in those cheap calendars and journals, in those canticles of beggars and old men that descend in a straight line from the stamp album?

XXXIV

After many sunny weeks came a series of cloudy, hot days. The sky grew dark as in old frescoes, and stacks of clouds swirled in the stifling silence like tragic battlefields in pictures from the Neapolitan school. Against the background of these leaden and dark gray swirls the houses shone bright with a chalky, burning whiteness, made even more prominent by the acute shadows of their cornices and pilasters. People walked about with lowered heads, filled inside with the darkness that was piling up in them, as before a storm, amid quiet electrical discharges.

Bianka no longer appears in the park. They are guarding her, apparently, not allowing her to go out. They have smelled danger.

Today I saw in the city a group of gentlemen dressed in black dress coats and top hats, diplomats gliding across the market square with measured steps. Their white shirtfronts shone brightly in the lead-hued air. They were looking at the houses in silence as if assessing their value. They walked in step with one another at a slow, rhythmic pace. They had mustaches black as coal on their smoothly shaved cheeks, and shining eyes that rolled smoothly in their sockets as if oiled and full of eloquence. From time to time they removed their top hats and wiped the sweat from their brows. They were all tall, thin, middle-aged, and had the swarthy faces of gangsters.

XXXV

The days have become dark, cloudy, and gray. Day and night, a far-off, potential storm lies on the distant horizon without discharging itself in a downpour. In the great silence there sometimes passes through the steely air a breath of ozone, the smell of rain, a damp, fresh breeze.

But then once again the gardens only inflate the air with enormous sighs and grow a thousandfold greater with foliage, racing one another, day and night, completing one piecework job after the other. All the flags are hanging heavily, darkened now, and they feebly pour the last waves of color into the thickened atmosphere. Sometimes, in an opening in the street, someone turns toward the sky a garish half face carved out of the darkness, with a terrified, shining eye—and he listens intently to the sound of the skies, the electric silence of the scudding clouds, and black-and-white swallows cut across the depths of the air like arrows, trembling and pointed.

Ecuador and Colombia are mobilizing. In menacing silence ranks of infantry, white trousers, white straps across their chests, throng onto wharves. The Chilean unicorn has reared up. It is seen in the evenings against the backdrop of the sky, a pathetic beast, frozen with terror, its hooves in the air.

XXXVI

The days are descending deeper and deeper into shadow and reverie. The sky has shut down, barricaded itself, swelling with an ever darker steel storm, and, hanging low and turbulent, maintains its silence. The earth, scorched and streaked, has stopped breathing. Only the gardens are growing breathlessly; dazed and drunk, they pour down foliage and overgrow every free crack with cool leafy substance. (The papules of the buds were gluey, prickly, and blistery like a scabby rash—now they are healing with cool greenery, building up scabs leaf upon leaf many times over, compensating with health a hundred times greater, for the future, more than is necessary, and without keeping count. They have already covered over and muffled beneath dark greenery the lost call of the cuckoo; only its distant, stifled voice can be heard stitched into the deep cloisters, lost under a flood of joyous flowering.)

Why do the houses shine so in their darkened landscape? The gloomier the sound of the parks, the sharper the lime-whiteness of the buildings, and without sunshine it glows with the burning reflection of scorched earth, ever more brightly, as if any minute now it will be speckled with the black splotches of some garish, spotted illness.

Dogs are running about intoxicated, their noses in the air. Rummaging around in the greenery, they are dazed and excited, picking up the scent of something.

Something wants to ferment out of the concentrated noise of these darkening days—something sensational, something immense beyond measure.

I test and I calculate what kind of event might match this negative sum of expectations that is building up into an enormous load of negative electricity, what might equal this catastrophic barometric drop.

Somewhere, the thing is already growing and gathering strength for which in all our nature this concavity, this form, this breathless hiatus that the parks cannot fill in with the intoxicating fragrance of lilacs is preparing itself.

XXXVII

Negroes, Negroes, crowds of Negroes in the city! They have been seen here and there, simultaneously in different points of the city. They run across the streets in a great, raucous, shabby mob, barge into grocery stores, ransack them. Jokes, jabs, laughter, whites of widely rolling eyes, guttural sounds, and white, glistening teeth. Before the militia could be mobilized, they vanished into thin air.

I had a premonition of this, it could not be otherwise. It was the natural consequence of meteorological tension. Only now do I realize that I felt it from the start: this spring is underlain with Negroes.

From where did Negroes arise in this zone, from where had these hordes of Negroes in striped cotton pajamas migrated? Had the great Barnum set up his camp nearby, pulling behind it a countless train of people, animals, and demons? Were his wagons parked somewhere close by, crammed full with the interminable clamor of angels, beasts, and acrobats? No; never. Barnum was far away. My suspicions point in an entirely different direction. I shall say nothing. For you I remain silent, Bianka, and no torture will extract a confession from me.

XXXVIII

That day, I spent a long time dressing carefully. Ready at last, I stood in front of the mirror and composed my face into an expression of calm and implacable resoluteness. I carefully loaded my pistol before slipping it into the back pocket of my trousers. I glanced once more at the mirror, touched my hand to my frock coat beneath which the documents were concealed on my chest. I was ready to confront him.

I felt calm and determined to my very core. After all, it concerned Bianka, and what would I not have been capable of doing for her! I decided not to confide in Rudolf at all. The better I got to know him, the stronger was my conviction that he was a low-flying bird incapable of rising above the commonplace. I had already had enough of that face, stiff with consternation and growing pale with envy, with which he greeted my every revelation.

Sunk in thought, I quickly covered the short distance. When the great iron gate slammed behind me, shuddering with a muffled vibration, I stepped immediately into a different climate, into a different blowing of the air, into an alien, cool region of the great year. The black branches of trees branched out into a distinct, detached time; enclosed on all sides by avenues, their still-leafless tops forked like black wicker into the white sky of a different, alien region floating high above—cut off and forgotten like a bay without an outlet. Birds' voices, lost and hushed in the distant expanses of this vast sky, were cutting the silence differently; sunk in thought, they took it into their workshop, heavy, gray, reflected upside down in the silent fishpond, and the world flew madly into this mirrored reflection, gravitated toward it blindly, violently, into the great universal gray reverie, into the inverted corkscrews of trees escaping endlessly, the great, wind-tossed pallor without limit or end.

With my head held high, utterly cold and calm, I demanded that they announce me. I was conducted into a dim hall. A semidarkness vibrating with silent splendor reigned inside there. Through an open high window, as if through the opening in a flute, air from the garden flowed in gentle waves, balmy and temperate, as if into a room in which someone incurably ill was lying. From these quiet influences penetrating invisibly through the gently breathing filters of the curtains, slightly puffed up by the garden's atmosphere, objects came back to life, awoke with a sigh, and a lustrous premonition ran in anxious passages through rows of Venetian glass inside a deep display case, while the leaves of the wallpaper, startled and silvery, rustled.

Then the wallpaper faded away, subsided into shadow, and its strained reverie, confined for years in these thickets full of dark speculation, broke free, imagining impulsively in a blind delirium of aromas like that of old herbariums across whose dried prairies fly V formations of hummingbirds and herds of bison, fires on the steppe, and pursuers racing past with scalps on the saddle.

It is strange that these old interiors cannot find peace above their own agitated, dark past, how in their silence they keep attempting to stage anew their doomed and lost history, arranging the same situations in endless variants, turned every which way by the sterile dialectic of wallpaper. Thus does this silence unfold, spoiled and thoroughly demoralized in a thousand reflections, in lonely deliberations, crazily circling the wallpapers in lightless lightning flashes. Why conceal this? Was it not required here night after night to soothe these excessive disturbances, these mounting paroxysms of fever, to resolve them with injections of secret drugs that led them into expansive, comforting, pleasant landscapes, filled—amid the parted wallpaper—with distant waters and reflections?

I heard a rustle. Preceded by a footman, he was descending the stairs, stocky and compact, sparing in his movements, blinded by the gleam of his large, horn-rimmed eyeglasses. For the first time, I stood before him face-to-face. He was inscrutable, but not without satisfaction did I detect two furrows of grief and bitterness biting into his features as soon as my first words were uttered. While he was draping his face into a mask of splendid inaccessibility behind the blind glare of his eyeglasses, I saw between the folds of the mask a stealthily flitting pale panic. He gradually became interested; it was evident from the more serious look on his face that only now was he beginning to appreciate me. He invited me into his adjacent office. As we entered, a female figure in a white dress jumped back from the door, startled, as if she had been eavesdropping, and retreated into the depths of the apartment. Was it Bianka's governess? It seemed to me, crossing the threshold into that room, that I was entering a jungle. The murky-green semidarkness of the room was striped with watery shadows produced by lowered Venetian blinds in the windows. The walls were hung with botanical illustrations, and small colorful birds fluttered in large cages. Wishing, evidently, to gain time, he explained the specimens of primitive weapons—javelins, boomerangs, and tomahawks—displayed on the walls. My heightened sense of smell caught the scent of curare. While he was handling a particular type of barbaric halberd, I advised him to employ extensive caution and restrained movements, and I supported my warning with my suddenly drawn pistol. He smiled unpleasantly, somewhat disconcerted, and put the weapon back in its place. We sat down beside a huge ebony desk. I thanked him for the cigar he offered me, pleading abstinence. So much caution, however, gained me his respect. With a cigar in the corner of his drooping mouth he looked intently at me with a menacing benevolence that did not awaken trust. Then, as if distracted, leafing inattentively through his checkbook, he suddenly proposed a compromise, naming a figure with many zeroes, while his pupils fled to the corners of his eyes. My ironic smile inclined him to rapidly drop the subject. With a sigh, he opened his ledgers. He started explaining to me the state of his businesses. Bianka's name was not mentioned once between us, although she was present in every one of our words. I looked at him without trembling, the ironic smile never leaving my lips. Finally, he leaned weakly against his armrest.

"You are implacable," he said as if to himself. "What do you really want?"

I started speaking again. I spoke in a muted voice, with restrained fire. My cheeks became flushed. Several times, I uttered the name Maximilian with a tremor; I named him with emphasis, observing each time how the face of my opponent became a shade paler. Finally, I finished, breathing heavily. He sat there crushed. He no longer had control over his face, which had suddenly become old and weary.

"Your decisions will show me," I finished, "if you have matured to the point of understanding the new state of things and if you are ready to acknowledge it in deeds. I demand facts and again facts . . ."

With his trembling hand, he tried to reach for the bell. I stopped him with a gesture, and with my finger on the trigger of my pistol I backed out of the room. At the door, a servant handed me my hat. Still full of whirling darkness and vibrations in my eyes, I found myself on a terrace awash with sunshine. I descended the steps without looking back, feeling triumphant, and certain now that a treacherous shotgun barrel would no longer track me through the closed shutters of the palace.

XXXIX

Important matters, matters of state of the utmost importance, now compel me frequently to conduct confidential conferences with Bianka. I prepare for them scrupulously, sitting at my desk late into the night over these dynastic matters of the most delicate nature. Time passes, the night pauses quietly in the open window above the table lamp, ever later and more ceremonious, it slices off later and darker layers, cuts through ever deeper stages of initiation, and, helpless, discharges in the window with inexpressible sighs. In long, slow drafts, the dark room absorbs deep into itself the park's dense woods; in cool transfusions, with an inoculation of feathery seeds, dark grains of pollen, and silent plush moths flying around the walls in quiet panic, it exchanges its contents with the approaching great night, which is swollen with darkness. The thickets of the wallpaper bristle with fear in the darkness, silvery and on alert, sifting through the streaming foliage the errant, lethargic shudders, the cool ecstasies and flights, the transcendental fears and irrational follies with which the May night is filled beyond its margins, long past midnight. The night's transparent glass fauna, the light plankton of mosquitoes, settles on me as I sit bent over papers, overgrowing space higher and higher with that frothy, delicate, white embroidery with which night embroiders itself long after midnight. Grasshoppers and mosquitoes composed, it would seem, of the transparent tissue of nocturnal speculation, alight on the papers—glass Farfarellos, delicate monograms, arabesques dreamed up by the night, ever larger and more fantastic, as large as bats, as vampires, made from calligraphy itself and from air. The curtain is swarming with erratic lace, with the silent invasion of that imaginary, white fauna.

On such an extramarginal night that knows no boundaries, space loses its meaning. Encircled by that bright whirling dance of mosquitoes, with the sheaf of papers completed at last, I take a few steps in an uncertain direction, into a blind alley of night that must end at a door, at, precisely, Bianka's white door. I press down on the handle and go in to her, as if from room to room. Despite this, my black Carbonaro's hat flaps as if in the wind of distant wandering; when I cross the threshold my tie, fantastically twisted, rustles in the draft, and I press to my breast my folder filled with the most secret documents. It is as if I have entered from the vestibule of night into true night! How deeply one breathes in this nocturnal ozone! Here is the hidden lair, here is the heart of night overflowing with jasmine. Only here does it begin its true story. A large lamp with a pink shade is burning at the head of the bed. In its pink semidarkness Bianka lies among enormous pillows, borne by overflowing bedding as if on the high tide of night beneath a wide-open, respiring window. Bianka is reading, propped up on her pale arm. She answers my deep bow with a brief glance over the top of her book. Seen up close, her beauty is as if restrained, entered in upon itself, like a turned-down lamp. With sacrilegious joy I notice that her little nose is not quite so nobly fashioned, and her complexion is far from ideal perfection. I observe this with a certain relief, although I know that the restraint of her radiance is only born of mercy, as it were, and only so that it not take one's breath and speech away. Afterward, this beauty regenerates rapidly through the medium of distance and becomes painful, unbearable, and beyond all measure.

Emboldened by her nod I sit down near the bed and begin my account, making use of the prepared documents. Through the open window behind Bianka's head the wild noise of the park flows in. The entire forest, crowded outside the window, flows by in a procession of trees, penetrates the walls, spreads out, omnipresent and all-encompassing. Bianka listens rather distractedly. It is really irritating that she does not stop reading while this is happening. She permits me to elucidate each matter from every angle, to point out all the pro and contra, then, lifting her eyes from the book and fluttering her lashes rather absentmindedly, she settles the matter quickly, summarily, and with astonishing accuracy. Alert and attentive to every one of her words, I eagerly pick up on the tone of her voice in order to penetrate to her hidden intention. Then I humbly submit the documents for her signature and Bianka signs, casting a long shadow with her lowered eyelashes, and with slight irony watches from under them as I inscribe my countersignature.

Perhaps because the hour is late, long past midnight, it is not conducive to concentration on affairs of state. Night, having passed its last boundary, inclines toward a certain dissoluteness. While we are conversing like this, the mirage of this room becomes more and more disconnected; we are actually in the woods, every corner is overgrown with clumps of ferns, and right behind the bed the wall of undergrowth, active and entangled, is shifting. From this wall of leaves large-eyed squirrels, woodpeckers, and nocturnal animals emerge in the light from the lamp and stare motionless into the light with shining, protuberant eyes. Starting from a particular hour we enter into illegal time, into a night lacking in control and subservient to all nocturnal caprices and whims. What is still happening is already somehow beyond reckoning, it does not count, it is full of insignificance, of incalculable transgressions and nocturnal dalliance. I can ascribe the strange changes that take place in Bianka's mood only to that. She, always so controlled and serious, the very personification of discipline and beautiful decorum, is now becoming full of caprices, perversity, and irresponsibility. The papers lie scattered about on the great plain of her quilt; Bianka picks them up carelessly, reluctantly casts a glance at them, and drops them indifferently from her loose fingers. With swollen lips, having placed her pale arm under her head, she delays her decision and makes me wait. But she turns her back to me, covers her ears with her hands, deaf to my pleas and persuasions. Suddenly, without a word, with one thrust of her foot beneath the quilt, she shoves the papers onto the ground and glances across her arm from the height of her pillows with enigmatically widened eyes as I, bending down, feverishly gather them up from the ground, blowing the pine needles off them. These caprices, albeit full of charm, do not ease my already difficult and responsible role as her regent.

During our conversations the soughing of the woods overflowing with cool jasmine wanders through the room as miles upon miles of landscapes. New sections of the woods keep moving past and wander on, processions of trees and bushes, complete forest sceneries flow by, spreading out across the room. Then it becomes clear that from the outset we have actually been in a train of sorts, a forest night train rolling slowly along the edge of a ravine through the wooded district of the city. This is the source of the intoxicating, deep draft that flows through the compartments in an ever renewed thread, extending as an endless perspective of premonitions. Even a conductor with a lantern turns up from somewhere, emerging from among the trees, and perforates our tickets with his ticket punch. And so we ride into ever deeper night, we open up entirely new enfilades of clanging doors and drafts. Bianka's eyes grow deeper, her cheeks are aflame, an enchanting smile widens her little mouth. Does she wish to confide something in me? Something most secret? Bianka speaks of betrayal and her face burns with ecstasy, her eyes narrow from a flood of delight, as, writhing like a lizard under her quilt, she hints that I should betray my most sacred mission. She persistently searches my face, which has grown pale, with her sweet squinting eyes.

"Do it," she whispers insistently. "Do it. You will become one of them, those black Negroes . . ."

And when I place my finger over my lips with a pleading gesture, full of despair, her little face suddenly turns mean and venomous.

"You are ludicrous with your unshakable loyalty and that entire mission of yours. God only knows what you imagine about being indispensable. If only I had chosen Rudolf! I prefer him to you a thousand times more, you boring pedant. Ah, he would have been obedient, obedient to the point of committing a crime, to erasing his very being, even to self-annihilation . . ."

Then suddenly, with a triumphant look on her face, she asks, "Do you remember Lonka, the daughter of Antosia the washerwoman, with whom you used to play when you were little?"

I look at her, astonished.

"That was me," she says, giggling, "only I was still a boy at the time. Did you like me then?"

Ah, in the very heart of spring something is rotting and disconnecting. Bianka, Bianka, will you, too, disappoint me?

XL

I am afraid of revealing my final trump cards too soon. I am playing for rather too high a stake to take such a risk. It's been a long time since I gave Rudolf an accounting of how things are playing out. His behavior changed a while back, after all. Envy, which was the dominant trait in his character, has yielded to a certain magnanimity. An eager kindliness combined with embarrassment manifests itself in his gestures and awkward words whenever we chance to meet. Formerly, beneath his gruff guise as a man of few words, beneath his expectant reserve, the curiosity that devoured him was still concealed, hungry for every new detail, every new version of the affair. Now he is strangely calm, no longer thirsting to learn anything from me. Actually, this suits me very well since night after night I have been holding extremely important sessions in the waxworks that for the time being must be held in deepest secrecy. The attendants, knocked out by the vodka that I don't begrudge them, sleep the sleep of the just in their cubicles while I, by the light of several smoky candles, confer in this noble gathering. After all, there are even crowned heads among them here, and negotiating with them is no easy matter. From ancient times they have maintained that abstract heroism, empty now and lacking a text, that flame, that self-immolation in the fire of some concept, that staking of their entire life on a single card. The ideas for which they lived discredited themselves, one after the other, in everyday prose, their fuses burned out, and now they themselves stand empty and full of unsatisfied dynamism, vacantly flashing their eyes, waiting for the final word of their role. How easy it is at this moment to falsify that word, to slip them the first good idea, when they are so uncritical and defenseless! This makes my task so marvelously easy! On the other hand, however, it is exceedingly difficult to penetrate their minds, to kindle in them the light of any thought; there is such a draft in their spirit, such an empty wind blows straight through them. Just waking them up from their sleep cost me a great deal of effort. They were all lying in their beds deathly pale and not breathing. I leaned over them, uttering in a whisper words that were the most essential for them, words that ought to have gone through them like an electric current. They opened one eye. They were afraid of the attendants, they pretended to be dead and deaf. Only when they had convinced themselves that we were alone did they prop themselves up on their beds, swathed in bandages, constructed from pieces, clutching their wooden prostheses, their imitation, fake lungs and livers. At first they were very distrustful and wanted to recite the roles they had memorized. They could not understand that something different might be desired of them. And so they sat there dully, groaning from time to time, these splendid men, the flower of humanity, Dreyfus and Garibaldi, Bismarck and Victor Emmanuel I, Gambetta and Mazzini, and many others. The one for whom understanding was most difficult was Archduke Maximilian himself. When I kept repeating Bianka's name near his ear in a fervent whisper, he blinked his eyes vacantly, an expression of incredible astonishment appeared on his face, and not a glimmer of comprehension penetrated his features. Only when I uttered the name of Franz Joseph I slowly and precisely did a wild grimace flit across his face, a pure reflex already without a counterpart in his soul. This complex had long since been driven out of his consciousness; how, after all, could he have lived with it, with this explosive pressure of hatred—he, put together with such difficulty, badly scarred after that bloody execution by firing squad in Veracruz? I had to teach him his life again from the beginning. His anamnesis was exceedingly weak; I was attempting to connect with subconscious glimmers of feeling. I implanted in him elements of love and hatred. But the following night it turned out that he had forgotten. His colleagues whose comprehension was greater assisted me, suggesting to him the reactions with which he should respond, and thus his education inched forward with slow steps. He was very neglected, quite simply devastated internally by the attendants; despite this, I brought him to the point at which, at the sound of Franz Joseph's name, he drew his saber from its sheath. He even almost stabbed Victor Emmanuel I, who did not get out of his way quickly enough.

It turned out that the rest of this excellent council grew enthusiastic and accepted the idea much more quickly than did the unfortunate archduke, who was having difficulty keeping up. Their fervor knew no bounds. I had to employ all my strength to restrain them. It is impossible to say if they fully understood the idea that they were to fight for. The merits of the affair did not concern them. Destined to immolate themselves in the fire of some dogma or other, they were delighted that thanks to me they had acquired a slogan in the name of which they could die in battle, in a whirlwind of ecstasy. I calmed them with hypnosis, with difficulty drilled into them that they must keep this secret. I was proud of them. What leader had ever had under his command such an excellent staff, a group of generals composed of such fiery spirits, an honor guard—composed, to be sure, only of cripples, but such brilliant ones!

Finally the night arrived, stormy and swollen with a windstorm, shaken to its very depths by the immense and boundless thing that was building inside it. Lightning flashes ripped apart the darkness time and again, the world was opening up; cleaved to its innermost viscera, it was revealing its interior, vivid, horrifying, and breathless, and slamming it shut again. And it flowed onward, with the noise of the parks, with a parade of the woods, with a procession of circling horizons. Under cover of darkness we left the museum. I walked at the head of this inspired cohort, moving along amid violent limping, sweeping movements, the clatter of crutches and of wood. The lightning flashes flew across bared saber blades. Thus did we make our way in the darkness to the gates of the villa. We found them open. Anxious, anticipating a trap, I gave the order to light the torches. The air grew red from the pitchy wood chips, the birds, startled, soared high up in the red radiance, we could see the villa clearly with its terraces and balconies in that Bengal light, as if it stood within the glow of a conflagration. A white flag waved from the roof. Touched by a bad premonition, I crossed into the courtyard at the head of my gallant men. The majordomo appeared on the terrace. He came down the monumental stairs, bowing, and approached hesitantly, pale and uncertain in his movements, becoming progressively more visible in the fiery glow of the torch. I aimed the sharp edge of my blade at his breast. My faithful men stood motionless, raising high the smoking torches; in the silence one could hear the roar of the horizontally streaming flames.

"Where is M. de V.?" I asked.

He spread his hands wide in a vague gesture.

"He drove off, sir," he said.

"We shall see for ourselves right now if this is true. And where is the infanta?"

"Her Highness also left, they all left . . ."

I had no reason to doubt this. Someone must have betrayed me. There was no time to lose.

"To horse!" I cried. "We must cut them off."

We broke down the stable doors; in the darkness, the air was redolent with warmth and the odor of animals. A moment later we were all seated on rearing and neighing steeds. Carried by their galloping, we emerged onto pavement amid the clatter of hooves in a cavalcade stretching into the nighttime street.

"Through the woods toward the river," I cried over my shoulder and turned into the forest avenue. Around us the dense woods were raging. In the darkness landscapes of catastrophes and floods opened up as if stacked upon one another. We were racing amid waterfalls of sound and agitated woodland masses; the flames of our torches separated out in great flakes behind our extended gallop. A hurricane of thoughts was flying through my head. Had Bianka been abducted, or had the lowly heritage of her father triumphed over her mother's blood and the mission that I had, in vain, strived to inculcate in her? The avenue was growing narrower, changing into a gorge at the outlet of which a great forested plain opened out. There, we caught up with them at last. They had already noticed us from afar and had halted their carriages. M. de V. got out and crossed his arms on his chest. He walked toward us slowly, grim, his eyeglasses glittering, crimson in the torches' radiance. Twelve shining blades were aimed at his breast. We approached in a great semicircle, in silence, the horses moving at a walk; I shaded my eyes with my hand in order to see more clearly. The radiance of the torches fell on the carriage and I beheld Bianka, deathly pale, sunk into the seat, and next to her—Rudolf. He was holding her hand and pressing it to his breast. I got down slowly off my horse and walked unsteadily toward the carriage. Rudolf rose slowly, as if he wanted to come out and meet me.

Standing beside the carriage, I turned back to the cavalcade, which was following me slowly, having spread out in a broad front line, their swords ready for the thrust, and I said, "Gentlemen, I have troubled you unnecessarily. These people are free and are at liberty to depart, undetained by anyone. Not a hair shall fall from their heads. You have fulfilled your obligation. Put your sabers back in their sheaths. I do not know to what extent you accepted the idea in whose service I engaged you, nor to what extent it entered into you and became the blood of your blood. That idea, as you see, is bankrupt, bankrupt in every respect. As for you, I believe that you will survive this bankruptcy without any major harm, since you have already survived the bankruptcy of your own idea. You are already indestructible. As for me . . . but, let me not talk about myself. I would only want you"—and here I addressed those in the carriage—"not to think that what has happened finds me completely unprepared. That is not so. I foresaw all of this long ago. If outwardly I continued in my error for such a long time, if I did not allow better knowledge to reach me, it is only because I had no right to know things that exceed my purview, I had no right to anticipate events. I wanted to remain at the post where my fate had placed me, I wanted to fulfill my program to the end, to stay faithful to the role that I had usurped. Because, I confess this now contritely, despite the promptings of my ambition, I was only a usurper. In my infatuation, I undertook the exposition of a script, I wanted to be a translator of God's will, with false inspiration I grasped at the circumstantial evidence and contours threaded through the stamp album. Alas, I connected them only into a free-form figure. I imposed on this spring my own staging, I placed my own program under its unconstrained flowering, and I wanted to make it conform to my own plans. Patient and indifferent, scarcely noticing me, for a time it carried me along on its blossoming. I took its insensitivity for tolerance, bah, for solidarity, for agreement. I thought that I could guess from spring's features, better than spring herself could, her deepest intentions, that I was reading her soul, anticipating what she, seduced by her own unembraceability, is incapable of expressing. I ignored all the signs of her wild and unbridled independence, I overlooked the unpredictable and violent perturbations agitating her to the core. I slipped so deeply into my megalomania that I dared to enter into dynastic matters of the highest powers, I mobilized you, gentlemen, against the Demiurge, I abused your susceptibility to ideas, your noble credulity, in order to instill in you a false and world-shattering doctrine, to spur your burning idealism for mad deeds. I do not wish to decide if I was summoned to the highest things that my ambition strove for. Most likely, I was summoned only to initiate, I was opened up and then discarded. I overstepped my boundaries, but that, too, was foreseen. As a matter of fact, I knew my fate from the outset. Like the fate of the unfortunate Maximilian, my fate was Abel's fate. There was a moment when my sacrifice was fragrant and dear to God, and your smoke, Rudolf, did not rise. But Cain always wins. The game was determined beforehand."

At that moment a distant explosion shook the air, a pillar of fire rose above the woods. They all turned their heads.

"Be calm," I said. "It's the waxworks burning. Leaving the museum, I left a cask of powder there and a lit fuse. You no longer have a home, noble gentlemen, you are homeless. I hope this does not disturb you overmuch?"

But those powerful individuals, those select representatives of humanity, remained silent, with helplessly glittering eyes, standing there in the distant glow of the fire, half conscious in their battle formation. They exchanged glances, fluttering their eyelashes without conveying any meaning.

"You, Sire," and here I addressed the archduke, "were wrong. It was probably megalomania on your part, too. It was wrong of me to want to reform the world in your name. Most likely, that was not at all what you intended. The color red is just a color like others, and only all of them together create the fullness of light. Forgive me for misappropriating your name for aims that were not yours. Long live Franz Joseph I!"

The archduke shuddered at the sound of that name and reached for his saber, but in a moment he seemed to come to his senses, a more lively red colored his rouged cheeks, the corners of his mouth rose as if in a smile, his eyes began rolling in their sockets, and rhythmically and with dignity he performed a *cercle*, moving from one person to the next with a radiant smile. Scandalized, they distanced themselves from him. This relapse into imperial manners in such inappropriate circumstances made the worst possible impression.

"Forbear, Sire," I said. "I do not doubt that you are well versed in the ceremony of your court, but now is not the time for that."

"I want to read to you, distinguished gentlemen, and you, Infanta, my decree of abdication. I abdicate in every regard. I disband the triumvirate. I place the regency in the hands of Rudolf. And you, noble gentlemen," here I turned to my staff, "are free. You had the best intentions and I thank you fervently in the name of the idea, of our dethroned idea"—tears flooded my eyes—"which, despite everything . . ."

At that moment the boom of a gun going off resounded close by. We all turned our heads in that direction. M. de V. was standing there with a smoking pistol in his hand, strangely stiff and obliquely elongated. His face was horribly contorted. Suddenly, he swayed and collapsed onto his face.

"Father, Father!" Bianka cried out and flung herself onto the prostrate man.

There was instant commotion. Garibaldi, an old hand at this, knew about wounds and examined the unfortunate man. The bullet had pierced his heart. The king of Piemonte and Mazzini lifted him carefully by the shoulders and placed him on a stretcher. Bianka, supported by Rudolf, was sobbing. The Negroes, who only now were gathering under the trees, surrounded their master.

"Massa, massa, our kind massa," they wailed in unison.

"This night is truly fatal!" I cried. "This will not be the final tragedy in its memorable history. I confess, however, that I did not foresee this. I wronged him. Truly, a noble heart beat in his breast. He was obviously a good father, a good master to his slaves. In this, too, my concept meets with bankruptcy. But I sacrifice it without regret. It is for you, Rudolf, to assuage Bianka's pain, to love her with a double love, to take her father's place. You will surely wish to take him onboard with you, so let us form a procession and proceed to the harbor. The steamboat has long since been sounding its siren for you."

Bianka got back into the carriage, we mounted our horses, the Negroes lifted the stretcher onto their shoulders, and we set off for the harbor. A cavalcade of riders brought up the rear of this sad procession. The storm had abated during my speech, the light from our torches opened up deep clefts in the forest, and elongated, black shadows flashed past by the hundreds to the side and above us, forming a great semicircle behind our backs. At last, we were riding out of the forest. Already visible in the distance was the steamboat with its paddle wheels.

Little remains to be added now; our story is drawing to its conclusion. The dead man's body was carried onboard to the sound of Bianka's and the Negroes' weeping. For the last time, we formed ranks on the bank.

"One more thing, Rudolf," I said, grabbing him by a button on his frock coat. "You depart as heir to an immense fortune. I do not wish to impose anything on you; rather, it should be my duty to provide for the old age of these homeless heroes of humanity, but alas, I am a pauper."

Rudolf instantly reached for his checkbook. We consulted briefly on the side and quickly came to an understanding.

"Gentlemen," I cried, turning to my guard, "this noble-minded friend of mine has decided to make good my action that has deprived you of bread and a roof over your head. After what has occurred no waxworks will receive you, the more so because the competition is great. You will have to lower your ambitions somewhat. In exchange, you will be free, and I know that you are able to appreciate this. Since you, alas, have not been taught any practical trades, my friend is providing for you who were predestined to pure representation a sum sufficient for the purchase of twelve barrel organs from Schwarzwald. You will disperse throughout the world, playing for the people in order to give them courage. The choice of arias belongs to you. Why waste many words? You are not real Dreyfuses, Edisons, and Napoléons. You are they, if I may say so, only for want of better men. Now go and add to the collective of your many predecessors, those anonymous Garibaldis, Bismarcks, and Mac-Mahons, who roam by the thousands, unrecognized, throughout the world. In your hearts you will be them forever. And now, dear friends and worthy gentlemen, join me in raising this cry: 'Long live the happy newlyweds, Rudolf and Bianka!'"

"Long live!" they cried in chorus.

The Negroes struck up a Negro song. When quiet returned, I again gestured to them to form a group, after which, standing in the center, I drew my pistol and cried out, "And now, farewell, gentlemen, and take heed from what you will see in a moment, so that no one should attempt to interpret divine intentions. No one has ever plumbed the designs of spring. *Ignorabimus*, gentlemen, *ignorabimus!*"

I had placed the pistol against my temple and was firing it when at that very moment someone knocked the weapon out of my hand. Beside me stood a Feldjäger officer with documents in his hand, asking, "Are you Józef N.?"

"Yes," I replied, astounded.

"Did you, a while ago," asked the officer, "dream the standard dream of the biblical Joseph?"

"Perhaps . . ."

"It checks out," said the officer, looking at the document. "Do you know that this dream was noticed in the highest location and was severely criticized?"

"I do not answer for my dreams," I said.

"Of course you do. In the name of His Imperial and Royal Highness you are arrested!"

I smiled.

"How slow is the machinery of justice. The bureaucracy of His Imperial and Royal Highness is quite unwieldy. I long ago distanced myself from that early dream with deeds of much greater caliber for which I wished to mete out justice on myself, and now that obsolete dream has saved my life. I am at your service."

I caught sight of an approaching Feldjäger column. I held out my arms for the shackles. Once more, I turned my head. I saw Bianka one last time. Standing on deck, she was waving her handkerchief. The guard of invalids saluted me in silence.

A July Night

I became familiar with summer nights for the first time in the year of my high school graduation, during our vacation. Our house, through whose open windows the breezes, noises, and brightness of hot summer days wafted all day long, held a new tenant, a small, cranky, whimpering little creature, my sister's baby boy. He brought down upon our house a certain return to primitive relations; he reverted sociological development to the nomadic, haremlike atmosphere of a matriarchy with its encampment of bedding, diapers, and linens being forever laundered and dried, with a negligence of feminine toilette aiming at ample exposure of an asexually innocent character, with the sour smell of infancy and of breasts swollen with milk.

After a difficult lying-in my sister left to take the baths, my brother-in-law appeared only at mealtimes, and my parents stayed in the shop until late at night. The infant's wet nurse unleashed her rule over the house; her expansive femaleness multiplied many times over, deriving its sanction from her role as mother-provider. In the majesty of her dignity, with her broad, weighty existence, she impressed on the entire house the stamp of gynocracy, which was at the same time the dominance of a sated, luxuriant corporeality distributed in wise gradation among herself and the two serving girls, whose every activity allowed them to unfold like the fan of a peacock's tail the entire range of self-sufficient femaleness. The quiet flowering and maturing of the garden filled with the rustling of leaves, silvery gleams, and shady reveries was answered by our house with the aroma of femaleness and maternity rising above the white linens and blooming flesh, and when at the frightfully glaring hour of noon all the curtains on the wide-open windows would rise up in terror and all the diapers pinned on clotheslines stand in a shining double row, winged seeds, specks of dust, and lost petals would stream straight through this white alarm of foulards and cloth, and the garden with its flow of lights and shadows, with its wandering of murmurs and reveries, would move slowly through the room as if at that hour of the Lord all the partitions and walls would rise into the air and a shudder of all-encompassing oneness pass through the world in an outflowing of thought and feeling.

I spent the evenings of that summer in the town's movie theater, leaving after the final showing.

From the blackness of the cinema hall riven by a flurry of flying light and shadows one entered the quiet, bright vestibule as if from the boundlessness of a stormy night into a cozy tavern.

Following a fantastic chase across the rough terrain of a film, the pursued heart would calm down after the excesses on the screen in the bright waiting room, walled off from the pressure of the great, pathetic night, in that safe harbor where time had stopped long ago, and in vain did the lightbulbs emit their feeble light, one wave after another in a rhythm set once and for all by the dull clattering of a motor that made the ticket booth tremble slightly.

That vestibule, submerged in the boredom of late hours like railway waiting rooms long after the trains have departed, appeared at times to be the last backdrop of life, that which will remain when all events have passed, when the din of multitudes is depleted. On a great, colorful poster Asta Nielsen was forever staggering with the black stigma of death on her brow, her mouth was forever open in her final scream, and her eyes superhumanly intense and permanently beautiful.

The cashier had long since wended her way home. She was no doubt bustling about in her little room near her carefully made bed, which awaited her like a boat ready to carry her off into the black lagoons of sleep, into the imbroglios of dream adventures and scandals. The woman who sat in the booth was only her outer layer, an illusory phantom observing with bored, brightly made-up eyes the emptiness of the light, unconsciously fluttering her eyelashes in order to shake off the golden dust of drowsiness that drifted down unceasingly from the electric lights. Sometimes she smiled weakly at the fire brigade sergeant who, having long ago been abandoned by his reality, stood propped up against the wall, forever motionless in his glittering helmet, in the sterile splendor of his epaulets, silver cords, and medals. From afar, the panes of the glass doors leading into the late July night rattled in time to the motor's rhythm, but the reflection of an electric chandelier blinded the glass, negated the night, patched up as best it could the illusion of a safe haven unthreatened by the elements of enormous night. After all, in the end the spell of the waiting room had to dissipate; the glass doors opened and the red portiere swelled with the breath of the night, which suddenly became everything.

Can you sense the secret, profound meaning of this adventure when a frail, pale, high school graduate exits all alone through the glass doors of that safe haven into the boundlessness of a July night? Will he someday slog through those black swamps, quagmires, and abysses of endless night, will he land in a safe port one morning? How many decades will this black odyssey last?

No one has yet written the topography of a July night. Those maps have not been inscribed in the geography of the inner cosmos.

A July night! What can it be compared to, how describe it? Shall I compare it to the interior of an enormous black rose covering us with the hundredfold sleep of a thousand velvet petals? The night wind fans open its fluffiness to the core and in its fragrant depths the gaze of the stars reaches us.

Shall I compare it to the black firmament of our tightly closed eyelids, full of wandering particles of dust, the white poppy seeds of stars, rockets, and meteors?

Or perhaps compare it to a night train, long as the world, riding through an endless black tunnel? To walk through a July night is to make one's way with difficulty from car to car, between sleepy passengers, through crowded corridors, stuffy compartments, and crisscrossing currents of air.

A July night! The mysterious fluid of darkness, the vital, alert, and energetic matter of gloom, incessantly forming something out of chaos and instantly discarding every form! Black building material piling up caverns, arches, recesses, and niches around the sleepy wanderer! Like an importunate bab-bler the night accompanies the solitary wanderer, confining him in the circle of its phantoms, indefatigable in its inventiveness, delirium, its fantasizing— hallucinating astral distances, white milky ways, labyrinths of endless colosseums and forums before him. The night air, that black Proteus arrang-ing for its amusement velvet concentrations, bands of jasmine fragrance, cascades of ozone, sudden airless dead spots expanding like black bubbles into infinity, monstrous grapes of darkness swollen with dark juice. I push my way through narrow doorframes, bow my head beneath low-hanging arches and vaults, and then suddenly the ceiling breaks off, a bottomless cupola opens up for a moment with an astral sigh only immediately to lead me again between narrow walls, passages, and doorframes. In these secluded refuges without a breath of air, in these gulfs of darkness, scraps of conversations remain, abandoned by nocturnal wanderers, fragments of inscriptions on posters, lost beats of laughter, bands of whispers that the night breeze has not dispersed. Sometimes the night confines me as if in a narrow room without an exit. Drowsiness overwhelms me; I cannot tell if my feet are still walking or if I have been resting in this small hotel room of night. But now I sense a velvet, burning kiss lost in space by fragrant lips, the blinds open, and lifting my foot high I cross the windowsill and wander on under the parabolas of falling stars. Two wanderers emerge from the labyrinth of the night. They are weaving, extracting from the darkness a lengthy forlorn braid of conversa-tion. One of them carries an umbrella that taps monotonously against the pavement (such umbrellas are carried for protection from a rain of stars and meteors), they meander like great drunken heads in their spherical bowler hats. Another time, the conspiratorial glance of a black squinting eye stops me and a great bony hand with prominent joints hobbles through the night on the crutch of a cane, clutching the hand grip made out of deer antler (in such canes long thin swords are often concealed).

Finally, at the city limits night gives up on its little games, casts off its veil, reveals its serious, eternal face. It no longer builds its deceptive labyrinth of hallucinations and phantoms around us; it opens its starry eternity before us. The firmament grows into infinity, the constellations burn in splendor in their eternal positions, sketching magical figures in the sky as if they wished to herald something, to proclaim something ultimate by their terrifying silence. From the flickering of those distant worlds comes the croaking of frogs, a silvery astral murmur. The July heavens sow the inaudible poppy seed of meteors that silently infiltrate the universe.

At some unknown hour of the night (the constellations were dreaming their eternal dream in the sky) I found myself once again on my street. A star was positioned at its outlet, fragrant with a foreign aroma. A draft moved through the street as if through a dark corridor when I opened the door to my house. It was still light in the dining room; four candles were smoking in the bronze candelabra. My brother-in-law was not yet there. Since my sister's departure he was always late for supper, arriving late at night. Waking from sleep, I often saw him removing his clothes with a dull, distracted gaze. Then he would snuff out the candle, undress completely, and lie there for a long time unable to sleep in his chilly bed. Eventually, a restless half sleep would descend on him, gradually overpowering his great body. He still muttered something, wheezed, sighed deeply, wrestled with some burden that was crushing his chest. It happened sometimes that he would burst out with a sudden quiet, dry sob. Terrified, I would ask him in the darkness, "What's the matter, Karol?" But in the meantime he was already wandering farther along his heavy dream road, laboriously climbing up a steep hill of snoring.

Through the open window the night was breathing in slow pulses. In its great, unformed mass a cool, fragrant fluid was spilling out, the joints of the night's dark solid forms were relaxing, and narrow trickles of fragrance leaked out. The dead matter of the darkness was seeking its liberation in inspired flights of jasmine fragrance, but the infinite masses in the depths of the night still lay there, not freed and dead.

A gap in the door leading to the adjoining room shone like a golden string, resonant and sensitive, like the sleep of the infant who was fussing in his cradle. From there came the twitter of endearments, an idyll between wet nurse and child, a pastorale of first love, of the suffering and sulking of lovers, pressed on all sides by the demons of the night who condensed the darkness outside the window, lured by the warm spark of life smoldering there.

On the other side, an empty, dark room adjoined our room, and beyond it was my parents' bedroom. Straining my ears, I could hear how my father, suspended in the bosom of sleep, gave himself over to being transported in ecstasy onto his aerial paths, committed with his entire being to that distant flight. His musical, distant snoring narrated the history of his wandering across the unknown rough terrain of sleep.

Thus do souls slowly enter the dark aphelion, the sunless side of life whose forms no living person has seen. They lie as if dead, snoring horribly and weeping while a black eclipse lies like unresponsive lead on their soul. But when they finally pass the black nadir, itself the deepest Orcus of souls where they battle in mortal sweat across its most amazing promontories, the bellows of their lungs begin to swell again with a different melody that rises with inspired snoring to greet the dawn.

Mute, dense darkness pressed the earth, its hulks lay slaughtered there like inert black cattle with lolling tongues, saliva pouring out of their helpless mouths. But some other fragrance, some other color of darkness was heralding the distant approach of dawn. From the poisoned fermentation of the new day the darkness was swelling, its fantastic dough was rising as if fed by yeast, it grew wildly into crazy shapes, overflowed every watering trough and kneading trough, fermented hastily, in a panic, so that the dawn would not take it by surprise at this dissolute fecundity and nail down for all eternity these excrescences of sick men, these monstrous children of spontaneous generation arisen from the bread pails of night like demons bathing by twos in bathtubs meant for children. This is the moment when drowsy befuddlement alights for an instant on the most sober, sleepless head. The sick, the very sad, and the heartbroken have a moment of relief then. Who knows how long that moment lasts during which night lowers the curtain on what has happened in its depths, and that brief entr'acte suffices to rearrange the stage, to remove the enormous apparatus, to liquidate the great affair of night with all its dark, fantastic pomp. You wake up terrified with a feeling that you are late for something, and, indeed, you see on the horizon the bright stripe of dawn and the black, solidifying mass of the earth.

My Father Joins
the Firefighters

During the first days of October Mother and I would return home from a summer resort in the neighboring district, in the forested Słotwinka River basin, which was saturated with the murmuring of a thousand springs and streams. With the rustling of the alder grove punctuated by birdsong still in our ears, we rode in an old expansive landau with an enormous body like a dark, branching inn; we sat crowded in among bundles, in a deep velvet-upholstered alcove into which colored pictures of the landscape fell through the window, card after card, as if they were being slowly shuffled from one hand to the other.

Toward evening we arrived on a windswept plateau, the great, puzzled crossroads of the country. The sky stood above the crossroads deep, out of breath, rotating at its zenith like a colorful wind rose. Here was the country's most distant tollgate, the final bend, beyond which there opened up, down below, an expansive, late-autumn landscape. Here was the border, and here stood an old, rotten border post with a faded sign, playing on the wind.

The great wheels of the landau screeched and were mired in the sand; the chattering, glittering spokes fell silent, only the great carriage body thundered dully, flapping darkly in the crisscrossing winds of the crossroad like an ark come to rest in a wilderness.

Mother paid the toll, the arm of the tollgate rose, creaking, and the landau rode heavily into autumn.

We entered into the withered boredom of an immense plain, into a faint, pale breeziness that opened out its pleasant, bland boundlessness over the golden distance. A kind of belated, immense eternity was blowing, arising from the faded distances.

As in an old romance the yellowed pages of the landscape grew paler and weaker while they turned as if they had to put an end to some great, wind-blown void. In that windblown nothingness, in that yellow nirvana, we could have driven beyond time and reality and remained forever in that landscape, in that warm, barren breeziness—a motionless stagecoach on huge wheels, mired among clouds on the parchment of the sky, an old illustration, a for-gotten woodcut in an old-fashioned, disintegrating romance—when the coachman, with his last bit of strength, snapped the reins and drove the lan-dau out of the sweet lethargy of those winds and turned into the forest.

We rode into thick, dry fluffiness, into withering tobacco. Suddenly it became snug and brown around us as in a box of Trabucos. In that cedar semidarkness the dry and fragrant tree trunks moved past us like cigars. We rode on, and the forest grew darker and darker, grew more and more fragrant with tobacco, until at last it enclosed us as if inside the dry box of a cello that the wind was hollowly tuning. The coachman had no matches and could not light the lanterns. The horses, snorting in the darkness, followed the road by instinct. The rattling of the spokes slowed and grew quiet, the rims of the wheels rode softly over the fragrant needles. Mother fell asleep. Time passed uncounted, creating strange knots and abbreviations in its passing. The dark-ness was impenetrable, the dry noise of the forest was still roaring above the body of the coach, when the ground suddenly turned into clods under the horses' hooves and became the hard pavement of a street; the carriage turned in and stopped. It stopped so close to a wall that it practically rubbed against it. Opposite the landau's small doors Mother was groping for the entrance-way to our house. The coachman was unloading our bundles.

We entered the great branching hall. It was dark there, warm and cozy as in an old, empty bakery toward morning after the oven fire has been extin-guished, or as in a bathhouse late at night when the baths are deserted and the buckets are growing cold in the darkness, in silence measured by the patter of drops. A cricket was patiently opening up deceptive seams of light from the darkness, a slight stitch that made it no lighter. We found the stairs by touch.

When we reached the creaking landing at the turn, Mother said, "Wake up, Józef, you're dead on your feet, it's just a few more steps." But barely con-scious with drowsiness, I snuggled closer against her and fell sound asleep.

Afterward, I could never find out from Mother how much reality there was in what I saw that night through my closed eyelids, overcome as I was by deep sleep and continually falling into profound oblivion, and how much was the fruit of my imagination.

There was a great debate here between my father, mother, and Adela, the protagonist of that scene, a debate of fundamental significance, as I under-stand it today. If I am trying in vain to guess its continually elusive meaning, certain gaps in my memory bear the guilt, blind spots of sleep that I strive to fill by conjecture, supposition, hypothesis. Torpid and barely conscious, I kept drifting into profound unawareness while the light breeze of the starry night, stretched out in the open window, settled on my closed eyelids. The night was breathing in pure pulsations and suddenly it cast down a transparent veil of stars and was peering from on high into my sleep with its old, eternal visage. A distant star's ray, enmeshed in my eyelashes, overflowed as silver on the blind whites of my eyes, and through the cracks of my eyelids I saw the room in the light of a candle entangled in a maze of golden lines and zigzags.

It may be, however, that the scene occurred at some other time. Many things point to my having been witness to it only much later, when Mother, the salesclerks, and I returned home one day after closing the shop.

On the threshold of our apartment Mother let out a cry of amazement and delight and the salesclerks, dazzled, froze. In the middle of the room stood a splendid brass knight, a true Saint George made gigantic by his cuirass, the gold bucklers of his armlets, a complete jangling suit of armor made of polished gold metal plates. With amazement and joy I recognized the erect mustache and bristling beard of my father protruding from under the heavy praetorian helmet. The breastplate heaved on his chest, brass rings breathed in the gaps like the body of an enormous insect. Made gigantic by his armor, in the radiance of the golden metal sheets he resembled an archstrategist of the heavenly hosts.

"Alas, Adela," Father was saying, "you have never had any understanding of matters of a higher order. Everywhere and always you have thwarted my actions with outbursts of mindless malice. But encased in armor, today I scoff at your tickling with which you used to drive me, a defenseless man, to despair. Today, impotent rage will carry away your tongue to a pitiable fluency whose boorishness and primitiveness are mixed with obtuseness. Believe me, it fills me only with sorrow and pity. Deprived of a noble flight of fancy, you burn with unconscious jealousy toward everything that rises above the commonplace."

Adela measured Father with a gaze full of boundless contempt and, turning to Mother, said in an excited voice while, despite herself, she let fall tears of irritation, "He takes all our juice! He carries out of the house all the bottles of raspberry juice that we made together last summer! He wants to give it to those good-for-nothing pumpers to drink. And to top it all off he's been showering me with impertinences."

Adela briefly burst into sobs.

"Captain of the fire brigade, captain of the rascals," she shouted, fixing Father with a hateful glance. "I'm fed up with them. In the morning, when I want to go out to buy bread, I can't open the door. Naturally, two of them have fallen asleep on the threshold in the entry hall and are blocking the exit. On the staircase, there's one of them in a brass helmet lying on every step, asleep. They beg to be let into the kitchen, they thrust their rabbit faces in those brass tin pots through a crack in the door, they make scissor signs with two fingers like schoolboys and whimper beseechingly: sugar, sugar . . . They grab the bucket from my hands and run to bring me water, they dance around me, they simper, they practically wag their tails. While doing this they blink their red eyelids over and over again and lick their lips disgustingly. All I have to do is look at one of them for a second and immediately his face swells up like red, shameless flesh, like a turkey. And I'm supposed to give our raspberry juice to such creatures! . . ."

"Your common nature," said Father, "pollutes everything that it touches. You have sketched a picture of these sons of fire worthy of your shallow mind. As for me, all my sympathy resides with that unhappy race of salamanders, those poor, disinherited fiery beings. The only guilt of that once holy race was that they devoted themselves to the service of humans, that they sold themselves to people for a teaspoon of miserable human pabulum. For that they have been repaid with contempt. The obtuseness of the common people is boundless. These delicate beings have been driven to the deepest ruin, to ultimate degradation. Why is it surprising that they do not relish the fare, that tasteless, coarse fare prepared by some caretaker's wife at a city school in a common cauldron for them and for the municipal convicts? Their palates, the delicate, brilliant palates of fiery spirits, demand noble dark balsams and aromatic, colorful fluids. That is why on that solemn night when we shall be seated festively at tables covered with white cloths in the great hall of the city's Stauropigian Institute, in that hall with its tall, brightly illuminated windows casting their radiance into the depths of the autumn night, while all around the city is swarming with thousands of illuminating lights, every one of us will dip a roll in a goblet of raspberry juice and with the pietism and gourmandism characteristic of the sons of fire will slowly sip that noble, thick liquor. In that manner the essence of the fireman is fortified, the wealth of colors that that race emits in the form of fireworks, rockets, and Bengal lights is regenerated. My soul is filled with pity for their penury, for their undeserved degradation. If I have accepted from their hands a captain's sword, it is only in the hope that I will succeed in raising up this tribe from ruin, leading them out of degradation, and unfurling above them the banner of a new idea."

"You are completely changed, Jakub," said Mother; "you are magnificent. But you will not leave the house for the night. Don't forget that since my return we have not had an opportunity for a good conversation. As for the pumpers," she said, addressing Adela, "in fact it seems to me that you are guided by a certain prejudice. They are nice lads even if they're good-for-nothings. I always look with pleasure at these slender youths in their shapely uniforms that are a bit too tightly cinched at the waist. They have a great deal of natural elegance; their zeal and the enthusiasm with which they are ready at any moment to assist a lady is touching. Whenever my umbrella slips from my hand in the street or a shoelace comes untied, one of them always comes running, full of emotion and ardent readiness. I don't have the heart to disappoint such burning desire and I always wait patiently until he runs up and assists me, which, it seems, makes him very happy. When he moves off after completing his knightly obligation, a crowd of his comrades immediately surrounds him, discussing the entire incident with him in a lively fashion while the hero re-creates through mimicry how everything happened. If I were you, I would happily avail myself of their gallantry."

"I consider them to be parasites," said Teodor, the elderly salesclerk. "After all, because of their childish irresponsibility we don't permit them to put out fires. It is sufficient to observe with what envy they always join any group of boys who are throwing buttons against a wall for us to judge the maturity of their rabbit minds. Whenever wild shrieking during a game reaches me from the street it is almost a certainty that if I look out the window I will see among the crowd of boys those restless, wildly running, strapping fellows, almost unconscious in the exuberance of the chase. At the sight of fires they go mad with joy, they clap their hands and dance like savages. No, it is impossible to employ them to extinguish fires. For that we employ chimney sweeps and city policemen. The only occasions for which they are indispensable are parties and popular holidays. For example, in the autumn during the so-called storming of the capitol, they dress up as Carthaginians and with an infernal racket besiege the Basilian Hill in the dark of daybreak. Then they all sing, 'Hannibal, Hannibal ante portas.'

"Furthermore, in late autumn they become lazy and somnolent, they fall asleep on their feet, and when the first snow falls there's neither hide nor hair of them. An old stove fitter told me that when he works on chimneys he finds them clinging to the inside of the flue, immobile as chrysalids in their scarlet uniforms and glittering helmets. They sleep standing up like that, drunk on raspberry juice, filled up inside with sticky sweetness and fire. Then they are pulled out by the ears and conducted to the barracks, drunk with sleep and unconscious, through the autumnal morning streets, bright with the first light frosts, while the street rabble throw stones at them, but they smile their embarrassed smile full of guilt and bad conscience and stagger like drunks on their feet."

"Be that as it may," said Adela, "I am not giving them juice. That is not why I ruined my complexion at the stove, cooking it so that these good-for-nothings can drink it up."

Rather than answer, my father raised a whistle to his lips and whistled terrifyingly. As if they had been listening at the keyhole, four slender youths rushed in and lined up against the wall. The room grew bright from the radiance of their helmets while they, adopting a military pose, dark and sun-tanned under their bright casques, waited for a command. At a sign from Father, two of them grabbed hold of a wicker-wrapped demijohn filled with the purplish fluid and before Adela could intervene they had already run clattering down the stairs, carrying away their precious loot. The two remaining men gave a military salute and went after the others.

For a moment it seemed that Adela was about to take off after them on an insane mission, her beautiful eyes were flashing such fire. But Father did not wait for the explosion of her anger. With one leap he was on the windowsill, spreading out his arms. We ran over to him. The market square, bestrewn with lights, swarmed with colorful crowds. Below our house eight firemen were spreading out a large sailcloth in a circle. Father turned to face us once more; saluting us silently, he blazed with all the splendor of his gear, and then with arms outspread he leaped bright as a meteor into the night, which was burning with a thousand lights. It was such a beautiful sight that everyone clapped their hands in rapture. Even Adela, forgetting her grudge, applauded that leap, which was performed with such elegance. My father, in the mean-time, jumped up elastically from the sheet and, shaking his metal carapace with a clanking sound, took his place at the head of the squad, which, falling out of formation by twos, unfolded during their march into a long line and slowly receded down the dark avenue of the crowd, the brass cans of their helmets sparkling.

A Second Autumn

Among the many scientific works undertaken by my father in rare moments of peace and inner calm amid the blows of defeats and catastrophes that his adventurous and stormy life abounded in, the closest to his heart were his studies of comparative meteorology, especially the specific climate of our province, which was full of unique characteristics. It was he, my father, who laid the foundation for the expert analysis of climatic formations. His *Outline of a General Taxonomy of Autumn* clarified once and for all the essence of that season of the year that in our provincial climate assumes the protracted, branching, parasitically overgrown form that under the name "Chinese summer" extends far into the depths of our colorful winters. What is there to say? He was the first to clarify the secondary, derivative character of that late formation that is nothing other than a poisoning of the climate by the miasmas of the overripe, degenerating baroque art stuffed into our museums. This museum art, decomposing in boredom and oblivion, locked up without any outlet, becomes too sugary, oversweetens our climate like old jam and is the cause of that beautiful malarial fever, those colorful deliriums, with which the protracted autumn struggles as it dies. Beauty is an illness, my father taught, it is a type of shivering caused by a mysterious infection, a dark portent of decay arising from the depths of perfection and welcomed by perfection with a sigh of deepest happiness.

Let several factual observations about our provincial museum serve at this point for a better understanding of the matter . . . Its beginnings reach back to the eighteenth century and are connected with the admirable collecting passion of the Basilian Fathers, who bestowed upon the city that parasitic growth, burdening the city budget with an excessive and unproductive expense. For some years the Treasury of the republic, having purchased these collections for a song from the impoverished order, ruined itself magnanimously by patronage worthy of a royal house. But already the next generation of city fathers, who were more practically oriented and did not close their eyes to economic necessity, after futile negotiations with the board of trustees of the archduke's collections, to whom they were attempting to sell the museum, closed it down, dissolved the directorate, and designated a lifelong

pension for the last curator. At the time of these negotiations experts confirmed beyond any doubt that the value of these collections had been grossly
overrated by the local patriots. The worthy fathers in their laudable fervor
had acquired more than one forgery. The museum contained not a single
painting by a first-rate master; instead, it held entire collections of third- and
fourth-rate artists, entire provincial schools known only to specialists, forgotten, blind alleys of art history.

An amazing thing: the worthy monks had had military inclinations; a
large part of the paintings depicted battle scenes. A scorched golden murk
showed darkly on these canvases that were deteriorating with age, on which
flotillas of galleys and caravels and ancient forgotten armadas rotted in bays
without outlets, rocking the majesty of long-since vanished republics on their
wind-swelled sails. From beneath smoke-dimmed, darkened varnish, barely
visible outlines of skirmishes on horseback emerged. Across the emptiness of
burned Campanias, under a dark and tragic sky, swirling cavalcades stretched
out in ominous silence, caught on both sides in a buildup and eruption of
artillery fire.

In paintings of the Neapolitan school, swarthy, smoke-dried afternoons
are forever growing old as if seen through a dark bottle. A darkened sun
appears to wither before one's eyes in those doomed landscapes as if on the
eve of a cosmic catastrophe. And that is why the smiles and gestures of the
golden fisherwomen are so futile as with mannered charm they offer bundles
of fish for sale to itinerant comedians. That entire world was long since condemned and resides in the distant past. Hence that boundless sweetness of a
final gesture that alone still endures—distant from itself and lost, continually
renewed but already immutable.

Still deeper in that land inhabited by a carefree race of jesters, harlequins,
and bird fanciers with cages, in that land without solemnity and without reality, little Turkish girls with chubby hands slap together honey cakes arranged
on boards, two boys in Neapolitan caps carry a basket of noisy pigeons on a
stick that sags slightly under the cooing, winged weight. And even deeper,
on the very edge of evening, on the last scrap of earth, where on the border
of hazy golden nothingness a wilting bunch of acanthus sways—a card party
is still in progress, a final human stake before the great night that is drawing near.

That entire storeroom of old beauty was subjected to painful distillation
under the pressure of entire years of boredom.

"Are you capable of understanding," asked my father, "the despair of that
condemned beauty, its days and nights? It is forever making new attempts
at illusory auctions, staging successful clearance sales, noisy and crowded

bidding, it is passionate about wild gambles, selling short, handing out money with a profligate's gestures, squandering its wealth, only to realize once it has sobered down that all this is in vain, that it does not lead beyond the closed circle of perfection to which it is condemned and cannot alleviate the painful excess. It is not at all surprising that the impatience, the helplessness of beauty finally had to mirror itself in our sky, had to flare up as a glow above our horizon, and degenerate into that atmospheric jugglery, those cloud arrangements, immense and fantastic, that I call our second, our pseudo-, autumn. This second autumn of our province is nothing other than a sickly fata morgana, radiated in an exaggerated projection onto our sky by the dying, confined beauty of our museums. This autumn is a great traveling theater dissembling through poetry, an enormous, colorful onion shedding layer after layer in a continually renewed panorama. One can never reach its core. Behind every coulisse as it wilts and folds with a rustling sound, a new and radiant prospect appears, alive and true for a moment before, dying out, it betrays its paper nature. And all perspectives are painted and all panoramas are made of pasteboard, and only the smell is true, the smell of wilting coulisses, the smell of a great dressing room full of greasepaint and incense. And at dusk, great disorder and the jumble of the coulisses, the disarray of discarded costumes among which one flounders endlessly as among rustling, wilted leaves. And there is great anarchy, and everyone pulls the curtain ropes, and the sky, the great autumn sky, hangs in scraps of prospects and is filled with the creaking of pulleys. And that hasty fever, that breathless, late carnival, that panic of predawn ballrooms and Tower of Babel of masks that cannot retrieve their real garments.

"Autumn, autumn, the Alexandrian era of the year, collecting in its enormous libraries the sterile wisdom of three hundred and sixty-five days of revolving around the sun. Oh, those senile mornings, yellow like parchment, sweet with wisdom like late evenings! Those slyly smiling forenoons, like clever palimpsests, multilayered like old yellowed tomes! Ah, autumn day, that old jester-librarian, climbing ladders in his worn bathrobe and sampling the jams of all ages and cultures! For him, every landscape is an entrance into an old romance. How wonderfully he amuses himself, releasing the heroes of ancient novels for a stroll beneath that smoky, honey sky, into that murky, sad, late sweetness of light! What new adventures will Don Quixote experience in Soplicowo? How will Robinson Crusoe's life play out after his return to his native Bolechów?"

On sultry, still evenings, golden from sunsets, Father would read us excerpts from his manuscript. The stirring flight of ideas allowed him to forget for a while the threatening presence of Adela.

The warm Moldavian winds arrived, the immense golden monotony approached, that sweet, sterile blowing from the south. Autumn did not want to end. Like soap bubbles, the days arose more beautiful and ethereal every time, and each seemed so extremely refined that every moment it lasted was a miracle extended beyond measure and almost painful.

In the silence of those deep and beautiful days the substance of foliage was changing imperceptibly until one day the trees were standing in the straw-colored fire of dematerialized leaves, in loveliness delicate as an efflorescence of chaff, as a dusting of colorful confetti—splendid peacocks and phoenixes that have only to shake themselves and flap their wings in order to shed their glorious feathers, lighter than tissue paper, already molted, and no longer needed.

The Dead Season

I

At five in the morning, a morning brilliant from early sunshine, our house had already been bathed for a long time in ardent and quiet morning radiance. At that solemn hour, unobserved by anyone—while across the room in the semidarkness of lowered drapes the peaceful breathing of sleeping people still moved in solidarity—in total silence it entered into the facade that was blazing in the sunlight, into the silence of the early heat, as if its entire surface were made of blissfully slumbering eyelids. Thus, profiting from the silence of those solemn hours, it swallowed the very first fire of morning with a blissfully slumbering face, fainter in the radiance, with the arrangement of its features trembling slightly in the dream-filled sleep of that intense hour. The shadow of the acacia in front of the house, waving brightly on those burning eyelids, repeated on their surface as if on a piano, over and over again, the same glittering phrase washed away by a breeze, vainly attempting to penetrate the depths of that golden dream. The canvas drapes absorbed the morning heat, portion after portion, and grew darkly suntanned, swooning in the boundless radiance.

At that early hour, my father, no longer able to find sleep, descended the stairs, laden with his books, in order to open the shop, which was located on the ground floor of our apartment building. He stood motionless in the entrance for a moment, withstanding with tightly closed eyes the powerful attack of fiery sunshine. The sun-bright wall of the house drew him sweetly into its blissfully leveled flatness, smoothed down to the point of disappearance. For a moment he became a flat father, grown into the facade, and he felt his arms, branching out, trembling and warm, fuse flat amid the golden stucco decorations of the facade. (How many fathers have already grown permanently into a facade at five in the morning, at the moment when they stepped off the bottom step of a staircase? How many fathers have become in this way forever the keepers of their own door, flatly sculpted onto the frame, with a hand on the door handle and a face unfolded into the same parallel, blissful grooves over which their sons' fingers would later travel lovingly, seeking the last traces of their fathers now merged forever into the universal smile of the facade?) But then he detached himself with his last bit of will, regained the third dimension, and turned into a man once again, freeing the shackled shop door from its padlocks and iron bars.

When he opened the heavy, ironclad wing of the shop door the grumbling gloom retreated one step from the entrance, drew back a few inches into the depths of the shop, changed its place, and lay down lazily inside. Invisibly giving off steam from the still-cool paving stones of the sidewalk, the morning freshness stood timidly on the threshold as a faint, trembling strip of air. Deep inside, the darkness of many previous days and nights lay in the unopened bales of cloth that were arranged in layers and ran in rows into the interior, in muffled parades and pilgrimages, until it came powerlessly to a stop in the very heart of the shop, in the dark stockroom, where, already undifferentiated and replete with itself, it dissolved into the silent, looming, ur-matter of cloth.

Father walked along that tall wall of cheviot wools and twills, trailing his hand along the edges of cloth bales as if along the slits of women's dresses. Under his touch, the rows of blind torsos that were always ready to panic, to break out of line, would calm down and consolidate in their cloth hierarchies and order.

For my father our shop was a place of never-ending anguish and remorse. As it grew, this creation of his own hands had for a long time been exerting pressure upon him, ever more insistently from one day to the next, had begun to outgrow him threateningly and inexplicably. It was an excessive task for him, a task beyond his strength, a sublime, unending task. He was horrified by the immensity of this claim upon him. Staring with dread at the enormity of this demand, which, with his entire life staked on this one card, he could not satisfy, he saw with despair the recklessness of the salesclerks, their frivolous, carefree optimism, their mischievous, mindless manipulations taking place on the margins of this great cause. With bitter irony he observed the gallery of faces untroubled by a single care, brows not beset by a single idea; he plumbed to the very bottom those eyes whose innocent confidence was undisturbed by the slightest shadow of suspicion. Of what help to him was Mother with all her loyalty and devotion? No reflection of that excessive thing reached her simple, unthreatened soul. She was not created for heroic tasks. Could he not see how she came to an understanding behind his back with a quick glance exchanged with the salesclerks, how glad she was of every unsupervised moment during which she could participate in their mindless buffoonery?

Father distanced himself further and further from that world of carefree unconcern; he escaped into the hard rule of his order. Terrified by the dissoluteness that was rampant everywhere around him, he locked himself up in his lonely service to a high ideal. His hand never lost its tight grip on the reins, he never permitted himself a slackening of rigor or the convenience of cutting corners.

Bałanda & Co. and those other dilettantes of the trade for whom the hunger for perfection, the asceticism of high mastery was an alien thing, could allow themselves this slackness. Father looked on with sorrow at the decline of the trade. Who among the present generation of cloth merchants still knew the fine tradition of the ancient art, who among them still knew, for example, that a stack of cloth bales arranged on shelves according to the principles of the merchant's art had to emit a tone like a piano scale under a finger traveling from top to bottom? Who among them today could manage the most up-to-date finesse of style in exchanges of notes, memoranda, and letters? Who still knew all the charm of merchant diplomacy, the diplomacy of the good old school, all the tension-filled process of negotiations from irreconcilable stiffness, from closed reserve at the appearance of a plenipotentiary minister of a foreign firm, through slow thawing under the influence of the indefatigable solicitations and blandishments of a diplomat, to finally a mutual supper with wine served on the desk, on papers, in an elevated mood, amid the pinching of the servant girl Adela's buttocks, and spicy, free conversation as between men who know what they owe to the moment and surroundings—concluded with a mutually profitable deal?

In the silence of those morning hours, during which the scorching heat was ripening, my father anticipated discovering the happy, inspired stratagem that he needed to conclude the letter to Chrystian Seipel & Sons, Mechanical Spinning and Weaving Mills. It was to be a trenchant retort to the unfounded claims of those gentlemen, a reply broken off precisely in the decisive place where the style of a letter ought to rise to a powerful, witty, culminating point, to a moment followed by an electric shock, palpable as a slight internal shudder, after which it could only subside into a phrase composed with panache, with elegance, already conclusive and definitive. He could feel the shape of that witticism that had been eluding him for days, he had it almost between his fingers, always evading his grasp. He lacked that moment of happy humor, that moment of happy gusto that was required in order to take by storm the obstacle against which he had crashed time after time. He kept reaching for a clean sheet of paper in order to conquer with fresh momentum the difficulty that kept mocking his efforts.

In the meantime the shop was gradually filling up with the salesclerks. They arrived red from the early heat, skirting Father's desk at a distance, glancing at him anxiously, filled with a guilty conscience.

Filled with shame and weakness, they felt on themselves the weight of his silent disapprobation, having nothing with which they could counter it. Nothing could appease that boss who was locked in his own troubles; it was impossible to mollify him with any display of fervor, lurking as he was like a scorpion behind his desk, his eyeglass lenses glittering venomously as he rustled in his papers like a mouse. His excitement grew, his indefinite passion increased along with the intensifying heat of the sun. A quadrangle of radiance blazed on the floor. Metallic, shiny flies cut across the entrance to the shop like flashes of lightning, stopped for a moment on the door casements as if they were blown from metallic glass—glass bubbles breathed out of the sun's burning pipette, from the glass foundry of the fiery day—hovered full of flight and speed, their little wings extended, and traded places in frantic zigzags. In the door's bright quadrangle the distant linden trees of the city park were fainting in the radiance and a faraway church bell tower loomed very close in the transparent, trembling air as if in the lens of a telescope. Metal roofs blazed. An enormous, gold basin of heat was swelling over the earth.

Father's irritation was growing. He glanced about helplessly, painfully doubled over, worn-out from diarrhea. In his mouth he had a taste more bitter than hemlock.

The heat was intensifying, it sharpened the frenzy of the flies, struck bright points on their metallic abdomens. The quadrangle of light reached the desk and the papers burned like the Apocalypse. Eyes illuminated by the excess of light could no longer endure its white uniformity. Through his thick chromatic lenses Father sees every object edged with purple, with violet and green borders, and despair overcomes him at this explosion of colors, this anarchy of hues, rampaging over the world in incandescent orgies. His hands tremble. His palate is bitter and dry as before an attack. In the crevices of his wrinkles his hidden eyes attentively follow the development of events deep inside the shop.

II

When at noon Father, already on the verge of madness, disoriented from the heat and trembling with aimless agitation, withdrew to the upstairs rooms, and the ceilings of the ground floor creaked here and there under his surreptitious squatting, a moment of pause and decompression ensued in the shop—the hour of the midday siesta had arrived.

The salesclerks turned somersaults on the bales of cloth, pitched cloth tents on the shelves, hung up swings made from heavy fabrics. They unwound dense bales, released into freedom the fluffy, century-old darkness folded a hundred times over. Now that it was released into freedom, the felt darkness, musty for years, filled the upper space with the odor of a different time, with the smell of bygone days arranged patiently in innumerable layers during long-ago cool autumns. Blind moths spilled out into the darkened air, fluffs of feather and wool circled around the entire shop, seeding the darkness, and the smell of finishing, deep and autumnal, filled the dark campground of cloth and velvet. Bivouacking in the middle of the campground, the sales-clerks thought up pranks and tricks. They allowed their colleagues to wrap them up to their ears, snug in dark, cool cloth, and they lay there like that in a row, blissfully motionless, under a stack of bales—living bolts, cloth mummies, rolling their eyes with feigned terror at their own immobility. Or they let themselves be swung and bounced up to the ceiling on enormous outspread tablecloths. The dull flapping of these sheets and the breeziness of the stirred-up air moved them to uncontrolled delight. It seemed as if the entire shop were taking flight, the cloths were rising inspired, the salesclerks flying up with unfurled coattails like prophets in short-lived ascensions to heaven. Mother turned a blind eye to these pranks; as she saw it, the relaxation of those siesta hours justified the worst escapades.

In the summer the shop was wildly and messily overgrown with weeds. From the courtyard side, from the stockroom, the window looked completely green with weeds and nettles, submerged and sparkling with leafy shimmering, with reflections. As if on the bottom of an old green bottle, in incurable melancholy, flies buzzed inside it in the semidarkness of the long summer afternoon—sick, monstrous specimens bred on Father's sweet wine, hairy loners lamenting their accursed fate all day long in lengthy, monotonous epopees. That degenerate race of shop flies prone to wild and unexpected mutations abounded in bizarre specimens, the fruits of incestuous hybridizations; it was deteriorating into a kind of superrace of unwieldy giants, veterans with deep, mournful timbres, wild, morose druids of their own sufferings. Toward the end of summer these lonely posthumous children, already the last of their race, finally hatched out, resembling great blue beetles, already mute and voiceless, with stunted wings, consummating their sad lives by racing continuously over the green panes in indefatigable, errant wanderings.

The rarely opened door became overgrown with spider webs. Mother slept behind the desk in a hammock made from cloth suspended between the shelves. The salesclerks, pestered by the flies, shuddered and made faces, tossing about in their restless summertime sleep. In the courtyard, in the meantime, the weeds were growing everywhere. Under the wild, sweltering heat of the sun, the garbage pile bred generations of enormous nettles and mallows.

From the sun's touch and drops of groundwater a virulent substance from the weeds was fermenting on this bit of earth, a cantankerous broth, a poisonous derivative of chlorophyll. That feverish ferment soured in the sunshine and effervesced into light, leafy formations, multiple, serrated, and wrinkled, repeated a thousand times over following a single pattern, according to the sole idea concealed within them. Having seized its moment, this infectious concept, this perfervid, ferocious idea spread like wildfire— ignited by the sun, it grew beneath the window as empty, papery twaddle of pleonasms, herbaceous trash multiplied one hundred times over into indiscriminate egregious ravings—a tawdry paper patchwork covering the wall of the shop with ever larger, rustling pieces that swelled shaggily, wallpaper upon wallpaper. The salesclerks woke up from their fleeting nap with their faces flushed. Strangely excited, they got out of their beds full of feverish industriousness, imagining heroic buffoonery. Consumed by boredom, they swung on the high shelves and drummed with their feet, vainly watching the empty expanse of the market square, swept clean by the scorching heat, for any adventure at all.

Then it happened that a village yokel, barefoot and dressed in coarse cloth, was standing hesitantly inside the shop door, timidly peeking into the interior. For the bored salesclerks that was quite a treat. Lightning fast, they descended from the ladders like spiders at the sight of a fly, and the bumpkin, suddenly surrounded, pulled and pushed, sprinkled with a thousand questions, responded to the interrogations of the importunate men with an embarrassed smile. He scratched his head, smiled, looked distrustfully at the terribly kind Lovelaces. So, was it tobacco he wanted? But what kind? The very finest, Macedonian, amber-gold? No? Would ordinary pipe tobacco do? Coarse shredded tobacco? Just come closer, closer, please. Nothing to be afraid of. The salesclerks directed him with light pokes and compliments toward the rear of the shop to a side counter near the wall. Leon, a salesclerk, went behind the counter and attempted to pull out a fictitious drawer. Oh, how he struggled, poor man, how he gnawed his lips with fruitless effort. No! It was necessary to hammer at the counter with his fists, take a wide swing at it with all his strength. The yokel, urged on by the salesclerks, followed suit excitedly, full of attentiveness and concentration. Finally, when that did not help, he climbed onto the table, stamping his bare feet, hunchbacked and graying. We exploded with laughter.

It was then that the regrettable incident happened that filled us all with sadness and shame. None of us was innocent, no matter that we had not acted from ill will. Rather, it was our frivolousness, our lack of seriousness and understanding of Father's high worries, it was, rather, our imprudence, combined with Father's unpredictable, vulnerable nature, so inclined to extremes, which led to those truly fatal consequences.

While we stood in a semicircle, fooling around for all we were worth, Father had quietly slipped into the shop.

We missed the moment of his entry. We noticed him only when the sudden comprehension of the connection between things pierced him like a lightning bolt and distorted his face with a wild paroxysm of dread. Terrified, Mother ran over to him.

"What is it, Jakub?" she cried, gasping for breath.

Desperate, she wanted to slap his back as one does for someone who is choking. But it was already too late. Father bristled all over and glared, his face rapidly disintegrating into symmetrical parts of horror, metamorphosing unrestrainedly in front of our eyes beneath the weight of boundless defeat. Before we could understand what had happened, he started vibrating violently, and as we watched he buzzed and wafted toward us as a monstrous, buzzing, hairy, steel-blue fly, striking against all the walls of the shop in his mad flight. Aghast, we listened to his hopeless lament, the hollow grievance modulated expressively, running down and up through all the registers of unfathomable pain, of inconsolable suffering under the dark ceiling of the shop.

We stood there confounded, profoundly mortified by this pitiful fact, avoiding one another's gaze. Deep in our hearts we felt a certain relief that at the critical moment he had, however, found this way out of deep disgrace. We marveled at the uncompromising heroism with which he threw himself unhesitatingly into that blind alley of desperation from which, it seemed, there was no longer any return. Still, it was necessary to take that step of Father's *cum grano salis*. It was, rather, an internal gesture, an impetuous, desperate demonstration that operated, however, on a minimal dose of reality. One should not forget: the majority of what we relate here can be attributed to those seasonal aberrations, that semireality of the dog days of summer, those irresponsible marginalia proceeding without any guarantee on the borders of the dead season.

We listened intently, not saying a word. It was Father's refined vengeance, retaliation against our consciences. From then on we were condemned forever to hear that pitiful, low buzzing, complaining more and more insistently, more and more painfully, and suddenly falling silent. For a moment we savored the silence with relief, the benevolent pause during which a timid hope awoke in us. But a moment later it was back, inconsolable, increasingly plaintive and irritated, and we understood that for this boundless pain, this droning anathema condemned to homeless beating against every wall, there was neither an end point nor liberation. That plaintive monologue, deaf to every persuasion, and those pauses during which he seemed to be forgetting about himself for a moment only to awaken afterward with a louder, angry crying, as if he was retracting with despair the preceding moment of solace, exasperated us to the core. Suffering without end, suffering stubbornly enclosed in a circle of its own mania, suffering with fervor, whipping itself with fury, in the end becomes unbearable for the helpless witnesses of unhappiness. That constant, angry appeal to our mercy contained within itself an overly explicit reproach, a too-clear accusation of our own felicity not to arouse our resistance. Full of rage instead of contrition, we all retorted in our souls. Was there really no other way out for him than to fling himself blindly into that pitiful, hopeless state and, having fallen into it from his own or from our fault, remain incapable of finding greater stoutness of spirit, greater dignity, to bear it without complaint? Mother was controlling her anger only with difficulty. The salesclerks, seated on the ladders in a dull stupor, were daydreaming bloodily, racing along the shelves in their thoughts with a leather flyswatter, their eyes bloodshot. The canvas awning above the portal was flapping brightly in the heat, the scorching afternoon air sped across miles of bright plain, laying waste the distant world beneath it, and in the semidarkness of the shop, under the dark ceiling, my father was circling, snared in the noose of his fate with no way out, frantic, entangling himself in the desperate zigzags of his pursuit.

III

When it comes down to it, despite all appearances what little significance such episodes have stems from the fact that in the evening of that very day my father was sitting over his papers as he usually did in the evening; the incident appeared to be long since forgotten, the profound trauma overcome and erased. Naturally, we refrained from any allusion to it. We looked on with pleasure as in seemingly total spiritual equilibrium, in apparently serene contemplation, he sedulously covered page after page with his even, calligraphic handwriting. On the other hand, it became all the more difficult to erase traces of the compromising personage of the poor yokel; it is well known how stubbornly aftereffects of this sort take root in certain soils. During the course of those empty weeks we deliberately did not notice him dancing on the counter in that dark corner, growing smaller from day to day, grayer from day to day. Already almost imperceptible, he was still at his post hopping constantly in that same spot, smiling benevolently, hunched over the counter, tapping tirelessly, listening attentively, saying something quietly to himself. Tapping became his true calling, in which he lost himself irreversibly. We did not call him back. He had already gone too far; it was no longer possible to catch up with him.

Summer days have no twilight. Before we looked around it was already night in the shop, the great oil lamp was lit, and the business of the shop went on. On the short summer nights it did not pay to return home. While the night hours passed, Father sat in apparent concentration and marked the margins of letters with touches of his pen in black, flying stars, little devils of ink, shaggy bits of fluff whirling mistakenly in the field of vision, atoms of darkness torn from the great summer night outside the door. Outside the door that night was sifting down like a puffball, the black microcosm of darkness scattering its seed in the shadow cast by the lampshade, a contagious rash of summer nights. His spectacles blinded him, the oil lamp hung behind them like a fire surrounded by a tangle of lightning flashes. Father was waiting, waiting impatiently, and listening, staring at the bright whiteness of the paper across which those dark galaxies of black stars and dust particles sailed. Behind Father's back, in a sense without his participation, the great contest for the shop kept on; it kept on, strangely enough, in the painting hanging behind his head between the file cabinet and the mirror in the bright light of the oil lamp. It was a talisman painting, an enigmatic painting, a mystery painting, endlessly interpreted, wandering from generation to generation. What did it represent? It was an endless dispute carried on for generations, a never-concluded trial between two divergent principles. Two merchants stood facing each other, two antitheses, two worlds. "I sold on credit," cried the thin one, ragged and dazed, his voice breaking in despair. "I sold for cash," replied the fat one in an armchair, one leg draped over the other, twiddling the thumbs of his interlocked hands on his belly. How Father hated the fat one. He had known them since childhood. Already at his school bench that potbellied egoist devouring an endless quantity of buttered rolls during recess had filled him with disgust. But he did not side with the skinny man. He watched with astonishment as the entire enterprise escaped from his hands, appropriated by those two quarreling men. Holding his breath, with a frozen squint from behind his spectacles that were askew, Father awaited the outcome, bristly and deeply dismayed.

The shop, the shop was unfathomable. It was the goal of all thought, of nighttime investigations, of Father's terrified pensive moods. Impenetrable and boundless it was beyond everything that was taking place, gloomy and universal. During the day those cloth generations, full of patriarchal gravity, lay there, arranged in order of seniority, ranked by generation and lineage. But at night the rebellious cloth blackness would break free and storm the sky in pantomime tirades, in Luciferian improvisations. In autumn, the shop soughed, flowed out of itself, swollen with a dark assortment of winter wares, as if entire hectares of forests were setting out from their place into a great, soughing landscape. In the summer, in the dead season, it grew dusky and retreated to its dark reservation, unapproachable and surly in its lair of cloth. At night the salesclerks pounded at the dull wall of bales with wooden yard-sticks, wielding them as if they were flails, listening intently as he roared mournfully in its depths, immured in the bearlike cloth heart.

Father descended these mute steps of felt into the depths of genealogy, onto the bottom of time. He was the last of his race, the Atlas on whose shoulders rested the weight of an immense testament. Day and night Father pondered the thesis of that testament, struggled to understand its *meritum* in a flash. Often, he looked questioningly, full of expectation, at the salesclerks. Without signs in his own soul, without any glimmers, without directives, he expected that the meaning of the shop, hidden from him, would sud-denly reveal itself to those young and naive men, only recently emerged from a larval state. He pressed them to the wall with his insistent winking, but they, dull and gibbering, evaded his gaze, averted their eyes, babbling utter nonsense in their confusion. In the mornings, leaning on his tall walking stick, Father wandered like a shepherd among that blind, woolen flock, those crowded obstacles, the undulating, bleating, headless trunks beside a water-ing hole. He was still waiting, delaying the moment when he would lift up all his people and move out into the noisy night like that oppressed, teeming, hundredfold Israel . . .

The night outside the door seemed made of lead—without space, without a breeze, without a road. After a couple of steps it just ended. One toddled along as if in a half sleep, in the place at that instantaneous border, and while one's feet were trapped, having exhausted the meager space, one's thoughts raced on endlessly, continuously interrogated, grilled, led down all the false byways of that dark dialectic. The differential analysis of the night flowed on of its own accord. Until at last one's feet came to a stop in that remote alley without an exit. One stood there in the dark, in the most intimate corner of the night, as if in front of a pissoir, in dead silence, for hours on end, with a feeling of blissful disgrace. Only thought, left to itself, unwound slowly, the convolute anatomy of the brain unwound as if from a ball of yarn, and amid the scathing dialectic the abstract treatise of the summer night rolled on endlessly, turning somersaults amid logical contortions, supported on both sides by indefatigable, patient interrogations, sophistic questions to which there were no answers. Thus did it philosophize with difficulty through the speculative expanse of that night and enter, already incorporeal, into the ultimate emptiness.

It was already long past midnight when my father abruptly raised his head from his papers. He stood up full of importance, his eyes wide-open, his ears straining for sound.

"He's coming," he said, his face radiant. "Open up."

Before Teodor, the senior salesclerk, reached the glass door, which was barricaded at night, the long-awaited guest, splendid and smiling, with a black beard and weighed down with bundles, had squeezed through it. Jakub, profoundly moved, ran to meet him, bowing and holding out both hands. They embraced. For a moment it seemed that a black, low, glittering locomotive had driven silently up, right to the shop door. A porter wearing a railway cap carried in an enormous trunk on his back.

We never learned who the guest really was. The senior salesclerk, Teodor, steadfastly insisted that it was Chrystian Seipel & Sons, Mechanical Spinning and Weaving Mills, in person. Very little supported that; Mother did not conceal her reservations about that notion. However that might be, there was no doubt that he must have been a powerful demon, one of the pillars of the Regional Creditors' Association. A black, aromatic beard rimmed his fat, glistening, dignified face. With Father's arm around his shoulder, he walked, exchanging bows, toward the desk.

Not understanding foreign speech, we listened respectfully to that ceremonious conversation full of smiles, averted eyes, and delicate, tender backslapping. After the exchange of these introductory courtesies, the gentlemen passed on to the main thing. Ledgers and papers were spread out on the desk, a bottle of white wine was uncorked. With pungent cigars in the corners of their mouths, with faces contorted into grimaces of peevish satisfaction, the gentlemen exchanged short code words, monosyllabic knowing signs, convulsively marking with a finger the right place in the ledger, with the cunning gleam of augurs in their gaze. Slowly, the discussion grew more heated; it was clear that their agitation was being restrained with difficulty. They chewed their lips, the cigars hung bitter and extinguished from faces suddenly disappointed and full of antipathy. They trembled with internal agitation. My father was breathing through his nose, there was a red flush under his eyes, his hair bristled over his sweaty brow. The situation was growing heated. There was a moment when both gentlemen leaped up from their seats and stood there dazed, wheezing heavily, with their spectacle lenses glittering blindly. Mother, terrified, started patting Father's back imploringly, wishing to avert a catastrophe. At the sight of a lady, both gentlemen came to their senses, recollected the social code, bowed to each other with a smile, and sat down to further work.

Around two A.M. Father finally slammed the heavy cover of the main ledger. Anxious, we monitored the faces of both interlocutors, watching to see whose side victory was inclining toward. Father's good humor struck us as artificial and forced, whereas the man with the black beard lounged in his chair with his legs crossed and gave off an air of goodwill and optimism. With ostentatious generosity he distributed gratuities to the salesclerks.

Having folded up the papers and accounts, the gentlemen rose from behind the desk. Their looks were highly promising. Winking knowingly at the salesclerks, they let it be understood that they were full of initiative. Behind Mother's back they mimed a desire for a mighty spree. It was empty bragging. The salesclerks knew what to think about this. The night was leading nowhere. It ended at the gutter, in a well-known spot, along a blind wall of nothingness and shameful mortification. All paths leading to it led back to the shop. All escapades undertaken deep in its expanses had broken wings from the outset. The salesclerks returned their winks out of politeness.

The man with the black beard and Father, taking each other by the arm, left the shop filled with eagerness, seen off by the indulgent glances of the salesclerks. Right outside the door the night's guillotine cut off their heads with a single stroke and they splashed into the night as into black water.

Who has investigated the bottomlessness of a July night, who has measured how many fathoms deep one falls into a void in which nothing is happening? Having flown through that entire black infinity, they stood once again before the doors of the shop as if they had only just walked out, retrieving their lost heads with yesterday's word still unused on their lips. Standing thus, it is impossible to know how long, they chatted in monotones, as if returning from a distant expedition, connected by the friendship of so-called nocturnal adventures and brawls. They shoved their hats back with a gesture common to those who are tipsy and staggered along on wobbly legs.

Avoiding the illuminated entrance to the shop, they entered furtively through the door of the house and began stealthily ascending the main floor's creaking stairs. Thus they arrived at the rear porch in front of Adela's window and tried to peek at the sleeping woman. They were unable to spot her; she was lying in shadow with her thighs apart, sobbing unconsciously in the embrace of sleep with her head thrown back and burning, fanatically sworn to her dreams. They knocked at the black windowpanes, sang bawdy songs. But she, with a lethargic smile on her open lips, was wandering torpid and cataleptic on distant roads, miles away and inaccessible.

Then, sprawled on the balcony's railings, they yawned broadly and noisily, already resigned, and drummed with their feet against the boards of the balustrade. At some late and unknown hour of the night they discovered their bodies by some unknown means on two narrow cots, supported on bedding piled up high. Asleep, they drifted side by side into races, overtaking each other by turns with the arduous gallop of snoring.

At some kilometer of sleep—had the sleep current united their bodies, did their dreams merge imperceptibly into one?—they sensed at some point in that black boundlessness that they were lying in each other's arms and fighting in a heavy, unconscious struggle. They were panting in each other's faces amid futile efforts. The man with the black beard lay on top of Father like the Angel on top of Jacob. But Father squeezed him with his knees with all his might, and floating away numbly into mute absence, he secretly stole another brief restorative nap between one round and another. Thus they fought. For what? For a name? For God? For a contract? They wrestled in their mortal sweat, drawing upon their last strength—while the current of sleep carried them away into ever more distant and strange regions of the night.

IV

The next day, Father was limping slightly on one leg. His face shone. At the break of day he had found the prepared and dazzling conclusion for his letter, which he had struggled over in vain for so many days and nights. We never saw the man with the black beard again. He drove off before morning with his trunk and bundles, without taking leave of anyone. It was the last night of the dead season. Counting from that summer night, there began for the shop seven long years of abundance.

The Sanatorium under the Hourglass

I

The journey went on for a long time. Barely a couple of passengers were traveling on that forgotten spur line that carries a train only once each week. I had never seen such archaic carriages, long since withdrawn from other lines—spacious as rooms, dark, and full of nooks and crannies. The corridors, bending at various corners, the empty compartments, labyrinthine and cold, contained something strangely deserted, something almost terrifying. I moved from one car to another in search of a cozy corner. There was wind blowing everywhere, cold drafts cleared the way for one another through the interior spaces, drilled right through the entire train. Here and there people were sitting on the floor with their small bundles, not daring to occupy the empty, exceptionally high settees. In any event, those oilcloth-covered, bulging seats were as cold as ice and sticky from age. Not a single passenger boarded at the empty stations. Without a whistle, without puffing, the train moved on slowly, seemingly lost in thought.

For a while, a man wearing the tattered uniform of a railroad worker kept me company, sunk in thought. He was pressing a handkerchief to his swollen, sore face. Then he, too, disappeared somewhere, having gotten off at one of the stops without my noticing. What remained after him was a depressed place in the straw that covered the floor and a black, dilapidated valise that he had forgotten.

Wading through straw and rubbish, I walked unsteadily from car to car. The compartment doors, wide-open, were swaying in the draft. There wasn't a single passenger anywhere. Finally, I met a conductor wearing the black uniform of that line's railway employees. He was winding a thick scarf around his neck, packing up his personal belongings, a lantern, and an official book.

"We're almost there, sir," he said, having glanced at me with his completely white eyes.

The train was slowly coming to a stop, without any puffing, without the rumbling of wheels, as if life was slowly leaving it along with its last breath of steam. We stopped. Silence and emptiness, no station building. Getting off, he pointed out the direction in which the sanatorium stood. Carrying my valise, I set off along a white, narrow road that soon disappeared in the dark thicket of a park. With some curiosity, I scrutinized the landscape. The road I was following rose to the crest of a gentle knoll that commanded a view of a grand horizon. The day was completely gray, gloomy, without any features. And perhaps under the influence of that heavy, colorless atmosphere the entire great basin of the horizon loomed dark; an extensive, forested land-scape composed itself on it like a stage set made from stripes and strata of forestation that were increasingly distant and gray, flowing along trails and gentle slopes, now from the left, now from the right. This entire dark solemn landscape appeared to be barely perceptibly flowing within itself, slipping past itself, like a cloudy, towering sky filled with hidden movement. The fluid stripes and trails of the woods seemed to be soughing and rising on this noise like an ocean tide imperceptibly gathering strength as it flows toward land. Amid the dark, forested dynamic of the terrain the raised white road meandered like a melody along a crest of broad chords, crushed by the pres-sure of powerful musical masses, which were finally engulfing it. I snapped off a twig from a roadside tree. The green of its leaves was completely dark, almost black. It was an amazingly saturated black, deep and beneficial, like a dream full of power and nourishment. And all the grays of the landscape were derivatives of that one color. Our landscape often takes on such a color in a cloudy summer twilight saturated with long rains. The same profound, calm abnegation, the same resigned and ultimate numbness that is no longer in need of the consolation of colors.

In the woods, it was as dark as night. I groped my way over silent pine needles. When the trees thinned out, the planks of a bridge thudded under my feet. At the other end, amid the blackness of the trees, the gray, many-windowed walls of a hotel loomed up, advertising itself as the sanatorium. The double glass doors at the entrance were open. One entered directly from the little bridge that was enclosed on both sides by shaky balustrades of birch branches. Semidarkness and solemn silence reigned in the corridor. I started moving on tiptoe from door to door, reading in the darkness the numbers placed above them. At a turning, I finally came across a chambermaid. She came running out of a room, breathless and agitated, as if she had just torn herself away from insistent arms. She barely understood what I said to her. I had to repeat. She fidgeted helplessly.

Had they received my telegram? She spread wide her hands, her gaze wandering off to the side. She was only waiting for an opportunity to be able to leap at the half-open door that she was looking at out of the corner of her eye.

"I have come from far away; I reserved a room in this building by telegram," I said with a certain impatience. "Whom should I speak to?"

She did not know.

"You can go to the restaurant," she said, confused. "Everyone is sleeping now. When the doctor gets up, I will register you."

"Sleeping? But it's daytime, a long time until night . . ."

"They sleep all the time here. Didn't you know?" She glanced up with curious eyes. "After all, it is never night here," she added flirtatiously. She no longer wanted to escape; she was fidgeting, plucking at the lace of her apron.

I left her. I entered a half-dark restaurant. There were little tables and a large buffet occupying the width of an entire wall. After a long time I once again was feeling some appetite. The sight of the cakes and tortes with which the surface of the buffet was generously covered cheered me up.

I set down my valise on one of the tables. They were all empty. I clapped my hands. No answer. I looked into the neighboring room, which was larger and brighter. That room was open with a wide window or loggia onto the landscape with which I was already familiar and which, with its deep sadness and resignation, was framed by the window like a funereal memento. The remains of a recent meal, uncorked bottles, half-emptied glasses, could be seen on the tablecloths. There were even tips lying about that the staff had not picked up. I returned to the buffet and examined the cakes and patés. They looked exceedingly tasty. I considered whether I should serve myself. I felt a rush of unaccustomed gluttony. In particular, a certain type of shortbread with apple marmalade was making my mouth water. I already wanted to pry up one of those cakes with a silver spatula when I sensed someone's presence behind me. The maid had entered in silent slippers and was touching my back with her fingers.

"The doctor is asking for you," she said, examining her fingernails.

She walked ahead of me, and, confident of the magnetism exerted by the play of her hips, she did not turn around at all. She amused herself by intensifying the magnetism, regulating the distance between our bodies while we passed dozens of doors with numbers affixed to them. The corridor was growing darker and darker. Already in total darkness, she leaned against me for an instant.

"Here is the doctor's door," she whispered. "Please go in."

Dr. Gotard received me standing in the center of the room. He was a short man, broad in the shoulders, with black stubble.

"We received your telegram yesterday," he said. "We sent our institution's carriage to the station, but you arrived on a different train. Alas, the railway network is not the best. How are you?"

"Is Father alive?" I asked, sinking my anxious gaze into his smiling face.

"He's alive, naturally," he said, calmly holding my feverish glance. "Of course, within the boundaries conditioned by the situation," he added, screwing up his eyes. "You know as well as I that from the point of view of your home, from the perspective of your fatherland, your father died. That cannot be entirely undone. This death casts a certain shadow on his existence here."

"But Father does not know, does not guess?" I asked in a whisper.

He shook his head with deep conviction.

"Rest assured," he said in a hushed voice, "our patients do not guess, they cannot guess . . ."

"The entire trick depends," he added, ready to demonstrate the mechanism on his fingers, which were already prepared for this, "on the fact that we have turned back time. We are late by an interval whose length is impossible to define. This boils down to a simple relativism. Here, your father's death, the death that already reached him in your fatherland, has simply not taken effect."

"In that case," I said, "Father is dying or close to death . . ."

"You do not understand me, sir," he responded in a tone of tolerant impatience. "We reactivate past time here with all its possibilities, including the possibility of recovery."

He looked at me with a smile, holding his beard.

"And now you will surely wish to see your father. In accordance with your order, we reserved another bed for you in your father's room. I shall take you there."

When we emerged into the dark corridor, Dr. Gotard was already speaking in a whisper. I noticed that, like the maid, he had felt slippers on his feet.

"We allow our patients to sleep as long as they need to, sparing their life energy. Anyway, they have nothing better to do here."

He stopped in front of one of the doors and placed a finger on his lips.

"Go in quietly, sir; your father is sleeping. Why don't you lie down, too. That is the best thing you can do at this moment. Good-bye."

"Good-bye," I whispered, feeling the beating of my heart rising into my throat. I pressed down on the handle, the door surrendered, opening slightly like lips that part without resistance in sleep. I went inside. The room was practically empty, gray and bare. On an ordinary wooden bed under a small window my father was lying in abundant bedding, asleep. His deep breathing discharged entire layers of snoring from the depths of sleep. The entire room seemed to be already lined from floor to ceiling with this snoring, and new items were still arriving. Full of emotion, I looked at Father's emaciated, haggard face entirely swallowed now by that labor of snoring, the face that in a distant trance, having discarded its earthly covering, somewhere on a distant shore had confessed its existence by solemn enumeration of its minutes.

There was no second bed. Penetrating cold blew in through the window. The stove was not lit.

"It appears that they don't pay too much attention to patients here," I thought. "Such a sick man exposed to drafts! And apparently no one cleans here. A thick layer of dust has carpeted the floor, covered the night table with its medicines and a glass of coffee that had grown cold. Stacks of cakes on the buffet, but they give patients plain black coffee in place of something nourishing! But in relation to the blessings of time forced into retreat, this is, naturally, a trifle."

I undressed slowly and slipped into Father's bed. He did not wake up. Only his snoring, already towering too high, descended an octave lower, giving up on the grandiloquence of his declamation. It became, as it were, private snoring, for his own use. I tucked a duvet around my father, protecting him as much as possible from the draft blowing in from the window. I soon fell asleep beside him.

II

When I awoke it was dusk inside the room. Father, already dressed, was seated at the table, drinking tea into which he dipped frosted rusks. He was wearing a still-new black suit of English cloth that he had had made for himself the previous summer. His tie was knotted rather carelessly.

Seeing that I was awake, he said with a kindly smile on his face, which was pale from illness, "I am truly happy that you've come, Józef. What a surprise! I feel so lonely here. It's true that in my situation one cannot complain; I have already experienced worse things and should one wish to extract a result from all these positions . . . But enough of that. Imagine, the first day here they immediately served me a splendid *filet de boeuf* with mushrooms. It was an infernal piece of meat, Józef. I warn you most emphatically—should they ever try to serve you *filet de boeuf* here . . . I still feel the fire in my belly. And diarrhea upon diarrhea . . . I couldn't manage at all. But I have to inform you of a piece of news," he went on. "Don't laugh, I've rented a place for the shop here. That's right. And I congratulate myself on the idea. I was thoroughly bored, you know. You have no idea what boredom prevails here. And now at least I have a pleasant occupation. But don't imagine anything splendid. Nothing of the sort. A much more modest space than our old store. Just a booth in comparison with it. I would have been ashamed of such a stall in our city, but here, where we have had to let go of so many of our pretensions . . . that's right, isn't it, Józef?"

He laughed sorrowfully.

"Even so, one lives somehow."

I was upset. I felt ashamed of Father's embarrassment at realizing that he'd used an inappropriate word.

"I see that you're sleepy," he said after a moment. "Sleep a little longer, and then you'll visit me in the shop—right? I'm off now to see how business is doing. You have no idea how difficult it was to get credit, how distrustfully they treat old merchants here, merchants with a respectable past . . . Do you remember the optician's office in the market square? Our shop is right next to it. It doesn't have a sign yet, but you'll find it anyway. It's hard to mistake it."

"Are you going out without a coat?" I asked anxiously.

"They forgot to pack it for me . . . imagine . . . I didn't find it in the trunk, but I don't miss it at all. The mild climate, the sweet atmosphere! . . ."

"Take my coat, Father," I urged him, "please, do take it."

But Father was already putting on his hat. He waved good-bye and left the room.

No, I was no longer sleepy. I felt rested . . . and hungry. I recalled with pleasure the buffet stocked with cakes. I got dressed, thinking how I would pamper myself with various samples of those delicacies. I intended to give priority to the shortbread with apples, but I had not forgotten the splendid sponge cake with orange-peel filling I had seen there. I stood in front of the mirror in order to knot my tie, but its surface, like a spherical mirror, concealed my image somewhere deep inside, swirling in its murky depths. In vain did I adjust my distance from it, approaching, retreating—no reflection wished to emerge from the silvery, liquid fog. "I have to tell them to supply a different mirror," I thought, and left the room.

It was utterly dark in the corridor. The impression of solemn silence was strengthened even more by the dim gaslight burning with a bluish flame at the bend. In this labyrinth of doors, frames, and nooks, I found it difficult to recall the entrance to the restaurant. "I'll go into the city," I thought with sudden determination. "I'll eat somewhere in town. Probably I'll find a good café there."

Outside the gate the humid, sweet air of this peculiar climate enveloped me. The chronic grayness of the atmosphere became several shades deeper still. It was like day seen through a funeral pall.

I could hardly feast my eyes enough on the velvety, luscious blackness of the darkest parts, on the gamut of muted grays, of plush ashes, unfolding in passages of muffled tones, broken off by the keyboard's damper—the nocturne of that landscape. The abundant, voluminous air fluttered against my face like a soft sheet of cloth. It contained the sickly sweetness of stale rainwater.

Again, the soughing of the black woods circling upon itself, the dull chords disturbing the air beyond the range of the audible! I was in the rear courtyard of the sanatorium. I looked around at the high walls of the annex to the main building, which was laid out in the shape of a horseshoe. Black shutters covered all the windows. The sanatorium was sound asleep. I passed the gate in the iron picket fence. Next to it there was a doghouse of unusual dimensions—deserted. Again the black woods swallowed and held me while I groped my way through the darkness on the silent pine needles as though walking with my eyes closed. As dawn broke, outlines of buildings appeared among the trees. A few more steps and I was in a spacious city square.

A strange, confusing similarity to the market square of our native city! How similar, in fact, are all the market squares in the world! Virtually the same houses and shops!

The sidewalks were practically empty. A mournful, late, semidawn of an indeterminate time was drifting down from a sky of indefinite grayness. I had no trouble reading all the posters and signs, and yet I would not have been surprised had I been told that it was late at night! Only a few shops were open. Others had their shutters halfway down; they had been locked up in a hurry. Intense, lush air, air that was intoxicating and rich, was swallowing up part of the view in some places, like a wet sponge washing away a couple of houses, a streetlight, a piece of a sign. At times it was difficult to raise my eyelids, which were drooping from some peculiar enervation or sleepiness. I began searching for the optician's shop that Father had mentioned. He had talked to me about it as if it was something I was familiar with, as if alluding to my familiarity with local conditions. Did he not know that I was here for the first time? Without a doubt everything was confused in his head. But what could be expected of Father, only half real, living a life that was so provisional, so relative, limited by so many conditions! It is hard to conceal that it required a lot of goodwill to grant that he had some kind of existence. It was a pitiful surrogate of a life, dependent on universal indulgence, on that *consensus omnium* from which he drew his feeble juices. It was clear that only thanks to everyone's turning a blind eye, to a collective refusal to see the obvious glaring shortcomings of this state of affairs, could this pathetic appearance of life be sustained for even a moment within the fabric of reality. The slightest opposition would shake him, the weakest gust of skepticism would knock him down. Could Dr. Gotard's sanatorium guarantee him the hothouse atmosphere of well-meaning tolerance, protect him from cold gusts of sobriety and criticism? One had to marvel that in this endangered, contested state of things Father still managed to maintain such a splendid attitude.

I was pleased when I saw the café's display window full of pound cakes and tortes. My appetite revived. I opened the glass door with its ICE CREAM sign and entered the dark establishment. It smelled of coffee and vanilla. A young lady, her face blurred by the dusk, emerged from the back of the shop and took my order. Finally, after such a long time, I could sate my hunger with excellent doughnuts that I dunked in coffee. In the darkness, with the whirling arabesques of dusk dancing all around me, I wolfed down more and more cakes, sensing how the whirling of the darkness was insinuating itself under my eyelids, stealthily taking over my insides with its warm pulsing, its countless swarm of delicate touches. Finally, only the rectangle of the window shone like a gray blemish in the total darkness. In vain did I bang with a spoon on the tabletop. No one appeared to take what I owed for the meal. I left a silver coin on the table and walked out into the street. A light was still on in the bookstore next door. The salesclerks were busy sorting the books. I inquired about Father's shop. "It's the second shop down from us," they explained. A helpful lad even ran over to the door to point it out to me. The portal was glass, the display window not yet ready, covered over with gray paper. Already at the door I observed with surprise that the shop was full of customers. My father was standing behind the counter, repeatedly licking his pencil, and adding up the items on a lengthy bill. The gentleman for whom this bill had been prepared was leaning over the counter, moving his index finger behind every additional figure, and counting under his breath. The rest of the guests looked on in silence.

My father cast a glance at me from over his spectacles and said, keeping his finger on the item where he'd stopped, "There's a letter for you here; it's on the desk among the papers."

And again he immersed himself in counting. In the meantime the salesclerks were setting aside the purchased goods, wrapping them in paper, tying them with string. The shelves were only partly filled with cloth. Most of the space was still empty.

"Why aren't you sitting down, Father?" I asked softly, going behind the counter. "You are so sick, and you're not taking care of yourself at all."

He raised his hand defensively as if pushing away my arguments and did not stop counting. He looked very haggard. It was clear as day that only his artificial excitement and feverish activity sustained his strength, delaying the moment of total collapse.

I searched the desk. It was more of a parcel than a letter. A few days before I had written to a bookstore about a certain pornographic book and here it was, sent to me here; my address had already been discovered, or rather the address of Father, who had only just opened his shop without a sign or a firm. In truth, it was an astonishing system of intelligence, shipping efficiency worthy of amazement! And such extraordinary speed!

"You can read all you like in the back, in the office," said Father, casting a dissatisfied glance at me. "You can see for yourself that there's no room here."

The office behind the shop was still empty. A small amount of light from the shop entered it through the glass door. The salesclerks' coats hung on the walls. I opened the letter and started reading in the weak light from the door.

I was informed that, alas, the book I had ordered was not in stock. A search for it had been undertaken, but, without anticipating the outcome, the firm was allowing itself to send me in the meantime without obligation a certain item in which my undoubted interest was foreseen. There followed a convoluted description of a collapsible astronomical refracting telescope with great light power and various advantages. My curiosity aroused, I extracted from the envelope an instrument made of black oilcloth or stiff canvas folded into a flat accordion. I have always had a weakness for telescopes. I began to expand the multiple folds of the instrument's outer cover. Stiffened with thin little rods, the enormous bellows of the telescope expanded under my hands, extending its empty box across the entire length of the room; it was a labyrinth of black chambers, a lengthy complex of darkrooms inserted halfway into one another. It was in the shape of an elongated automobile made of lacquered canvas, a theatrical prop of sorts imitating in the light material of paper and stiff denim the solidity of reality. I looked into the black funnel of the eyepiece and observed in its depths the faintly visible outlines of the sanatorium's courtyard facade. Intrigued, I slipped deeper into the rear chamber of the apparatus. Now, through the telescope's field of vision, I followed the chambermaid walking along the semidark corridor of the sanatorium with a tray in her hand. She turned around and smiled. "Can she see me?" I thought to myself. An overpowering drowsiness shaded my eyes with mist. Actually, I was sitting in the rear chamber of the telescope as if in a limousine. A slight movement of the lever and the apparatus started rustling with the fluttering of a paper butterfly, and I sensed that it was moving with me and turning toward the door.

Like a great black caterpillar the telescope rode out into the illuminated shop—a many-limbed torso, an enormous paper cockroach with two imitations of lanterns in front. The customers crowded together, retreating before this blind paper dragon, the salesclerks opened the doors to the street, and I rode out slowly in this paper automobile amid a lineup of guests escorting with indignant glances this truly scandalous departure.

III

Thus does one live in this city, and time goes on. Most of the day one sleeps, and not only in bed. No, one is not too fastidious on this point. In any place and at any time of day a person is ready to take a delicious nap here. With one's head resting on a restaurant table, in a droshky, and even standing up during a journey, in the hallway of some house where one drops in for a moment in order to succumb for a while to the overpowering need for sleep.

Waking up, still groggy and shaky, we resume the interrupted conversation, continue the arduous road, carry forward the convoluted affair without beginning or end. As a consequence, sometimes entire intervals of time get lost accidentally along the way, we lose control over the continuity of the day, and in the end we stop relying on it; without regret we give up on the skeleton of uninterrupted chronology to whose attentive oversight we had in days past become accustomed out of habit and from mindful daily discipline. Long ago we sacrificed that incessant readiness to render an account of time past, that scrupulousness in calculating to the last groschen the hours spent—the pride and ambition of our economics. We long ago gave up on those cardinal virtues for which in days past we knew neither hesitation nor transgression.

May a few examples serve as illustration of this state of things. At some hour of day or night—a barely perceptible nuance of sky distinguishes between these times—I awaken near the balustrade of the little bridge leading to the sanatorium. It is dusk. I must have wandered about the city unknowingly, overcome with drowsiness, before I dragged myself, dead on my feet, to this bridge. I cannot say whether Dr. Gotard, who stands before me now finishing a lengthy disquisition with final conclusions, had accompanied me on this path the entire time. Carried away by his own eloquence, he takes me under the arm and drags me after him. I go with him and before we have walked across all the thudding planks of the bridge I am already asleep again. Through my closed eyelids I dimly see the doctor's astute gestures, the smile deep inside his black beard, and in vain do I attempt to comprehend the splendid logical trick, the final trump card, with which at the peak of his argument, standing still with arms outstretched, he is triumphant. I do not know how much longer we have been walking side by side like this, engrossed in a conversation full of misunderstandings, when at a certain moment I am suddenly completely awake. Dr. Gotard is no longer here, it is completely dark, but only because I am keeping my eyes closed. I open them and I am in bed, in my room to which I returned by I don't know what means.

An even more drastic example:

At dinnertime I walk into a restaurant in the city, into the chaotic buzz of voices and disarray of diners. And whom should I meet in the middle of the room before a table bending under the weight of dishes? Father. All eyes are turned toward him, and he, his diamond tiepin glittering, unusually animated, rapturous to the point of ecstasy, bows affectedly in all directions in an overflowing conversation with the entire hall at once. With artificial bravado, which I cannot observe without the highest anxiety, he keeps ordering new dishes, which pile up in heaps on the table. He gathers them around himself with delight, although he has not yet coped with the first course. Smacking his tongue, chewing and talking at the same time, with gestures and mimicry he fakes the greatest contentment with this feast, with an adoring gaze following Pan Adaś, the waiter, to whom he constantly calls out new orders with an infatuated smile. And when the waiter, waving a napkin, runs to fulfill them, Father appeals with an imploring gesture to everyone, takes everyone as witness to the irresistible charm of this Ganymede.

"A priceless lad," he cries with a blissful smile, half closing his eyes. "An angelic lad! Admit it, gentlemen, he's charming!"

I withdraw from the room, filled with distaste, not noticed by Father. If he had been deliberately assigned by the hotel administration for reasons of publicity and to enliven the guests, he could not have behaved more provocatively and ostentatiously. My head swimming from drowsiness, I stagger through the streets, aiming for home. I rest my head on a mailbox for a moment, giving myself a brief siesta. Finally, I fumble my way in the darkness to the sanatorium gate and enter. It is dark in our room. I turn the switch, but the electricity isn't working. A cold draft is blowing in through the window. The bed creaks in the darkness.

Father lifts his head from the bedding and says, "Ah, Józef, Józef! I have been lying here for two days already without any attention, the bells have been disconnected, no one looks in on me, and my own son abandons me, a seriously ill man, and gallivants about town after girls. Look how my heart is thumping."

How to reconcile this? Is Father sitting in the restaurant, overcome with unhealthy ambition in his gluttony, or is he lying in his own room, seriously ill? Is he two fathers? Nothing of the sort. The fault of everything is the rapid disintegration of time that is not supervised with constant vigilance.

We all know that this undisciplined element avoids trouble only by keeping a tight rein on itself thanks to continual cultivation, solicitous attention, and diligent regulation and correction of its excesses. Deprived of this supervision, it inclines immediately to transgressions, to wild aberration, to playing innumerable tricks, to amorphous buffoonery. The incongruence of our individual times becomes ever clearer. My father's time and my own time no longer coincided.

Parenthetically speaking, Father's accusation of dissoluteness in my behavior is an unfounded insinuation. I have not yet approached any girl here. Stumbling like a drunk from one dream to another, I barely pay attention in my sober moments to the local fair sex.

Besides, the chronic dusk in the streets here does not permit one even to distinguish faces clearly. The one thing I have managed to notice as a young man who still, after all, has a certain interest in this area, is the peculiar walk of these young ladies.

It is a walk in an inflexibly straight line that does not take into account any obstacles and is obedient solely to some inner rhythm, some law that they unwind as if from a ball of yarn into a straightforward little trot, full of meticulousness and measured grace.

Each one carries within herself, like a tightly wound spring, a different, individual, regulation shoe tree.

When they walk straight ahead like that, eyes fixed on that rule, full of focus and dignity, it seems that they are preoccupied with only one worry— not to leave anything out, not to break the difficult rule, not to deviate from it by even a millimeter. And then it becomes clear that what they carry above themselves with such care and excitement is but a certain idée fixe of their own perfection, which through the power of their conviction almost becomes reality. It is a kind of anticipation decided upon at their own risk, without any guarantee, an inviolable dogma raised beyond all doubt.

What shortcomings and defects, what snub or flattened little noses, what freckles and pimples they smuggle defiantly under the flag of this fiction! There is no ugliness or ordinariness that cannot be carried away on the wings of this faith into the fictional sky of perfection.

Sanctioned by that faith the body becomes visibly more beautiful and the feet, truly shapely, elastic, feet in immaculate footwear, speak with their gait; with alacrity they explicate in a fluid, glittering monologue of stepping, the richness of the idea that the closed face, out of pride, leaves unspoken. They keep their hands in the pockets of their short, tight-fitting jackets. In the café and in the theater they cross their legs, exposed all the way up to the knee, and remain suggestively silent with them. So much, in passing, for just one of the city's peculiarities. I have already mentioned the black local vegetation. A certain species of black fern, enormous bunches of which adorn vases in every local apartment and every public place, is especially deserving of attention. It is almost a symbol of mourning, the funeral coat of arms of this city.

IV

Relationships in the sanatorium are becoming more unbearable with every day. It is hard to deny that we have simply fallen into a trap. Since the moment of my arrival, during which certain appearances of hospitable thoughtfulness were spun out for the newcomer's sake, the administration of the sanatorium has not troubled itself in the least to give us even the illusion of some kind of care. We are simply turned over to ourselves. No one concerns himself with our needs. I have long since verified that the wires to the electric bells break off directly above the door and lead nowhere. Staff are nowhere to be seen. Day and night, the corridors are steeped in darkness and silence. I have a strong conviction that we are the only guests in this sanatorium and that the secretive, discreet face with which the chambermaid firmly closes the doors of rooms when entering or leaving is simply a mystification.

I might have had a desire on occasion to open wide the doors of those rooms one after another and to leave them wide-open in order to unmask this ignoble intrigue in which we have been entangled.

However, I am not entirely certain of my suspicions. Sometimes late at night I see Dr. Gotard in the corridor hurrying somewhere in his white surgical coat with an enema syringe in his hand and preceded by the maid. It is difficult to stop him then in his haste and to press him to the wall with determined questioning.

Were it not for the restaurant and café in the city, one could die of hunger here. To this day I have not been successful in my request for a second bed. Fresh linens are out of the question. I must admit that the general disregard for cultured habits has not spared us either.

For me as a civilized man, getting into bed in my clothing and shoes was always simply an unthinkable act. Now, I come back late to the house, drunk with drowsiness, the room is in semidarkness, the curtains on the window billowing from a cold wind. I collapse unconscious onto the bed and bury myself in the feather bed. I sleep like that for an entire irregular expanse of time, for days or weeks, traveling across empty landscapes of dream, always on the road, always on the steep high roads of respiration, now riding down gently and elastically on gentle slopes, then crawling back up with difficulty onto the perpendicular wall of snoring. Once having gained the summit, I embrace the immense horizons of this rocky, soundless wilderness of sleep. At some point, at an unknown time, somewhere on a sudden bend of snoring, I wake up half conscious and feel Father's body at my feet. He is lying curled up into a ball, little, like a kitten. I fall asleep again with my mouth open and the entire immense panorama of mountain landscape glides by me sinuously and majestically.

In the shop, Father develops animated activity, conducts transactions, exerts all his eloquence to persuade his customers. His cheeks are flushed with animation, his eyes shine. In the sanatorium he lies gravely ill just as in his last weeks at home. It is hard to conceal that the process is rapidly approaching its fatal end. He speaks to me in a weak voice.

"You should drop in to the shop more often, Józef. The salesclerks are stealing from us. You can see that I am no longer able to cope with the task. I have been lying here sick for weeks and the shop is going to ruin, consigned to the mercy of fate. Wasn't there any mail from home?"

I am beginning to regret this whole affair. I can't say it was a good idea that, misled by a pretentious advertisement, we sent Father here. Time turned back . . . indeed, it sounds lovely, but in reality what does it turn out to be? Does one receive high-value, reliable time here, time somehow unwound from a fresh length of cloth, smelling of newness and dye? On the contrary. It is threadbare time, worn out by people, tattered time with holes in many places, transparent as a sieve.

It is no wonder that it is, so to speak, regurgitated time—please understand me—it is secondhand time. God have mercy! . . .

In addition, there is all this highly inappropriate manipulation of time. These immoral dealings, this sneaking into its mechanism from behind, the reckless fingering near its sensitive mysteries! Sometimes one would like to bang the table and yell at the top of one's voice, "Enough of this, leave time alone, time is inviolable, you're not allowed to provoke time! Isn't space enough for you? Space is for man, you can roam as much as you like in space, turn somersaults, roll over, leap from star to star. But for the love of God, don't touch time!"

On the other hand, is it possible to demand that I should have broken the agreement with Dr. Gotard myself? Whatever Father's miserable existence may be, I still see him after all, I am with him, I speak with him . . . Actually, I owe Dr. Gotard endless gratitude.

On several occasions I wanted to speak openly with him. But Dr. Gotard is elusive.

"He just left for the restaurant," the chambermaid informs me.

I am on my way there when she catches up with me to say that she was mistaken, Dr. Gotard is in the operating room. I hasten upstairs, speculating about what operations can be performed here, enter the vestibule, and in fact they tell me to wait. Dr. Gotard will come out in a second, he has just completed the operation and is washing his hands. I can almost see him, short, taking big steps, hurrying in his open coat through a row of hospital wards. A moment later what do I learn? Dr. Gotard wasn't here at all, no operations have been performed here in years. Dr. Gotard is asleep in his room, his black beard jutting up into the air. The room fills with his snoring as if with clumps of clouds that grow, pile up, lift up Dr. Gotard along with his bed on their swirling stacks ever higher and higher—a great, pathetic ascension into heaven on waves of snoring and of swollen bedding.

Even stranger things happen here, things that I conceal from myself, things that are fantastic simply because of their absurdity. Whenever I walk out of our room it seems to me that someone hastily retreats from outside the door and turns into a side corridor. Or someone is walking in front of me without looking back. It is not a nurse. I know who it is! "Mama!" I cry, my voice trembling with excitement, and Mother turns her face and looks at me for a moment with an imploring smile. Where on earth am I? What is going on here? What trap have I become ensnared in?

V

I do not know if it is the influence of the late time of year or if the days are becoming more serious in color, growing murkier and darker. It is as if one were looking at the world through totally black glasses.

The entire landscape is like the bottom of an immense aquarium—of pale ink. Trees, people, and buildings merge into black silhouettes, undulating like submerged plants against the background of this inky deep.

The neighborhood of the sanatorium is swarming with black dogs. Of various sizes and shapes, running low to the ground, they cut across all the roads and paths in the twilight, absorbed in their canine business, silent, full of intensity, and alert.

They fly by in twos, in threes, with alert outstretched necks, their ears pricked straight up, with a mournful sound of soft whimpering that is wrenched from their throats against their will, signaling the highest excitement. Intent on their affairs, full of haste, always on the road, always consumed by an incomprehensible goal, they pay scarcely any attention to a passerby. Sometimes, they only give him a quick glance while flying by, and then from that black, wise gaze fury peers out, checked in its intended action only by a lack of time. Sometimes, indulging their malice, they even start running over to one's feet with lowered head and sinister snarling, only to abandon their intention halfway there and race on in their great canine capers.

There is no coping with this plague of dogs, but why in the devil's name does the administration of the sanatorium keep an enormous German shepherd on a chain, a terrifying beast, a veritable werewolf of simply demonic ferocity?

My skin crawls whenever I pass his kennel, next to which he stands motionless on his short chain, with his wildly erect collar of shaggy fur around his head, bewhiskered, bristly, and bearded, with the machinery of his powerful jaws filled with fangs. He doesn't bark at all, but his wild face becomes even more terrifying at the sight of a person, his features stiffen into an expression of boundless fury, and, slowly lifting his terrible muzzle, he erupts in silent convulsion with an utterly low, passionate howl extracted from the depths of hatred, in which the sorrow and despair of impotence resonate.

My father passes by this beast with indifference when we walk out of the sanatorium together. As for me, I am shaken to my core every time by the elemental manifestation of impotent hatred. Now I am growing two heads taller than Father, who toddles along beside me, short and thin, with his tiny old man's step.

Approaching the market square we already see unusual movement. Crowds of people are running in the streets. Improbable news reaches us about the incursion of an enemy army into the city.

Amid the general consternation, people share alarming and contradictory news. It is hard to understand this. A war not preceded by diplomatic moves? War in the middle of blissful peace, not disrupted by any conflict? War with whom and about what? They inform us that the invasion of the enemy army emboldened a party of malcontents in the city who poured out into the streets with weapons in hand, terrorizing the peaceful inhabitants. In fact, we caught sight of a group of these attackers in black civilian suits with white straps across their chests moving along silently with rifles at the ready. The crowd was retreating before them, crowding onto the sidewalks, while they walked on, casting ironic dark glances from under their top hats, glances in which was revealed a feeling of dominance, a gleam of nasty amusement, and a certain knowing winking as if they were restraining outbursts of laughter that would unmask all this mystification. The crowd recognizes some of them, but joyous exclamations are stifled by the threat of the lowered gun barrels. They pass by us without accosting anyone. Again, all the streets overflow with the frightened, sullenly silent crowd. A muffled din floats over the city. It seems that the rattle of artillery can be heard in the distance, the thudding of munitions wagons.

"I have to get to the shop," says Father, pale but determined. "You don't need to accompany me. You'll only get in my way," he adds. "Go back to the sanatorium."

The voice of cowardice counsels me to be obedient. I see Father squeezing into the tight wall of the crowd and lose sight of him.

In a rush, I steal along side streets to the upper reaches of the city. I realize that on these steep roads I'll succeed in making a semicircle to avoid the city center, which is blocked by a human crush.

There, in the upper part of the city the crowd was thinner and finally disappeared completely. I walked calmly along empty streets to the city park. There were streetlights there burning with a dark blue flame, like funereal asphodels. Each of them was surrounded by a dancing swarm of cockchafers, heavy as bullets, carried along on the oblique, sideways flight of their vibrating wings. Some who had dropped down were scrambling stiffly on the sand, their backs convex, hunched over with hard coverings beneath which they were attempting to fold the extended, delicate membranes of their wings. People were strolling on the lawns and paths, immersed in carefree conversations. The last trees drooped over the courtyards of houses down below, backed up against the park wall. I wandered alongside this wall, which on this side barely came up to my chest, but on the other side fell away to the level of the courtyards on one-story-high escarpments. At one spot, a ramp made of firm soil emerged from between the courtyards and led up to the height of the wall. I easily stepped over the barrier and by means of this causeway I reached the street, squeezing between the closely built houses. My calculations, supported by outstanding spatial intuition, were accurate. I found myself almost directly across from the sanatorium building, whose wing showed up indistinctly white against the black setting of trees. As usual, I enter from the rear, cross the courtyard, go through the gate in the iron fence, and already from a distance I see the dog at its post. As always, a shudder of aversion passes over me at this sight. I want to pass him as quickly as possible in order not to hear that groan of hatred drawn from the depths of his heart, when to my horror and not believing my own eyes, I see him bounding away from his box, not tethered, running around the courtyard in a desire to cut off my retreat, with a hollow bark that seems to come from inside a barrel.

Numb with terror I withdraw into the opposite, farthest corner of the courtyard and, instinctively seeking some kind of hiding place, take shelter in a little bower that stands there, absolutely convinced that my efforts are in vain. The shaggy beast approaches in leaps and bounds and now its muzzle is already at the entrance to the alcove, trapping me. Barely alive with fear, I observe that he has unwound the entire length of the chain, which he has dragged behind him across the courtyard, and that the bower itself is beyond the reach of his teeth. Beaten down, crushed by horror, I barely register relief. Staggering on my feet, close to fainting, I raise my eyes. I had never seen him so close up and only now do the scales fall from my eyes. How great is the power of prejudice! How mighty the suggestion of terror! What blindness! For it was a man. A man on a chain, whom in reductive, metaphoric, undifferentiated abbreviation by some inconceivable means I had taken for a dog. Please don't misunderstand me. It was a dog, most assuredly—but in human form. Canine quality is an internal quality and can manifest itself just as well in human and in animal form. The one who stood before me in the opening of the bower with his muzzle apparently contorted, with all his teeth bared in terrible growling, was a man of medium height, with a black beard. A yellow, bony face, black eyes, evil and unhappy. Judging from his black suit and the civilized form of his beard one might take him for an intellectual, an educated man. He could have been the elder, unsuccessful brother of Dr. Gotard. But that first appearance was deceptive. His great hands, filthy with glue, the two brutal, cynical furrows around his nose that disappeared into his beard, the horizontal, coarse wrinkles on his low brow swiftly erased that first illusion. He was, rather, a bookbinder, a tub thumper, a speaker at rallies, a party activist—a violent man with dark explosive passions. And precisely there, in those jaws of passion, in that convulsive bristling of all his fibers, in that mad fury insanely barking at the end of the stick aimed at him—he was one hundred percent a dog.

If I were to crawl across the rear barrier of the bower, I think, I could completely escape the reach of his fury and reach the sanatorium gate by the side path. I am already throwing my leg across the railing when suddenly I stop in the midst of what I am doing. I feel that it would be too cruel simply to walk away and leave him like that with his helpless uncontrollable rage. I imagine his terrible disillusionment, his inhuman pain, if he were to see me walking away from the trap, distancing myself once and for all. I stay there. I approach him and say in a natural, calm voice, "Please calm down, sir, I will unchain you."

At that, his face, cleaved by convulsions, disrupted by the vibration of his growling, becomes whole and smooth, and an almost thoroughly human countenance emerges from its depths. I approach without apprehension and unfasten the catch on his neck. Now we walk side by side. The bookbinder is dressed in a decent black suit, but he is barefoot. I attempt to start a conversation with him but only incomprehensible gibberish comes out of his mouth. Only in his eyes, in those black eloquent eyes, I read a wild enthusiasm for attachment, for fondness, which relieves me of terror. From time to time he stumbles over a rock, a clod of earth, and then because of the shock his face instantly fractures, disintegrates, dread rises halfway to the surface, prepared to leap, and right behind it comes fury, only awaiting the moment to once again change this face into a tangle of hissing vipers. I call him to order then with a sharp, collegial reprimand. I even pat him on the back. And sometimes an astonished, suspicious smile, not trusting itself, attempts to form on his face. Ah! how this terrible friendship weighs me down. How this weird affection terrifies me. How to rid myself of this man walking beside me, his gaze hanging on my face with all the fervor of his canine soul? I cannot, however, betray my impatience. I take out my wallet and say in a matter-of-fact voice, "You probably need money; I will lend you some with pleasure," but at sight of the money his face takes on such terrible wildness that I put away my billfold as fast as I can. And for a long time he remains incapable of calming down and controlling his features, which are contorted by convulsions of howling. No, I can stand this no longer. Anything but this. Matters have already gotten so complicated, so hopelessly tangled. Over the city I see the red glow of a fire. Father somewhere in the fire of revolution inside a burning shop, Dr. Gotard unreachable, and on top of all this Mother's inconceivable appearance, incognito, on some secret mission! These are the links of some great, incomprehensible intrigue tightening around my person. To flee, to flee from here! Anywhere at all. To shed this hideous friendship, this bookbinder who stinks like a dog, who does not let me out of his sight. We are standing in front of the sanatorium gate.

"Come to my room, please," I say with a polite gesture. Civilized movements fascinate him, lull his wildness. I let him go ahead of me into the room. I settle him in a chair.

"I am going to the restaurant to fetch some cognac," I say.

At that, he leaps up with terror, wishing to accompany me. I calm his panic with gentle firmness.

"You will sit, you will wait calmly," I say to him in a deep, vibrating voice at the base of which my concealed fright is resonating. He sits down with a hesitant smile.

I leave and walk slowly down the corridor, then down the stairs, through the corridor to the exit, I pass the main gate, cross the courtyard, slam the iron wicket behind me, and now I start to run breathlessly, with thumping heart, with pounding temples, along the dark avenue leading to the railway station.

Images pile up in my head, one more terrifying than the next. The monster's impatience, his terror, despair when he realizes that he has been duped. The return of fury, the recurrence of rage erupting with unrestrained force. My father's return to the sanatorium, his unsuspecting knock at the door and unexpected face-to-face encounter with the terrifying beast.

It's fortunate that Father is, for all intents and purposes, no longer alive and this won't really touch him, I think with relief, and already I see before me a black string of railway cars stopped at the departure point.

I board one of them and the train, as if it had been waiting for this, slowly moves off without a whistle.

In the window, the immense bowl of the horizon moves past again and turns slowly, inundated with dark, rustling woods amid which the walls of the sanatorium loom white. Farewell, Father, farewell, city, which I shall not see again.

Ever since that time I have been riding, continually riding, I have made my home as it were on the railroad and they tolerate me here, wandering from car to car. The cars, immense as rooms, are full of trash and straw, drafts penetrate right through them on gray, colorless days.

My clothing has grown threadbare and tattered. I have been presented with a railroad employee's shabby uniform. My face is tied up with a dirty rag because of my swollen cheek. I sit on the straw and doze, and when I am hungry, I stand in the corridor in front of the second-class compartments and sing. And people throw coins into my conductor's cap, into the black cap of a railway man with a ripped-off visor.

Dodo

He came to us on Saturday afternoons, wearing a dark frock coat that complemented his white piqué vest, and a bowler hat that must have been specially made for his head size; he came to sit for a quarter of an hour or two nursing a glass of water and raspberry juice, to meditate with his chin resting on the bone knob of the walking stick that he held between his knees, to be lost in thought over the azure smoke of his cigarette.

As a rule other relatives were also visiting, and during the freely flowing conversation Dodo would somehow slip into shadow, fall into the passive role of an extra in this animated gathering. Never speaking up, he would fix his eyes, which were full of expression beneath his splendid eyebrows, on one speaker and then the next, while his face gradually grew longer, emerging from its joints, as it were, and turned utterly stupid, as if uncontrolled in this elemental, rapt listening.

He spoke only when spoken to and then he would answer the question, in monosyllables, to be sure, and somewhat reluctantly, gazing in a different direction, and only insofar as the questions did not go beyond a certain range of simple, easily resolved matters. Sometimes he succeeded in maintaining a conversation for a few more questions beyond that range, but then only thanks to a supply of expressive faces and gestures that he had at his disposal and that, owing to their ambiguity, served him universally by filling in the gaps of articulated speech and supporting with lively mimicry a suggestion of a reasonable response. That was an illusion, however, that soon vanished, and the conversation broke off pitifully while the interlocutor's gaze turned away slowly and meditatively from Dodo, who, left to himself, fell back into his proper role as an extra and a passive observer against the background of the gathering's conversation.

For how was it possible to continue a conversation when, for example, in answer to a question as to whether he had accompanied his mother on her journey to the country, he replied in a minor key, "I don't know," and that was his sad, embarrassing truthfulness, since Dodo's memory did not, in fact, reach beyond the present moment and the most recent reality.

Long ago, while still a child, Dodo had suffered a serious brain disease during which he had lain unconscious for many months, closer to death than to life, and when despite this he finally recovered, it turned out that he had already been withdrawn from circulation, as it were, and that he no longer belonged to the community of reasonable people. His education took place privately, pro forma as it were, with great circumspection. Hard, uncompromising demands made of others softened, as it were, with respect to Dodo, restrained their severity, and were thoroughly indulgent.

Around him a sphere of strange privilege was created that sheltered him with a safety belt, a neutral zone, from the pressures of life and its demands. Everyone outside this zone was attacked by its waves, floundered in them noisily, allowed themselves to be transported, affected, carried away in strange abandon; inside this zone there was peace and a pause, a caesura, in the general tumult.

Thus he grew up, and the exceptional nature of his fate grew with him as if it were self-explanatory, and without opposition from any quarter.

Dodo never received new clothing; he always wore only the well-worn clothes of his older brother. While the life of his peers was separated into phases and periods marked off by boundary events, by sublime and symbolic moments—name days, examinations, engagements, promotions—his life flowed along in undifferentiated monotony, undisturbed by anything pleasant or unpleasant, and the future appeared as an entirely straight, monotonous highway without events or surprises.

Anyone who believed that Dodo rebelled internally against this state of things would have been mistaken. He accepted it with simplicity as his appropriate way of life, without amazement, with matter-of-fact acceptance, with dignified optimism, and he organized his life, arranged its details, within the boundaries of this uneventful monotony.

Every morning he went for a stroll into town and he always walked the same circuit along three streets that he followed to the end and then returned by the same route. Dressed in his brother's elegant but well-worn suit, his hands behind his back clasping his walking stick, he moved with distinction and without haste. He looked like a gentleman who was traveling for pleasure, visiting the city. This lack of haste, direction, or goal, which could have been expressed in his movements, sometimes acquired compromising forms, because Dodo displayed a tendency to fall into a trance—in front of shop doors, in front of workshops in which there was hammering and tinkering, and even in front of a group of people conversing with one another.

His physiognomy began to mature early on and, an amazing thing, whereas life's experiences and shocks hesitated on the threshold of this life, sparing his vacant imperturbability, his marginal uniqueness, his features were formed on the experiences that passed him by, they anticipated a kind of unrealized biography that, barely sketched in the sphere of possibility, molded and sculpted that face into the illusory mask of a great tragedian, full of the knowledge and the sorrow of all things.

His brows curved in magnificent arcs, plunging in shade his great, sad eyes surrounded by deep circles. Two furrows full of abstract suffering and illusory wisdom were inscribed around his nose and ran down to the corners of his mouth and even farther. His small, swollen lips were painfully closed, and the coquettish "beauty spot" on his long Bourbon chin gave him the appearance of an elderly, experienced bon vivant.

He did not escape having his privileged uniqueness tracked down, predatorily sniffed out by cunningly concealed human malice always hungry for prey.

Thus, more and more often it happened that he would acquire companions during his morning strolls and, as part of the conditions of his privileged uniqueness, these were companions of a special sort, not in the sense of friendship and commonality of interests, but in a highly problematic sense that brought no honor. They were mainly from much younger age groups, attracted to someone full of dignity and gravity, and the conversations they conducted had a special tone, merry and jocular, and for Dodo—there's no denying it—that tone was pleasant and stimulating.

When he walked along, a head taller than the merry, harebrained troop, he looked like a peripatetic philosopher surrounded by his pupils, and a frivolous smile, struggling with the tragic dominant of that physiognomy, broke out on his face from beneath the mask of dignity and sorrow.

Dodo came home late now from his morning strolls, returning from them with his mop of hair disheveled, his clothing slightly *dérangé*, but he was animated and inclined to a jolly dispute with Karola, his poor cousin, whom Aunt Retycja had taken in. Anyway, as if sensing the paltry distinction of those meetings, at home Dodo observed complete discretion on this topic.

Once or twice events occurred in this monotonous life that by reason of their format loomed above the shoals of daily events.

Once, having gone out in the morning, he did not come home for dinner. He did not come home for supper either, nor for dinner on the following day. Aunt Retycja was on the verge of despair. But he arrived that evening, a little rumpled, with his bowler hat crushed and somewhat askew, but in any event healthy and full of spiritual calm.

It was difficult to reconstruct the history of that escapade about which Dodo maintained total silence. Most likely, having fallen into a trance during his stroll, he had wandered into an unfamiliar district of the city; perhaps the peripatetic youth helped him do this, eagerly inserting Dodo into new and unfamiliar conditions of life.

Perhaps it was one of those days when Dodo sent his poor, overburdened memory on vacation—and forgot his address, and even his name, his personal details, which, after all, at other times were always clear to him.

We never did learn the specific details of that adventure.

Whenever Dodo's older brother went abroad, the family would shrink to three or four individuals. In addition to Uncle Hieronymus and Aunt Retycja, there was also Karola, who played the part of housekeeper in my uncle and aunt's large household.

Uncle Hieronymus had not left his room for many years now. Since the time when Providence had gently removed from his hands the helm of this ship of life, run aground on the shoals and shattered, he had led the life of a pensioner on a narrow strand between the entryway and a dark alcove that was set aside for him.

Wearing a long bathrobe that reached to the floor, he sat in the back of the alcove and from day to day grew ever more fantastic facial hair. His long beard, the color of pepper (almost white toward the ends of its long wisps), floated around his face, reached halfway onto his cheeks, leaving uncovered only his sparrow-hawk nose and two eyes, their whites rolling in the shade of his bushy eyebrows.

In the dark alcove, in that cramped prison in which like a wild, predatory cat he was condemned to pace back and forth in front of the glass doors leading to the drawing room, there stood two immense oak beds, the nocturnal lair of his aunt and uncle; a large Gobelins tapestry looming as a vague shape in the dark interior covered the entire rear wall. When one's eyes grew accustomed to the darkness, an enormous lion emerged among the bamboos and palms, powerful and gloomy as a prophet and majestic as a patriarch.

Seated back to back, the lion and Uncle Hieronymus each knew the other was there and were filled with hatred. Without looking, they threatened each other with their bared, exposed fangs and a menacingly growled word. At times the lion, agitated, half rose on its front paws, the mane on its outstretched neck bristling, and its threatening roar echoed around the cloudy horizon.

Then again Uncle Hieronymus would rise above him with a prophetic tirade and his face would take on a menacing shape from the great words with which he swelled while his beard waved in inspiration. Then the lion would narrow his pupils painfully and slowly turn his head away, limping beneath the power of the word of God.

That lion and that Hieronymus filled my aunt and uncle's dark alcove with eternal disputation.

Uncle Hieronymus and Dodo lived in this cramped apartment despite each other, as it were, in two different dimensions that intersected without ever coming into contact. When they met, their eyes moved past each other, as happens with beasts of two different and distant species who do not recognize each other at all and are incapable of arresting an alien image that speeds past their consciousness if they cannot visualize it in themselves.

They never spoke to each other.

When they sat down to eat, Aunt Retycja, seated between her husband and son, served as the border between two worlds, an isthmus between two seas of lunacy.

Uncle Hieronymus ate agitatedly, his long beard falling onto his plate. If the door in the kitchen creaked he would jump up from his chair and grab hold of his soup plate, ready to flee to the alcove with his portion should anyone unknown to him enter the apartment. Then Aunt Retycja would calm him.

"Don't be afraid, no one is coming, it's the maid."

Then Dodo would direct a glance from his glittering eyeballs, full of anger and indignation, at the terrified man, muttering to himself disconsolately, "A serious madman . . ."

Before Uncle Hieronymus received absolution from the exceedingly intricate complications of life and was granted permission to withdraw into his lonely refuge in the alcove, he was a man of an entirely different cut. Those who knew him in his youth affirmed that his ungovernable temperament knew no restraints, considerations, or scruples. To the incurably ill he spoke with satisfaction about the death awaiting them. He made use of condolence calls to subject the life of the deceased, for whom their tears had not yet dried, to harsh criticism before the bewildered family. To people who were concealing some unpleasant, sensitive personal matters, he mentioned these out loud and abusively. But one night he came home from a journey entirely changed and unconscious from fear and tried to hide under the bed. A few days later the news spread in the family that Uncle Hieronymus had abdicated from all his complicated, dubious, and risky business affairs that had grown too much for him, abdicated down the entire line and definitively, and had begun a new life, a life encompassed by a strict, precise rule—albeit one that we found incomprehensible.

On Sunday afternoons we all came to Aunt Retycja's for a small family tea. Uncle Hieronymus did not recognize us. Sitting in the alcove, he would cast wild, terrified glances at the company through the glass door. Sometimes, however, he would come out unexpectedly from his hermitage in a long bathrobe that reached the floor, with his beard fluttering around his face, making a motion with his hands as if to divide us, and say, "And now I beg you, just as you are, disperse, run away stealthily, silently, and imperceptibly . . ."

Then, threatening us mysteriously with his finger, he would add in a hushed voice, "They're already saying everywhere, 'Dee, da.'"

My aunt would shove him gently back to the alcove, and in the doorway he would turn to address us again threateningly and repeat with raised finger, "Dee, da."

Dodo understood everything with a delay, slowly, and several moments of silence and consternation would pass before the situation became clarified in his mind. Then, turning his gaze from one person to the next, as if making sure that something jolly had occurred, he would burst out laughing, and laugh loudly and with satisfaction, shaking his head pityingly, and repeat amid his laughter, "A serious madman . . ."

Night descended over Aunt Retycja's house, the cows, already milked, rubbed against the boards in the darkness, the servant girls were asleep in the kitchen, and bubbles of nighttime ozone floated in from the garden and burst in through the open window. Aunt Retycja slept in the depths of her great bed. On the other bed, Uncle Hieronymus sat like a tawny owl amid pillows. His eyes glittered in the darkness, his beard flowed onto his raised knees.

He slowly got down from the bed, tiptoeing over to my aunt. He stood over the sleeping woman like that, poised like a cat ready to jump, his eyebrows and mustache bristling. The lion on the wall yawned briefly and turned its head away. My aunt, awakened, was terrified of that head blazing with its eyes and snorting.

"Go, go to bed," she said, gesturing with her hand and shooing him away like a rooster.

He retreated, snorting and looking around with nervous movements of his head.

In the other room lay Dodo. Dodo was unable to sleep. The sleep center in his brain did not function properly. He fidgeted, wallowed in the bedding, turned from side to side.

The mattress creaked. Dodo sighed heavily, snored, lifted himself up, baffled, amid his pillows.

Unlived life tormented itself, agonized in despair, fidgeted like a cat in a cage. In Dodo's body, in that body of a half-wit, someone was growing old without experiences, someone was ripening to death without a crumb of contents.

Suddenly he started sobbing horrendously in the darkness.

Aunt Retycja ran over to him from her bed. "What is it, Dodo, is something hurting you?"

Dodo turned to her in astonishment.

"Who?" he asked.

"Why are you groaning?" my aunt asked.

"It's not me, it's him . . ."

"What him?"

"The walled-up one . . ."

"Who?"

But Dodo waved his hand resignedly. "Eh . . . ," and turned onto his other side.

Aunt Retycja tiptoed back to her bed. Uncle Hieronymus shook his finger at her threateningly as she passed by. "Everyone's already saying, 'Dee, da . . .'"

Edzio

I

On the same floor as us, in a narrow long wing off the courtyard, lives Edzio with his family. It's a long time since Edzio was a little boy; Edzio is a grown man with a stentorian masculine voice in which he sometimes sings operatic arias.

Edzio is inclined toward corpulence, not to the spongy, soft form, however, but to the athletic, muscular variety. He is strong in his arms like a bear, but what does that matter when his totally degenerate, misshapen legs are unusable.

Looking at Edzio's legs one really does not know what is the basis of this strange deformity. It appears that they have too many joints between knee and ankle, at least two joints more than normal legs. It is not surprising that they bend pitifully in these supernumerary joints, and not only sideways but also to the front, and in all directions.

So Edzio moves with the aid of two crutches, crutches of excellent craftsmanship, beautifully varnished to look like mahogany. On these crutches he goes downstairs every day to buy the newspaper, and that is his only walk and his only diversion. It is pitiful to watch his struggle with the stairs. His legs bow out irregularly, now to the side, now to the rear, bend in unexpected places, and his feet, short and high like horses' hooves, thump like logs against the boards. But once he is on a flat surface, Edzio is unexpectedly transformed. He straightens up, his torso swells impressively, and his body gathers momentum. Leaning on his crutches as if on parallel bars, he swings his legs out far ahead of him; they strike the ground with an uneven clatter and then he moves the crutches from their place and with new momentum he again flings himself forcefully forward. By such throws of his body he conquers space. Quite often, maneuvering with his crutches in the courtyard in an excess of strength stored up by long sitting, he is able to demonstrate this heroic method of locomotion to the amazement of the servant girls from the first and second floors. At those times the nape of his neck swells, the two folds of his double chin are outlined under his beard, and on his face, which he holds at an angle, its lips pressed tightly together in concentration, there stealthily appears a painful grimace. Edzio has no profession or occupation, as if fate, having encumbered him with the burden of deformity, freed him on the sly from that curse of the children of Adam. In the shadow of his deformity Edzio profits completely from an exceptional right to idleness and in the quiet of his soul he is satisfied with his private, so to speak, individually concluded transaction with fate.

Quite often, however, we think about how this young man in his twenties fills his time. Reading the newspaper offers a lot to occupy him. Edzio is a thorough reader. Not a single notice or a single advertisement escapes his notice. And when he finally makes his way to the last page of the daily paper, it is not boredom that awaits him during the rest of the day, oh no, not in the least. Only then does the real work begin, which Edzio has already been enjoying ahead of time. In the afternoon, when other people lie down for an after-dinner nap, Edzio takes out his great, thick volumes, opens them on the table near the window, prepares glue, a brush, and scissors, and begins his pleasant, interesting work of cutting out the most interesting articles and incorporating them according to a certain system into his books. The crutches stand ready just in case, leaning against the windowsill, but Edzio does not need them since he has everything close to hand, and so, amid diligent labor, the several hours until afternoon tea are passed.

Every third day Edzio shaves his red beard. He likes this activity and all its paraphernalia: hot water, foaming soap, and a smooth, gentle razor. Mixing up the soap, sharpening the razor on a leather strop, Edzio sings, not learnedly, not artistically, but rather unpretentiously, and from his whole chest, and Adela confirms that he has a pleasant voice.

However, not everything appears to be all right in Edzio's home. Unfortunately, between him and his parents a very serious discord reigns whose background and basis are unknown. We are not going to repeat conjectures and gossip and will limit ourselves to empirically confirmed facts.

It usually happens toward evening, during the warm time of the year when Edzio's window is open, that the sounds of these misunderstandings reach us. Actually, we hear only one-half of the dialogue—namely, Edzio's part— since the response of his antagonists, concealed in the farthest rooms of the apartment, do not reach us.

It is hard to conjecture from this what they accuse Edzio of, but one can conclude from the tone of his reaction that he is hurt to the quick, driven almost to extremes. His words are vehement and reckless, dictated by excessive indignation, but the tone, although irascible, is cowardly and miserable.

"That's right," he cries in a plaintive voice, "what of it? . . ." —"When yesterday?" —"Not true!" —"And if it is?" —"Then Papa is lying!" And so it goes for a full quarter of an hour, varied only by outbursts of grief and indignation from Edzio, who hits his head and tears out his hair from hopeless fury.

But at times, and this is the true point of these scenes, which supplies them with a specific little shudder, what we have been waiting for with bated breath occurs. In the depths of the apartment something seems to crash, a door opens with a bang, some piece of furniture falls over with a loud noise, and then Edzio's piercing screech resounds.

We listen to this, shaken and filled with shame but also with unbelievable satisfaction such as awakens at the thought of the wild, fantastic violence carried out on the person of this athletic young man, even though he is limp in his legs.

II

At dusk, when the dishes are already washed after an early supper, Adela sits on the courtyard-side balcony not far from Edzio's window. Two long U-shaped balconies wrap around the courtyard, one on the ground floor, the other at the second-floor level. Grass grows in the cracks in these wooden balconies, and in one crevice between two beams a small acacia tree shoots out and sways high above the courtyard.

In addition to Adela, neighbors are sitting here and there in front of their own doors, drooping on chairs and stools, fading indistinctly in the dusk; they sit there full of the drudgery of the day like sacks tied up and mute, waiting for the dusk to gently untie them.

Down below, the courtyard is rapidly soaking up the darkness, wave after wave, but up above the air does not want to renounce the light, and the more everything grows charred and turns funereally black, the more brightly it shines—it shines bright, shimmering and glittery, glimmering from the blurry flights of bats.

But down below the rapid, silent work of dusk has already begun, it is swarming there with those rapid, voracious ants that disassemble and distribute the substance of things into scraps, gnaw them down to the white bones, to the skeleton and the ribs phosphorescing hypnotically on that sorrowful battlefield. Those white papers, rags on top of the trash bin, the undigested shin bones of light, survive the longest in the worm-eaten darkness and cannot die. Time after time it seems as if the dusk has finally swallowed them, and once more they are still there and shining, lost from sight from moment to moment by eyes filled with vibrations and ants, but it is already becoming difficult to distinguish between these remains of things and the hallucinations of an eye that just then is starting to rave as if in its sleep, until everyone is sitting in his own aura as in a cloud of mosquitoes, surrounded by a dancing, stellar swarming pulsating in his brain, with the mesmerizing anatomy of hallucinations.

Then from the bottom of the courtyard the fine veins of breezes begin rising, as yet uncertain of their existence and already relinquishing it before they can reach our faces, streaks of freshness with which the underside of the undulating summer night is lined as if with silk. And while in the sky the first twinkling and continuously blown-out stars are being lit, the stifling veil of dusk, woven of swirling and phantoms, very slowly parts, and with a sigh the deep summer night opens up, filled to its depths with star dust and the distant croaking of frogs.

Without a light Adela goes to bed in the crumpled, tangled bedding from the night before, and scarcely has she closed her eyes when a chase begins on all the floors and in all the apartments in the building.

Only for the uninitiated is a summer night a time of rest and oblivion. Scarcely is the day's work done, the weary brain wanting to fall asleep and forget, then the chaotic comings and goings, the tangled, enormous disorder of the July night begins. All the apartments in the building, all the rooms and alcoves, are full then of voices, of wandering, of going in and going out. There are table lamps with shades in every window; even the corridors are brightly illuminated, and the doors open and shut continuously. One great, chaotic, half-ironic conversation becomes entangled and branches off amid constant misunderstandings through all the chambers of the hive. The people on the second floor have no clear idea what is being talked about on the ground floor and they send emissaries with urgent instructions. Couriers fly through all the apartments, up the stairs, down the stairs, forgetting their instructions on the way, continually being called back for new commissions. And there is always something to be added, always one more matter remains unclear, and all the rushing about amid laughter and jokes does not lead to a resolution.

Only the side rooms, not drawn into the great shambles of the night, have their own separate time, measured by the ticking of clocks, the monologues of silence, the deep breathing of sleepers. Wet nurses sleep there, ample and swollen with milk, they sleep sucking greedily at the bosom of night, their cheeks burning in ecstasy, and through their dreams ramble infants with their eyes closed, they wander caressingly like sniffing baby animals along the azure map of veins on the white plains of those breasts, they crawl delicately, seeking with blind faces a warm opening, an entrance into that deep sleep until with their sensitive mouths they find the nub of sleep, the trusted teat full of sweet oblivion.

And those who have seized sleep in their beds don't let it go, and they wrestle with it as with an angel who struggles to get free until they subdue it and smother it in the bedding and take turns snoring as if they were quarreling and angrily reproaching one another with the history of their enmity. But when the complaints and bickering are appeased and subside, and all the chasing around disperses and gets lost in various corners, and room after room sinks into silence and nonexistence—then Leon the salesclerk furtively ascends the stairs, comes in slowly with his shoes in his hand, and in the darkness searches with his key for the hole in the lock. As he does every night, he is returning from the lupanar with bloodshot eyes, shaken with hiccups, and with a thread of saliva dangling from his parted lips.

In Jakub's room a table lamp is burning, and, hunched over the table, he is writing a letter to Chrystian Seipel & Sons, Mechanical Spinning and Weaving Mills, a lengthy letter of many pages. A long train of writing-covered sheets is already lying on the floor, but there is still a long way to go until the end. Every so often he leaps up from the table and runs around the room with his hands in his tousled hair, and while he is circling the room like this it sometimes happens that he climbs the wall in his flight, flies across the wallpaper, crashing deliriously against the arabesques of the wallpaper patterns like a great shadowy mosquito, and runs down again onto the floor, continuing his inspired circling race.

Adela is sleeping soundly, her lips are parted, her face elongated and absent, but her lowered eyelids are transparent and on their thin parchment the night is writing its pact with the devil, half text, half images, full of sketches, corrections, and scribbles.

Edzio is standing in his room naked to the waist and lifting weights. He needs a lot of strength, double a lot of strength in his arms, which stand in for his feeble legs, and so he exercises assiduously, exercises secretively all night long.

Adela is drifting backward, beyond herself, into nonexistence and cannot scream, cry out, or interfere with Edzio's climbing out through the window.

Edzio gets out onto the porch without the protection of his crutches and Adela watches with horror to see if his legs will move him. But Edzio does not try to walk.

Like a great white dog he approaches in four-legged squat jumps, in great shuffling bounds along the thudding boards of the porch and is already at Adela's window. As he does every night, with a pained grimace he presses his pale, fat face to the windowpane, luminous with moonlight, and he says something plaintively, insistently; weeping, he reports that at night they lock up his crutches in the wardrobe and now he has to run like a dog on all fours through the night.

But Adela is inert, surrendered entirely to the deep rhythm of sleep that flows through her. She does not even have the strength to pull the quilt over her naked thighs, and she can do nothing to cope with the bedbugs, the rows and columns of bedbugs, wandering across her body. These light, thin little leaf torsos run across her so delicately that she does not feel their slightest touch. They are flat little purses for blood, dark red bags for blood, without eyes and without features, and now they are advancing in entire clans, a great migration of peoples divided into generations and tribes. They run from her legs by the millions, in a countless promenade, ever larger, as large as moths, like flat wallets, like great red vampire bats without heads, light and papery on little legs more delicate than a spider's web.

But when the last slow bedbugs have run across and vanished, one more gigantic one and then the last, it becomes completely silent, and while the rooms slowly absorb the grayness of dawn, deep sleep flows through the empty corridors and apartments.

In every bed people are lying with their knees drawn up, their faces flung violently to the side, profoundly focused, immersed in sleep and surrendered to it without limits.

When someone gets his hands on sleep, he holds on to it convulsively with a fervent, unconscious face, while his breath, getting far ahead of him, wanders on its own along distant roads.

And this is really one great story divided into parts, into chapters and rhapsodies apportioned among the sleepers. When one stops and falls silent another picks up the thread, and so the narrative moves here and there in a broad, epic zigzag while they lie in the rooms of this house inert as poppy seeds in the sections of a great, hollow poppy head and rise on this breathing toward the dawn.

The Pensioner

I am a pensioner in the literal, total meaning of that word, very far advanced in that estate, seriously advanced, a pensioner of high quality.

Perhaps, even in that regard, I have crossed certain final, acceptable boundaries. I do not wish to conceal it; what, after all, is so unusual about this? Why immediately make big eyes and watch with that hypocritical regard in which there is so much concealed joy at a fellow human being's hurt? Indeed, how little of even the most primitive tact do people possess! Such facts must be accepted with the most ordinary expression on one's face, with a certain absentmindedness, and with the insignificance inherent in these matters. One should disregard this effortlessly, humming under one's breath, as it were, just as I disregard it effortlessly and blithely. Perhaps that is I why I am slightly unsteady in my legs and have to place my feet slowly and carefully, one foot in front of the other, and pay careful attention to the direction. It is so easy to deviate in this state of things. The reader will understand that I cannot be too explicit. My form of existence is dependent to the highest degree on discernment, it demands in this regard a good deal of free will. I will appeal to that many times, to its very delicate nuances that one may lay claim to only with a certain discreet winking, made difficult for me especially because of the stiffness of a mask no longer habituated to facial expressions. Anyway, I do not impose myself on anyone, I am far from melting out of gratitude for the asylum kindly afforded me in someone's discernment. I acknowledge this concession without emotion, coolly and with total indifference. I do not like it when someone presents me with a bill of gratitude along with his benevolence. What is best is when I am treated with a certain lightness, a certain healthy severity, jokingly and in a collegial fashion. In this respect, my honorable simplehearted office colleagues, my younger colleagues in the department, have struck the proper tone.

I drop in there sometimes out of habit, around the first of the month, and stand silently next to the railing waiting for them to notice me. Then the following scene plays out. At a certain moment the head of the department, Pan Kawałkiewicz, lays down his pen, signals to the clerks with his eyes, and suddenly says, looking past me into the void of the air with his hand close to his ear, "If my hearing doesn't betray me, sir, it's you, Councillor, who is somewhere in our midst!"

His eyes, focused high above me on the void, change to a squint when he says this, his face smiling playfully.

"I heard a voice in the skies and immediately thought to myself that it must be our beloved councillor!" he cries out in a loud voice, forcefully, as if to someone very far away. "Please make a sign, sir, at least disturb the air where you are hovering."

"Jokes are free, Pan Kawałkiewicz," I say to him quietly right to his face. "I came for my pension."

"For your pension?" Pan Kawałkiewicz shouts, squinting into the air. "You said, 'for my pension.' You are joking, dear Councillor. You have long since been crossed off the list of pensioners. How long do you want to keep collecting your pension, dear sir?"

In that way they make fun of me in a warm, lively, human way. The crude coarseness, the unceremonious grabbing of my arm gives me surprising relief. I leave there strengthened and livelier and hurry home in order to carry into my apartment a bit of that nice internal warmth that is already evaporating.

But, on the other hand, other people . . . the meddlesome, never-uttered question that I constantly read in their eyes—it is impossible to get rid of it. Let us assume that this is the case—then why those long facial expressions right away, those solemn faces, that retreating silence seemingly out of respect, that frightened guardedness? Just so as not to hurt with even a little word, to delicately say nothing about my condition . . . How I see through that game! On the part of those people it is nothing other than a form of sybaritic delectation in oneself, savoring one's own, thank goodness, difference, a violent distancing of themselves from my situation that is masked by their hypocrisy. They exchange expressive glances and are silent and allow those things to grow in silence. My situation! Perhaps it isn't entirely correct. Perhaps there is a certain insignificant defect in it of a fundamental nature! My God! What of it? That is not grounds for immediate and terrified submissiveness. Sometimes I am overcome with hollow laughter when I see that sudden, serious understanding, that eager recognition with which they make room, as it were, for my condition. As if it were simply an irrefutable, decisive, conclusive argument. Why are they so insistent on this point, why is it more important than anything for them, and why does ascertaining this afford them profound satisfaction that they conceal behind a mask of startled sanctimoniousness?

Let us assume that I am, so to speak, a lightweight passenger, in truth, exceedingly lightweight, let us assume that certain questions embarrass me—for example, how old I am, when I celebrate my name day, and so forth. Is that cause for incessantly circling around those questions as if the heart of the matter rested in them? Not that I am ashamed of my condition. Not at all. But I cannot bear the exaggeration with which they inflate the significance of a certain fact, a certain difference that in actuality is as thin as a hair. That entire false theatricality makes me laugh—the solemn pathos that is piled up over this matter, the draping of the moment in a tragic costume full of gloomy pomposity. Whereas in reality? Nothing is more devoid of pathos, nothing more natural, nothing more banal in the world. Lightness, independence, irresponsibility . . . And musicality, the exceptional musicality of the limbs, if I may put it that way. It is impossible to walk past a barrel organ without dancing. Not from gaiety, but because it is all the same to us, and melody has its own will, its insistent rhythm. So I yield. "Margaret, treasure of my soul . . ." It is too light, too irresistible, for one to oppose it, and anyway in the name of what should one oppose such a nonbindingly enticing, such a modest, proposition? So I dance, or rather, I mince in time to the melody with the little trotting step of a pensioner, hopping from time to time. Few people notice this, occupied as they are with their daily running about. One thing I should like to prevent is my reader creating exaggerated notions about my condition. I explicitly caution against overestimating it, *in plus* as well as *in minus*. No romanticism, please. It is a condition like any other, carrying within itself like any other the mark of the most natural intelligibility and ordinariness. All paradoxicality disappears as soon as one is on the other side of the matter. A great disillusionment—that is how I would label my condition—a divesting of all burdens, a dancelike lightness, emptiness, irresponsibility, leveling of differences, loosening of all bonds, a disregard for boundaries. Nothing holds me and nothing restrains me, a lack of resistance, freedom without boundaries. A strange indifference, with which I slip lightly across all the dimensions of being—it ought to be truly pleasant, what do I know? That bottomlessness, that ubiquitousness, as if carefree, indifferent, and lightweight—I don't want to complain. There's a saying: "Don't let the grass grow under your feet." That's it exactly: I long ago stopped cultivating grass.

When from the window of my room located high above I look at the city from a bird's-eye perspective, at the roofs, the fiery walls, and chimneys in the dark gray light of an autumn dawn, at the entire densely built-up landscape only just brought to life out of the night, dawning pale toward yellow horizons that are sliced into bright tatters by the flapping black scissors of the cawing of crows, I feel: this is life. Everyone is lodged in himself, in whatever day to which he awakens, at whatever hour belongs to him, at whatever moment. Somewhere out there in a semidark kitchen coffee is brewing, the cook has gone away, the dirty reflection of a flame dances on the floor. Time, deceived by the silence, flows backward for a moment, and during those uncounted moments night returns and grows on the undulating fur of a cat. Zosia from the second floor yawns for a long time and stretches languorously before she opens the window to do the cleaning; the night air, well rested, having snored its fill, wanders lazily over to the window, crosses it, enters slowly into the dun-colored, smoky grayness of the day. The girl languidly sinks her hands into the dough of the bedclothes, still warm and yeasty from sleep. Finally, with an inner shudder, with eyes filled with the night, she shakes out a large, ample feather bed through the window and fluffs of down float onto the city, tiny down stars, a lazy sowing of nighttime dreams.

Then I dream about becoming a baked-goods delivery man, an electric company lineman, or a bill collector for the health service. Or even a chimney sweep. In the morning, as soon as it's dawn, by the light of the custodian's lantern one enters a gate that is opened only slightly and, carelessly raising two fingers to one's hat brim, with a joke on one's lips, one steps into that labyrinth only to leave it at some late evening hour, on the other side of the city. To make one's way from apartment to apartment for the entire day, conducting a single unfinished, elaborate conversation, from one end of the city to the other, a conversation divided into parts among the tenants, to ask about something in one apartment and receive an answer in the next, to make a joke in one place and long after in more distant places to collect the fruits of laughter. To make one's way amid the slamming of doors through narrow corridors, through bedrooms stacked with furniture, to overturn chamber pots, to bump into creaking baby carriages in which infants are crying, to bend down to retrieve the babies' dropped rattles. To linger longer than necessary in kitchens and hallways where the servants are doing the housework. The girls, bustling about, flex their young legs, tighten their arched soles, play and shimmer with their cheap footwear, clatter with their loose slippers . . .

Such are my daydreams during the irresponsible, marginal hours. I do not repudiate them, although I see their absurdity. Everyone ought to be acquainted with the limits of his condition and know what is appropriate for him.

For us pensioners, autumn is generally a dangerous season. Those who know with what difficulty one arrives in our state at some degree of stability, who know how difficult it is for us pensioners especially to avoid distraction and losing our grip on ourselves, will understand that autumn, with its windstorms, turbulence, and atmospheric confusions, is not helpful in our already imperiled existence.

There are, however, other days in autumn, full of peace and musings, that are kind to us. Now and then there are days like that without sunshine, warm, cloudy, and amber colored at their farther edges. In the gap between buildings a view suddenly opens up deep into the expanses of a sky that is descending lower, ever lower, down to the final windswept goldenness of the farthest horizons. In those perspectives that open out into the very heart of the day, one's gaze wanders as if into the calendar's archives, observes the strata of days as if in cross section, the unfinished registries of time escaping in rows into golden, bright eternity. All of this accumulates and forms ranks in the flaxen, fading formations of the sky, while in the foreground the day is present and the moment, too, and rarely does someone lift his gaze toward the distant shelves of this illusory calendar. Hunched over toward the ground, everyone is rushing somewhere, people are passing one another impatiently and the street is thoroughly crazed with the lines of these pursuits, encounters, and the rushing past. But in that arc of buildings, from where one's gaze soars over the entire lower reaches of the city, over the entire architectonic panorama lit up from behind by a streak of brightness that fades away toward the dull horizon, there is a break and a pause in the tumult. There, on an expanded, bright square they are sawing wood for the city school. Stacked there in squares and cubes are cords of a healthy, vigorous tree, slowly diminishing, log after log, under the saws and axes of the woodcutters. Ah, wood, trusted, honest, estimable material of reality, clear all the way through and dependable, the embodiment of decency and of the prose of life. However deep you may search into its deepest core, you will find nothing that it will not already have revealed on its surface, simply and without reservation, always evenly smiling and bright with the warm, sure brightness of its fibrous pulp woven together into a likeness of the human body. In each fresh cut of a split log a new face appears, but it's always the same, smiling and golden. Oh, that most wondrous complexion of wood, warm without exaltation, healthy through and through, fragrant and dear.

A truly sacramental activity full of dignity and symbolism. The chopping of wood! I could stand for hours like this in the bright arc opened into the heart of a late afternoon and look at those melodiously playing saws, the steady labor of the axes. Here is a tradition as old as the human race. In the bright gap of the day, in the arc of time opened onto yellow, withered eternity, beech trees have been sawn into cords of wood since the time of Noah. The same patriarchal, eternal movements, the same blows and stooping. They stand up to their armpits in that golden carpentry and slowly slice into the cubic meters and cords of wood, sprinkled with sawdust, with a slight reflected spark in their eyes, they chop deeper and deeper into the warm, healthy pulp, into the solid mass, and with every blow they have a golden glimmer in their eyes as if they were seeking something in the core of the wood, as if they wished to hack their way to a golden salamander, a squeaky, fiery little creature always escaping into the very heart of the wood's core. No, they are simply dividing time into small logs, they are husbanding time, filling the cellars with a good, evenly split future for the winter months.

Oh, just to survive this critical time, these couple of weeks, and soon the morning frosts and winter will begin. How I love this entry into winter, still without snow, but with the smell of frost and smoke in the air. I remember such Sunday afternoons in late autumn. Let us suppose it has been raining for the entire week before then, a prolonged spell of nasty autumn weather, until finally the earth, replete with water, begins to dry out and turn dull on its surface, exuding a brisk, healthy coolness. The weeklong sky with its covering of clouds in rags has been raked like mud onto one side of the horizon, where it grows dark in heaps, voluminous and crumpled, and from the west healthy, robust colors of an autumn evening slowly begin to penetrate and color the gloomy landscape. And while the sky slowly cleanses itself from the west, radiating transparent clarity, the servant girls are out walking, dressed in their Sunday best, walking in threes and fours, holding one another's hands down the empty street, which is Sunday clean and drying out between the cottages of the city's outskirts, cottages colorful in the pungent vividness of air that is turning red before dusk; the girls are walking, their dusky faces rounded from the healthy cold, moving their feet elastically in their tight new shoes. A pleasant, moving recollection extracted from the recesses of memory!

Recently, I have been going to the department almost daily. It happens at times that someone falls ill and they allow me to work in his place. Sometimes someone simply has some urgent business in the city and it is possible to substitute for him in the office. Alas, this is not regular work. It is pleasant to have, even for just a couple of hours, one's own chair with its leather cushion, one's own rulers, pencils, and pens. It is pleasant to be jostled or even scolded in a friendly way by one's colleagues. Someone turns to you, someone says a word or two, jokes, banters—and for a moment one blossoms anew. You latch on to someone, hook your homelessness and worthlessness against something alive and warm. The other person walks away and does not feel my weight, does not notice that he is carrying me on himself, that for a moment I am parasitizing his life . . .

But ever since the new office head arrived that, too, came to an end.

Now, if the weather is good, I often sit on a bench in the little square across from the city school. From the neighboring street the thud of axes chopping wood reaches me. Girls and young women are returning from the market. Some have serious, regularly drawn eyebrows, and, gazing out from under them menacingly, slender and glum, they walk along—angels with baskets full of vegetables and meat. Sometimes they stop for a moment in front of the shops and look at themselves in the panes of the display windows. Then they walk away, first casting a proud, commanding glance behind them at the backs of their own shoes. At ten o'clock the janitor walks out to the school doorstep and his clamorous bell fills the street with its din. Then the interior of the school seems suddenly to erupt with a noisy tumult that almost explodes the building. Like fugitives from the general uproar little ragamuffins come flying out of the gate as if from a catapult; shrieking, they race down the stone steps only to undertake some crazy leaps once they find themselves free, flinging themselves into crazy performances improvised blindly between two blinks of an eye. Sometimes they run as far as my bench in these mindless pursuits, hurling unintelligible abuse at me as they run. Their faces seem to come unhinged from the violent grimaces they make at me. Like a herd of preoccupied monkeys commenting parodically on their own clownish stunts, the mob flies past, gesticulating with infernal shrieking. Then I see their upturned, slightly prominent noses incapable of holding back leakage, their mouths opened in a shout and covered with pimples, their small, clenched fists. It happens on occasion that they stop near me. An amazing thing: they take me for a peer. My height has been diminishing for a long time now. My face, slackened and flabby, has acquired a childish appearance. I am somewhat perplexed when they touch me familiarly. The first time one of them suddenly struck me on the chest, I rolled under the bench. But I didn't take offense. They pulled me out from under there blissfully confused and delighted by such fresh, invigorating behavior. This quality of mine—that I don't take offense at any of the violence of their impetuous savoir vivre—gradually wins me respect and popularity. It is easy to guess that since then I have been stocking my pockets diligently with an appropriate collection of buttons, pebbles, empty spools of thread, pieces of gum. This simplifies immeasurably an exchange of thoughts and acts as a natural bridge in establishing friendship. Besides which, absorbed in material interests, they pay less attention to me. Shielded by the arsenal extracted from my pocket I need not fear that their curiosity and inquisitiveness about me will become importunate.

In the end, I resolved to introduce into action a certain thought that had been rankling me more and more insistently for some time.

It was a day without wind, mild and pensive, one of those days in late autumn when the year, having exhausted all the colors and shades of the season, appears to be reverting to the springtime registers of the calendar. The sunless sky had arranged itself into colorful streaks, pleasant layers of cobalt, verdigris, and celadon, framed at the very edge with a streak of whiteness pure as water—the color of April, ineffable and long since forgotten. I put on my best clothes and went into the city not without a degree of stage fright. I walked quickly, with nothing blocking my way in the day's quiet atmosphere, not deviating even once from a straight line. Breathless, I ran up the stone stairs. *Alea iacta est*—I said to myself after knocking at the office door. I assumed a humble posture in front of the headmaster's desk as befit my new role. I was rather flustered.

The headmaster removed a cockchafer on a pin from a glazed little box and brought it obliquely to his eye, looking at it under the light. His fingers were stained with ink, his nails short and cut straight across. He looked at me from behind his spectacles.

"Councillor, you wish to enroll in the first grade?" he asked. "Very praiseworthy, and deserving of recognition. I understand, Councillor, that you wish to rebuild your education from the basics, from the foundations. I always repeat: grammar and the multiplication table are the basics of education. Naturally, we cannot treat you like a pupil subject to school discipline. Rather, like a guest student, like a veteran of the alphabet, so to speak, who after a lengthy exile has somehow called in at the school bench for a second time. He has steered his shattered vessel to that port, if I may put it that way. Yes, yes, Councillor, few people show us this gratitude, this recognition of our merits by returning to us after an age of work, after an age of difficulties, to take their seats here permanently as voluntary, lifelong repeaters. You will be here on exceptional terms, Councillor. I have always said—"

"Excuse me," I interrupted him, "but I would like to mention that as for exceptional terms, I renounce them entirely . . . I do not wish to be privileged. Quite the opposite . . . I would not want to be singled out in any way; it is, of course, important to me that I fit in to the extent possible, disappearing in the gray mass of the class. My entire intention would fall short of its goal if I were in any way privileged in comparison with the others. Even if it is a matter of corporal punishment," and here I raised a finger, "I acknowledge completely its salutary, morally uplifting influence; I stipulate explicitly that in this regard no exceptions should be made regarding me."

"Very praiseworthy, very pedagogical," said the headmaster appreciatively. "In addition, I think," he added, "that in fact your education demonstrates certain gaps as a result of prolonged disuse. In this regard, as a rule we tend to give ourselves over to optimistic illusions that it is easy to dispel. Do you remember, for example, how much five times seven is?"

"Five times seven," I repeated, flustered, feeling confusion welling up to my heart in a warm, blissful wave and veiling the clarity of my thoughts in fog. Dazzled by my own ignorance as if by a revelation, I began to stammer and repeat, half from delight at really returning to childhood ignorance, "five times seven, five times seven . . ."

"As you see," said the headmaster, "it is high time you enrolled in school."

Then, taking me by the hand, he led me to a classroom where a lesson was in progress.

Once again, as half a century ago, I found myself in that uproar, in that room teeming and dark with a swarm of lively heads. I stood there, tiny, in the center, holding the headmaster's coattail, while fifty pairs of young eyes stared at me with the indifferent, cruel objectivity of young animals who see an individual of the same species. From many sides they contorted their faces at me, made faces in rapid, summary enmity, stuck out their tongues. I did not react to these provocations, mindful of the good upbringing I had once received. Looking around at these lively faces, full of clumsy grimaces, I recalled the same situation from fifty years before. At that time, I had stood like this next to Mother while she settled matters with a woman teacher. Now, instead of Mother, it was the headmaster whispering something into the ear of a professor, who nodded his head and stared solemnly at me.

"This is an orphan," he finally said to the class; "he has no father or mother; don't tease him too much."

Tears welled in my eyes at this speech, true tears of tender emotion, and the headmaster, himself deeply moved, tucked me into the front bench.

At that moment a new life began for me. At once, the school completely absorbed me. Never in my old life had I been so preoccupied with a thousand affairs, intrigues, and interests. I was living in a grand state of agitation. A thousand most various interests intersected above my head. I was sent signals, telegrams, was given knowing signs, hissed at, winked at, and reminded every which way in signs of the thousands of obligations I had incurred. I could hardly wait for the end of the lesson, during which out of innate decency I stoically endured all the attacks in order not to miss a word of the professor's lectures. As soon as the bell sounded, the shrieking mob piled on me, attacked me with spontaneous force, practically pulling me apart. They ran up from behind me across the benches, their feet thudding on the desks, they jumped over my head, turned somersaults across me. Everyone yelled his complaints into my ear. I became the center of all deals; the most important transactions, the most complex and sensitive affairs could not be managed without my participation. I walked down the street surrounded always by a rowdy rabble gesticulating urgently. Dogs passed us at a distance, their tails down; cats jumped onto roofs as we approached, and lone youngsters encountered on the way drew their heads down between their shoulders with passive fatalism, resigned to the worst.

School lessons did not lose any of the charm of novelty for me. For example, the art of syllabification. The professor simply appealed to our ignorance, was able to extract it with great skill and cunning, finally reaching that tabula rasa in us that is the foundation for all instruction. Having in this way eradicated in us all our prejudices and habits, he began his teaching from the basics. Laboriously and tensely we melodically stammered out resonant syllables, sniffing during the pauses, and imprinting letter after letter onto the book with our fingers. My primer bore just the same traces of my index finger, concentrated next to the harder letters, as did my classmates' primers.

Once—I no longer remember what the problem was—the headmaster entered the classroom and in the silence that suddenly ensued pointed his finger at three of us, including me. We had to go with him immediately to the office. We knew what that smelled of, and my two accomplices had already started blubbering in anticipation. I looked at their belated remorse impassively, at their faces suddenly transformed by crying as if the human mask had dropped off them with their first tears and laid bare a shapeless pulp of weeping flesh. As for me, I was calm, and with the determination of moral and just natures I submitted to the course of things, prepared to bear with stoicism the consequences of my deeds. That strength of character, which looked like intransigence, did not please the headmaster when we three accomplices stood before him in the office. The professor assisted in this scene with a cane in his hand. With indifference, I unfastened my belt, but the headmaster, taking one look, shouted, "Shameful! Is this possible? At your age?" and gave the professor a scandalized look. "A strange freak of nature," he added with a grimace of disgust. Then, having dismissed the kids, he had a long and grave sermon for me, full of sorrow and disapprobation. But I did not understand him. Chewing my fingernails unconsciously, I looked straight ahead dully and then said, "Pwease, pwofessuh, it was Wacek who spitted on your roll." Already, I was truly a child.

We went to a different school for gymnastics and drawing, where there were special rooms and equipment for those subjects. We marched in pairs, chatting heatedly, introducing into every street that we crossed the sudden uproar of our agitated soprano voices.

That school was a large wooden building converted from a theater hall, old and full of annexes. The interior of the art room resembled an enormous bathhouse, its ceiling supported by wooden columns, and beneath the ceiling a wooden gallery that encircled the room. We ran over to it immediately, storming the stairs, which thudded like a storm under our feet. Numerous side toilets were perfectly suited for playing hide-and-seek. The drawing professor never came; we fooled around without constraint. From time to time the headmaster of this school would drop by the room, place a few of the most raucous among us in a corner, twist the ears of a couple of the wildest ones, but scarcely had he turned to the door than the tumult arose again behind his back.

We did not hear the bell signaling the end of class. It had turned into an autumn afternoon, short and colorful. Mothers came to get some of the boys and led the unruly ones away, scolding and beating them. But for the others, deprived of such loving domestic care, true amusement began only then. Only late at dusk did the old janitor lock up the school and chase us away.

At that time of year, dense darkness still persisted in the morning; when we left for school, the city still lay deep in sleep. We groped our way with outstretched arms, our feet rustling the dry leaves that covered the street in piles. As we walked we held on to the walls of buildings so as not to lose our way. Unexpectedly, in some niche we would brush the face of a schoolmate who was walking in the opposite direction. How much laughter, guessing, and surprises ensued from this! Some had tallow candles; they lit them and the city was seeded with the journeys of these candle ends, sidling along low near the ground in a trembling zigzag, encountering one another and stopping for a moment in order to illuminate a tree, a circle of earth, a pile of withered leaves in which little kids were looking for chestnuts. Also, already in some houses the first lamps were being lit on the second floor, their dim light, magnified, falling into the city night through the squares of windowpanes and lying down in large shapes on the square in front of the houses, on the city hall, on the blind facades of buildings. And when someone, picking up a lamp, goes from room to room, in the courtyard those enormous rectangles of light turn like the pages of a colossal book, and the square seems to roam along the apartment houses and to rearrange shadows and buildings as if laying out a game of solitaire from a great deck of cards.

At last, we arrived at school. The candle stubs were burning out, we were enveloped in the darkness in which we groped our way to our places on the benches. Then the teacher entered, stuck a tallow candle into a bottle, and the boring questioning about vocabulary and declensions began. In the absence of light, lessons were oral and by rote. While someone recited in a monotone, we watched, screwing up our eyes, as golden arrows, tangled zigzags, shot out of the candles and, rustling like straw, intersected in our tightly closed lashes.

The professor poured ink into our inkwells, yawned, looked out into the dark night through the low window. Deep shadow lay under the benches. We dived under there, giggling, moving around on all fours, sniffing one another like animals, carrying out ordinary transactions in the dark and in a whisper. Never shall I forget those blissful early morning hours in school while dawn was slowly breaking outside the windowpanes.

At last, the season of autumn gales arrived. On that day already in the morning the sky was yellow and late, modeled against that background in dull-gray lines of imaginary landscapes, of great, hazy wastelands withdrawing in perspective along diminishing coulisses of hills and folds, crowding together and growing smaller far to the east, where it broke off abruptly like the wavy hem of a soaring curtain and revealed yet another plane, a deeper sky, a gap of frightened whiteness, the pale and terrified light of the most distant distance—colorless, as clear as water, with which as if in final stupefaction the horizon ended and closed down. As in Rembrandt's etchings, on those days, under that streak of brightness, you could see microscopically distinct lands that had never been seen before but now were arising from beyond the horizon under that bright cleft in the sky, flooded with a vividly pale, panicky light, as if they had emerged from another era and another time like a promised land revealed for only a moment to homesick peoples. In this miniature, bright landscape one could see with surprising clarity a train, barely discernible in that distance, moving along on a wavily meandering track, puffing out a silvery white trail of smoke, and vanishing in bright nothingness.

But then the wind rose. It seemed to fall out of that bright gap in the sky, circled, and dispersed across the city. It was composed entirely of softness and gentleness, but in its peculiar megalomania it pretended to be a brute and a bully. It churned, overturned, and tortured the air so that it was dying from bliss. Suddenly, it stiffened in space and reared up, spread out like canvas sails, like enormous, taut sheets that seemed to be cracking a whip; with a fierce mien it tied itself into sturdy knots that shuddered from the tension as if it wanted to fasten the entire atmosphere to the void, but then it pulled on a deceptive end and untied the fake noose, and already a mile farther on it threw its whistling lasso, an entangling lariat that caught nothing.

But what didn't it do with the smoke from the chimneys! The poor smoke did not know how to escape its scoldings, how to bow its head under the blows, whether to right or to left. Thus did it rampage throughout the city, as if it wanted once and for all to establish on that day a memorable example of its unrestrained lawlessness.

Since morning I had had a presentiment of misfortune. I made my way through the windstorm with difficulty. On the street corners, at the intersections of wind gusts, my classmates held me by my coattails. Thus did I cross the city and everything went well. Then we set out to the other school for gymnastics. Along the way we bought pretzels. The long snaking line of us, chattering away, was marching by twos through the gate and into the interior. Another moment and I would have been safe, in a protected place, secure until the evening. If necessary, I could even have spent the night in the gymnastics room. My loyal classmates would have kept me company through the night. Bad luck would have it that Wicek had gotten a new top that day and with a flourish he set it spinning right in front of the school's threshold. The top was whirring, a traffic jam formed near the entrance, I got shoved outside the gate, and at that moment I was snatched away.

"Dear classmates, help!" I cried, already hanging in the air. I could still see their outstretched arms and their screaming, open mouths, and then a minute later I turned a somersault and was drifting in a splendid, ascending line. Already I was flying high above the rooftops. Flying like that and out of breath, with the eyes of imagination I saw my classmates stretching out their arms, wildly pricking up their fingers, and shouting to the teacher, "Professor, Szymek's been swept away!"

The professor looked through his spectacles. He walked calmly over to the window and, shading his eyes with his hand, carefully studied the horizon. But he could no longer see me. In the dull glare from the flaxen sky his face became entirely made of parchment.

"He'll have to be stricken from the directory," he said with a bitter look on his face and walked over to his desk. But I was being carried higher and higher into yellow, unexplored autumn space.

Loneliness

Now that I can go out into the city doing so has been a great comfort for me. But for how long did I not leave my room! Those were bitter months and years.

I cannot explain the fact that it is my old room from childhood, the room farthest from the porch, rarely visited already in those days, continually forgotten, as if it did not belong to the apartment. I no longer remember how I wandered into it. It seems to me that it was a bright night, a watery-white, moonless night. I saw every detail in a gray glow. The bed was unmade, as if someone had just left it; I listened intently in the silence to check if I could hear slumbering people breathing. Who could possibly be breathing here? I have lived here ever since. I have been sitting here for years feeling bored. If only I had thought beforehand of stocking up on things! Ah, you who are still capable, who have been given your own time for this, gather up supplies, hoard grain, good and nourishing sweet grain, because a great winter will come, years lean and hungry will come, and the earth in the land of Egypt will not bear fruit. Alas, I was not like a provident hamster; I was like a careless field mouse, living from day to day without a care for tomorrow, confident in my talent as a starveling. Like a mouse, I thought, "What can hunger do to me? As a last resort I can even gnaw on the wood or shred paper into tiny pieces with my tiny snout. The poorest animal, a gray church mouse—at the tail end of the Book of Creation—I will manage to live on nothing." And so I do live on nothing in this dead room. The flies have long since died out in it. I place my ear against the wood, to check if perhaps a grub might be scratching inside it. The silence of the grave. Only I, an immortal mouse, a lonely posthumous child, am rustling about in this dead room, endlessly running across the table, the étagère, the chairs. I glide like Aunt Tekla in a long gray dress reaching to the ground, nimble, swift, and small, dragging my rustling tail behind me. I am sitting now in broad daylight motionless on the table, as if stuffed, my eyes, like two beads, bulging and glittering. Only the end of my little snout pulses, barely visibly, chewing daintily out of habit.

This is to be understood metaphorically, of course. I am a pensioner, not a mouse. It is a characteristic of my existence that I parasitize metaphors; I am so easily carried away by the first fine metaphor. Having gone too far with this I must now withdraw with difficulty, returning slowly to reason.

What do I look like? Sometimes I see myself in a mirror. An amazing, laughable, and painful thing! It is shameful to admit it. I never see myself *en face*, face-to-face. But a bit deeper, a bit farther away, there I am, standing in the depths of the mirror seen slightly from the side, slightly in profile, standing there sunk in thought and glancing off to the side. I stand there motionless, glancing off to the side and slightly behind myself. Our gazes no longer meet. When I move, he moves, too, but turned halfway to the back, as if he is not aware of me, as if he has gone beyond many mirrors and can no longer return. Grief grips my heart when I see him so alien and indifferent. After all, it is you, I want to cry, who were my faithful reflection, you accompanied me for so many years, and now you don't recognize me! O God! Alien, and looking somewhere off to the side, you stand there and seem to be listening intently somewhere in the depths, waiting for a word, but from over there, from the glass depths, obedient to someone else, awaiting orders from somewhere else.

I sit like this at the table and leaf through old, yellowed university lecture notes—my only reading.

I look at the faded, threadbare curtain, I see how it billows slightly from the cold breath from the window. I could do exercises on that curtain rod. An excellent barre. How easily one turns somersaults on it in the sterile, so often reused air. Almost casually one performs an elastic *salto mortale*—coolly, without inner participation, purely speculatively, as it were. When one stands acrobatically on this barre, on the tips of one's toes, touching the ceiling with one's head, one feels that it is somewhat warmer at this height, one has a faintly tangible illusion of a milder atmosphere. Since childhood I have liked to look at the room from a bird's perspective.

I sit and listen to the silence. The room is whitewashed simply with lime. At times, crow's-feet-like cracks break out on the white ceiling, at times a flake of plaster drops down with a rustling sound. Must I reveal that my room is walled in with bricks? How can that be? Walled in? By what means could I get out? That's it exactly: there is no barrier to goodwill, nothing will resist intense desire. I have only to imagine doors, good, old doors, as in the kitchen of my childhood, with an iron handle and a bolt. There is no room so walled up that it cannot be opened with such a trusted door if only one has enough strength to insinuate it.

Father's Final Escape

This was in the late, dismal period of total disorder, during the period of the final liquidation of our business. The sign above the door to our shop had long since been taken down. Near the half-lowered blinds Mother was carrying on an illicit trade in the remnants. Adela had left for America. It was said that the ship she sailed on sank and all the passengers lost their lives. We never confirmed this rumor; news of the girl vanished, and we heard no more about her. A new era began, empty, sober, and joyless—as white as paper. A new servant girl, Genia, anemic, pale, and boneless, crept softly through the rooms. If someone stroked her back, she writhed and stretched like a snake and purred like a cat. She had a dull-white complexion that even under the lids of her enamel eyes was not pink. Sometimes, in a distracted state, she made a roux from old invoices and ledger sheets—sickening and inedible.

At that time my father had already died definitively. He had died numerous times, always not yet entirely, always with certain reservations that forced a revision of this fact. This had its good side. By breaking up his death into installments, Father was accustoming us to the fact of his departure. We grew indifferent to his ever more diminished returns, which were more pitiful each time. The physiognomy of the already absent man dispersed, as it were, in the room in which he lived; it branched out, creating in certain spots the most amazing knots of resemblance of an unbelievable clarity. In some places the wallpaper imitated the shudders of his tic, arabesques formed themselves into his laughter's painful anatomy, arranged as symmetrical limbs like the petrified imprint of a trilobite. For a while we kept a great distance from his polecat-lined fur coat as we walked past. The fur coat breathed. The panic of the animals biting one another and sewn together blew through them in feeble shudders and was lost in the folds of cloth. Pressing one's ear to it one could hear the melodious purring of their amicable slumber. In that well-tanned form, with the slight odor of polecat, murder, and nocturnal rutting, he would have been able to survive for years. But here, too, he did not last long.

Once, Mother came home from the city with a troubled look on her face.

"Look, Józef," she said, "what a happy coincidence. I caught him on the stairs, jumping from step to step." And she lifted a handkerchief off something she was carrying on a plate. I recognized him at once. The resemblance was unmistakable, although he was now a crab or a large scorpion. Profoundly struck by the clarity of the resemblance that, through such changes and metamorphoses, continued to impose itself with simply irresistible force, we confirmed this for each other in an exchange of glances.

"Is he alive?" I asked.

"It goes without saying; I can hardly restrain him," said Mother. "Should I release him onto the floor?"

She placed the plate on the floor, and, leaning over him, we observed him more attentively now. Sunken among his many arched legs, he was moving them almost imperceptibly. His slightly raised pincers and antennae seemed to be listening intently. I tipped the saucer and Father stepped cautiously, with a certain hesitation, onto the floor, but once he'd touched the flat ground under himself, he suddenly set off running with all his dozen or so legs, clattering with his hard little arthropod's bones. I blocked his path. He hesitated, touching the obstacle with his waving antennae, after which he raised his pincers and turned sideways. We allowed him to run in his chosen direction. On that side, no furniture could shelter him. Running like that in wavering shudders on his many legs, he made it to the wall and, before we could realize it, climbed it lightly without stopping, with all the armature of his limbs. I shuddered with instinctive revulsion, following the multilegged journey advancing and flapping across the wallpaper. In the meantime, Father reached the small kitchen cabinet mounted on the wall, hung over its edge for a moment, explored with his pincers the interior terrain of the cabinet, and then all of him crawled inside.

It was as if he were becoming newly acquainted with the apartment from this new crab's perspective, getting to know objects by smell, perhaps, since despite close observation I was unable to discover any organ of sight in him. He appeared to deliberate slightly over the objects he encountered on his way, stopping near them for a moment, touching them lightly with his waving antennae, even embracing them, as if testing with his pincers whether he was familiar with them, and only after a moment would he disengage from them and run on, dragging behind him his abdomen, raised slightly off the floor. He behaved the same way with the bits of bread and meat that we tossed onto the floor for him in the hope that he would eat them. He only felt them hastily and ran on, not recognizing edible things in these objects.

One might think, seeing his patient reconnaissances in the space of the room, that he was searching for something assiduously and tirelessly. From time to time he ran into a corner of the kitchen under the water bucket, which was leaking, and when he reached the puddle he appeared to be drinking. Now and again he gave promise of lasting for entire days. He seemed to be capable of getting along without food, and we did not notice his vital signs decreasing at all as a result. With mixed feelings of shame and revulsion we nourished a secret fear during the day that he might visit us in bed during the night. But that did not happen even once, although during the day he wandered all over the furniture and liked especially to spend time in the space between the wardrobes and the wall.

Certain manifestations of intelligence, and even of a certain teasing play-fulness, could not be overlooked. Never, for example, did Father fail to appear in the dining room at mealtime, although his participation at dinner was purely platonic. If the dining room door was closed by accident during dinner and Father found himself in the adjoining room, he would keep scratching under the door, running back and forth along the crack, for as long as it took until it was opened for him. Later, he learned to insert his pincers and legs into this lower crack, and, after rather intense rocking of his body, he would succeed in pushing himself sideways under the door and into the room. That seemed to make him happy. Then he would be motionless under the table, lying absolutely quiet, with only his abdomen lightly pulsing. What that rhythmical pulsing of his glossy abdomen meant we were unable to figure out. It was something ironic, indecent, and mean that seemed to express at one and the same time a kind of low, salacious satisfaction. Nimrod, our dog, would walk up to him slowly and without conviction, sniff him carefully, sneeze, and walk away indifferently, not having reached a decisive conclusion.

The disorder in our home spread in wider and wider circles. Genia slept for days on end, her slender body undulating flaccidly with her deep breath-ing. We often found in the soup spools of thread that she had tossed in along with the vegetables because of her inattentiveness and a peculiar absent-mindedness. The shop was open *in continuo* day and night. The clearance sale by the half-lowered blinds followed its intricate course day after day amid haggling and arguments. On top of everything, Uncle Karol arrived.

He was strangely disconcerted and uncommunicative. He declared with a sigh that after the last sad experiences he had decided to change his way of life and take up the study of languages. He did not leave the house, locked himself up in the last room, from which Genia, filled with reproof for this new guest, dragged out all the carpets and tapestries, after which he immersed himself in the study of old price lists. Several times he maliciously attempted to step on Father's abdomen. With shouting and horror, we for-bade him to do this. He only laughed maliciously to himself, unconvinced, while Father, unaware of the danger, cautiously came to a stop over some spots on the floor.

My father, nimble and lively as long as he was standing on his legs, shared with all crustaceans the characteristic that, if turned over onto his back, he became completely defenseless. It was a bitter, pitiful sight when, desperately waving all his little legs, he rotated helplessly on his back around his own axis. It was impossible to look without bitterness at this too-evident, articulated, almost shameless mechanics of his anatomy, lying, so to speak, on the surface and not veiled by anything from the side of his naked, multilegged belly. At such moments Uncle Karol was roused to the point of trampling him. We would run to the rescue and give Father some object that he could grasp convulsively with his pincers and skillfully regain his normal position, immediately setting off running back and forth in a lightning-fast zigzag, with redoubled speed, as if he wanted to erase the memory of his compromising fall.

I regret that I must master myself in order to relate truthfully an inconceivable fact from which my entire being recoils. To this day I cannot comprehend that we were, to the fullest extent, conscious perpetrators of this fact. In this light the event acquires the character of some strange fate. For fate does not bypass our consciousness and will but incorporates them into its own mechanism so that we permit and accept, as in a lethargic dream, things before which under normal conditions we recoil.

When, shaken by the fait accompli, I asked Mother in despair, "How could you have done that! If at least it was Genia who had done it, but you yourself . . ." Mother wept, wrung her hands, was unable to give me an answer. Did she think that it would be better for Father that way, did she see in this the only exit from his hopeless situation, or did she simply act out of incomprehensible carelessness and thoughtlessness? . . . Fate finds a thousand devices when it is a matter of carrying out its incomprehensible will. Some tiny, momentary eclipse of our intellect, a moment of blindness or inattention suffices to smuggle a deed between the Scylla and Charybdis of our resolutions. Afterward, one can endlessly interpret and explain motives ex post, investigate the motives—but the fait accompli remains irreversible and foredoomed once and for all.

We came back to our senses and shook off our blindness only when my father was carried in on a platter. He lay there large and swollen as a consequence of boiling, pale gray and gelatinous. We sat in silence, mortified. Only Uncle Karol extended his fork toward the platter, but he dropped it uncertainly halfway there, looking at us in astonishment. Mother ordered that the platter be set aside in the salon. He lay there on the table covered with a plush cloth, next to a photograph album and a music box that held cigarettes, lay there avoided by us and motionless.

However, the earthly journey of my father was not to end there, and the continuation, the prolongation of his story beyond its apparently final permissible borders is the most painful point. Why did he not give up at last, why did he not recognize in the end that he was defeated when, truthfully, he already had every reason to do so and fate could go no farther in its utter subjugation of him? After several weeks of lying motionless he somehow became consolidated and appeared to be slowly coming back to himself. One morning we found the platter empty. Just one leg was lying on the edge of the plate, dropped on the congealed tomato sauce and aspic trampled during his escape. Boiled, losing legs along the way, he had dragged himself onward with his remaining strength, on to his homeless journey, and we never laid eyes on him again.

Other Stories

Autumn

Do you know that time when summer, recently so lush and full of vigor, universal summer embracing in its expansive sphere everything that can be imagined—people, events, and objects—one day acquires a barely perceptible flaw? The sun's radiance still falls plentifully and profusely, there is still a grand, classical gesture in the landscape that the genius of Poussin has bequeathed as a legacy to this time of year, but—strange to say—we return from a morning outing strangely bored and unproductive: could it be that we are ashamed of something? We feel a bit uneasy and avoid one another's glances. Why? And we know that at dusk one person or another will go with an embarrassed laugh to a secluded corner of the summer to knock, knock at the wall, to see if the tone is still entirely full, reliable. There is in that attempt the perverse delight of betrayal, of unmasking, a slight shiver of scandal. But officially we are still full of respect, full of loyalty: such a solid firm, such an excellently endowed firm . . . And despite this, when on the next day the news of insolvency spreads, it is already yesterday's news and there is no longer the explosive power of scandal. And while the sale at auction takes its sober, invigorating course, the profaned apartments empty out and are stripped and become filled with a clear, sober echo; this does not awaken any regret or sentiment—the entire liquidation of summer contains within itself the lightness, indolence, and insignificance of a delayed carnival that persisted until Ash Wednesday.

And yet pessimism is perhaps premature. Negotiations are still going on, the summer's reserves are still not exhausted, it may still come to full restitution . . . But deliberation and composure are not characteristic of vacationers. Even hoteliers, hoteliers up to their eyeballs in the shares of summer, capitulate. No! So little loyalty and reverence toward a faithful ally does not testify to a great merchant style! They are sellers at market stalls, little, cowardly people who do not think about the long term. Each one of them clutches his purse with its hoarded savings against his belly. They have cynically cast off the mask of courtesy, shed their dinner jackets. Out of each of them crawls a former payer.

And we, too, are packing our trunks. I am fifteen years old and not in the least burdened with the obligations of practical life. Because there is still an hour remaining before departure, I run out one more time to bid the summer resort farewell, to reassess the summer's goods, to see what can be taken with me and what must be left forever in this town condemned to annihilation. But in the small roundabout of the park, empty now and bright in the afternoon sunshine, near the monument to Mickiewicz the truth about the summer is revealed to me in my soul. In the euphoria of this revelation I climb the two steps of the monument, describe with my gaze and outspread arms a broad arc as if addressing the entire resort, and say, "Farewell, Season! You were very beautiful and rich. No other summer can compare with You. Today, I admit this, although often I was very unhappy and sad because of You. I leave to You as a souvenir all my adventures scattered through the park, the streets, the gardens. I cannot take with me my fifteen years; they will remain here forever. In addition, on the veranda of the villa in which I lived I inserted into a chink between two beams a drawing I made for You as a souvenir of me. Now You are descending into the shadows. Together with You this entire town of villas and gardens will descend into the land of shadows. You have no offspring. You and this town will die, the last of your race.

"But You are not without fault, O Season. I shall tell You wherein lay Your fault. You did not wish, O Season, to confine Yourself to the boundaries of reality. No reality satisfied You. You looked beyond every realization. Not finding satisfaction in reality, You created superstructures out of metaphors and poetic figures. You moved about in the associations, allusions, imponderabilia between things. Every thing alluded to some other thing, and that one appealed to another farther off, and so on, without end. Your eloquence was boring in the end. People became fed up with that coming and going on waves of endless phraseology. That's right, phraseology—pardon the word. This became clear when, here and there, a yearning for relevance began to awaken in many souls. At that moment You were already defeated. The boundaries of Your universality became visible, and Your great style, Your beautiful baroque, which was appropriate for reality during Your good times, now turned out to be a mannerism. Your sweetness and Your pensiveness bore the mark of youthful exaltation. Your nights were immense and endless, like the megalomaniacal sighs of lovers, but they were swarms of apparitions, like the ravings of hallucinators. Your fragrances were excessive and beyond the capacity of humans for rapture. Under the magic of Your touch everything dematerialized and grew toward its more distant, always higher, forms. Your apples were eaten while dreaming about the fruits of heavenly landscapes, and near Your peach trees people thought about ethereal fruits that could be consumed by the sense of smell alone. You had on Your palette only the highest registers of colors; you did not know the satiety and the firmness of dark, earthy, rich browns. Autumn is the yearning of the human soul for materiality, for relevance, for boundaries. When for obscure reasons people's metaphors, projects, dreams begin yearning for realization, the time of autumn arrives. These phantoms, which until then were dispersed in the most distant spheres of the human cosmos, coloring its high vaults with their specters, now draw close to man, seek the warmth of his breath, the close, cozy shelter of his home, the alcove where his bed stands. A man's home becomes, like the stable in Bethlehem, the heart around which all the demons, all the spirits of the higher and lower spheres condense space. The time of beautiful, classical gestures, of Latin phraseology, of southern theatrical curves has passed. Autumn seeks firmness for itself, the rustic strength of Dürers and Bruegels. The form cracks from an excess of matter, hardens into knots and burls, it grasps matter in its jaws and pincers, harasses it, violates it, crushes it, and releases it from its hands with traces of the struggle, logs half worked on with the mark of extraordinary life in the grimaces it has stamped into the wooden faces."

This and much more I said to the empty semicircle of the park, which seemed to be retreating in front of me. I tossed out from myself only several words of this monologue, either because I could not find the appropriate words or because I was only feigning a speech, supplementing the missing words with gestures. I pointed out the walnuts, the classical fruits of autumn related to the furniture in the room, nutritious, tasty, and long-lasting. I mentioned chestnuts, those polished models of fruits, bilboquets created for the amusement of children, autumnal apples, turning red with that good, homey, prosaic red on the windows of apartments.

Dusk had already begun to stifle the air when I returned to the pension. In the yard, two large carriages designated for our departure were already in position. The unsaddled horses were snorting, their heads plunged into feed bags. All the doors were wide-open and the candles burning on the table in our room flickered in the draft. The rapidly descending darkness, the people who were losing their faces in the dusk and hastily carrying out chests, the disorder in the open, ravaged room—all this gave the impression of a kind of hasty, sad, belated panic, a tragic, startled catastrophe. At last, we took our seats in the deep carriages and set off. The dark, deep, robust air of the fields blew across us. With their long whips, the coachmen fished out succulent cracks from the intoxicating air and carefully regulated the horses' rhythm. Their powerful, magnificent withers bearing us away swayed in the darkness amid the fluffy beating of their tails. Thus, one after the other, did these two conglomerations of horses, thudding coach bodies, and wheezing leather bellows travel on through the lonely nighttime landscape without stars or lights. At times they appeared to be disintegrating, coming apart like crabs dividing into pieces in flight. Then the coachmen took up the reins more tightly and gathered together the disorganized hoofbeats, closing them up into disciplined, regulated teams. From the lighted lanterns elongated shadows fell into the depths of the night, lengthened, broke free, and vanished in great leaps into the wild wasteland. They escaped stealthily on their long legs in order to—somewhere far off, at the edge of the forest—mock the coachmen with derisive gestures. The coachmen cracked their whips at them with broad movements and did not permit themselves to be thrown off balance. The city was already asleep when we drove in among the houses. Here and there lanterns were burning in the empty streets as if created for the purpose of illuminating a certain building with a low second story and a balcony, or to imprint on one's memory the number above a locked gate. Taken by surprise at this late hour, the tightly shuttered shops, the entrances with their slippery thresholds, the signs tossed about by the night wind, all displayed a hopeless abandonment, the profound orphanhood of things left to themselves, things forgotten by people. My sister's carriage turned into a side street while we drove on toward the market square. The horses changed the rhythm of their pace when we drove into the deep shade of the square. A barefoot baker on the threshold of an open doorway shot a glance at us with his dark eyes; the apothecary's window, still vigilant, was serving and retracting the raspberry lotion in a large show globe. The pavement thickened under the horses' feet, individual and doubled clatter of horseshoes emerged out of the jumble of hoofbeats, growing more distinct and less frequent, and our house with its shabby facade slowly moved out of the darkness and stopped in front of the carriage. The servant girl opened the door for us, holding in her hand an oil lamp with a reflector. Our immense shadows appeared on the stairs, breaking against the vaulted ceiling of the stairwell. The apartment was illuminated only by a candle whose flame wavered in the breeze from an open window. The dark wallpaper was overgrown with the mold of afflictions and the bitterness of many sick generations. The old furniture, awakened from sleep and extracted from lengthy loneliness, seemed to look at the returnees with bitter knowledge, with patient wisdom. "You will not escape from us," they seemed to be saying; "in the end you must return to the circle of our magic, for we have already divided up among ourselves all your movements and gestures, your standing up and your sitting down, and all your future days and nights. We are waiting, we know . . ." The huge, deep beds, piled high with cool bedding, were waiting for our bodies. The floodgates of night were already creaking under the pressure of dark masses of sleep, the dense lava that was threatening to break out, to pour out from the sluice gates, the doors, the old wardrobes, the stoves, in which the wind was sighing.

The Republic of Dreams

Here on the streets of Warsaw, in these tumultuous days, fiery and intoxicating, I am transported in thought to the distant city of my dreams, I soar with my gaze above this low land, expansive and undulating like a coat of God's thrown down as a colorful canvas at the threshold of heaven. For this entire land underpins the sky, holds it upon itself, the colorfully vaulted, manifold sky, full of cloisters, triforia, rosaces, and windows onto eternity. Year after year, this land grows into the sky, merges with the dawns, turns entirely angelic in the reflected gleams of the great atmosphere.

Where the map of the land is already very southern, tawny from the sun, darkened and scorched from the summer weather, ripe as a pear, there it lies—like a cat in sunshine—this chosen region, this singular province, this city unique in all the world. It is futile to speak of this to the uninitiated! Futile to explain that with the long, wavy tongue of earth with which this land pants in the scorching heat of summer, with this canicular promontory toward the south, this spur inserted alone between swarthy Hungarian vineyards—this hinterland detaches itself from the entirety of the region and proceeds unaccompanied, single-handed, along an untried road, attempting on its own to be a world. This city and this region locked themselves into a self-sufficient microcosm, installed themselves at their own risk on the very brink of eternity.

The gardens on the city outskirts stand as if on the edge of the world and look across the fences into the infinity of an anonymous plain. Just beyond the tollgates the country's map becomes nameless and cosmic, like Canaan. Above this narrow, doomed scrap of earth the sky opened up once again deeper and more expansive than anywhere else, a vast sky, like a cupola, many storied and engulfing, filled with unfinished frescoes and improvisations, flying draperies and violent ascensions into heaven.

How to express this? When other cities expanded into economics, grew into statistical figures, into numbers—our city descended into essentiality. Here, nothing happens in vain, nothing occurs without profound meaning and without premeditation. Here, events are not an ephemeral phantom on the surface, here they have roots in the heart of things and reach for what is essential. Here, every minute something is resolved in exemplary fashion and for all time. Here, all matters happen only once and irrevocably. That is why there is such gravity, a deep accent, sorrow in what takes place here.

Now, for example, the courtyards are drowning in nettles and weeds, the sheds and storerooms, crooked and moss covered, are sinking up to their armpits in enormous burdocks that tower as high as the eaves of their shingled roofs. The city is under the sign of the weed, of wild, passionate, fanatical vegetation shooting out cheap, shoddy greenery, poisonous, virulent, and parasitic. The weeds are on fire, ignited by the sun, the leaves' windpipes gasping from the burning chlorophyll—armies of nettles, lush and voracious, devour the floral cultures, invade the gardens, overgrow at night the unguarded rear walls of houses and barns, multiply in roadside ditches. It is amazing what frenzied vitality, vain and unproductive, inheres in that passionate bit of green substance, that derivative of sun and groundwater. From a pinch of chlorophyll it brings forth and expands in the fire of these days that lush, vacant tissue, the green pulp disseminated a hundred times onto millions of leafy surfaces, greenly pierced with light and veined, diaphanous with watery, vegetative, herbal blood, moss covered and hairy, with a pungent, weedy, rustic odor.

In those days the rear window of the shop's stockroom facing the courtyard was blinded with a green film, full of green shinings, leafy reflections, spongy flutters, undulating pieces of greenery, the monstrous profusion of this courtyard, its hideous abundance. Descending into deep shade, the stockroom leafed glimmeringly through all the hues of greenery, green reflections diffused in it like waves through the entire depth of its vaulting as in a soughing forest.

The city fell into this profusion as if into a hundred-year sleep, unconscious from the heat, deafened by the glare, and slept cocooned a hundred times over in a spiderweb, overgrown with weeds, breathless and empty. In rooms green from the bindweed on the windows, submarine and murky, as if on the bottom of an old bottle, tribes of flies were taking their final breaths, imprisoned forever and locked in a painful mortal agony, reduced to monotonous, long-winded lamentations, to angry and pitiful buzzing. Slowly, the window collected this entire lacy, scattered fauna for a final, deathbed sojourn: enormous, long-legged mosquitoes that for a long time knocked at the walls with the quiet vibrations of errant flights before they landed on the windowpanes for the final time, immobile and dead, an entire genealogical tree of flies and insects grown in this window and branching into a slow journey along the panes, the multiplied generations of these mysterious winged seedpods, azure, metallic, and vitreous.

On the shop's display windows large, bright, blind awnings flap silently in the hot breeze and blaze with their stripes and undulations in the radiance. The dead season runs rampant in the empty squares and on streets swept clean by the wind. The distant horizons, swollen with gardens, stand in the radiance of the sky, dazzled and unconscious, as if they had only just flown down as an immense, garish canvas from the celestial void—bright, blazing, tattered in flight—and in a moment already spent, awaiting a new blast of radiance in which to be renewed.

On these days what can one do, where can one escape from the heat, from the heavy sleep that pounds one's chest like a nightmare in the burning hour of noon? On these days, Mother would hire a carriage and we would all drive out, crammed inside its black box—the salesclerks on the coachman's seat with their bundles or clinging to the springs—outside the city, to "the Hillock." We drove into a hilly, undulating landscape. The carriage, alone on the road, climbed for a long time in the scorching heat between the humps of the fields, burrowing in the golden, hot dust of the high road.

The horses' backs tensed into arcs, their glistening rumps surged laboriously, brushed off at every moment by the fluffy strokes of their tails. The wheels rolled along slowly, squeaking on the axles. The landau passed flat pastures sown with molehills among which cows were distributed everywhere—forked and horned—immense, shapeless skins full of bones, knots, and pinnacles. They lay monumentally, like burial mounds, the distant, floating horizons reflected in their peaceful gaze.

At last, we would come to a stop at "the Hillock" beside a wide tavern with stone walls. It stood by itself in the watershed, standing in relief against the sky with its extensive roof, on the towering border of two sloping expanses of land. The horses made it to the high edge with difficulty, halted there on their own, lost in thought, as if at a tollgate dividing two worlds. Beyond the toll-gate the view opened out onto a vast landscape that was cut by high roads, faded and opalescent like a pale Gobelins, and wrapped in immense, empty, azure air. A breeze rose from that distant, undulating plain, lifted the horses' manes from their necks, and flowed on beneath the high, pure sky.

We would stop here for the night, or else Father would give a sign and we would drive into that country, vast as a map, branching out expansively with high roads. Ahead of us on distant, winding roads moved the carriages, barely visible at this distance, that had overtaken us. They proceeded down the bright high road among the cherry trees and straight to the spa, which was still small at that time and was snuggled in a narrow forested valley full of the murmurs of streams, running water, and the rustling of leaves.

In those distant days for the first time my friends and I adopted the impossible, absurd idea of wandering even farther, beyond the spa, into a land that was no one's and God's, into a disputed, neutral borderland where the boundaries of countries got lost and a wind rose spun mistakenly under a high, towering sky. We wanted to dig in there, be independent of the adults, go out entirely beyond the limits of their sphere, proclaim a republic of the young. Here we would constitute a new, independent legislature, erect a new hierarchy of measures and values. It was to be a life under the sign of poetry and adventure, ceaseless brainstorms and astonishment. It seemed to us that all we needed to do was push aside the barriers and borders of convention, the old riverbeds in which the course of human affairs was confined, so that the elements, the great deluge of the unforeseen, the flood of romantic adventures and plots would force their way into our lives. We wanted to submit our lives to the stream of the plot-weaving elements, the inspired high tide of history and events, and to allow ourselves to be carried by the swollen waves, passive and devoted to them alone. The spirit of nature was fundamentally a great storyteller. From its core the eloquence of fables and novels, romances and epopees flowed out in an unstoppable stream. The entire great atmosphere was full of plot elements milling about. One had only to set snares under a sky full of phantoms, drive in a stake that would play the wind, and already the scraps of the novel trapped by it would be flapping around its top.

We decided to become self-sufficient, to create a new basis of life, to establish a new era, to once again constitute the world on a small scale—for us alone, to be sure, but according to our taste and likes.

It was to be a fortress, a *Blockhaus*, a fortified post commanding the vicinity—half citadel, half theater, half visionary laboratory. All of nature was to be harnessed into its orbit. As in Shakespeare, this theater ran out into nature, was not fenced off by anything, grew into reality, taking into itself impulses and inspiration from all the elements, undulating with the great high tides and ebb tides of natural cycles. Here was to be the crucial node of all the processes running through the great body of nature, here all the threads and plots that wandered deliriously in its great, misty soul were to enter and exit. We wanted, like Don Quixote, to admit into our lives the riverbed of all stories and romances, to open its borders to all intrigues, imbroglios, and peripeteias that join together in the great atmosphere that outbids itself in fantasticality.

We dreamed that the vicinity would be threatened by some undefined danger, winnowed by a mysterious threat. Against this danger and threat we found safe shelter and asylum in our fortress. Thus, packs of wolves ran through the vicinity, bands of highwaymen prowled the forests. We planned security and fortifications; filled with delightful shivers and pleasant anxiety we prepared for a siege. Our gates swallowed up fugitives from the ruffians' knives. They found shelter and safety with us. Calèches chased by wild beasts galloped up to our gates. We played host to distinguished, mysterious strangers. We got lost in conjectures, yearning to penetrate their incognito. At night they all gathered in the great hall by the light of flickering candles; we listened to stories and confidences one after another. At a certain point the intrigue pervading these stories left the frames of narratives and entered among us—alive and hungry for victims, entangling us in its dangerous whirlpool. Unexpected recognitions, sudden revelations, an improbable encounter invaded our private lives. We lost our footing, threatened by peripeteias that we ourselves had unleashed. The howling of wolves reached us from afar, we reflected upon romantic imbroglios, half drawn in ourselves into their whirlpools, while outside the window the unfathomable night was soughing, full of unformulated aspirations, ardent and unlimited confessions, bottomless, inexhaustible, entangled a thousandfold within itself.

It is not without cause that such long-ago dreams are returning today. It occurs to me that no dream, no matter how absurd and preposterous, goes to waste in the universe. A kind of hunger for reality is enclosed in dreaming, a kind of pretension that obligates reality, grows imperceptibly into a liability and a claim, a bill of indebtedness that demands to be covered. We renounced our dreams of a fortress long ago, but then years later someone turned up who grasped it, took it seriously, someone naive and faithful in his soul, who took it literally, at face value, took it into his hand like a simple, unproblematic thing. I saw him, I spoke with him. He had unbelievably azure eyes, created not for looking but only for turning endlessly blue in daydreams. He told me that when he arrived in this region about which I am speaking, in this anonymous land, virginal and belonging to no one, it immediately smelled to him of poetry and adventure, he noticed in the air the prepared contours and the phantom of myth hanging over the vicinity. He discovered in the atmosphere the preformed shapes of that concept, plans, elevations, and tables. He heard a summons, an inner voice, like Noah when he received his orders and instructions.

He was visited by the spirit of this concept, lost in the atmosphere. He proclaimed a republic of dreams, the sovereign territory of poetry. On such and such a number of hectares, on a canvas of the landscape thrown into the forests, he announced the indivisible dominion of fantasy. He marked the borders, laid the foundations of a citadel, changed the environs into a single immense rose garden. Guest rooms, cells for solitary contemplation, refectories, dormitories, libraries . . . solitary pavilions among the park, bowers and belvederes . . .

Anyone chased by wolves or brigands who makes it to the gates of this citadel is saved. He is led inside triumphantly, his dust-covered clothing is removed. Festive, blissful, and happy, he enters into Elysian breezes, into the rosy sweetness of the air. Cities and affairs, days and their fever remain far behind him. He has entered a new, festive, glittering normality, shed his body like a shell, cast off the grimacing mask adhering to his face, he has pupated and liberated himself.

The Blue-Eyed One is not an architect; rather, he is a director. A director of landscapes and cosmic scenery. His artistry is based on his catching the intentions of nature, his ability to read her secret aspirations. For nature is full of potential architecture, planning, and building. What did the builders of the great centuries do that was different? They overheard the broad pathos of expansive squares, the dynamic perspective of distances, the silent pantomime of symmetrical avenues. Long before Versailles, clouds arranged themselves in expansive summer evening skies into expansively developed Escorials, aerial, megalomaniacal residences; they tried out in stage productions, in towering stacks, in immense, universal compositions. This great theater of the unconstrained atmosphere is an inexhaustible source of ideas, planning, aerial preliminary budgets; it hallucinates an architecture immense and inspired, city planning that is cloudlike and transcendental.

Human works have this characteristic: completed, they close in on themselves, cut themselves off from nature, stabilize according to their own laws. The work of the Blue-Eyed One did not emerge from great cosmic ties; it inheres in them, made half human like a centaur, harnessed into the great periods of nature, not yet ready and still maturing. The Blue-Eyed One invites everyone to continuation, to building, to cocreation—we are all, after all, dreamers by nature, brothers under the sign of the trowel, we are by nature builders . . .

The Comet

I

That year, the end of winter was under the sign of an especially propitious astronomical conjuncture. Colorful harbingers of the calendar blossomed red in the snow on the boundaries of early mornings. From the burning red of Sundays and holidays a reflection fell onto half a week and those days burned cold with a false, straw fire; deceived hearts beat more vigorously for a while, dazzled by that heralding red that heralded nothing and was only a premature alarm, a colorful calendar sham, painted in garish vermilion on the cover of the week. Beginning on Three Kings' Day we sat night after night around the white pageantry of a table glistening with candlesticks and silver, laying out endless games of solitaire. With every passing hour the night outside the window became brighter, frosted and glistening throughout, full of endlessly sprouting almond trees and candies. The moon, an inexhaustible quick-change artist, entirely immersed in its late lunar doings, performed its phases in turn, ever brighter and brighter, dealing out all the tricks of preference, duplicated in every color. Already, it often stood to the side during the day, ready ahead of time, brass colored and with no radiance—a melancholy jack with its glossy clubs—and awaited its turn. In the meantime, entire skies of fleecy clouds passed across its lonely profile in a quiet, white, expansive wandering, barely covering it with the changing, mother-of-pearl fish scale into which the colorful firmament congealed toward evening. Then the days were already turning the pages emptily. A gale flew through with a roar above the rooftops, blew out the cooled-down chimneys all the way to the bottom, erected imaginative scaffolds and stories over the city, and demolished the rumbling, overhead structures with a crashing of rafters and beams. At times a fire broke out in a distant suburb. Chimney sweeps ran across the city at the height of roofs and porches under the verdigris, riven sky. Crossing from one expanse of roof to another, beside the promontories and flags of the city they dreamed in that aerial perspective that for a moment the gale was opening up for them the lids of the roofs above the servant girls' alcoves and soon afterward slamming them shut over the great, agitated

251

book of the city—intoxicating reading for many days and nights. Then the gale winds grew tired and stopped. In the shop window the salesclerks hung up springtime materials and the atmosphere became gentler with soft colors of wool, turned lavender, blossomed with pale reseda. The snow contracted into itself, folded up into an infant's fleece, turned dry, and vanished in the air, drunk up by cobalt breezes, swallowed again by the expansive, concave sky without sun and without clouds. Here and there oleanders were already blossoming in apartments, windows were opened, and the mindless chirping of sparrows filled the room in the dull pensiveness of an azure day. Over the clean squares violent squabbles of chaffinches, bullfinches, and tits came together for a moment with a piercing cheeping—then they flew off in all directions, swept by a puff of wind, erased, annihilated, in the empty azure. For a moment what remained after them in one's eye were colorful flecks—a handful of confetti thrown blindly into bright space and then drowned at the bottom of the eye in neutral azure.

The premature spring season began. Lawyers' apprentices wore small mustaches curled upward in spirals and high, stiff collars and were models of elegance and chic. On days undermined by a windstorm as if by a flood, when a gale raged noisily high up above the city, they braced their backs against the wind and with coattails flying they doffed their colorful bowler hats to ladies they knew, returned glances, full of determination and delicacy, so as not to expose their goddesses to slander. The ladies lost their footing for a moment, uttered terrified shrieks, their dresses flapping against them, and, regaining their balance, replied with a smile to their bows.

In the afternoon, the wind usually died down. On the porch, Adela cleaned the great copper saucepans that rattled metallically under her touch. The sky stood motionless above the shingled roofs, breathless, branching out with blue roads. The salesclerks, dispatched from the shop on some errand, lingered near her for a long time at the entrance to the kitchen, leaning against the porch balustrade, drunk with the daylong wind and the confusion in their heads from the deafening chirping of sparrows. From far away a breeze carried the lost refrain of a barrel organ. It was impossible to hear the quiet words they formed under their breath as if reluctantly, with an innocent look on their faces, but which were in fact calculated to scandalize Adela. Pierced to the quick, thoroughly irritable, she reacted violently, reviled them passionately, and her face, gray and clouded over with springtime dreams, turned crimson from anger and amusement. They lowered their eyes with sordid devotion, with vile satisfaction at having succeeded in throwing her off balance.

Days and afternoons came and went, everyday events flowed on in the turmoil above the city viewed from the height of our porch, above the labyrinth of roofs and houses in the murky glow of those gray weeks. Tinkers raced around, proclaiming their services, occasionally in the distance one of Shloma's mighty sneezes punctuated the city's distant, scurrying tumult like a witty punch line; on some remote square, Tłuja the madwoman, driven to despair by the boys' bantering, would start dancing her wild saraband, flinging her skirt high to the delight of the mob. A gust of wind would smooth and even out these outbursts, blend them into a monotonous, gray din, and spread them uniformly over the sea of shingled roofs in the milky, smoky air of afternoon. Adela, leaning against the porch balustrade, looking out over the distant, agitated noise of the city, would pick out all the louder accents, assemble the lost syllables with a smile, attempting to connect them, to discern some meaning from the great, gray, rising and falling monotony of the day.

The age was under the sign of mechanics and electricity, and an entire swarm of inventions was spilling onto the world from under the wings of human genius. In bourgeois homes cigar boxes equipped with an electric lighter appeared. A switch was turned and a swarm of electric sparks ignited a wick dipped in gasoline. This aroused unprecedented hopes. A music box in the shape of a Chinese pagoda, wound with a key, instantly began playing a miniature rondo, rotating like a carousel. Little bells trilled on the corners, the wings of tiny doors opened wide, displaying a revolving core of a barrel organ, a snuffbox-style triolet. Electric bells were installed in every house. Home life was under the sign of galvanism. A coil of insulated wire became the symbol of the time. Elegant youths demonstrated Galvani's phenomenon in drawing rooms and received the radiant gazes of the ladies. An electric conductor opened a path to women's hearts. The heroes of the day blew kisses over their successful experiment amid the drawing rooms' applause.

There wasn't long to wait before the city was teeming with velocipedes of various sizes and shapes. A philosophical outlook on the world held sway. Whoever professed the idea of progress drew the conclusion and mounted a velocipede. The first were, naturally, the apprentice lawyers, that avant-garde of new ideas, with their curled-up mustaches and colorful bowler hats, the hope and flower of our youth. Scattering the boisterous mob, they rode into the crowd on enormous bicycles and tricycles, their wire spokes twanging. Resting their hands on their wide handlebars, from their high perches they maneuvered the enormous wheel that sliced into the frolicking rabble along a wavy, crooked line. Some of them were seized by an apostolic frenzy. Rising on their revolving pedals as if in stirrups, they addressed the people from on high, proclaiming a new, happy era for mankind—salvation through the bicycle—and rode on amid the applause of the public, bowing to them on all sides.

And yet there was something pitifully compromising in those splendid, triumphant rides, a painful, pitiful dissonance to which they inclined at the peak of triumph and then descended into their own self-parody. They must have sensed this themselves when, suspended like spiders among the filigreed apparatus, astride their pedals like great leaping frogs, they executed their waddling movements among the broadly rolling hoops. Only one step separated them from ridiculousness and they took it despairingly, leaning on their handlebars and doubling their speed—a gymnasticized knot of violent acrobats turning somersaults. Is that surprising? Through the power of an impermissible joke, here man entered a realm of unprecedented conveniences achieved too cheaply, below cost, almost free, and the disproportion between the investment and the result, the obvious cheating of nature, the excessive payment of the brilliant trick, was evened out by self-parody. These lamentable conquerors, martyrs to their own genius, rode among spontaneous bursts of laughter—so great was the comedic power of these miracles of technology.

When for the first time my brother brought home from school an electromagnet, when with an inner shudder we all experienced the touch of secretly vibrating life locked up in the electric circuit, Father smiled with superiority. In his head a far-reaching idea was maturing, a chain of long-since accepted suspicions was concentrating and closing. Why did Father smile to himself, why did his eyes, filling with tears, roll back into their orbits in comically mocking devotion? Who could say? Did he sense a crude trick, a vulgar intrigue, a transparent machination beyond the amazing manifestations of secret power? Father's turn to laboratory experiments dates from that moment.

Father's laboratory was simple: a few pieces of wire twisted into coils, a couple of jars of acid, zinc, lead, and coal—that was the entire workshop of this most peculiar esoteric.

"Matter," he said, lowering his abashed eyes over his muffled sniggering, "matter, gentlemen . . ."

He did not complete the sentence, allowing us to surmise that he was on the trail of a coarse joke, that all of us who were sitting there had been thoroughly duped. With lowered eyes Father quietly sneered at this perennial fetish.

"*Panta rhei!*" he exclaimed and indicated with a movement of his hands the eternal circulation of substance. Long ago he had yearned to mobilize the hidden powers circulating in it, to liquefy its stiffness, to pave the way for its universal penetration, transfusion, circulation, the only thing appropriate to its nature.

"*Principium individuationis* is rubbish," he said, and by this he expressed his boundless contempt for this chief human principle. He dropped those words in passing, running along the wire, half closed his eyes, and with a delicate touch palpated various places in the circuit, sensing a faint difference in potency. He made notches in the wire, leaned down, listening intently, and was already ten steps farther along in order to repeat this activity at another point in the circuit. He seemed to have ten hands and twenty senses. His scattered attention worked in a hundred places simultaneously. Not a single point in space was free from his suspicions. He would lean down, pricking the wire at some point in the circuit, and, with a sudden glance behind him, he would pounce like a cat at the prepared spot and, embarrassed, miss.

"Excuse me," he would say, turning suddenly to the astounded witness who was closely observing his manipulations, "excuse me, I need precisely that bit of space that you are occupying with your person—would you be so kind as to yield it for a moment?" And he would hastily perform his instantaneous measurements, nimble and skillful as a canary hopping dexterously on the tremors of his specific nerves.

Metals immersed in solutions of acids, briny and growing tarnished in that painful bath, began to transmit in the darkness. Awakened from numb torpor, they hummed monotonously, sang metallically, glowed intramolecularly in the endless dusk of those funereal, late days. Invisible charges surged at the poles and crossed them, disappearing into the whirling darkness. A barely audible tingling, blind swarming currents ran across the polarized space into concentric lines of power, into the circulation and spirals of the magnetic field. Now here, now there, the apparatuses sent signals from their sleep, responding to one another with a delay, too late, in hopeless monosyllables, dash, dot, in intervals of profound lethargy. Father stood among these wandering currents with a painful smile, shaken by the stammering articulation, the wretchedness pent up once and for all, with no way out, signaling monotonously in crippled semisyllables from unliberated depths.

As a result of these experiments, Father reached amazing conclusions. He demonstrated, for example, that an electric bell, based on the principle of the so-called Neeff hammer, is an ordinary mystification. It was not man who broke into the laboratory of nature but nature that dragged him into her own machinations, achieving by means of his experiments her own aims that led who knows where. During dinner, my father touched the nail of his thumb to the handle of a spoon immersed in soup and Neeff's bell started clattering in the lamp. The entire apparatus was an unnecessary pretext, it did not pertain to the issue; Neeff's bell was a place at which certain impulses of substances converged, seeking their path through a man's quick wits. Nature wanted and made it happen that man was an oscillating arrow, a shuttle in the weaving workshop, shooting now here and now there according to nature's will. Man himself was only a component, a part of Neeff's hammer.

Someone dropped the word *mesmerism* and Father grasped it greedily. The circle of his theory had closed; it had found its final link. Man, according to this theory, was only a transitional stage, a temporary knot of mesmeric currents entangled here and there in the bosom of eternal matter. All the discoveries with which he had triumphed were traps into which nature lured him, they were snares of the unknown. Father's experiments began to take on the character of magic and prestidigitation, the taste of a parodic juggling. I will not mention the various experiments with pigeons, which in the course of waving a wand he manipulated into two, three, ten, in order afterward, gradually and with difficulty, to manipulate them back into a wand. He tipped his hat and they flew out one after the other with a flutter, returned to reality in their complete number, filling the table with a waving, bustling, cooing flock. Sometimes he would interrupt himself at an unexpected point in his experiment, standing indecisively with his eyes half shut, and after a moment would trot with tiny steps to the hall, where he would stick his head into the chimney flue. It was dark there, muffled with soot and blissful as in the very heart of nothingness; warm currents wandered up and down. Father would close his eyes and stand there for some time in that warm, black nothingness. We all felt that this incident did not belong to things, it was somehow outside the wings of the matter; we turned a blind eye internally to that supramarginal fact that belonged to an entirely different order of things.

My father had in his repertoire truly disconcerting arts, impressive in their genuine melancholy. In our dining room the chairs had high, beautifully carved backs. They were some kind of garlands of leaves and flowers in realistic taste, but Father's light touch sufficed for the carving to suddenly acquire unusually witty physiognomy, a vague appearance; it would begin to twinkle and wink knowingly, and it was inexpressibly embarrassing, almost unbearable, until the winking stopped taking on an entirely defined direction, an undefeated irrefutability, and one or another of those present would begin to cry, "Aunt Wanda, as God is my witness, it's Aunt Wanda!"—and the ladies would begin to squeal, because it was like a living Aunt Wanda, no, she herself was already paying a visit, already sitting and engaging in her endless discourse, not allowing anyone else to say a thing. Father's miracles self-destructed, because it was no specter, it was the real Aunt Wanda in all her ordinariness and commonness, which did not permit even the thought of a miracle.

Before we move on to further events from that memorable winter, it is necessary to touch briefly upon a certain incident that is always shamefully hushed up in our family chronicle. What had happened to Uncle Edward? He had come to visit us, not suspecting anything, bubbling with health and industriousness; he had left his wife and daughter in the country longing for his return; he arrived in the best of humor in order to have some fun, to enjoy himself away from his family. And what happened? Father's experiments had an electrifying impact on him. Right after his first tricks he stood up, took off his coat, and placed himself entirely at Father's disposal. Without reservation! He uttered this phrase with an intense glance and powerful handshake. My father understood. He ascertained that Uncle had no traditional prejudices as to *principium individuationis*. It turned out that no, he had none, none at all. Uncle was liberal and without superstition. His only passion was to serve science.

Initially, Father left him a modicum of freedom. He did the preparations for a basic experiment. Uncle Edward made use of his freedom by taking in the city's sights. He bought a velocipede of impressive size and rode in an enormous circle around the market square, peering into second-floor windows from the height of his seat. Riding past our house, he doffed his hat elegantly before the ladies standing at the window. His mustache ends were turned up in spirals and he had a little pointed beard. Soon, however, he became convinced that a velocipede was not capable of leading him into the deeper mysteries of mechanics, that this brilliant apparatus was in no condition to reliably supply metaphysical shudders. And that is when the experiments began for which Uncle's lack of prejudices as to the *principium individuationis* turned out to be so indispensable. Uncle Edward had no reservations about giving himself physically, for the good of science, to reduce himself to the bare foundation of the Neeff hammer. He agreed without regret to the gradual reduction of all his qualities with the goal of baring his deepest essence, identical, as he had long since felt, with the aforementioned principle.

Having locked himself in his study, Father began the gradual disassembling of Uncle Edward's complicated essence, a torturous psychoanalysis spread over a series of days and nights. His study table began to fill with the disassembled complexes of his ego. In the beginning, Uncle was still partaking of our meals; extremely reduced, he attempted to participate in our conversations, he rode his velocipede one more time. Then he gave that up, seeing himself as more and more depleted. A certain variety of shame appeared in him, which was characteristic of the state in which he found himself. He avoided people. At the same time, Father was coming closer and closer to the goal of his procedures. He reduced him to the essential minimum, removed one after another everything that was nonessential. He placed him high up in a niche in the wall of the stairway cupboard, organizing his parts according to the principles of the Leclanché cell. The wall was covered with mold at this spot, a fungus had spread out its whitish plaits. Without any scruples, Father made use of Uncle's entire capital of enthusiasm, extended his thread along the entire length of the hall and the left wing of the house. Moving on a ladder along the wall of the dark corridor, he drove little nails into the wall along the entire track of his present life. Those smoky, yellowish afternoons were almost completely dark. Father used a lit candle with which, from close up, he illuminated the moldy wall, inch by inch. There are versions of the story in circulation that have Uncle Edward, so heroically self-controlled up to this point, at the last moment demonstrating a certain impatience. People even say that it actually came to a violent, although belated, explosion that nearly shattered the almost completed work. But the installation was ready and Uncle Edward, who had been a model man, father, and businessman all his life, now in this final role, too, submitted in the end to higher necessity.

Uncle functioned excellently. There was no occasion on which he refused obedience. Emerging from his intricate complication, in which he had so often gotten lost and confused in the past, he at last found the purity of a uniform, straightforward principle to which he would submit unfailingly from then on. At the cost of his multiplicity, administered with such difficulty, he had now achieved a simple, unproblematic immortality. Was he happy? There's no point in asking. That question has meaning if it is a matter of beings in whom a wealth of alternatives and possibilities is concealed, thanks to which present reality can be opposed to partially real possibilities and be reflected in them. But Uncle Edward had no alternatives; the contrast—happy/unhappy—did not exist for him, because he was identical to himself to the outermost limits. It was impossible to refrain from a certain recognition, seeing him so punctually, so precisely functioning. Even his wife, Aunt Teresa, when she arrived after a while on her husband's trail, could not refrain from pressing the button in order to hear that sonorous, shrill voice in which she recognized the former timbre of his voice when he was irritated. As for their daughter Edzia, one might say that her father's career delighted her. True, later she took a form of revenge on me, avenging herself for my father's deed, but that belongs to a different story.

II

Days passed, the afternoons became longer. There was nothing to be done with them. The excess of still-raw time, still unfilled and without practical application, prolonged the evenings with empty twilights. After washing the dishes early and cleaning up the kitchen, Adela, forlorn, stood on the porch, looking vacantly at the evening distance turning a pale red. Her beautiful eyes—prominent, large, shining—so expressive at other times, stared fixedly in a dull reverie. Her complexion, faded and gray by the end of winter from fetid kitchen odors, was growing younger now under the influence of the springtime gravitation of the moon, which was swelling from one quarter to the next and was gathering milky reflections, opalescent tones, the sheen of enamel. She was triumphing now over the salesclerks, who had lost their self-confidence under her dark glances, had fallen out of their roles as the blasé frequenters of saloons and brothels, and, shocked by her new beauty, were seeking a different platform for closeness, ready for concessions on the matter of the new state of relations, for recognizing positive facts.

Father's experiments, despite all expectations, did not introduce a revolution in our common life. The grafting of mesmerism on the body of modern physics did not turn out to be fruitful. It was not that there was no grain of correctness in Father's discoveries. But truth is not what determines the success of an idea. Our metaphysical hunger is limited and quickly succumbs to satiation. Father was standing right on the threshold of revelatory discoveries just when in all of us, in the ranks of his followers and adherents, reluctance and demoralization began to creep in. The signs of impatience were ever more frequent, going as far as open protests. Our nature rebelled against the relaxation of fundamental laws, we had had enough of miracles, we yearned to return to the old, trusted, solid prose of eternal order. And Father understood this. He understood that he had gone too far and he arrested the flight of his ideas. The company of elegant female disciples and male adherents with their twisted mustaches was melting away from one day to the next. Father, desiring to retreat with honor, intended to pronounce his final, conclusive lecture when suddenly a new event turned everyone's attention in an entirely unexpected direction.

One day, my brother, upon returning from school, brought the improbable and yet true news about the near end of the world. We ordered him to repeat it, judging that we had misheard. But no. That is exactly what that unbelievable news, incomprehensible in every respect, proclaimed. Indeed, just as it was, unprepared and unfinished, at some chance point in time and space, without a settling of accounts, not having made it to any finish line, as if in the middle of a sentence, without a period or exclamation point, without divine judgment and wrath—somehow on the best of terms, loyally, according to mutual agreement and mutually recognized principles—the earth was supposed to meet its end, just like that and irreversibly. No, it was not the eschatological end long since predicted by prophets, the tragic finale and final act of the divine comedy. No, it was rather a bicycling circus act, an upsy-daisy-prestidigitating, splendidly hocus-pocus, edifyingly experimental end of the world—amid the applause of all the spirits of progress. There was almost no one who would not be instantly persuaded. The horrified and protesting were instantly shouted down. Why could they not understand that it was simply an unprecedented chance, the most progressive, freethinking end of the world, astride the height of time, plainly honorable and bringing honor to the Most High Wisdom? People persuaded one another fervently, they drew *ad oculos* on pages torn out of notebooks, demonstrated irrefutably, opponents and skeptics were beaten on the head. In the illustrated magazines full-page prints appeared, images foreseeing the catastrophe in impressive mise-en-scènes. One could see in them populated cities in nighttime panic under a sky magnificent with luminous signals and phenomena. People had already seen the astonishing influence of the distant bolide whose parabolic apex, directed continuously at the earth's globe, remained in the sky in motionless flight, approaching with the speed of so many, many miles per second. As in a circus farce caps and bowler hats flew into the air, hair stood on end, umbrellas opened by themselves, and bald spots were bared beneath flying wigs—under the black, enormous sky, twinkling with the simultaneous alarm of all the stars.

Something festive poured into our life, a certain enthusiasm and ardor, a certain importance and solemnity entered into our movements, expanded our chests with cosmic breathing. The globe of the earth hummed at night from a ceremonial din, from the unanimous ecstasy of thousands. The nights became black and immense. Galaxies of stars coalesced around the earth in countless swarms. In the black planetary spaces the swarms were randomly arranged, showering the dust of meteors from one abyss to another. Lost in the infinite expanses, we felt the globe of earth slip out from under our feet; disoriented, confusing directions, we hung upside down like antipodeans above the inverted zenith and wandered among the astral swarms, running a licked finger from star to star across entire light-years. Thus, we wandered across the sky in a disorderly, extended line, running in every direction over the infinite rungs of night—émigrés from a deserted globe, ransacking the infinite swarms of stars. At last the barriers opened and the bicyclists rose into the black starry expanse; performing wheelies on their velocipedes, they continued in motionless flight in the planetary void that kept opening up with ever newer constellations. Flying like that along a blind track, they traced the roads and paths of a sleepless cosmography, in actuality, however, remaining in planetary lethargy, black as soot, as if they had stuck their heads into the opening of a stovepipe, the final finishing line and goal of all those blind flights.

After a short, disorderly, half-slept day, the night opened up like an enormous swarming fatherland. Crowds poured into the street, spilled into the squares, head to head, as if barrels of caviar had been broken open and were rolling along like streams of shining buckshot, flowing in rivers under a night black as tar and tumultuous from the stars. Stairways broke beneath the weight of thousands, in every window distressed figurines appeared, human matches on moving pieces of wood were crawling across the parapet in a somnambulistic frenzy, forming living chains like ants, mobile pileups and columns—standing atop one another's shoulders—pouring down from the windows onto the platforms of the squares, bright from the radiance of tar barrels.

Please forgive me if in describing these scenes full of enormous pileups and tumult I fall into exaggeration, modeling myself inadvertently on certain old etchings in the great book of defeats and catastrophes of the human race. After all, they aspire to a single ur-image, and this megalomaniacal exaggeration, the enormous pathos of these scenes, indicates that here we have knocked out the bottom of the age-old barrel of memories, a kind of ur-barrel of myth, and have broken into the prehuman night full of babbling elements, of burbling anamnesis, and we can no longer hold back the swelling flood. Ah, those piscine, swarming nights, stocked with the fry of stars and glittering with scales; ah, these schools of little mouths indefatigably swallowing in tiny gulps, in hungry swallows all the swollen, undrunk streams of those black, torrential nights! To what fatal fykes, what wretched seines, were these dark generations multiplied a thousand times over drawing close?

Oh, the skies of those days, all in luminous signals and meteors, marked by the calculations of astronomers, traced over a thousandfold, initialed and marked with watery algebraic signs. With faces blue from the glories of those nights, we wandered through skies pulsing with the explosions of distant suns, amid sidereal illuminations—human swarms flowing in a wide band along the shoals of the Milky Way spilled over the entire sky, a human stream above which the cyclists towered on their spidery apparatuses. Oh, the starry arena of night, etched by acrobatics to the outermost peripheries; oh, the spirals, arcana, loops of those elastic rides, the cycloids and epicycloids executed in inspiration along the diagonals of the sky, losing wire spokes, indifferently dropping gleaming rims, already racing naked, now solely on a pure idea of a bicycle, to the luminous finish line! After all, a new constellation dates from those days, a thirteenth constellation accepted forever into the community of the zodiac, radiant from then on in the sky of our nights: "the Cyclist."

During those nights apartments were wide-open in the light of wildly smoking lamps. Window curtains fluttered, flung far into the night, and the enfilades of rooms stood like that in the all-embracing, incessant draft that cut right through them in one unceasing, wild alarm. It was Uncle Edward sounding the alarm. Yes, he'd finally lost patience, broken off all ties, trampled the categorical imperative, broken away from the rigors of his high morality, and sounded the alarm. He was hastily stoppered by means of a long rod and kitchen rags, an attempt was made to stem his violent explosion. But even gagged like that, he clamored wildly, rattled unconsciously, rattled unrestrainedly; he was indifferent to everything now, and life was leaving him with that rattling, he was bleeding in front of everyone without help in his fatal fury.

Occasionally, someone dropped in for a moment to the empty rooms pierced with this violent alarm, among lamps burning with a high flame; he would run a couple of steps on tiptoe from the threshold and stop hesitantly, as if seeking something. The mirrors took him without a word into the transparent depths and divided him silently among themselves. Uncle Edward clamored at the top of his lungs through all the bright and empty rooms, and the lone deserter from the stars, filled with a bad conscience as if he had come to commit a wicked deed, would retreat stealthily from the apartment, deafened by the alarm, and aim for the door, escorted out by the sensitive mirrors that let him pass between their gleaming rows, while in their depths a swarm of startled doubles raced around on tiptoe in various directions with a finger to their lips.

Again, the sky opened above us, its vastnesses strewn with star dust. In this sky the fatal bolide was already appearing night after night at an early hour, tilted to one side, suspended from the peak of its parabola, aimed motionlessly at the earth, swallowing to no avail so many thousands upon thousands of miles per second. All eyes were focused on it while it, shining metallically, cylindrical in shape and somewhat brighter in its convex core, performed its daily pensum with mathematical precision. How difficult it was to believe that this tiny worm, shining innocently amid the countless swarms of stars, was the fiery finger of Balthazar inscribing on the tablets of the sky the destruction of our globe. But every child knew by heart the fatal formula framed in the pipelike symbol of the multiple integral from which, after the insertion of the limits, our inevitable doom resulted. What could possibly save us?

While the rabble ran wild in the great night, getting lost among astral radiances and phenomena, Father remained covertly at home. He alone knew the secret way out of this snare, the rear wings of cosmology, and he was smiling slyly. While Uncle Edward was desperately sounding the alarm, gagged with rags, Father was silently sticking his head into the stovepipe vent. It was hollow and too black in there to see straight. It smelled of warm air, soot, seclusion, and a refuge. Father settled down comfortably and blissfully closed his eyes. Into that black diving suit of the house, protruding above the roof into the starry night, fell the faint glimmer of a star and, refracted as if in the lenses of a telescope, it sprouted as light in the focal point of the lens and germinated like an embryo in the dark retort of the chimney. Father carefully turned the screw of the micrometer, and that fatal creature, bright as the moon, slowly emerged into the telescope's field of vision, brought as close as one's hand by the lens, plastic and shining like a limestone statue in the silent blackness of the planetary void. It was somewhat scrofulous and riddled with pockmarks—the moon's very own brother, a lost double returning after a thousand years of wandering to its maternal globe. My father moved it close up in front of his bulging eye like a round of Swiss cheese cratered with holes, pale yellow, brightly illuminated, covered with white spots like leprosy. With his hand on the micrometer screw, his eye dazzled by the light of the eyepiece, Father cast his cold gaze across the limestone globe; he saw on its surface the intricate drawing of the sickness shaping it from inside, the tortuous little channels of the spruce bark beetle excavating its cheeselike, worm-eaten surface. Father shuddered, spotted his mistake: no, it was not Swiss cheese, it was most obviously a human brain, an anatomical section of a brain in all its intricate construction. Father saw clearly the borders of the lobes, the ganglia of gray matter. Narrowing his gaze even more intensely, he read even the faint letters of the inscriptions running in various directions on the intricate map of the hemisphere. The brain appeared to be chloroformed, deeply put under, and blissfully smiling in its sleep. Reaching the core of that smile, through the tangled sketch on the surface Father caught sight of the essence of the phenomenon, and he smiled to himself. What is not revealed to us by our own trusted chimney, black as black can be! Through the ganglia of gray matter, through the minute granulation of infiltrations, Father clearly distinguished the translucent contours of an embryo in the characteristic head-over-heels position, with its little fists against its face, on its back, sleeping its blissful sleep in clear amniotic fluid. Father left it in that position. He stood up with relief and closed the stovepipe's vent.

This far and no farther. How can that be, and what happened to the end of the world, with that glorious finale after such a splendidly developed introduction? A lowering of the eyes and a smile. Had an error crept into the calculations, a tiny mistake in addition, a printer's typo while entering the digits? Nothing of the sort. The calculation was exact, no error had stolen into the columns of ciphers. Then what on earth happened? Please pay attention. The bolide raced bravely, reared up like an ambitious stallion in order to reach the finish line in time. Current fashion ran along beside it. For some time it flew at the head of the age to which it gave its shape and name. Then these two brave steeds drew even and galloped even faster parallel to each other, our hearts beating in solidarity with them. But then fashion slowly edged ahead by the length of a nose, overtaking the indefatigable bolide. That millimeter decided the comet's fate. It was already doomed, outdistanced once and for all. Our hearts were already running with fashion, slowly leaving behind the glorious bolide; we watched indifferently as it grew pale, diminished, and finally stopped, resigned, on the horizon, tilted sideways, already taking its final turn on its curving path in vain, distant and pale blue, forever harmless. Powerless, it dropped out of the competition, the power of up-to-dateness was exhausted and no one worried about the one that had been outrun. Left to itself, it shriveled silently amid universal indifference.

We returned with bowed heads to our everyday occupations, richer by one disillusionment. Cosmic perspectives were hastily furled, life returned to its usual paths. We slept uninterruptedly night and day during those days, sleeping off the wasted time. We lay side by side in already dark apartments, overcome with sleep, carried away on our own breathing along the blind path of starless reveries. Floating like that, we billowed—squeaky bellies, bagpipes and hornpipes, fighting with melodious snoring through all the rough terrain of the already closed and starless nights. Uncle Edward had fallen silent forever. There was still an echo of his alarmed despair in the air, but he himself was no longer alive; life had escaped from him in that rattling paroxysm, the circuit had opened, he himself had ascended without hindrance into ever higher degrees of immortality. In the dark apartment Father alone remained vigilant, wandering around silently in rooms full of melodious sleeping. Occasionally, he would open the chimney vent and look with a smile into the dark maw where an eternally smiling homunculus, locked in a glass ampule, slept his luminous sleep, circumnavigated by the fullness of light as by neon, already doomed, crossed out, set aside for the files—an archival entry in the great registry of the sky.

Fatherland

At last, after many vicissitudes and turns of fate that I do not intend to describe here, I found myself abroad, in a country fervently yearned for in the reveries of my youth. The fulfillment of lengthy dreams came too late and in circumstances entirely different from the ones I had imagined. I entered there not as a victor but as a castaway from life. That country, imagined as the stage set of my triumphs, was now the terrain of miserable, inglorious little defeats in which I was losing, one after the other, my high, proud aspirations. Now I was struggling only for bare life itself and, knocked about, rescuing my wretched little bark as best I could from shipwreck, driven here and there by fate's changing inclinations, I finally stumbled upon the provincial city of medium size where in my youthful daydreams the villa, the refugium of an old and famous master from the turmoil of the world, was supposed to stand. Not even noticing the irony of fate in the confluence of accidents, I intended to stop there now for a time, to perch somewhere, perhaps to spend the winter, until the next gust of events. I did not care where fate would carry me. The charm of that land was extinguished irreversibly for me; depressed and emaciated, by now all I yearned for was peace.

It turned out differently, however. Apparently, I had reached a certain turning point in my road, a particular turn in my fate, and my existence unexpectedly began to stabilize. I felt as if I had entered an auspicious current. Everywhere I turned I found a situation that seemed to have been made for me; people immediately tore themselves away from what they were doing as if they had been waiting for me, and I would notice an unconscious gleam of attention in their eyes, an immediate decision, a readiness to serve me as if under the dictate of a higher authority. It was, naturally, an illusion, evoked by an appropriate coming together of circumstances, the skillful linking of the elements of my fate under the capable fingers of chance that led me as if in a somnambulistic trance from event to event. There was scarcely time to marvel; along with that auspicious streak of fate a certain resigned fatalism set in, a blissful passivity and trustfulness that ordered me to submit without resistance to the gravitation of events. Hardly had I sensed this as the fulfillment of a long-unsatisfied need, as a profound satiation of the eternal hunger of a rejected and unrecognized artist, than I was finally recognized here for my abilities. From a café fiddler seeking any kind of work I rapidly advanced to first violin in the city orchestra; exclusive circles enamored with art opened before me and I entered the best company as if on the basis of a right achieved long ago—I, who until then had existed half in the underground world of déclassé existences, of stowaways beneath the deck of society's ship. Aspirations that had led a tormenting underground life in the depths of my soul in the form of repressed and rebellious pretensions, rapidly became legal, entered life on their own. The mark of usurpation and vain grandiosity fell from my brow.

I am relating all of this in abbreviated form, rather as one aspect of the general line of my fate, without going into the details of that strange career, since all these incidents actually belong to the prehistory of the events narrated here. No, my happiness had nothing at all in it of excess and profligacy as one might assume. Only, a feeling of profound peace and certainty came over me, a sign by which I, an experienced physiognomist of fate sensitized by life to all the twitches on its face, recognized with profound relief that this time fate would not conceal from me any criminal intentions. The quality of my happiness was of the lasting and dependable sort.

My entire past as a wanderer, the homeless, subterranean misery of my past existence, broke away from me and flew back like an expanse of land, bent slantwise in the rays of the setting sun, once again looming above the late horizon, while the train carrying me away, taking the final curve, carried me straight into the night, its breast full of the future beating against its face, the stalwart, intoxicating, slightly smoke-seasoned future. Here is the place where I should mention the most important fact that closed and crowned this epoch of industriousness and happiness—Eliza, whom I met at that time during my travels and whom, after a brief, intoxicating engagement, I took as my wife.

The bill for my happiness is closed and full. My position in the opera is unshakable. The conductor of the philharmonic orchestra, Maestro Pellegrini, values me and consults my opinion in all decisive matters. He is an old man on the brink of retirement and there is an unspoken agreement between him, the opera's board of trustees, and the city's musical society that after his retirement the conductor's baton will pass into my hands without any fuss. I have already held it many times, whether conducting the monthly philharmonic concerts or in the opera as replacement for the sick maestro, or when the kindly old man did not feel strong enough to cope with a new, fashionable score whose spirit was alien to him.

The opera is among the best paid in the country. My salary is entirely sufficient for life in an atmosphere of prosperity not deprived of the gilding of a certain luxury. Eliza has arranged the couple of rooms that we occupy according to her taste, whereas in my case, I am lacking in any desires and entirely without initiative in this direction. In contrast, Eliza has very decided although constantly changing desiderata that she realizes with energy suitable for more important matters. She is constantly in negotiations with suppliers, fights valiantly for the quality of goods, for the price, and also achieves success in this field and is quite proud of this. I look upon her thriftiness with indulgent tenderness and, at the same time, with some apprehension, as at a child playing heedlessly at the edge of a precipice. What naïveté it is to imagine that by fighting over a thousand trivia in our lives we are molding our fate!

I, who have fortunately tucked myself into this peaceful bay, now wish only to lull its vigilance, to not attract its attention, to cling unnoticed to my happiness and become inconspicuous.

The city in which fate allowed me to find such a peaceful, blissful harbor is famous for its old, venerable cathedral, erected on a high platform at some remove from the last of the houses. Here, the city ends abruptly, falls away steeply down bastions and escarpments, with wooded groves of mulberry and walnut trees and a view opening up onto a distant land. It is the final, waning elevation of an upland chalk massif guarding the province's vast, bright plain, open across its entire breadth to the warm western breezes. Exposed to this mild flow, the city enclosed itself in the sweet, quiet climate, creating, as it were, its own miniature meteorological circulation within the sphere of the larger, general climate. Year-round, barely perceptible, gentle air currents blow here that toward autumn slowly transform into a single constant, mellifluous course, something like the bright, atmospheric Gulf Stream, into universal and monotonous blowing, so sweet as to erase memory and lead to blissful disappearance.

The cathedral, carved over the course of centuries in the costly darkness of its endlessly multiplied stained-glass windows, scraped together for generations from jewels implanted upon jewels, now attracts crowds of tourists from all over the world. They can be seen in every season with their Baedekers in their hands running down our streets. It is they who inhabit the lion's share of our hotels, rummage through our shops and antique stores for curios, and fill our nightclubs. They bring from the distant world the smell of the sea, occasionally the inspiration of great projects, a wide range of businesses. It happens that, enchanted by the climate, the cathedral, the tempo of life, they settle here for a longer time, become acclimated, and stay forever. Others, departing, carry away with them wives, the comely daughters of our merchants, factory owners, restaurateurs. Thanks to these ties, foreign capital is frequently invested in our enterprises and strengthens our industry.

The economic life of the city has been proceeding for years without shocks and crises. The strongly developed sugar industry feeds three-fourths of the inhabitants from its sweet artery. In addition, the city has a famous porcelain factory with a beautiful, old tradition. It produces for export, and in addition every Englishman returning to his country considers it a point of honor to order one of these sets with such and such a number of porcelain pieces the color of ivory, with views of the cathedral and the city executed by the female students of our art school.

In any case, it is a city like many others in this rich and well-managed country—moderately thrifty and devoted to business, moderately devoted to comfort and bourgeois prosperity, and also moderately ambitious and snobbish. The ladies display an almost metropolitan excess in their dress, the gentlemen imitate the capital's way of life, taking pains to support with the help of a couple of cabarets and clubs a sort of faint nightlife. Card playing is blooming. Even the ladies nurture it and there is scarcely an evening when we, too, have not ended the day in one of the elegant homes of our friends at a card game that sometimes continues deep into the night. Again, the initiative in this falls to Eliza, who justifies her passion by concern about our social prestige, which demands frequent appearances in the world so as not to drop out of circulation; in fact, however, she yields to the charm of this mindless and mildly stimulating squandering of time.

Sometimes I observe her as, excited by the game, with a flush on her face and glittering eyes, she participates with all her soul in the changing fortunes of the gambling. From under its shade, a lamp sheds a gentle light on the table around which a group of people, absorbed in the fan of cards held in their hands, run an imaginary race after the deceptive trace of Fortune. I see her sometimes, a delusory figure, elicited by the tension of a séance and revealed almost imperceptibly behind the back of one or another person. It is quiet, and half-whispered words are uttered indicating the changing, tortuous paths of good luck. As for me, I wait for the moment when a silent, passionate trance enfolds all minds, when, having lost their memory, they become motionless, bent cataleptically as over a spinning table, in order to withdraw unnoticed from that damned circle and escape into the solitude of my thoughts. Sometimes, getting up from the game, I can leave the table without drawing anyone's attention and pass silently into the other room. It is dark there; only a streetlamp sends its light from afar. With my head resting on the windowpane I stand like that for a long moment and ponder . . .

Above the park's thicket, which is turning autumnal, the night grows light with an indistinct reddish dawn. In the ravaged thicket of trees startled crows awaken with dazed cawing, misled by the symptoms of this false dawn; they rise with a start in great numbers and noisily, and this plaintive, circling anarchic mob fills with tumult and undulation the ruddy darkness, which is full of the bitter aroma of tea and flying leaves. Slowly, the mayhem of circling and soaring, flapping across the entire sky, settles and calms down, slowly it subsides and perches throughout the thinned-out thicket of trees in a restless, provisional swarm, full of anxiety, of quieting conversations, of plaintive questions, and little by little it grows calm, settling down for good and slowly merging with the silence of that rustling wilting. And again, the night, deep and late, installs itself. Hours pass. With my burning brow pressed to the pane I sense and I know: nothing bad can happen to me now, I have found a harbor and peace. Now a long series of years heavy with happiness and replete, an unending train of good and blissful times will arrive. In several final, shallow, sweet sighs my breast fills to the brim with happiness. I stop breathing. I know: just like all of life, someday death, nurturing and sated, will take me into its open arms. I will lie sated to my depths among the greenery in the beautiful, well-tended local cemetery. My wife—how beautifully her widow's veil will adorn her—will bring me flowers on bright, quiet, local mornings. From the depths of that boundless plenitude, music will arise, seemingly heavy and deep, the funereal, solemn, profound cadence of a majestic overture. I feel the powerful beats of the rhythm rising from the depths. With raised eyebrows, staring at a distant point, I feel my hair rising slowly on my head. I stiffen and listen . . .

A louder hubbub of conversations awakens me from my trance. They are asking about me amid laughter. I hear my wife's voice. I return from my asylum to the brightly lit room, squinting my eyes that have been washed with darkness. The company is already going its way. The hosts stand in the doorway, chatting with the departing people, exchanging farewell pleasantries. At last, we are alone in the night street. My wife adapts her elastic, free gait to my steps. We walk companionably, and going up the street, her head slightly lowered, she disturbs the rustling carpet of withered leaves covering the roadway. She is animated by the game, by her good luck, she is drunk with wine, and full of little womanly projects. On the basis of an unspoken convention she demands absolute tolerance on my part for these irresponsible fantasies and is very angry with me for all my sober, critical comments. A green streak of dawn is already visible above the dark horizon when we enter our apartment. The fine aroma of a heated, well-cared-for interior sweeps over us. We do not turn on the light. The distant streetlamp sketches a silver pattern of curtains on the opposite wall. Sitting on the bed fully dressed, I silently take Eliza's hand and hold it for a moment in mine.